WITHDRAWN

WHEN DIPLOMACY FAILS...

**Baen Books
by Michael Z. Williamson**

❋ ❋ ❋ ❋

Freehold
Contact with Chaos
The Weapon
Rogue
Better to Beg Forgiveness . . .
Do Unto Others . . .
When Diplomacy Fails . . .

The Hero (with John Ringo)

WHEN DIPLOMACY FAILS...

MICHAEL Z. WILLIAMSON

WHEN DIPLOMACY FAILS . . .

This is a work of fiction. All the characters and events portrayed in this book are fictional, and any resemblance to real people or incidents is purely coincidental.

A Baen Book

Baen Publishing Enterprises
P.O. Box 1403
Riverdale, NY 10471
www.baen.com

ISBN: 978-1-4516-3790-8

Cover art by Kurt Miller

First Baen printing, August 2012

Distributed by Simon & Schuster
1230 Avenue of the Americas
New York, NY 10020

Library of Congress Cataloging-in-Publication Data:

Williamson, Michael Z.
  When diplomacy fails-- / by Michael Z. Williamson.
     p. cm.
  ISBN 978-1-4165-3790-8 (hc)
  1. Mercenary troops--Fiction. 2. Politicians--Fiction. I. Title.
  PS3623.I573W47 2012
  813'.6--dc23
                            2012022344

Printed in the United States of America

10 9 8 7 6 5 4 3 2 1

※ ※ ※
For Jessica Schlenker
Webninja, sounding board, pack mule, event
assistant and general dogsbody. Sucker.
※ ※ ※

◎ CHAPTER 1 ◎

ALEX MARLOW acknowledged that he was one of the best bodyguards in the galaxy. "Best" was a relative term, but he and his team had managed to keep principals alive through battles, riots, poisonings with neural toxins and even nuclear attack. The company charged accordingly for their services, and they were paid concordantly. The company also covered the insurance, because no sane underwriter would take their odds.

In a matter of days, they'd be guarding someone again. They took short-term, high-risk assignments that would cause any other company to shriek. Ripple Creek would take the jobs, then present a contract rate that would cause most principals' accountants to shriek, and the rest to faint. Ripple Creek did, however, keep people alive, which was cheaper than the alternative.

He and his team were on down time after their last contract. Jason Vaughn was outsystem at Grainne Colony, his home, with his wife and kids. Eleanora Sykora was in the Czech Constituency of Europe, not far from Bart Weil in Germany. Horace Mbuto was from West Africa, but had moved to Hawaii and had a nice patch of property on the side of an extinct volcano. That left Aramis Anderson, who was in Wales, though there were reasons no one would mention that.

Alex was in New York. The company wasn't based in New York, but the fastest way for a face to face with the CEO had been for the two of them to meet there.

The café was right on Times Square, which had to cost a fortune in rent. It was an independent, not a chain. However, it had plenty of staff and machines to keep juice, pastries, soups and sandwiches moving to the steady influx of customers. It was 0730, and only a handful of people were present so far. The smell of pastries and bacon hit him. It was even real bacon.

CEO Don Meyer sat at a booth in the rear, facing the door. He had a fliptop comm out, and a doc case. Alex walked in, wove past four tables, and took a seat to Meyer's right. His back was to the hallway, but he could watch window and door. It was a professional paranoia in the industry and the military.

"Greetings," he offered.

"Hello," Meyer agreed. The ersatz office he sat in was reasonably safe, since there was a planter to his left and his doc case was layered with armor. It also offered some concealment to his wrestlerlike frame. That classy-looking suit was laced with shear armor as well. He had half an omelet on a plate to his right. Half a very large omelet.

On the screen of his fliptop, was a news load about Bureau of State Minister Joy Herman Highland. Once Alex made eye contact with it, and back to Meyer, Meyer switched loads to the stock market, clearing that story, and her image, from the screen.

Christ. They actually had an assignment involving *her*? It seemed hard to believe.

"I've got something for you, and you'll need to leave shortly. How fast can Vaughn get back?"

"It's probably better to have him meet us at the work location."

"Noted. The client would like discretion and to make releases on their own schedule."

Alex nodded. "This client didn't like us much last time." Actually, when they'd rescued a man that certain elements wanted and had declared as good as dead, it had caused a furor. Going back to work for that same government smelled of setup.

"No. However, different departments operate differently. Higher profile also gives a different outlook."

"You certainly know how to challenge us."

"Only the best."

The exchange had taken less than a minute. A human server,

young and cute if a little pale, arrived with a menu screen for him. He glanced over it.

"I'll take the toasted ham and cheese pocket, please, with guava juice."

She smiled and departed.

Meyer asked, "What's Vaughn's travel time to location?"

"Fourteen days, that I recall. He's braced for departure, though he doesn't get much time with his family."

"Then he can meet you there. You'll be DAIC." District Agent in Charge. That meant there'd be other teams to coordinate with, under his guidance.

"I'll get on it. Can you send a schedule?"

"Yes, and of course the client wants discretion," Meyer repeated. The client wanted secrecy until she decided to say otherwise. Marlow understood that.

"Absolutely. I'll arrange transport."

Meyer moved to close things down. The meeting was done. "That only leaves the question of Anderson," he said.

"Not a question. I'll message him and he'll be en route."

"A debrief would be in order, just for formality's sake."

"Of course," he agreed. Aramis was playing with fire, but it wasn't their fire, and Alex rather suspected they were safer with it than without.

Then after breakfast he'd have a day to sight see and act nonchalant, before flying out to round up his motley band of bruisers.

Jason Vaughn swung the gun smoothly after the birds, fired, fired again. The first round hit, the second missed.

"Nice looking front sight, isn't it?" his coach chuckled. Scott Vir was possibly the best action shooter alive. The second of the two targets faded from looking like a bird back to a small drone and settled from the sky into the weeds.

Jason grinned back. "Yes, I'm a rifleman first." His wife giggled, too.

He was spending a bit of money to learn sport shooting for birds and other fast targets, rabbits and bounders and such. The classic over and under shotgun was dissimilar from the combat shotguns he used for work, or carbines or pistols. One didn't aim.

One watched the target, aligned the body and the gun, and slathered pellets in its path. Two to three seconds was a long, relaxed time, far more than one usually got in combat. At the same time, there were definitely aspects of this he could take to the job. They'd apply even better when he used the optics functions of his "shooting glasses." They were turned off for now, but once activated they added to the spectra he could use, and offered some highlight and tracking functions.

Likewise, no one was shooting back at him, the day was warm with a sultry cloy of humidity, and shooting stuff was fun. Having Marisa along made it even better.

Each lesson was a div, a tenth of a local day. He liked Grainne's longer cycle, and the primal rawness. There were fewer than one percent of the people here than on Earth. It was more free, and more comfortable. In that context, he couldn't explain why he kept taking jobs in restrictive systems.

Two more birds erupted from the brush, rose and angled left. Marisa pivoted, pointed and shot. Even with damping weights, the recoil caused her slim frame to stagger a half step.

"Holy hell, I got them!" she exclaimed.

"Nicely done," he said. There was something exciting about a woman shooting, and he couldn't let it affect him on the job. Here, though . . .

In twenty segs he'd have her home. Now, if he could get the daughter to go see friends for a div or so, it would be a perfect day.

"And that's it," Vir said. "Twenty-five frames. What do you think of your movements?"

Jason switched his attention back to business and debriefed himself, with Vir's feedback.

Just as they were wrapping up, a triple beep told him he had a priority message, which he threw on his glasses to read while walking back to the car. Ah, work. The Earth pay rates went a long way toward basics here, and allowed him quite a few imported luxuries. So it was a mixed blessing, because he'd bring back another huge deposit, but he'd be leaving a few days earlier than he'd expected.

Well, it was a warm day, and he could afford to fly and set it on auto.

✖ ✖ ✖ ✖

Aramis Anderson had a life most men his age would kill for, and he knew it. That didn't make it easier to juggle.

In the recent past, he'd been contracted to protect Caron Prescot, heiress and now, tragically, the richest person in the universe, who personally owned a controlling interest in an entire star system of mineral wealth and the intellectual property on all modern space mining gear.

It was impossible for her to have a normal life. As a rebellious young principal, denied any real social interaction, she'd drunkenly propositioned him while he was on duty alone. Against every fiber of his hormones he'd refused, and been the ultimate professional. He'd helped her sprawl into bed, folded her clothes, and sat on the couch until his relief showed up.

Any typical relationship she might have would be tainted by distrust. She had trillions of dollars of personal wealth, substantial industrial knowledge worth stealing, and of course, there were major bragging rights to bagging her. She knew for certain she could trust him, that he wasn't after the money, and not an industrial spy. He was also a very effective bodyguard, even if not contracted to her, and she found him "decently attractive." By turning her down when she was stressed and drunk, he'd won gentleman points. All he had to do now was keep them.

There were unspoken but ironclad rules to their relationship. Eventually, he thought those rules might cause it to fail. For now, they added tension.

First, he could never, ever tell even his closest friends, "I'm banging the trillionaire." It would be disastrous for his career to be identified, because the public perception would be that he'd used his contracted position to go after her. The company wouldn't risk it, nor would any future employers. Career ending mistake. If he said such a thing publicly, Caron would believe she was just a prize to him, as she was to everyone else. Relationship ending mistake.

When out with her, he wore a suit and shades like her current security detail. He was just part of the entourage as far as anyone with a camera was concerned. The same rule applied when he was outside on her mansion grounds. No one must identify him.

To that end, he appreciated his own company's professionalism.

The current security detail knew who he was, of course, as did Caron's own staff, and neither would ever comment.

Nor could he ask for money. That wasn't really a problem. His income was quite impressive for what he did. She treated him to numerous meals and events and occasional gifts. He was grateful once per treat, and appreciative on the rare occasions she asked if he was happy. He didn't make a big deal out of it, and that kept things safe in that arena.

He understood he was with her at her sufferance. She ran, and owned, the largest corporation in history. When she was busy, he stayed out of the way. He was part of her life, she not part of his. His job was to provide her release, whether she wanted to bitch and scream, drink and have her back rubbed, go out for dinner, or have screaming, orgiastic sex.

Most men might think they'd kill for such a deal, but it was work. Challenging and rewarding work, but very much work, beyond that of a normal relationship. He was part friend, part assistant and part gigolo. If he tired of that, he could leave. For now, he thought he could handle it.

The only part he really had trouble with was the stress relief. Sex he was fine with, and quite a few variations. However, sometimes she wanted someone to consensually abuse. That wasn't particularly his thing, but if it involved her, he wasn't *un*willing. He could handle quite a bit without suffering.

Sometimes, though, she wanted to be the one abused. Nothing life threatening, but she liked being forced, choked, bruised. He'd had to do some reading on that subject to wrap his brain around it. A person with a lot of responsibilities might like to create a fantasy of being utterly controlled, to de-stress. The ironic counterpoint was that she dictated how it was to happen, so she was still very much in control. It was merely fantasy, but it kept her sane. He just had a hell of a hard time choking or causing pain even when he knew she wanted, craved, needed it. It was worse that she was a devastating actress who really got into the role, and he had to constantly remind himself she had safewords if he went too far, except she insisted he was just starting to get to where she really got the release she needed. Then, of course, his comrades on contract as her current security detail knew most of the details and monitored that, for her safety. He knew intellectually they'd never share that information in public, but he was now in the position he'd had her in last year, of being repressed by the presence of bodyguards.

The rules. They'd actually had to discuss the intimate details with the Agent In Charge. She had to tell them ahead of time she would be engaging in that kind of activity, so they'd know it wasn't a threat. They got more details than he did, and other safewords or unsafewords, because it just might turn out to be an assassination attempt. Then there were the cameras. It was like being a fucking porn star.

With all that, it was still worth it. She was a hell of a woman in every way, and he still felt sorry for her, because her wealth, looks and brilliance were a prison she could never escape from. He just hoped they could remain friends regardless of what turns life took.

Which bemused him that he was actually becoming a gentleman, not just faking it.

Well, sort of. He wasn't Caron's full time, and he made a point not to lurk too much. He had his own place, his own bills, and sometimes dates. Like Ayisha. And if he intended to go out with her this weekend, he should be thinking about her, and that. Then he needed to get in some exercise to keep his fitness up.

When his phone chirped, he wasn't too surprised to see Alex on screen, but even more than usual it caused him to tense up. It was hard not to feel guilty when one was in fact guilty.

Alex asked at once, "Are you being discreet?"

That caused a flush. Had something come out?

"As discreet as I can be."

"Then are you available for assignment?"

Damn. Work called. Still, disappointing as it was, he did enjoy his job, and that's what paid the bills. Being a kept man could only be a hobby.

"I am. Do I have transport?"

"You do now. Monday at oh six hundred."

He glanced at the itinerary that flashed on one side of the screen. He'd meet most of them in orbit. Where was Jason? Oh, right. And Cady was along again. Just like old times.

"I'll be there," he said.

"Later."

He closed the screen but kept the hush field on. He brought another other screen up.

To Caron's inquisitive look he said, "Work calls. Scheduling trouble, too."

"So you can't make it next week," she said. She sounded understanding, but a bit disappointed and frustrated.

"Right."

"Well, what about the weekend? I can clear a couple of things."

Clearing a couple of things would probably cost her several million dollars, and she could easily make that decision. He always kept that in mind. It was even more complicated this time.

"I don't know. I'll have to try."

"Is there a problem?"

"No, I'll have to adjust my schedule. I knew something was coming, but I figured on having that extra week. I actually had something planned this weekend."

"Family?"

"Uh, no. A girl, actually." He wasn't sure if he should discuss it, but he tried to be scrupulously honest with her.

"Oh. There's plenty of room. Bring her along and we'll find a place for her."

"Oookay," he agreed. He thought Caron liked keeping a low profile. She was apparently willing to trust his judgment. Still, no reason she shouldn't, after . . .

"See you then," she said, with a devastating twitch of her eyebrows.

"Bye."

Yeah, that was great. So, his regular woman, who he had to pretend didn't exist, told him to bring along the quick fling that had picked him up.

His plan had been Ayisha one night and Caron the next, though he wasn't going to say so. Now, it looked as if he'd be playing the gentleman at least one of those nights, if not both, right before shipping out. There was more than enough room at Caron's "estate" to give them all their own wing, never mind a room. He just couldn't see how he could be with one and not slight the other.

His only hope was for Ayisha to say no. He screened her.

"Well, hi!" she said. She was a little flaky, but honest and intelligent and fun. Right now she had fiberoptic highlights in her hair and a top that was shaded to match her skin. She was obviously clothed but looked nude.

"You look great," he said, and he meant it, though he said it largely to be polite.

"Thanks. What's up?"

"My job moved up to Monday early, so this weekend is going to involve some packing, too."

"Okay. Can I help?"

"Probably not. It'll all be battle gear."

"Oh, dear," she said, with wide eyes.

"It's fine. We carry it all as a precaution, and there's no particular risk. It's just not stuff anyone can really help with."

"Ah, right. Secret."

"Not really," he said. "Just complicated and specialized."

"We're still doing something, though, right?" Her smile promised something. He ardently hoped he'd find out.

"Something, yes, but I've got an invite to England. You're invited as well, if you like."

"I'd love to!" she said. "Do I need to bring anything?"

"I'd say one nice conservative outfit and something for Sunday. We'll be back late, I think. Oh, and a suit for travel."

"Can you afford this?"

"A friend of mine is covering it. A woman I know," he admitted.

"Ah," she said, with a glimmer of comprehension. "Well, it sounds interesting. I'll be there."

Luckily, they weren't serious enough for her to get jealous. Instead she was interested.

Unluckily, Aramis would have to juggle two scorching women and play an entire hand of gentleman cards. That couldn't be a good start to a high-stress mission.

Alex picked a lodge owned by the TanCorp conglomerate for staging. They were a very professional group, valued discretion, and Ripple Creek had no contracts with them; they had their own, quite respectable security, and their own star system—Grainne, actually. He sent out notices through anonymizers. There really wasn't any secrecy, but enough vagueness slowed down the intel gathering necessary to confirm anything. That, and when possible, messages sent openly were ironically safer. There were so many messages, and so few reasons to search them.

He let the car drive him down a sunny North American 95, off into the Appalachians, and into the site. He ignored the highway in favor of compiling packing lists and schedules, and studying their principal. He had a rough briefing package, but whoever put it together had different objectives. It contained a modest amount of personal information, but not enough data to determine threats or even objectives those threats might aim for, other than "politician."

He took a break and enjoyed the scenery in the mountains—hills, really, after sixty million years of erosion. Besides, he couldn't work well with the vehicle swaying over the switchbacks and around hilly curves.

Upon arrival at the site, he flipped to manual, slowed and stopped for security. After they scanned and approved his car at the real iron gate, he followed the map around more twists, fountains and flower beds, to the log-built cottage on a small pond. It wasn't cheap, but it was reasonably secure, and it would be approved on the invoice.

As requested, there was no staff. He climbed out with his bag, punched in the reservation code, and stepped inside. Nice. It was clean and plain, easy to sweep for bugs, and had just enough furniture to be comfortable. There were three sleeping rooms, a porch, and a loft overlooking the common room. It also had a fully stocked bar in the kitchen nook. He left his bag on the coffee table and mixed up a Clubbed Seal—Arctic Club whisky and club soda on the rocks, a mound of fluffy coconut and a bloody red splash of grenadine.

It was only a couple of hours before another car pulled up, and Bart Weil and Elke Sykora jumped out. She was above average height for a woman, but Bart was near two meters, and towered over her. They each had a personal bag, and a rolling softside trunk with the nonrestricted battle gear they'd take. Alex's gear was due to arrive as cargo the next day. Horace "Shaman" Mbuto would arrive late tonight, Aramis would show up for departure, and Jason would meet them on site. It wasn't how he preferred to do things, but staggering them out was less obvious. Even using this site made it seem less like an off-world mission, if anyone was watching.

Bart nodded and put his gear in a room. Elke took the loft, where she had a good, clear field of view, and fire. That was like her. She was always surgically precise and her gear spotlessly clean.

Bart came back through then, to the kitchen, grabbed a liter bottle of hefeweizen, and with a look for assent, sat on the couch and sprawled.

"It is good to stretch," he said.

"I imagine. I get uncomfortable. You must be crunched."

"It's worse in armor. Can we talk before the others arrive?"

Elke came through with a glass of juice, though he suspected she'd doctored it with liquor.

"We can. If we're not secure here we're in trouble anyway. And I'll still ask Elke to do a scan."

"It's secure," she said, holding up a box he knew generated interference for most bugs. She wasn't as expert as Jason, but she was more than proficient. They had enough layers.

He said, "We're protecting a high-ranking UN bureau official out of system."

Bart asked, "Are there specific threats?"

"Some. We'll be able to cover those during transport. We're traveling together."

Elke asked, "What restrictions do we have on weapons and gear, and rules of engagement?"

He understood she was asking if she could have explosives. "Unknown yet, but I do know the usual security contingent are armed."

"Then why us?" Bart asked.

"The threat level is perceived as higher than typical."

"So the free market is better at protecting the government than it is at protecting itself."

"Fundamentally, yes."

"Very amusing."

"We're going to Mtali for the Environmental Summit and some other meetings," he said.

Bart raised his eyebrows. Yes, if they were up to date on newsloads, that pretty well gave away who the principal was.

"Perhaps I will like this person," Elke said. "I respect ruthlessness."

"We'll have to see. The public presence is not very nice, but people are almost never how the media present them, and of course, we don't know how much is done as a public image."

Bart said, "Alex, you are hedging your bet."

He sighed. "Yeah, I expect we're not going to be on great terms. We'll see."

Elke said, "I don't need to like the principal. I just need to be able to do my job. This seems less of a problem than last time."

"We won't have time to run physical practice, but I do have sim programs we can play through. Bart, I'll want you to take lead on this."

"Is Aramis joining us?"

"A bit late, yes. There are political reasons."

"Ah. Those." The big man nodded understanding without expressing emotion.

"Yes, those. He's discreet, she's a friend of the company, and there's a certain level of public visibility. I didn't want him to rush. In fact, the six of us are more identifiable now, so we'll likely stagger our transit and arrival in future as well."

"A few more of these beers and I will stagger now," Bart joked.

"Practice first, then stagger."

"Of course."

⚙ CHAPTER 2 ⚙

"SO WHY AM I IN A SUIT?" Ayisha asked in the back of the auto cab, and damn, did she look good even in business wear. Though that was likely in part because he knew she wasn't wearing underwear. That made it even more aggravating. She looked very professional outside, her hair neatly up, and it was all a mask.

She hadn't said much while boarding the Airstreak 5. She probably hadn't known its actual value, but "expensive" was easy to figure. He'd expected that. She didn't ask details of where in England they were going. Actually, they were going to Wales.

An hour later they landed, and she was still cool. *I may have overplayed it*, he thought. This was far more exotic and money-laden than anything they'd done, and he imagined she was put upon, or jealous, or worried at what kind of personal tag it carried, or if it was merely to show off.

The Skoda limo didn't help, though she smiled politely as she accepted a third margarita. He'd mixed them light, for hydration more than intoxication. He preferred women alert and willing, not clumsy-drunk and pliable.

"Such pretty scenery," she said. "I didn't know there were still areas this undeveloped over here."

"Not many, but there are a few. A few kilometers of hills hide a lot of things."

"Yeah, I guess."

It also helps when you own all those kilometers and get to decide who builds what, he thought. At one time, this had all been coal country, and the Prescot family owned it all.

It was a lovely sunny day as they pulled into the apron, past the polished and manicured flower beds and under the perfectly transparent rain dome. Ron Schenk, his opposite number for this team, was waiting.

Aramis said, "Uh, we have to be searched before we go in. Thoroughly."

"Oh. Patted down?" she asked.

"'Felt up' is more like it. They'll have a female guard."

The driver opened the door, and Schenk said, "Hi, Aramis. And this must be Ayisha?"

"I am," she agreed with a nervous smile.

Aramis spread arms and legs and let them scan, flash and grope him. Besides clothes, he had nothing except his wallet, feeling very naked unarmed, but that was one of the rules. He didn't know who the female was, but she was Company, so she was a veteran and knew her stuff. It had taken him one tour with Elke to accept that there were women who measured up for this job, and he'd never questioned the idea since.

Then they were done and inside and Caron swept through the parlor in a dark blue dress.

"Aramis!" she said, and moved in for a hug and a warm kiss on the cheek. That was very nice of her, *very* nice of her, but probably wasn't going to make Ayisha relax enough for anything.

Sure enough, Ayisha said, "Oh, my, I recognize you, but I'm afraid I don't recall your name."

"Caron Prescot. You must be Ayisha." She extended a hand and smiled with a friendly crinkle of her eyes.

"You're . . . her." Yes, that had overloaded Ayisha's brain.

Yes, Ayisha, my other girlfriend is the richest person in the universe. Oh, and scorching hot. Sorry.

"I am. Welcome to Wales. I have refreshments out and my staff will move your things." She didn't say to where. Aramis assumed adjoining rooms, giving Ayisha a choice. It wasn't likely to help. And he wasn't going to visit Caron's room while Ayisha was here. Sigh, and dammit.

Caron continued, "Would you like a tour?"

Ayisha didn't hesitate this time. "I would."

"Then Aramis can mix drinks for us, and we shall be back soon." Caron smiled at him and led Ayisha away. One of the guards followed at a discreet distance.

Yes, but first he'd mix himself one, strong. The Penderyn honey finish whisky was wonderful stuff, something that was affordable on Earth, and potent enough to dull his jitters.

He was on the couch, halfway through a second glass, when he saw them pass through the palatial public kitchen, separate from the professional one Joanne Crandall, the chef, used.

The two women were giggling and muttering, hunched close.

On the one hand, he was glad Caron was able to relax so easily. Things had improved for her. On the other hand, that pretty well ensured he was going to spend the weekend being a gentleman, and trying not to arouse jealousy in either of them.

He went for a third drink.

Joy Highland was irritated, more than usual. Minister of State was not her first choice of job, nor her final goal, but until the election she was stuck with it, and with having to do her best. That was fine. It wasn't fine for her putative boss, that upstart little social climber, to load extra tasks on her. She wasn't needed for the Summit on Mtali. It was just an excuse to get her off planet for a while leading up to the election. The outsystem votes weren't enough to matter.

Some people would be happy managing international relations on Earth and in the colonies. Managing relations, however, was not directing or leading. Or not enough to suit her.

That upstart Cruk, when campaigning for secretary general, had violated plenty of finance and ethics policies and laws, and played the press off to his benefit. Fair enough, it got him, and the Equality Party, into power. It got her the position she held now, which was a good launching platform.

Now, though, he remained a cheat and thief, even to his own party and administration. He might get reelected, but it would wreck them as a party if he did. Hence her campaign. It was completely legitimate. The party caucus could decide if they wished to support another run by him, or by her. If they chose him, she was just young enough to run again on the next cycle.

Instead, he was trying to derail her early on, so he'd have minimal competition. Hunter was the only other candidate with a shot, and she could take him out any time with accumulated dirt. It wasn't that he was dishonest. He was dishonest *and* clumsy.

Cruk's solution? Get her off planet with a small staff, to block most of her public appearances and name recognition. Any comment of hers would be twelve hours or more after the fact of the event, and she'd have only recorded second-string facetime, nothing live or leading. Well done, fucker.

Still, if he wanted to play that game, she'd play it. Mtali was a war zone. That could be useful.

She checked through her list while alternately responding to deputy queries. James Jaekel, her chief of staff, was going to have to manage in her absence for a while. The fastest she'd be able to respond was twelve hours, and she'd be dealing with events on Mtali. There'd be no instant feedback to keep him on track. Of course, Cruk might have planned that. Or his staff. He certainly was neither that scheming, nor that intelligent. The bureaucrats had an empty suit they could puppet, and they still whined. If she could get in . . .

"My detail understands they are to be armed, yes?"

"They do," said her personal assistant, Jessie. "Does that include explosives?"

Joy turned, holding her brush halfway to her hair. "What? Oh, hell no. Whose fucked up idea was that?"

"An Agent Eleonora Sykora, who is a munitions disposal expert. She's one of the ones who identified the nuke on Salin."

"And she wants a nuke?" That couldn't have been what she just heard.

"No, she apparently had a nuke at the Prescot mine on Govannon. All she's asking for now is half a tonne of Composition G, Orbitol and Smithereen."

That was impressive in its arrogance. "What a bloodthirsty bitch. Maybe I can get her vote. But no, I don't need some militaristic nutjob with explosives. The guns will work better for visibility. We don't want to actually hurt potential voters, just make it obvious I'm actually in a hostile zone."

"Should I relay that message?"

"It's probably better to let them think it's agreeable, and stall until they accept it."

"They won't be loaded on the transport, then."

"Is there any way we can let . . . no, the stuff is traced, dammit. It will just have to get forgotten."

On Sunday morning, Alex was almost too content to be happy. Shaman—their nickname for Horace Mbuto—had arrived the night before, and rose early. He made smoked Scotch Eggs for breakfast. Everyone was accounted for. Transport was ready, and it was military-managed, with their client part of the same government. That meant there were standard protocols for safety and transfer. Highland's existing security detail would see her to the ship; they'd transfer responsibility in transit.

It seemed too good.

He chalked it up to nerves. They'd had easy missions, though eventually they always earned their pay.

A message chimed in, and he scanned it. Subject: security detail weapons. Requested: a long list of stuff they optimistically hoped would be one third approved. Approval: everything.

Everything.

Pistols, carbines with grenade launchers, a sharpshooter's rifle, two squad weapons, an autocannon, a Medusa system, ammunition, hand grenades, Jason's tomahawk, knives, demolition hammers, stunners, stun batons, stickybombs . . . ah, there. "Authorization for incapacitance gas denied." Fine. He could live with that. Someone had either been very agreeable, slightly greased, or smart, and they had all the firepower they needed to hold off an angry mob with torches. Possibly due to the fact that once they *had* fought an angry mob with torches.

No mention of explosives yea or nay. He frowned, sent a query back, and decided not to mention that to Elke just yet.

Elke was slicing up a Scotch Egg with a surgically sharp knife, and fork. "These are fantastic," she said. "Though I'll need something vegetable to go with it. It's just too much by itself."

"Peasant food," Shaman said. "For very rich peasants. Such a marvelous world we live in."

"Caron's people are doing very well with the vats. It even tastes like it was well-exercised range meat."

Bart said, "I will be happy to assist her in testing any food, liquor or beer she wishes before the market. All they care to send."

Shaman said, "You know, I'm fairly sure she'd take you up on that. You are a connoisseur of beer, and reasonably experienced with liquor. You'd give her people honest feedback, which is a problem she always has."

"It will not be a new job, but it might be a nice hobby," the big man said with a slow nod. "I will suggest it to someone."

It had been a good day, Aramis reflected. He wasn't really a garden person, but Caron's groundskeepers did some amazing things with plants, rocks, flowers and trees. It was done in part under her direction, a hobby to keep her sane. She'd devised digital machines to dig and plant according to a map. They already existed for agriculture, she'd just modified one for decorative landscaping. She'd probably get a few million more dollars she didn't need from that, too.

Fine weather, if a little gray early on, but sunny with puffy cumulus clouds now, had helped. Caron's domestic staff members were the same, and Joanne had brought regular drinks, cocktails, hors d'oeuvres and other snacks. It was hard not to eat too much.

Ayisha had the same problem, but was delighted, and seemed comfortable enough, once over the shock of Caron's insane wealth.

And here it was, evening, they were inside Caron's huge apartment with a real wood fire in a fireplace. It crackled and popped, and the broad couch he sprawled on was very comfortable. He could sleep here. Ayisha made a good pillow, too. His head was cradled on her middle, with her hips and chest in an arch around him.

The wood smoke was pleasant, and the sherry was delicious. He didn't inquire as to brand. There was no way he could afford a single bottle.

Caron's family were dead, her immediate friends gone in a scandal. Now that she was alone except for staff members, the house had been rebuilt inside, into a couple of large apartments in this wing, with the other wing set for visiting guests. He wondered if Ayisha realized that they were staying in the personal and family wing, not the guest wing. He also wondered if something might actually happen. Caron seemed relaxed, and she had put Ayisha's and his rooms adjoining. They connected, too.

Ayisha did seem to agree. She had her fingers inside his shirt and one of the buttons was undone. Well. It seemed it might be a good weekend after all.

Caron sat back with a coy smile, watching.

"You'll probably find the bed more comfortable," she said, and waved at the far end of the great room she used as bedroom, office and lounge.

Well, that was obvious consent. She didn't seem offended, and that was good.

Ayisha giggled as he lifted her over his shoulder, swatted her ass and carried her up the broad risers.

Her blouse and bra yielded without struggle, and he enveloped her in a kiss and embrace, warm flesh against him.

They were naked and tingly when he felt a familiar sensation. An amazing set of boobs against his shoulders.

"Caron?" he said in surprise. Dammit, he should have been more alert, too. He hadn't noticed her undressing and coming over. Yes, she'd dropped the gown, and her underwear.

"You can't imagine I'm just *watching*, can you? I expect equal attention."

Oh, the bitch. Already he was clinging desperately to self control.

In moments, her mouth was on his, her warm, supple breasts against him, and Ayisha shifted so her body was all over his lower half. He kept a steely grip on his nerves as they moved about, straddling and using him. The panting he heard wasn't entirely theirs.

He focused on one thing at a time, ignoring sensations, or trying to. Silken sheets, sweat-cooled skin, tumbling hair, and Ayisha, soft and slick and shivering in response to him.

Her hips were very nice, rounded rather than oval, her thighs supple, and her skin wore a hint of spice. It was much easier to give than receive like this. Much easier.

He reached out for Caron, who was next to him and waiting patiently for him. He ran a hand down her flank and rose to look across.

Caron was . . .

Yes, she really was. Her fingers and lips were on Ayisha's skin, and . . .

Holy shit.

He clamped down on every fiber in his body, and the rush that hit him was as intense as an adrenaline dump in combat, but far, far more pleasant. Endorphins ripped through him like never before. It was like falling off a cliff.

He slid his hand up, and traced her lips with a finger, a physical confirmation for his eyes, while trying to decide what to do.

Ayisha wrapped an arm around Caron and clenched, and clutched for him with the other. With the taboo broken, he collapsed on them and stopped thinking, in a burning, melting rush. He was beyond drunk, beyond lost, and only a thread of control remained, a glowing, sparkling line amidst the waves of fog in his brain.

Then two warm mouths collided on him and his brain jolted in disconnect.

He wasn't sure if he was the first to scream.

It didn't end with that, and he never got past it all feeling like a dream, an hallucination, an unreality that he couldn't wake up from and didn't want to.

An hour later they stopped, gasping and sweating and with unfocused eyes. Caron kissed Ayisha sloppily, then him, then bounded off the bed and into a kimono. She headed for the kitchen, as Ayisha headed for the bathroom. Ayisha came back with cool, damp towels. Caron returned with three glasses of tart limeade and a bucket of ice.

They wound up sitting in a triangle, and he gauged them. They seemed comfortable enough, neither fawning each other nor shying away. They grinned when they made eye contact.

Even if he wanted to tell anyone, no one would ever believe this.

"Thanks much," Ayisha said as she accepted a glass.

"You're welcome," Caron replied. "I'm feeling dehydrated. And worn." She ran a hand through her dark, tangled waves of hair.

Shortly, he was massaging Caron's feet with mint lotion, while Ayisha braided her hair, and they talked about chocolate. Aramis liked it darker, but wasn't an aficionado, really. Caron was, and could readily afford to be, and took a quick trip to the kitchen for several high-end mixes.

Ayisha didn't seem to have any complaints about the weekend. She tried nibbles of five different mixes, and fed the balance to Caron, whose head was in her lap.

"I'm not sure about the hazelnut," Ayisha said. "Wonderful, but I like the effect of straight chocolate. This is too good to blend."

"I like the contrast," Caron said. "Also the Guatemalan pure with the bare hint of jalapeño. I always wondered about that."

"It's all good," he said, to say something, trying to ignore her feet on his belly. "Some is better than others, depending on mood." He didn't say that he couldn't tell much difference in his current state.

"Well, I suppose," Caron said, sat up and reached behind him to the table. "Ayisha, do you know what Aramis really likes? Ice cubes."

He could have wrestled them both off if he tried, but why?

When he woke the next morning, he was alone. He clutched around as Caron called from the desk, "It's okay, I gave her a ride home."

"I'd hoped she'd say goodbye."

"She did, about an hour ago. Don't you remember?" She rose and came over.

He didn't. Damn, they'd worn him out.

Caron was dressed in a business pullover and blazer, and even that was sexy as hell on her. She had literally everything, and all the sorrow that went with it, not to mention her murdered parents, psychotic uncle, and occasional assassination attempts. Would she rather trade her beauty or her money for a normal life? But she was who she was.

"I have to report in soon," he said.

"Well, be safe," she said, taking his hand as he rose from the bed. "I'll expect you in one piece, and ready for dinner when you come back."

"I'll do my best," he agreed. Yeah, getting busted up was not on his list. He stretched.

"The weekend was great," she said with a grin. "I don't promise I'll ever do that again. It was a spur of the moment thing."

"No worries," he said, blushing a bit now. Yes, she looked amazing face down on another woman, but it required the right woman, right time and place, and right mindset. "I'm glad I was there for it."

"So am I. Thank you, Aramis, for being here for me. Be safe," she insisted again, firmly and with finality.

"I will," he said.

Her smile broke to a concerned frown as she turned. She probably hadn't wanted him to see that.

A half hour later, her goodbye kiss was warm, but hesitant. They definitely had something. That was a complication.

That, and he probably should have mentioned to Ayisha that the security detail was definitely watching via camera. They were utterly professional about it, but probably enjoyed at least some of it.

He wasn't sure if the regret was a reaction, or something deeper.

◈ CHAPTER 3 ◈

BART SIGHED. The trip up to orbit was the usual spine-grinder. It was possible to run at lower acceleration, but it used more fuel. That raised costs. They could have larger couches, same story. He always felt imprisoned by the close confines of the seats, and they were either sticky or coarse, depending on the covering. He never complained out loud, though Jason did, and it was amusing to hear complaints about shuttle seats from a man who would very casually return fire in combat.

Next to him, Aramis seemed caught in thought. He was not as cocky as he had been. Some of that was maturity, which also meant less edge. Still, he seemed introspective, not worried. Everyone assumed his relationship with Caron was intimate, but he'd never said, and his expression was thoughtful.

Elke and Shaman both had seemed their usual calm selves, but they were seated behind him and he couldn't tell. Alex was never relaxed, but never stressed. He was seated diagonally ahead, and had something encoded out to work on.

On their first mission, he'd had more executive protection experience than the others. They were all catching up now. Still, he went through mental exercises on procedures. It would probably again be his task to teach the principal the necessary movements for evacuations and relocations, though she might already know some of that, with her background. He also considered how her personality might clash with theirs. She was strong willed.

There were incidents in her background. It was one thing when a principal wanted more freedom than safety allowed. It was entirely different when they didn't like consulting with their detail, or ignored them.

Then there were potential threats, with a high-ranking bureaucrat and former assemblyperson who had made numerous people and groups unhappy. Fortunately, most of the more violent ones didn't have a significant dislike of her or a threat record against her.

Though it was often the quiet ones.

In the BuState compound on Mtali, Jason stretched out knots. He'd found the worst, most frustrating aspects of the job possible: Ignorance.

Not that people were ignorant, though he was sure a lot of them were. No, it was that they ignored him.

He had scaled responses for any contingency, from polite greeting, diplomatic request, urgent demand, rude insult, angry threat, punch to the face, shoot in the face, to "call Elke." Some issues here were simply not responsive. The people in question refused to respond to him, or acknowledge him in any fashion.

That was the most aggravating response possible. He could accept a "no," though he'd certainly try to manipulate it to a "yes." He could appeal up the chain as was indicated by the urgency of the matter. Completely ignoring him put him in a helpless corner.

He couldn't use any violent means at this juncture. His lesser means were being ignored. He didn't want to call Corporate. He was supposed to be able to handle this, and if he wanted promotion he certainly had better. Their response would also be delayed, and watered down by distance.

He had connections, and he had some responses. Cady's team had landed the day before, and were busy securing the Ripple Creek section of the diplomatic compound, which was the Minister's residence and their adjoining apartments. That went smoothly enough; the military, contractors and agencies had no choice but to do as the BuState letterhead demanded.

There were mild complications with Highland's assistant deputy chief of staff, a position he wasn't even cognizant of. It seemed the man's task was to handle all the routine requests from Very Important People with Something to Say to the Minister, and scheduling of meetings with such groups, around the stuff Highland and her deputy chief of staff, who was on Earth, scheduled first. Magerin Rausch was a nice enough guy, spotless background, and on the list to be admitted with minimal hindrance. On paper, his credentials were impressive. How much of that actually meant something, Jason didn't know. He was also filling in as Protocol head, and in that capacity they would need to talk to him.

"Good morning, Agent in Charge Vaughn," he said as Jason entered the area. He was always perfectly polite.

"Mr. Rausch, good morning. How are you?"

"I like this planet in a lot of ways," Rausch said. That was ironic. He was Jewish, and this pit of despair was full of people who'd kill him in a second. It did have nice sunrises, though, ruddy and streaked with clouds.

Jason said, "It's not bad. As to our hopefully final clarifications, I reviewed all your documents. We will try to pass everyone with a minimum of delay, after checking for weapons and other threats. By the time they get to you, they should be cleared. Agent in Charge Cady is responsible for the perimeter, and her second team will be at the doors inside. You will need to let her know, so she can let them know, on anyone to admit. They will still need either pass or escort from you, or to show ID and be on file."

"That's surprisingly easy. There are stories that Ripple Creek are very tough to deal with."

"It's our job to be tough with threats and potential threats. Anyone cleared through the Minister and yourself will be deemed a nonthreat, though we'll be ready to respond if that changes. You can always ask for them to have a courtesy escort, which means we'll smile and shake hands and make them feel we're at their service. We won't shoot them in the back unless they make a clear, definite, health- or life-threatening move toward the Minister."

"I do appreciate your dry sense of humor."

I appreciate that you think I'm joking.

"Well, that's the personal interaction issue. We all have maps of the facility and the relevant areas marked. Just keep any guests, junior staff, housekeepers or others out of those areas, and we'll do the rest. We try to be polite to everyone, just let us know of any specific titles or addresses."

"I will do so."

Really, it shouldn't be too bad. They had a military perimeter, a BuState perimeter, the building entrance, controlled elevators. By the time anyone got to this level of the building, it would be a nonissue. Likewise, the Colonial Liaison Office, the stand-in for an embassy, wasn't their problem.

The military remained a problem. Even the Intel office had passed the buck until he hinted at going over them. Then they'd assigned a captain. Captain Das seemed competent and helpful, but was hamstrung by other duties and limited authority. At the same time, he was earnest, and going over him wouldn't create any friends, might hurt the man's reviews, and wasn't likely to yield anyone more helpful or able.

He tabled that as Cady came in.

"Afternoon, Jace," he acknowledged.

"Hi, Jason. Do you have anything on the perimeter fence request? I still need to know what software they use to monitor those lines."

That issue. He said, "Yeah, I put in a third request to Colonel Goran. They're still ignoring it. I'm sure they'll respond when it's too late for us."

"I know you're working it. It's just very aggravating."

"I have said exactly the same. What's our status?"

Cady shrugged. "I can't approve the fence. I do have our barriers in place inside. They won't allow explosive."

"Elke may have something to say about that."

"Yes, so I've heard." She giggled. "We wouldn't keep getting in trouble if they'd just let us do our job."

He grinned. "Unfortunately, we can't use that as a marketing blurb."

"Well, not officially. Though in the right circles, it would work."

"Heck, we don't need advertising. 'Ask President Bishwanath or Ms. Prescot.' It's hard to argue with results."

"Indeed. Perhaps we should unionize for better bargaining potential." Her face was serious.

"I can never tell when you're joking."

"Good. I do appreciate our small arms arriving. Any word on the body armor?"

Sigh. That issue. "Somehow, the weapons were 'diplomatic' but the armor got tagged as 'military materiel.' Held up in Aerospace Force storage until local and BuMil 'inspect' it. I sent another request to Colonel Goran on that, too."

"An operations officer who doesn't bother with operations."

"Yeah, though he has plenty of time to smoke, play cards at the O club and organize cookouts."

"I have my updates here," she said, handing over a ramstick. They never sent anything through a network they didn't own, if they didn't have to.

"Great. I'll beat on them as best I can. The good part is that the more falls in place, the less targets for my irritation still exist, so I can apply more loving attention."

"I'd almost say you enjoy the fight."

Right then a klaxon sounded, the emergency light on the wall flashed, and Jason's phone buzzed. He glanced at it to see, "REAL. ATTACK IN PROGRESS, SEEK SHELTER."

He and Cady swapped looks, then jogged for the door. He heard an explosion high overhead. It cracked and boomed.

From the second floor, they bounded down the stairs and out, passing two men and two women coming in. Landscapers. The two mercenaries headed toward the compound entrance. It was secured, the two guards on duty nestled into their reinforced gatehouse. There weren't many people about outside, but those few were trying to get inside.

Jason checked his watch. Almost a minute. Granted, there were fewer BuState people than military, but they were mostly accounted for, while the base still swarmed, and much of it wasn't mission critical. Those people should have been sheltered in seconds.

High overhead, another rocket sought to fall, only to be splattered into fine debris. A brilliant flash and crack of artificial lightning shook the sky in its wake. He couldn't tell the incoming airframe, though it was on the larger end of short range stuff. The counterfire was definitely a combination of laser and particles. The laser marked the target for any physical followup, applied energy to it, and opened a plasma sheath. The particles ripped along that sheath and punched holes in the weakened missile.

Interesting. The military had refused to comment on air defense, even though it applied directly to Highland's safety. He'd seen a Cobra antiaircraft battery. The core buildings were around an improvised courtyard, and the missiles were hidden within, camo mesh and glittery distortion shields around them, that didn't hide them from engineers with experience building landing fields. Apparently though, the Cobras were backup to the Sentinel Dual Array. He was glad to see it.

Cady said, "It seems they have a lot of trust in their air defense, or a contempt for the local artillery."

"Any kind of counterbattery going out?"

"Not that my sensors can detect. Though if it's distant enough, they may have something more local to it."

"Or they may just be too snobbish and decadent to actually return fire."

"Earth culture? Snobbish and decadent?"

"Yeah. A stretch, I know."

"In other observations, I see that the perimeter fence became live, the gate is locked, but there's no supplemental forces, we remain unquestioned even though our presence and observations could theoretically be intel or terminal guidance."

She paused and he picked up. "The building has not been locked down. I bet our ID won't be checked on entry."

"Well, that makes my job easier," she said. "The local contractors aren't present and the State weenies are useless. Why don't we have Marine guards anymore?"

"It was deemed 'Amerocentric.' Everyone should have a chance. These are Egyptian."

"Even by Egyptian standards, they are sub par."

"So it's all up to you."

"I wouldn't have it any other way," she said, and giggled again. "I'd like Elke to consult with me once she's here."

"I'll relay that."

The flight was comfortable enough, Alex thought. From the shuttle they'd embarked on a cruise liner that was privately owned by BuState, operated by contract and civil service crew, almost all of them veterans. That didn't negate the possibility of attempts on their principal, but it did reduce the probability and change the factors.

Still, it was nice to be comfortable while assessing threats. They each had a stateroom with frills and real wood paneling, which was ridiculous, and felt really odd during maneuvers, but the privacy and minimal but real space was something he appreciated. They'd once traveled all six in a bunkroom, on constant watch. This was nice.

However, he didn't trust the security protocols, nor the risk of anyone snooping, so they rotated between staterooms to discuss business, and did so by hand-writing notes to pass around and then shred. The contrast between state of the art ship and pencil on paper was amusing.

Alex expected trouble at some point. They were hired for that reason. He didn't expect an attack just yet, but political sniping would probably start early on.

Eight days later, they were in system and prepared to transition to protection taskings. He had four of five shooters behind him, with Jason doing recon on Mtali, groundside. They were in what passed as a boardroom for this ship, on sparse but adequate furniture, as unarmed as anyone else. It was a policy brought about because of the risk of damaging the ship and causing leaks, even though the vessel was rated for meteorite impacts at ungodly velocity. Policies were usually based on emotion, not facts, and impossible to argue with.

He stopped musing as the hatch swung. One of BuState's guards was first, then the slight-looking redhead who was the assistant to Joy Herman Highland who came next, all 1.7 meters of her, projecting an attitude three meters tall, all of it bitch.

The BuState security detail looked all too happy to hand her over. One of them came over, presented a tablet to be signed, then nodded as he turned. The four of them left with barely a mumbled goodbye.

That left it all up to Alex, which, while it had downsides, also meant he didn't have to argue with anyone except the principal. He expected that to be enough of a chore.

"Minister Highland, I'm Alex Marlow."

She smiled cordially enough, though it was a politician's smile. It was as real as her hair color and probably her breasts.

"Thank you, Mr. Marlow," she said, as she extended a hand. He recalled that she insisted on the appearance of manners. He took it firmly but not too hard.

She continued, "Allow me to introduce Jessie Monroe, my personal assistant, publicist and factotum."

The elfin redhead offered a hand. He took it and said, "Of course we're familiar with JessieM's reports. It's good to meet you." He reflected he was lying as much as they were. JessieM was the unofficial voice of Highland's empire. She made an endless stream of location reports, cute little references, and posted fake "questions" that Highland could easily answer.

She was also not part of the contracted protection.

Monroe said, "A pleasure to meet you, too, Mr. Marlow. That's without an 'E', yes?"

"Yes," he said, then realized she was publicizing his name, company and location across the entire spectrum.

He wasn't going to address that in public, and it was too late for that incident. However, that shit could not be allowed. Jason wasn't here, so he looked over at Elke. She raised an eyebrow, raised and lowered her head, and turned to her own enhanced "phone."

Then he turned to Highland and said, "Ma'am, I'd like to introduce the rest of the team and get up to speed, if that's okay." He didn't clench his jaw or snarl.

"Of course," she said brightly. He wasn't sure if that was act or honest.

"Very well. Bart Weil is our most experienced VIP protection specialist, from Germany."

Bart let her offer her hand first. He knew all the manners. He even sometimes used them. Highland's expression didn't betray anything.

"Mr. Weil."

"Minister Highland," he said with a nod.

"Aramis Anderson handles most of our navigation and is responsible for quite a bit of logistics." Translation, the kid could plot and draw maps, and liked stashing guns and gear where it might be useful. He followed Bart's lead and let her offer her hand, and she held his a fraction too long. Yes, he was quite handsome. Someone in her position should barely notice, though.

"Mr. Anderson."

"Ma'am."

"Eleonora Sykora is from the Czech Constituency and handles all our explosive and other hazardous material threats. She'll also be your close escort in some areas."

Highland said, "Very good. Pleased to meet you, Miss Sykora."

"Elke is fine, if you wish."

"Very well."

"Jason Vaughn is from Grainne Colony, and is already on location, preparing and doing advance observation." Her expression went from confused to understanding at his nonpresence, and she nodded. "He's a technical specialist on mechanicals and electronics." Mechanic, gunsmith, lockcracker, and occasional pilot.

"Horace Mbuto is a surgeon in addition to being an executive protection specialist."

As she shook his hand, he said, "I have your medical files, ma'am, but if there's anything else I should know, please do tell me. You have full privilege, and I like to be prepared for any eventuality, no matter how rare."

"Thank you. I'll try to get you a load." She didn't seem bothered by it, which was good. At her level of government, she had to be familiar with general security protocols. However, she was probably also rather secretive and wouldn't share that info. People at her level were worried about any leaks of any kind, with good reason. Actually, to that end, Ripple Creek might be more reliable than her staff. They all cashed checks, but Ripple Creek's loyalty was bought and paid for, at least for the duration.

They moved through into the docking compartment. It was already cleared of crew, but Elke made another sweep, and Aramis physically checked hatches.

JessieM tapped away at her screen.

"I'm not getting any signal in here," she said.

There was the barest hint of a smile at the corner of Elke's mouth. Alex decided he owed her a drink for picking up on that and acting on it. They couldn't have many "problems" with reception, but hopefully they could talk about it and get JessieM to tone down the intel leak. Probably not, but he'd try.

Elke reported back, "It all seems clear."

Without Jason, she was the go-to person, and their physical checks hadn't shown anything. He preferred redundancy, but he trusted Elke.

"Then we'll stand by to transfer at Ms. Highland's pleasure," he said.

She smiled a polished, professional smile and said, "We may as well do so now, then."

He said, "Yes, ma'am. Elke, Aramis, lead."

They took up position and preceded Highland, with Bart alongside her and Alex and Shaman at the rear. They locked through three hatches with *chuff* sounds and pressure shifts, into the deluxe landing shuttle, and took very comfortable couches.

And how the hell did this luxoboat get insystem? It had to be hauled externally, and the energy cost would be insane. Even Caron Prescot never did that. She rode very basic shuttles up and down, and even the resort customers didn't have it this nice.

The UN government had the money, but there were better ways to spend it, he thought.

Highland and her assistant took seats far forward. Alex indicated a bit of space, and the team sat four rows back. These were deep rows, with very comfortable couches, enough leg room even for Bart, adjustable tables and screens, everything. There was just enough airflow and mechanical noise to make an effective privacy screen.

Aramis gave an inquiring look, Alex translated it and nodded assent for him to talk.

"What's the word on weapons?"

"They're approved."

"Approved?" Aramis asked, disbelieving. Yes, they actually had weapons.

"Yes, armor with spares, two armored transport vehicles. Full commo suites. Knives, Jason's hatchet, pistols, carbines, two squad weapons, that autocannon you like, a couple of sharpshooter rifles."

"And explosive?" Elke asked.

"It's supposed to be coming."

"Then I shall raise our principal's standing in my portfolio."

Aramis flared his eyes. Alex could read his thoughts. Real weapons, and no one whining about what the locals might think. There had to be a catch, but he'd deal with it. Elke, of course, used explosive for things people never anticipated. They always assumed big blasts, and she could do that, including low-yield nukes.

However, she started with firecrackers and smoke and escalated as needed. The only problem was that she used geometric or logarithmic progression. They tried not to share that fact.

Alex said, "Jason will be waiting on the ground, with Cady, and they should have a minimum battlefield kit ready for us. They'll bring it in before we go out."

Aramis said, "I like this gig better all the time."

"I'm just wondering when it will go south," Alex said guardedly. "We aren't getting a big check for nothing."

On his right, Shaman said, "Not all our contracts have been dangerous. Only about one in four. Though they tend to make up the difference in value. I'm considering that she certainly has a strong opinion of her value, and until the last ninety days before the election, she's not eligible for Special Service Branch protection. If she thinks there's a threat, we are arguably better than BuState security, and she's not the one covering the tab."

"There is that," Alex agreed. "And she's certainly made a lot of claims of enemies."

Aramis asked, "You think there's more to those stories than grandstanding?"

Alex shrugged. "There may be, which would justify us being here. It could also be that our presence is supposed to suggest there's more to those stories, for campaign purposes."

Bart said, "Let's hope that's the case, and run a tight operation. Either way, it's what we're paid for."

Aramis said, "And no quibbles over weapons. So it's certainly not one of our worst assignments."

⚙ CHAPTER 4 ⚙

JASON DIDN'T LIKE THE PLAN. Even inside the driver's compartment of a nicely climate-controlled Improved Attack Resistant Personnel Carrier outfitted as an executive transport. He watched the putatively secure feed of the landing shuttle, and fidgeted. He sweated in his suit.

Tactically, everything was sound. The rest of the team would land with their principal in a few minutes. He had good leads in the area and an advance recon.

The strategic questions were what triggered his senses. BuState had security guards, and there was no spoken, outright threat to her at this point. Keeping it in-house would make political and economic sense. The only reason he could come up with for using Ripple Creek was to make them some sort of cover. Either they expected threats of a level that would be politically infeasible to handle themselves, or they planned to toss the team to the wolves. Or both.

Of course, it was possible she was just using their image for political gain.

It seemed unlikely, though. They weren't popular in the press, so she wouldn't pick up votes from their presence. The perceived threat level, however . . .

In the compartment behind him were Agent Jace Cady and two of her people. It was possible to shimmy between the two areas, though not easily.

Cady always looked exotically elegant, and if you didn't know she'd started out male, you'd probably never guess. They'd even

35

adjusted her wrist angles, as well as her hips. If you watched, though, she had the residual habits of someone raised male.

Malcolm Lionel and Roger Edge were just suited goons to look at, but very good at their jobs. Malcolm was from Antigua, Roger very English.

"You seem agitated," Cady said.

He said, "Yeah, and I shouldn't be. Except there's no good reason for her to use us."

"It could be they're both cautious and wanting distance. They can blame us for being excessive and have it forgotten in the news a day later."

"True. I hope that's all it is. We're paid to take the blame."

Cady said, "Well, our perimeter, their perimeter and all non-physical perimeters are secure. I've got our own bugs in the commo, and they'll shriek if anyone else touches the lines."

"You always do a fine job. I've got no concerns about that." He idly ran hands over the controls, eager to do something.

"Thank you."

"No problem. I am worried about a less than friendly principal and unseen threats."

"Of course. You're also missing your accomplices."

He smiled. "Yeah, Elke's great company, and Aramis, even if still a bit cocky, is the man to have at your back. I like how the company has let us sort into teams and stick there."

She said, "It works with five hundred employees. It wouldn't work with five thousand."

"Exactly. Though we wouldn't be any more capable or earn any more, either. The smaller structure helps. Now I realize you've got me distracted from stressing out alone, and the lander's on its final approach. Thanks."

She giggled very softly. "You're welcome. Guys, check weapons and prepare to open up."

A moment later she said, "Jason, check your phone. Tag for Highland and live feed."

"Uh? Okay." He dug it from the pouch on his shoulder, spoke into it, thumbed it and let the feed load.

JessieM: We're here on the ground with Ripple Creek Security. Alex Marlow in charge, looking ruff."

JessieM: Agent Sykora, Ripple Creek bomb expert.—photo. Ms. Highland should be well-protected.

Oh, holy shit. Did she really churp their IDs into the seething morass of the nodes, openly and directly attached to the company and Highland? With current whereabouts?

"Good thing this vehicle is EM proof. It's unfortunate there's something wrong with the outside transmission antenna."

Behind him he heard a ripping, cracking noise.

"You know, you're right," Cady agreed.

He'd need to arrange some sort of personal scrambler for them to wear, and they might want to consider something to obscure their faces.

Then they waited patiently while the gull-like white monster was ferried across the apron, hosed in a nimbus of steam that carried the dreadful heat away to condense and rain out in an oval a half kilometer downwind, and was prepared for debarkation.

A private signal chimed softly, and he kicked the ARPAC engine to life. IARPC was too clunky an acronym to pronounce, so it had been mutated.

He pulled in a broad curve, slowing more than he liked to get around a tug, a cargo can crane, and some other vehicle. The ground crew hadn't been told to expect him and didn't know how to react. They did the next best thing; stayed still and let him work it.

Once through those, he turned and backed, bringing the rear of the vehicle right up to the edge of the obligatory red carpet. She'd want to make a speech first, of course.

Alex untensed as the craft rolled out. He was always nervous on landing, for no other reason than that was when most problems were likely to manifest, and there was no way to do anything about them for those few minutes.

It would take several more minutes for the craft to maneuver to the departure area. There was no modern gate here; they'd have to cross open apron. That was a prime time for an attack because it was a clear, predictable window. He was ready for that. Before then, though, the craft would have to cool a bit, then be hosed down, so the remains of the incandescent passage through the atmosphere didn't roast them on exit.

Highland was putting on "professional" clothing, and JessieM was in the lounge, so now would be a good time to discuss that lingering issue.

"Jessie, I need to ask a favor, regarding Ms. Highland's security."

"Yes?" the woman asked, looking alert and interested.

"The constant media chatter decreases her safety. It means any threat knows her location to a close degree."

She didn't look indignant, exactly, but certainly put upon.

"That's what I do—promotion. It's expected. Ms. Highland's ratings and electability depend on it."

"I understand, but it also increases risk."

"Well, that's what you're for."

"I'm here to make things as safe as possible, and that media chatter makes things less safe. This is why I'm bringing it up."

"It's my job, and what she needs for this election cycle." The woman was insistent and, as near as he could tell, clueless. He sighed mentally, while staying completely calm outside. He wondered if he could get a job as an actor.

"Can you at least wait until after an event before you note it? Or at least after arrival? The scheduled events are a known issue, and have multiple agencies for security. The impromptu events are where the threat is, and I don't believe a lot of outsiders actually make it. Only those in the immediate area. Which means anyone arriving has a strong motivation, with an increase in the negative side."

Chewing her lip, JessieM said, "I suppose. That's a hindrance."

"Yes, but it makes her, and you, more safe." Had he put just enough emphasis on that? He wasn't going to tell her she was dispensable, but if she perceived a potential threat, it might help.

"I will try, then," she said. "A few minutes might be okay."

"It all helps."

Highland came through right then, and hurried over to JessieM, who plucked at lint, pulled a stray hair, and tugged a lapel.

"You look great, ma'am," she said.

The cooloff cycle allowed the crowd to move closer, set up and take position. There was a red carpet unrolled from a large drum, a podium, flags, seat risers. The crowd included press, dignitaries from three of the factions and General Marsten, in charge of peacekeeping operations. They'd have to interact with him at some point. That would probably lead to some issues, they being armed, but under BuState, not BuMil.

A chime on the Ripple Creek commo algorithm sounded. Cady's voice said, "Playwright, this is Desi. On location, sweep complete, green."

"Desi, Playwright confirms."

Purser Sergeant Valko stood at the hatch controls, and had Highland even learned his name? It seemed unlikely. She was fussing with her hair again, and didn't acknowledge his presence at all.

Stepping around back, Alex drew the assistant aside and said, "Jessie, please don't broadcast our departure. It would pinpoint our location on landing for any hostiles."

"Of course not," she said, sounding put upon. "I'll wait until we're ready for Ms. Highland's statement on the ground. That's all I've told anyone to expect, and that was thirty minutes ago."

"Very good. Thank you." That was a reasonable accommodation. He appreciated it.

Highland finally turned and looked at Valko. "I'm ready," she said simply. He nodded and swiped his panel. The hatch popped, chuffed, raised and swung. From the hold underneath, a complicated mechanism rolled a flowing staircase. This was a BuState landing limo, built on a military lander chassis. It could take a pretty good hit, and was designed to look classy in austere environments.

The air was a little thin, but the gravity was light, so they should have no trouble operating. It was surprisingly clean air, and warm. There really hadn't been much development here.

Highland knew enough to wait. At a signal from Alex, Bart and Aramis stepped through and waited.

She looked at Alex expectantly, lips parted, obviously eager. He gave it a few more seconds while Cady's people swept for anything threatening.

He transmitted, "On your mark, Desi." She and Jason would coordinate with military on the ground.

"Playwright, go."

He pointed at Highland. She nodded back and stepped off, JessieM right behind her, and a hindrance they'd have to deal with. Bart and Aramis preceded her as a wall of meat, Elke and Shaman closed in behind, and Alex took the rear.

"Thanks, Olen," he said to Valko. "Good to travel with you."

The man smiled back. "You're welcome, sir. Be safe."

"That's the plan," he agreed as he stepped through and down.

The stairway really was nice, descending in a long curve and a slight sweep. It had sparkly highlights that looked like something exotic, but was only aluminum dust embedded in the polymer. The heat increased as they descended.

JessieM had sent her churp. Alex had his phone set to ping on her messages. If he couldn't stop them, he could at least read and hear them.

We're down on Mtali. Ms. Highland will start her greeting momentarily. Sorry for the delay. It was necessary for safety in this action zone.

"Action zone" was code for "war zone." It wasn't polite to use that word anymore. It was interesting, he reflected, how custom tailored language. Words came and went based on perception.

He reached the bottom as Aramis and Bart reached the podium and stepped aside. They had to leave her exposed in front for the cameras. They'd shield the rest, even though the bulk of the lander did much of that. The time you didn't was the time someone exploited it.

The rain shield overhead was also ballistic protection. Between that and the mass of the crowd was a very small window she might be attacked through, and no buildings that had line of sight within three kilometers. They'd chosen this position to maximize safety, and of course, to have natural sunlight, or whatever it was called here, on her best angle. People imagined he was overpaid. They had no idea what this job entailed.

There was still the small chance of a remotely piloted vehicle. Any engine signature should be noted, but gliders were also possible, so they had jamming . . .

They didn't think anyone hated her enough to shell the entire apron with artillery or rockets.

Cady's men kept up a steady patrol and scan. Outside that perimeter, the military had a Recon unit watching things. Recon and Ripple Creek didn't get along very well, but they could work together. Outside that, the Aerospace Force had a security and marshal squadron. Outside that, the locals had whatever security they wanted, and good luck to them.

The polished podium had been placed just so, for their security concerns, and for her presentation. The press were in a controlled area for safety, and to ensure they caught her at just the right angle of profile. Had politicians always been celebrities?

She stepped up, looked in exactly the right direction, and read from the scroll on the one-way screen in front of her.

"Thank you. It's wonderful to be here, as we try to resolve differences in policies on a galactic matter, and between neighbors locally." She paused, nodded slightly to acknowledge the applause that was being inserted electronically. There was no one close enough to be heard or seen. A camera pan of the spectators, watching her on remote video, would be merged in also.

"I look forward to meeting with all the factions, as we explore our common ground . . ."

He tuned her out. She was going to say absolutely nothing with a lot of words.

She didn't take long. At least she was a professional speaker, and knew to stick to high points and a simple message. Or maybe it was the baking heat of the flightline. Either way, she finished, stepped back, and paused for a few photos from the hovering drones.

Those were a serious point of contention. Any drone was a potential bomb. Neither Ripple Creek nor BuState Security approved of them, or wanted to allow them. It was simply impossible to ascertain safety on them. However, media was a practical necessity, and a matter of Charter Freedoms. Instead, these were owned by BuState itself, controlled by one of Cady's team, and the feed available to any news outlet. There was always a legal challenge demanding individual access, and it always failed, and the media always tried anyway.

Alex's professional paranoia didn't even like these. He had no direct control over them, so they were a potential threat, given the status of the principal.

In this case, they were safe. This time. They filled in around her.

He heard Jason in his earbuds. "Arriving, twenty." He saw the vehicle and acknowledged.

"Roger." Then, "Ma'am, our transport is over to the left."

"I see it. I'm ready when you are." It was nice having a principal experienced with security details. It simplified some things.

The ARPAC pulled up at the edge of the apron. It would have been legal and simple to roll all the way in, but Highland had insisted on a walk for visibility. Cameras continued to hover far back. So, theoretically, could snipers.

With a whine of power takeoff, the ramp lowered smoothly, and Jason stood there waiting, along with Cady and two of her men.

"Welcome to Mtali," Jason said as they approached. He smiled and seemed very glad to be together with his friends and teammates again.

"Ma'am, Jason Vaughn is our technical specialist, crosstrained as a paramedic."

"Pleased to meet you," she said with little emotion.

"Jace Cady is Agent in Charge of the Facilities Security team," he said, and introduced the tall Asian woman.

Highland paid attention now.

"Oh, Ms. Cady. So very good to meet you at last."

"Thank you, ma'am."

"I appreciate the opportunity you offer, to work with you."

"Thank you."

The effusive commentary had to be political, but unless . . . no, that had to be it. Highland knew Cady was trans, and wanted the political points, but wasn't going to say so, because any mention of trans status was rude and gauche. It would be funny watching her try to juggle the conflicting issues if it didn't make him ill to watch his friend being treated like a pawn over a very personal issue.

He stopped musing when he heard the rattle of machine gun fire. Long burst. Mid-caliber.

There was nothing wrong with Highland's reflexes. She took two leaping steps in the general direction of the vehicle and dove behind a portable shield set for that purpose. Only he'd not imagined it would actually be needed.

That's why they pay us, and why we do that, he thought. Elke and Bart were closest, dove down with her, and readied to sprint up the ramp on either side of her.

He pointed and shouted, "Contact left!"

Jason shouted, "Suppression. I need some kind of suppression!" Elke didn't have any explosives, no one had anything but light arms, and someone with a machine gun had them pinned.

Then as fast as it had started, the hostiles disappeared.

That was good, since they were alive and apparently unhurt. Just out of view, Shaman patted Highland down, and he knew that from the surprised yelp everyone made the first time that happened. It was bad, because they had no idea who the threat had been, and it was probable that others would follow.

Aramis made it into the ARPAC in two leaps, braced feet on either side of the turret station, yanked and slammed the charging handle on the cannon, and opened fire in methodical but rapid shots.

Highland started screaming.

"Stop! Stop shooting! Get down, you militaristic asshole!"

Aramis turned and stared, but didn't let go of the weapon.

"They're gone, and I don't want any bad press. Get down!"

Aramis glanced at Alex, who nodded. He shrugged and climbed down.

Highland lowered her voice, but not her intensity. "The whole point of a rating event is lost if someone gets hurt."

There were two ways to interpret that, but Alex keyed on the proper words, then replayed it again, both mentally and via his recorder, to be sure that's what was actually said. It was too surreal to anger him now, though he knew it would shortly. In the meantime, he wanted to triple check.

"Ma'am, please clarify for me. That attack was a fake, set to help with your image?"

"It's more than that," she said. "It's about presentation. Poise and confidence are critical to any race, or to any presentation. I needed to start this off on the right foot."

"Yes, ma'am, but I need to know about these things." He hadn't heard any cracks pass by, so either it hadn't been aimed this way, or they'd been blanks.

"I didn't know if you were trained enough as actors to be believable. It works better if it's unstaged."

Yes, this was a waking nightmare. "It doesn't really, ma'am. We can act appropriately, and without warning, our default appropriate response could have gotten someone shot. That won't help your ratings."

"It depends on whom, and that's what my publicists are for. That was just a show with some blanks. They're not even real guns."

Well, this mission had hit the bottom of the shaft in a hurry, and was now starting to dig.

"Ma'am, let me reiterate that we are trained, contracted and expected to use lethal force if necessary. That's based on our threat assessment. I strongly caution against these kind of displays. There will be enough legitimate threats."

"Yes, but presentation is critical. I'd rather not be attacked, but if so, I of course plan to develop the event to demonstrate my core competencies."

Alex thought that "exploit" fit better than "develop."

He said, "Elke and Jason are both very skilled with cameras, for intel and promotional purposes. I am quite willing to make their footage available after it has been examined for tactical purposes."

Highland considered a moment, and replied, "Very well. I suppose I can arrange for Jessie to take charge of that if and when it happens."

"Thank you for your understanding. That will help us a lot." He'd also make very sure that footage was edited to blur anything intel-worthy in the background. Jessie appeared to have little restraint on what she loaded.

Highland continued, "You have to understand, part of the reason I was sent here was to lower my visibility during this stage of the campaign. This is a remote area, none of the key geographies care if these peasants kill each other, and I need to be able to maintain visibility, and boost my ratings."

"I can see that, ma'am, and we'll do what we can to assist. Please keep us in the loop. We're here for you." *Within reason.* This bitch would actually stage a battle for vid ratings. Unbelievable.

Alex understood the pressure she faced. He was not, however, going to assist with her campaign, even if it would make protecting her easier. There were some things even a pig wouldn't do. He did need to learn about this, though, and work with it. That's why he was getting paid more than most top surgeons.

It didn't seem like much of a deal. After all, that was probably why they'd nixed Elke's explosives.

At least they had an armored vehicle for transit. Clearly now, Highland wanted that for its imposing presence and the implication of great danger. However, this at least worked in their favor for protection purposes.

There were cutouts in the contract to separate them from a client who refused to cooperate sufficiently. The problem was, those criteria were vague, though he had the final say, and their job was to protect the bitch, not play rules lawyer, there would be repercussions if they did so. Why this type of client? Because they paid a lot of money, which is what it came down to.

There was a lot more to being a mercenary than people outside the business realized.

◎ CHAPTER 5 ◎

JASON WAS GLAD to have been on the advance. He had a grasp of local conditions, or as much grasp as one could have from outside the insane clannishness and religious freakery that went on here. He'd made introductions, knew the rough lay of the base and the units, and had their billets set. Highland had choice quarters in the official VIP/diplomat/government section of the base. They had decent quarters a floor down. The rooms were spare and small, but they were private, and they had a roomy common area they'd convert into a ready room. It was better than most of the troops here would get. He idly wondered if any of those troops had been in Celadon on Salin when they were there.

They also had a floor reserved at a nearby hotel, for them and their principal, and she had official quarters at the UN Colonial Liaison compound across town, where he'd staked out the adjoining suite using her credentials, to the annoyance of the local lodging manager.

He led the way to their quarters and pointed to indicate rooms.

"Aramis, Elke, Shaman, Bart, Jason, me. Kitchen. Had only vegetarian stuff when we arrived. Default to avoid upsetting people with dietary restrictions. However, it upset me, so I fixed that. Beer is very limited. We have one each to unwind from today, and I'll purchase more on a very limited basis. That's per me, Alex, Corporate and the base commander."

Aramis said, "I wasn't going to argue the point, but Bart might."

"I will be fine," Bart said. "Business is business."

"You see the vault there." It was more a large cabinet than a real vault, but it would suffice. "I did encourage and assist both the Security Directorate and ACAMS—their electronic contractor—in wiring it. We can bypass it if need be. It will log and monitor all activity inside and immediately in front. There is no audio. I've already placed audio scramblers to make sure. I advised that we might discuss personal details of Ms. Highland, and certainly technical matters regarding her security and travel, and that any discovered leaks would lead to serious conspiracy investigations if something happened to her. They were reluctant even to give us the monitoring we have, so we should be safe."

Elke said, "Ah, there is the paranoia I'd missed so much when on Earth. It is so good to be normal again."

"Indeed. Everyone stow your personals, we'll take a tour and discuss security. Beer when we're back."

"Uniform up. We'll blend in better."

In ten minutes they were ready, as a gaggle who presented as military while looking nothing like a formation. It would be obvious to any troop with experience they were "Security contractors," and high-placing ones. They had a company combat uniform that would make them look like any one of dozens of regional or national contingents.

They went out the foot gate of their compound and onto the broad base itself. There were islands of palm trees, a few flowerbeds, both maintained by bored, off-duty troops, and the usual block billets, portable concessionaires and heavy impact barriers around all important buildings.

A squad of troops went past in an open-backed Grumbly, heading for what appeared to be guardmount at the nearest Entry Control Point. But . . .

Aramis gaped. "What in the name of every god there is *is* that?"

Jason said, "That's the new camo."

Alex asked, "What in the hell were they thinking?" They sounded as incredulous as Jason had felt when he first saw it.

"It's supposed to fool the eye."

"It's bloody pink and orange with purple highlights," Alex repeated.

"Yes, the theory is that the colors are designed for optical interference. They're as far from anything natural as possible, which throws the brain off for a moment. The contrast between them disrupts outlines, and the blotches are computer designed to create artificial depth. Their lab tests say it takes about point four seconds for any response, plus normal reaction time. It makes them harder to hit. In addition, tactical lighting or flares create similar illusions."

"It's bloody pink and orange."

Elke said, "With a reflective belt." She sounded amused.

Aramis said, "That's for safety in the dark. Regulations."

"It's a war zone and it's daylight."

"You're expecting logic?" Jason asked.

Alex said, "No, but I'd hope that someone with a clue and a spine and some brass would at some point in the process say, 'This is fucking stupid,' and put a stop to it."

Jason said, "Yeah, I wondered about that, too. Just as I think it can't possibly get stupider, it does."

Bart said, "At a guess, I can locate that three kilometers away, without optics."

"It's the best camouflage ever devised. Their official reports say so."

"Uh huh." Alex looked meaningfully at the Catafract pattern they wore. Jason tried to. This stuff was near impossible to focus on, with its lines fading in and out of the surface, the texture shifts and the treatment that reflected nearby coloring from its neutral gray areas between the colors.

Jason said, "Yeah, they were offered this and refused."

"I can't wait to find out why."

"Officially, it's not as good, per their tests. Unofficially, I suspect a combination of not-invented-here and production cost. This stuff is expensive, but it does work."

"While I guarantee that doesn't." Alex pointed in the general direction of the troops.

"The people in the Army Field Research Center say it does."

Shaman said, "Let's put one of them in it and find out."

"Believe me, you are not the first person to suggest that."

Alex waited for the reply from his boss. He had a local legal contact now, to respond to the issues that were certainly going to arise, including this one. Highland's stupid stunt was worthy of cancelling the contract on the spot and leaving her hanging, and he'd like nothing better. No one else could be on station in less than two weeks, no one was as good, and the administration apparently wasn't going to give her official escort.

The message chimed in, and he sat up. First, it had to be downloaded to his secure stick. That got transferred to the closed system, checked for security, then decrypted.

He waved the file open and read.

"Proceed as ordered. Principal will be extremely difficult. Invoice will reflect this. We're playing our own game as part of this, and need to maintain at least peripheral involvement for the future. Make all efforts to cooperate as far as your judgment indicates. There is potential long-term benefit regardless of how the election turns out."

Well, that was that. The boss knew she was an insane client, and wanted to proceed. So, those were his orders. He didn't have to like them. It did, however, color how he was to respond.

Elke really needed those explosives. She always asked for more than she needed, and she used them as often as she could, but they did keep the clients alive. Without them, she was just one more suited goon. With them, she was a logarithmic force exponentiator.

As to lethal force, they always had used it, and Highland had to know that. They didn't unless necessary, but the two key rules of executive protection were to stop the threat and evacuate the area. If one didn't want to evacuate, stopping the threat was more critical. If one was agreeable to it, and had good police support, the threat could be ignored. Ripple Creek got hired for events where the feasibility for both was reduced, which meant applying their own force—killing the threat. This was understood, historically observable fact.

With that in mind, Highland was not stupid, so she was self-obsessed. She really thought that her opinion would change their MO. Likely, she was very used to getting her way. That did fit her background.

His office chair was comfortable but he was nonetheless tense. This was going to be an aggravating mission.

He wiped the file, randomized the stick, and removed it.

※ ※ ※ ※

Elke thought the Security Directorate building was reasonably secure. It had a gated fence inside crash barriers, a double translucite overhead with a sloped and surface-hardened roof. They were locked in through three sets of doors, ID checked, scanned, their personal weapons hand-checked and returned. Elke reluctantly surrendered her glasses because of the built-in cameras. Then they were inside and in a much smaller function space.

"Good thickness," she said.

Jason said, "It is, and layered. They won't give details, but I think they're safe enough. Now here's where it gets confusing." He waved them into a small conference room, and followed.

"Team, this is Captain Jason Das. For obvious reasons, we will call him Captain or Das, not Jason. Sir, this is the team."

Elke nodded as she was introduced. Das sounded Canadian. He wore the older style uniform, not the pink *scračku*.

He shook hands all around, then said, "I'm tasked with liaising with you. Given your principal, I'd have expected one of the majors to take it, or even the colonel himself, but they're already multiply booked."

She wondered if they'd found a way to be too busy. The principal was a bitch even by Elke's standards.

Jason, their Jason, said, "He'll provide us with whatever intel security comes down, which of course comes from Intelligence first, then to here, then to us."

Das said, "I'll be as quick with it as I can, but it does have to be processed, and cleared for release. I can clear some of it, but the general has various subjects, which I can't discuss I'm afraid," he looked embarrassed, "that he wants a tight hold on. So the higher ups have to approve those items. Of course, no one wants to risk Minister Highland unnecessarily, but military operations do have their role, and the general will give those equal priority."

Elke hoped it was higher priority, really, even if it increased their risk on the ground. Highland was one person, and there were a lot of troops involved.

He seemed to pause for questions, so she asked, "Captain Das, through which channel should I inquire about my explosive? The weapons are here, my demolition gear is not."

He looked a bit surprised. "I wasn't told of any. I can check with logistics, customs and with the cargo office. It's probably there somewhere. Inter-agency communication has not been good, which is going to affect you. Sorry."

Aramis asked, "What AARs do you need from us?"

"Anything you can release that isn't restricted by State is intel for us, and useful for us. We'll gauge general and specific threats and weapons availability. Most of the active extremist groups here are dangerous by volume, not by intent. Of course, most of the residents are peaceful civilians with no intent to do harm." From his expression Elke assumed it was an officially mandated speech for political reasons. The SecGen's parents had lived here as teachers while he was young, too, which had to affect something.

She believed Captain Das was honest. She also believed someone had deliberately held up her materiel out of some kind of ridiculous worry about it. She'd have Alex contact Corporate as well. The *blbci* always thought of big explosions hurting bystanders, not as expertly placed and controlled tools.

In the meantime, this was a big base, they certainly had a Munitions Disposal element, and she had a bit of a reputation. She'd find something. The nice thing about explosive was it was consumed in use, and very hard to track.

She couldn't wait for this meeting to end.

After the briefing, back at their digs, Horace did a mental assessment of his teammates so far. Alex was very disturbed by the obvious leak and complication JessieM presented, with good reason. Jason seemed more relaxed than usual. He must like what he'd found so far. Horace himself felt comfortable enough. He had nerves, but the religious fruitcakes were at least monotheistic and not the insane butchers the animists in Cameroun had been. There wouldn't be any eating of eyeballs, just death. Elke had that twitch. She'd be off to find explosive as soon as she could, licitly or not. Bart was taciturn and calm, and not just his exterior. Aramis seemed to alternate between brooding and cheerful. That first must be something to do with Caron. The man was playing with acid in that relationship. The balance for them all was the clear but reasonably common threat. Straight combat with amateurs. They'd done that before, and had lots of weapons, and the backup didn't seem hostile.

Otherwise it was warmish and pleasant here, though the planet had short seasons and it would chill soon. If only every war zone could have a climate like Hawaii . . . but in that case, few people would be inclined to fight.

As to their principals, since they'd involuntarily picked up the spare, there was tension between the two, but it seemed to be up from JessieM and not down from Highland. Doting worship? Romantic? It wasn't really relevant, as JessieM only mattered as an aside. Highland was sociopathic and narcissistic, which was not at all healthy, but common enough at her level of power, and meant little would bother her unless her worldview got shaken down. If they did wind up in the brush in a tent, she'd possibly fall apart, or act even more regal and demanding. She'd largely disregard anyone else unless she felt they were controlling her, then he'd need a lot of tranquilizers. He had four types that overlapped in effect.

He sighed inside. On the one hand, he'd so much prefer to be back on the Big Island in his comfortable home, watching the lava. On the other, this not only paid for that, but led to personal growth. As lovely as Hawaii was, it was too pleasant to offer any challenge.

As to the team, they were healthy enough and would become their effective gestalt with some renewed association. He would recommend another bout of training after this. Real missions actually took the edge off, rather than honing it, much like using a scalpel dulled it.

Getting back to the present, he called the base clinic.

"Outpost Freedom Medical Facility, this is not a secure contact, how may I help you?"

"Yes, this is Doctor Mbuto. I am with the BuState element and need to talk to the administrator."

"Stand by, please, I will connect you to two four seven."

In only a moment, a pleasant female answered. Middle aged, likely Portuguese.

"This is Doctor Caoila."

"Yes, ma'am, I am Horace Mbuto, surgeon and medical contact for Ripple Creek Security. Our element is providing security for Ms. Highland."

"Yes, Doctor. Your Mr. Vaughn spoke to me a few days ago."

"Excellent. I hope that we will not have need of your services."

"As do I. Mr. Vaughn briefed me that in an emergency you will probably not identify a casualty, nor any details, but simply state what equipment you need on arrival."

"Correct. Neither the patient's name nor status is revealed as far as possible, much as with military OPSEC."

"I understand, and we are set up for similar events. I presume there is a relevant BuState clearance code similar to the military ones?"

"I'm positive there is, but I do not know it. I can have our Agent in Charge contact you regarding that."

"That would be appreciated. At some point, the admin details must be completed or someone will grind their teeth."

"Of course. Also, if there is a mass casualty event and we are not out on escort, it's possible I can be available to assist. Mr. Vaughn is also an experienced paramedic, so you may call us both. Please understand that we must place Ms. Highland's safety above anyone else's."

"That must be aggravating for you professionally, but I understand and appreciate it."

"I hope our encounters are all this relaxed. Good day."

"Thank you, Doctor."

He could only hope it really did work that smoothly, if needed. There were usually frictions between them and local authority, and between departments. Though Highland's obvious status might help, since any emergency might reasonably be assumed to involve her.

It would likely be interesting, which is why he got paid.

Jason was quite glad to be back with the team. He'd been a complete pariah upon arrival, though he'd made most of the connections he needed to. Now all the planning got gutted by reality.

He, Alex, Aramis and Elke sat in his room, since he, Jason could most easily clear this one against intrusion, and had done so twice today. So far, there were no signs of eavesdropping, but in this society, there would be sooner or later. Everyone wanted some kind of hold.

Alex still looked pissed from the fake attack earlier. If that's how this bitch was going to play things, Jason didn't blame him. He wondered if part of the reason they were hired was because BuState security had either had enough of antics like that, nixed the idea of using fake attacks for publicity, or if it was a combination of using Ripple Creek as a whipping bitch while playing for publicity at the same time.

Amusingly, if they pulled this off, they'd look even better.

However, Alex was talking and he should follow that.

Alex said, "The next problem is JessieM. Jason, we need to find a way to squelch that signal. If she won't stop, we may have to cut it off."

"She'll suspect after the second time at most. I've already done it once."

Elke said, "As have I."

Alex said, "Hopefully, it won't take more than that. If we wind up in real shit, I'm hoping it'll be a wakeup call."

Jason said, "Also, we're guarding her as well. She's a pain in the ass, not covered by contract, but I don't see any way to argue the point."

Alex replied, "Nope. We'll just have to cover both. She's secondary, though. Worst case, I suspect the b . . . principal will benefit from danger factor in the news."

Jason grinned. "Are we old enough to be that cynical?"

Aramis asked, "Are we young enough to deal with the repercussions if the flaky little sidekick gets iced?"

Alex said, "We shout for Corporate and hold up the contract. I suspect she'll be a hero of the Revolution, or whatever, we take our usual flogging in the press, and move on. Also, I don't trust them not to be spying on us. You and Elke need to run regular checks on our commo, our encryption, and our quarters."

"Yeah, they'd love dirt for PR, blackmail or politics."

Elke smiled. "You said the same thing three times." She continued, "I will keep things clear here, and will ensure we have full monitoring of our principal, for safety's sake."

And for intel for blackmail's sake, he thought. They understood each other.

"Okay, break and get to it. I'll have more in a bit."

Jason ushered them out of the room, because it was his room at least for now, and he felt responsible for it, liked his privacy, and wanted to ensure it stayed private. That was why he'd hand-removed the vid terminal, and used only his own gear to interface with the nodes. It wasn't that he didn't trust his own people. He just didn't trust anyone, and if he was to be accountable he wanted as much control as possible. Professional distrust ran in all directions.

He turned toward what constituted their armory. He had weapons to prep. That, at least, was enjoyable.

CHAPTER 6

ARAMIS SAW JASON come from the conference, and head into the side room. He assumed it was to visit their armory, and he was correct. He fell-to to assist Jason with the guns.

"Can I help?"

"Please, and thanks."

"What do you need?"

"Crates," Jason said, and pointed.

They had a pair of two-meter cargo crates that were supposed to contain all their weapons and then some. They had to check that. The bands were keyed to Jason's fingerprints and snapped off with the right combination of print and pull.

"Sweet," Aramis said as he saw inside. What a reassuring crate.

There were six carbines with attached launchers, and three spares of each. Three shotguns. One autocannon that would need to be pintle mounted. Two squad weapons. One marksman rifle in 8mm. One heavy machine gun to mount on their vehicle on top of the three Jason already had attached. Spare parts. Tools. Knives. Jason's tomahawk. Extra body armor. Smoke grenades. Flares. Batteries. Multispectrum vision units. Tactical harnesses.

"We're short on grenades and explosives," he said.

Jason replied, "Yeah, check the other one."

He reached over and popped the straps on the second, smaller crate.

"Medusa!" Aramis crowed. That multibarreled, multiheaded,

massive monstrosity on a backpack was instantly recognizable. "She'll never let us carry it if she sees it."

"That's why she won't see it. It was IDed in the inventory as 'gun system, soldier portable.' We didn't say, 'With four barrels of automated death ready to paint the walls with people's livers.'"

"I see bullion, cash, a bag of spangly jewelry, good cigars, enough for trade, some liquor . . . I'm not seeing grenades either hand or projectile."

Jason reached past him. "Yeah, and this shotgun drum is shot, slug and recon only, no flame or explosive rounds."

"I don't see any explosive kits for Elke."

"Please do not offer that information. We'll relay it through Alex."

"Yeah. So they shorted us on everything explosive. Does the Medusa have loads?"

"Not for the grenade launcher, no."

"Fuckers."

Jason indicated the crates. "They don't seem to have been opened, so the stuff was never loaded. I don't know if that was a military thing, a BuState thing, something personal from Highland, or just some kind of cock-up."

Aramis shrugged. "In the meantime, we do have small arms."

"And that," Jason said.

"Oh?" Aramis opened the box. Harness. Nozzles . . .

"A jump belt?" he asked to confirm.

"Good for about thirty seconds of lift. Between the need for recon, the apartment blocks and those stupid walls they're building between factions, I figured we might use one."

"Heck, only one?"

"One was all I could get them to unload," Jason said.

An hour later, Aramis was amazed. Jason knew more about small arms than any dozen armorers he'd met. He could rattle off from memory alloys, strengths, ranges, ballistic patterns, timing and torque specs, masses, generation upgrades. He could strip a carbine in twenty seconds without even looking at it. He had a small but detailed tool box, and Aramis helped him sort and lay out parts as he modded all their weapons.

"Since we have permission from the principal, money from Corporate, and the tools to do so, we'll go with the best, personalized."

Aramis asked, "How do you know how everyone wants them personalized?"

"From two years of operating with you," Jason said with a grin. He slapped retaining pins on the weapon he held, cycled through a function check, and shoved it at Aramis.

Aramis took it. He checked the chamber, settled it in his grip and . . .

Holy crap. That was awesome.

It fit his hands perfectly. Controls for the weapon, attached launcher, optics and accessories sat right under his thumbs and forefingers. Three easy clicks took him from scope to standard to battlesight, with a thumb flick for night vision or UV for seeing through smoke. It balanced exactly between his hands. Everything was mounted with quick detach keys. He'd already seen the compartments with spare parts, batteries and cleaning kit. It was self-contained light support for a squad, and they each had one, plus some spares.

"Damned good work, man," he said.

"Thanks. There may be some problems with the encryption. If so, let me know."

Aramis shifted his grip. The biometrics didn't disengage, as required by law. He still had a live weapon even when only his finger was on the trigger, no palm on the grip.

"It seems to be working fine," he said. Fine for what he needed it for.

"Good. I'll work on the others. Tell Elke I have hers almost ready."

"She'll be jealous that she wasn't first." He stretched and started to stand.

Jason grinned. "She'll be fine. We go way back."

"When did you first work with her, anyway?" He crouched back down for the story.

Jason leaned back and grabbed a rag to clean his hands. "I was actually still in service. We had an exercise going on, and mining charges set to do a hasty dig of some boulders. You've seen the OmniDig multipurpose engineer vehicle?" he asked. Aramis nodded. "Well, in addition to trench, grade and load blades, it has a high-speed pole drill. On pilot bore, it cuts five centimeters, and can reach down three meters. More than enough. We chased out, bored under this boulder field in our LZ, planted the charges, backed off and shot. Nothing happened."

"Ah, that always sucks."

"It does. We gave it the ten minutes as required, and started back to reset charges. Someone decided to test a cap. Nothing. So we secured another lot number and started out.

"Then something did happen. One of them blew. We got showered in rock frag. Six minutes later a second one detonated. At that point, no one wanted anything to do with it, except we needed the field clear, because we did have a ship de-orbiting."

"That's a pretty lifelike exercise, not to clear first, then land."

"Right. Don't take this the wrong way, but we do more of that than the Army. Most exercises are pretty real in the functional details."

It used to be a sore point, but Aramis had to agree anymore. "Yeah, my Army went to hell when it became part of the UN, rather than being distinctly American. I am a bit jealous of the other branches, and some other nations."

"Right. The U.S. wanted to keep Marines for distinction, needed its own Aerospace, though even that is coalescing with the others now, and of course, the colonial units have to be independent. You did get shafted. But anyway, we had two craft to land, the first already in descent, and we had to clear the rubble fast, and it was pretty clear the charges or the caps were unreliable. We told the landers to abort, then we screamed for help."

"Elke?"

"Yes, she showed up, alone, all sixty kilos of her—she's put a bit more muscle on—went to one of the live ones, poked an illuminator and camera down, while we sat there shivering. She asked to see the box, ran some numbers, and told us there'd been a packing error. We had random delay charges used for area denial."

"Oh, shit."

"Yes, very much. The LT was ready to abandon that section of the exercise, have the craft land at a proper port, and ferry everyone out.

"Elke told him to wait, walked back out, and started hand-rolling directional charges. She cut them off from Dynalene sticks, bored the ends with a knife, capped, planted and wired. A third one blew while she was doing this, and she just kept walking, stuffing, setting.

"We had about five minutes of our two hour exercise window left when she walked back, asked the commander to clear the range, let him get off his three calls, then called fire in the hole and the entire field lit up. It turns out she'd put shattering charges over them, too. All these car-sized boulders turned into hundred millimeter gravel in a couple of seconds. She hung around a couple of days. We met in the chow hall once. It was a heck of a surprise when I joined the company and we wound up on assignment together."

"Was she always a flake?" That wasn't the best way to phrase it, but . . . well, yes it was.

"Yes. Very much. She's asocial, dislikes people because they're not logical or predictable, is far more educated than anyone realizes. She has a doctorate in physics."

Aramis replayed that and said, "Huh?"

"Yeah, I didn't find out until a few weeks ago. She can crunch the numbers in her head as she goes."

Aramis said, "I figured she had the usual reference charts in her visor and lots of hands-on practice."

"She has that, too, but she really does do the math as she goes. Did her basics in electronics, worked in the lab for the Czech Regional Police, moved into Munitions, and did school while working."

"So when whatsisname on Govannon . . . Eggett . . . said he'd read her papers . . ."

"Yes, he was head of explosive mining for Caron's family, and he meant professional journal papers, not just industry notes."

"Damn. I feel very undereducated, with only cartography and navigation theory to my bio."

"Well, education isn't wisdom or intelligence. Look at any politician for proof of that."

"I'd rather be compared to someone worthy, thanks," Aramis replied.

There was noise at the door, and everyone else came through.

"Where are my explosives?" Elke asked at once.

Jason said, "Here, have a shotgun, a carbine, a pistol and a fighting knife." He handed them over.

"Very nice, thank you," she said without expression as she took them, checked the chambers on all three, did a couple of practice drills, and laid them on the couch, the sheathed knife atop them. "Where are my explosives?"

Aramis handed out knives and demolition hammers to the circle around him, then started on pistols.

Alex took his, cleared it, nodded and said, "No word on the explosives?"

Jason said, "No sign that they've been here at all. I'm betting they're in a separate box."

Elke paced a bit. She didn't make any comments, but she was obviously irritated, and . . . Aramis guessed vulnerable, except that sounded romantic. Insecure? He could see that. Explosives were her tools. It would be the same if he didn't have firearms or armor.

"Where is the armor?" he asked, realizing he hadn't seen that.

Jason said, "Screwup in transit and customs, Cady will deliver it tomorrow."

"Good." Assuming it happened. He looked back at Elke.

Shaman kept an eye on her, surreptitiously, and she probably noticed but didn't say anything. She helped check and clear weapons, stow them, tag them. She filled magazines and belts, checked batteries.

In short order they had it all done, and split up the bullion and cash into packs and pockets. Aramis found himself in possession of a contractor credit account, a prepaid card with a healthy limit, a roll of cash that would choke a medium sized alligator, several hundred grams of gold, some silver, and one each palladium and rhodium 30 gram bars. It was a good thing he'd be armed, because anyone getting a whiff of this just might consider murder.

Still, it reassured him on bugging out. It was a mark of trust from the company, too, as they'd provided that from their own assets, and would have to take his, and their collective, word on disposition.

Elke looked unhappy, but she checked over her hardware and very politely said, "Thank you, Jason, the customizing is excellent. I'm going to retire early." She slung them carefully and walked out silently.

He didn't think he'd ever seen her that pissed the entire time they'd worked together.

Bart broke the uncomfortable silence by saying, "I would like that beer now."

❊ ❊ ❊ ❊

Alex was mostly satisfied. Elke's gear and the heavier weapons were an issue, but almost everything else had been resolved, though not the way channels would approve.

That's their own damned fault for refusing to cooperate, he thought. When they'd first started this outfit, the military had been competitors and eventually the enemy. However, they'd never until now been hostile.

The medics and intel were cordial and professional, at least as far as they saw mutual benefit. The rest of the base so far was actively antagonistic. They'd have to find some way to smooth that out.

Their quarters were quite comfortable for the field. They had billets on par with officers or other high-end contractors: hard buildings, private rooms where enlisted personnel would have three to five, basic bunks and lockable closets. The problem, of course, was the weapons, which in theory were supposed to be secured whenever they were not on escort, which would mean a lot of back and forth to the armory. In practice, they usually left someone in the billet to watch things, armed. He also knew Aramis concealed a small pistol when out. He was sure Jason did, too, though he'd never seen it. He made do with a knife.

Elke was ostensibly sleeping, and certainly fuming about her mistreatment. The explosives were a necessary component, and he'd talk to Das about that in the morning. For now, they could use a non-alcoholic beverage on the military side, and a little noise and camaraderie.

"Just keep the attitudes from bothering you," he said. "Right, Aramis?"

"Understood. I speak their language. I can talk around any problems."

Good. The man took the hint.

"Jason?"

"No problem at all. I just remember that I am Aerospace Force, Grainne Colony, and therefore better than they are."

He grinned at the delivery. "Very good. Shaman is remaining here. Bart will simply sit quietly in the corner and drink, and no one would be stupid enough to start a fight with him."

Jason said, "I'm sure someone would, so watch out for idiots. The big guy is always wrong."

"On paper, at least," Bart said, and cracked his knuckles. "I shall be relaxed."

At the gate, Alex greeted the guard. "We need to sign out."

The guard stared at him. "Why?"

"So we're accounted for. It's policy for State and for our company."

The man rolled his eyes, but grabbed a screen and passed it over. They each printed it and waited for it to acknowledge, then Alex handed it back.

"Thank you," he said.

The response was a mumble.

It was less than a kilometer to the rec center, but they attracted some stares.

"Everyone drives, even here," Aramis noted.

"Yes," he agreed. "Want to go back, or remember that for next time?"

Bart said, "Next time we shall take a limo, just to show them up."

"Discreet, Bart."

"At two meters tall?" Yes, the man was huge, but they could at least try.

The weather was quite pleasant and the walk enjoyable. It was early enough that they were before shift change. That reminded him of the issue that presented.

The day here was 25 hours and change. The UN ran on Earth's 24 hour clock, "To avoid schedule-related accidents," and ran two 12 hour shifts. That meant a steady progression across the day. However, Highland's appearances were mostly local day, though she, or rather Jessie, had planned some so the transmission times would hit certain areas of Earth, notably North America and Coastal Asia, during prime viewer time there, after being transferred from surface to ship, through the Jump Point then down to Earth. That was going to be murder on their own schedule.

For now, though, they should appear, participate and relax. Aramis was slightly ahead and held the door.

There were other contractors on base, but the Ripple Creek team were certainly the highest profile. Also, they were effectively combatants, while most of the others were either strictly technical support, or guards with nonlethal weapons and no authority outside the perimeter. This had caused tension before, and they expected it now.

It was made worse by their military non-uniforms. For now, they were wearing field pants with adjustable color, turned to dull gray, and collared sport shirts that had the obvious shine of nonnewtonian mesh. That said to everyone, "Contractors with assets." Coupled with JessieM's casual release of details, pretty much everyone knew they were Ripple Creek and Highland's personal detail. It might be a good idea to not socialize until things had a chance to settle down and some favors were exchanged. Still, they were here now.

They picked a vacant sitting area, ignored the stares and offered an occasional polite nod, and sat down. There were a couple of mutters, but nothing seemed problematic. Of course, things might be better, or worse, after some action and interaction.

Or even right now. The lieutenant near the counter spoke loudly enough to be heard clearly.

"That's not your problem, soldier. Contractors are exempt from all regulations. Just ask them and they'll tell you. In exchange, they have to put up with more pay, better quarters and get to go to political banquets. It's a rough job."

Alex looked up and asked, in a quiet voice, "Is there a problem, Lieutenant?"

The officer turned, and his expression wasn't a smirk, but was provocative.

He said, "Pardon me for believing people like you should be under military discipline. It would change your attitude."

Alex said, "We're all veterans. It's company policy." He was irritated. Even a lieutenant should know better than to provoke a fight, though Alex wasn't going to mention so, because that would be provocative.

"Yeah, I understand you left under questionable circumstances." He pointed at Aramis and continued, "Anderson was asked to leave due to conflict of interest with your employer. Weil's a surface sailor, which stopped being militarily relevant a century ago."

Jason did smirk and said, "Want to say something about me, next?"

The lieutenant turned. "Yeah, you're a colonial wannabe. It's not like your forces will ever amount to anything. As to the others, Sykora is a glorified bureaucrat who joined a pseudo police force, and Mbuto's 'army' doesn't even exist anymore, nor does the second rate excuse of a nation it belonged to."

Alex was still ticked, but Jason took over and flashed a big grin.

"Thanks. It's always good to know where someone stands."

"That's it? That's all you have to say?"

Jason shrugged. "There's not much to say. You didn't offer anything to really argue about."

Alex came out of it. Jason had defused that brilliantly. The lieutenant stood looking quizzical, then turned and walked off.

After he was gone, Jason said, "I could see the wheels turning behind his eyes, and I think that was brain smoke trickling from his ears."

"Thanks for doing that."

Jason said, "No problem. We're going to get more of that, though."

"Yes, I believe we are."

"I'm also disturbed that he had that much background on us. It's searchable, if you know our names or get good face shots. Now, of course, we're outed forever. If he can search us, so can any threats."

"Yup. Thanks, JessieM."

"That was a power play."

"Yes. He wants us to know how connected he is, and that he thinks he's better thereby."

"How long are we staying?"

"Thirty minutes. Want to play a game of pool?"

"Sure. I'm terrible at it and will laugh at myself."

"Can't hurt."

Aramis was eager to get on with the mission, but there was always groundwork. He knew it was important, and he took pains to make sure it was done properly.

In addition to the bailout bullion and cash, he'd been assigned discreet assets to use for his part of the groundwork. He was expected to furnish maps of as many areas as possible, with photos, on a nonconnected system or actual paper. He usually went for both. Basic supplies of food, water, clothing and rucks would be stashed in several safe locations, along with weapons as they were able to acquire them by purchase, trade, battlefield pickups or outright theft from anyone who on paper wasn't allowed to have them. Once, they'd even robbed a military armory. That had been life and death at the time, though. Planning ahead meant it might be unlawful, but shouldn't come at a cost to anyone.

Cady and Jason had two safehouses arranged already, but he would like a third. No one else needed to know about it.

He reflected that three years before he'd been a pure mercenary, attracted by gobs of cash and the potential excitement. It now was more home to him than the military had been, still better paid, but with fantastic esprit de corps and a better sense of accomplishment. They kept people alive when no one else could. He took the task seriously. Still, there was a thrill of ancient gunslinging and swordselling in acquiring the assets they needed. Weapons, explosives and bullion made for a fine simulation of an adventure game, in the real world.

The beer wasn't very good, but he finished it rather than waste it. He finished cutting the current map, saved it on both the "phones" he had wire-connected to the unit, and ran six copies through the printer on tough polymer sheet. The phones had no circuits for communication, only memory storage and display. One printed copy would go to each bugout location, and one each to Jason, Alex and himself.

At some point he'd have to make a shopping trip.

❁ CHAPTER 7 ❁

ELKE ROSE EARLY. She was about to try something she hadn't much experience with. Diplomacy.

Neatly dressed complete to a blazer, she took an apple and a chunk of havarti cheese for breakfast, and went down to the vehicle apron.

They had access to several, but for now, that little three-wheel runabout was fine. It was different from the military's, but State had several. Dressed like this, no one should remark on her. She rolled for the gate.

The guard held up a pad, and she nodded, slowed and printed out.

It took only minutes to reach the engineer compound. It had nice landscaping and a proud sign they'd milled themselves. That was a positive indicator. She drove in carefully. There were no shop markers. That was decent OPSEC, but she'd know what she was looking for, and yes, that was it. She parked.

The shop in question was separated slightly from the others, had additional cofferdamming, and two items that were trophies. One was a section of nose cone off an H-17 rocket, the other a twisted corkscrew of metal that most people might take for mere fragmentation debris, but she knew had been explosively formed in a combination of practice and recreation. It was a reasonably good job, though she could do better.

She pushed the button and waited patiently. It was a full two minutes before someone opened a physical hatch and looked through. He was early thirties, lean and unremarkable.

"May I help you, ma'am?"

"I'm Eleonora Sykora, Executive Protection Agent and Munitions Disposal Specialist in Charge, Ripple Creek Security. I will be operating in your area and need to consult with your shop chief."

"One moment. And can I see your ID, please?"

She handed over her primary ID—she had a duplicate in case of emergencies, and several local and Earth IDs in case evasion was necessary. There was no reason it would be necessary here, but Jason issued the instructions and she concurred.

The man glanced it over and said, "Very well, please stand by." He closed the hatch.

Another full minute elapsed before the door was opened. The greeter stood next to a woman, a master sergeant.

She said, "Agent Sykora? I'm Master Sergeant Corbelle." She sounded French, though the accent was unusual. Caribbean? Quebecois?

"Pleased to meet you."

"Tea?" Corbelle indicated an office.

"Thank you."

Elke adjusted her seat to keep her back from the door, accepted a cup from the assistant.

"I didn't catch your name," she said.

"Sorry. Sergeant Lang. Welcome to Mtali."

"Thank you."

"Well, Agent Sykora, you're rather well known in some circles."

"More than I would like, on this tour, unfortunately."

"Yes, I figured that wasn't intentional publicity. What can I help you with?"

"I wish to be polite so that you know I am operating in your area. I am available for disposal work if not on post with my principal. I'm available for consult."

"We appreciate that. It's been quiet, though your last tour had an interesting outcome."

"Which do you mean? I've had several." Did they mean Govannon, where she'd used a small nuclear core as a distraction? Or . . .

"Celadon, where you did recovery work after that home-brewed device."

"Ah, yes. A poorly executed contraption that was most exciting for a while." She smiled slightly, then sipped her tea. It was quite good.

Corbelle said, "'Most exciting,' indeed. I wish I'd been there, but I'm also glad I wasn't."

"Are there any special rules or restrictions on operations here?"

"As far as demolitions?"

Elke nodded.

"The near range, outside the South Gate, is limited to two hundred kilos per shot. The far range is outside the city, and I mean outside. The city comes to a stop and the wilderness begins. Very colonial. Out there, we're unlimited."

"What about military engagements? Are they restricted on munitions?"

Corbelle took a long drink, then said, "Very. They require patrol commander approval for any release. He has a key. Lethal weapons require shift commander approval from here. Support weapons may not be unlocked for two minutes."

"And explosive munitions?"

"Prohibited except for artillery and Aerospace."

"There seems to have been a mixup. I have need of small charges for emergency escapes, disabling pursuit vehicles, entering safe buildings during emergencies. My request apparently got rolled into the military logistics, and was cancelled."

Corbelle smiled and shook her head. "No, Elke, 'Demigoddess of Destruction,' I am unable to furnish you with explosives. While I could obviously make some disappear, the tagants are unique and fresh and would positively identify the source. If any is stolen, I will have to mark you as a suspect."

Elke grew tight and cool inside. *Kurva drat.* That was not how she'd wanted to start the negotiations, nor end them. There was nothing she could do, however.

She stood and said, "I remain at your disposal if need arises. Thank you for the tea." She offered a hand briefly.

She kept the cool lump inside until she exited the building, at which point it became incandescent.

They'd lied to her all along. Even if they'd not known until arrival, Jason was the advance man, and would have had this information.

This would mean a shopping trip.

Alex didn't sleep well. He rarely did the first night, had a lot to worry about, and had few allies to back him up. There were the twelve Ripple Creek operators here, and another team of four protecting Ahmed Anjari, but while he was that team's putative boss, he was mostly liaison and would sign off on any logistics issues. Unless an incident called for lawyers, they weren't his problem.

Highland and JessieM made up for it, though. He figured this morning, the first outing, would add to the stress.

Highland's first trip was twofold. She was to meet with the Mtali Sufi Council, and to be interviewed for the Mtali release of her video presentation, "Family Across Cultures."

In fact, the trouble had started already. A Sunni group vowed to protest her appearance. An Amala group claimed they'd been promised her presence first. Someone called her an enabler of illicit occupation, regarding the military mission. They hadn't even had breakfast yet.

Well, it was time to do that, and decide how to proceed.

Elke had signed out to visit the base, with a note on return. As the five of them ate from a table nicely laid out by the unobtrusive staff, he broached the subject.

Bart said, "With Aramis's help, I can randomize the routes. Will we have support vehicles?"

"We do not. I'm not sure why yet."

Jason said, "She won't think of rescheduling."

"Nor should we. We can handle it. If we start being timid, we'll lose professional rating."

"Are we working on our own PR here?"

"No, but pretty much everything we do is PR. Our ability to deliver a principal safely is all we have. We certainly can't get anywhere with Bart's looks or Aramis's manners."

Aramis said, "Or Elke's subtlety."

"So we load up and do it."

"At least we have the ARPAC."

"Yup. Are we ready?"

"It's fueled and inspected. Cady's people and subcontractors have charge of the park. I want weapons for all of us, a spare of each and water and food. Aramis?"

"Yes, I have paper and RAMmed backup routes."

Alex asked, "What's status on body armor?"

"It was released last night, and Cady's bringing it up now."

He heard Cady's voice say, "I'm here, Alex. Jason pinged me." He pointed and Bart rose to get the door.

A dolly rolled in, boxes overflowing, with Cady following. Elke arrived behind.

"They're all here, but I suspect Bart's isn't fitted. Corcoran is on the way up to fit him now." Jason could do armor, but Corcoran on Cady's team was a specialist.

"Danke," said Bart. "I prefer not to use mass to stop bullets." He started unstacking the boxes and ripping their seals.

Aramis said, "Think of it as an ecological mission. You're a portable heavy metal collection point."

Jason said, "I like him better as a self-deploying sandbag."

Corcoran arrived with tools. "I'd forgotten how big you were," he said.

"No bigger than last time. One nine five centimeters, one four zero kilos."

"Yes, but that's a 4 X vest, and they only sent through 2 X. I can make it work." He opened up his box and started adding inserts to the 2X to fit Bart's frame. Girth was easy enough. Length required drilling holes in the carrier and threading in ballistic cord to hold extension panels. It didn't take long.

"The 4 X should be here in a week. This will have to do for now."

Bart shifted and stretched. "It's no more uncomfortable than other stuff I have worn. I have my inside vest. This will work, thank you."

Alex kept a side eye on the process as he chose a route, planned movements and deployment positions, and checked the rest. It looked good, and still looked good, so he made the call.

"Minister Highland, we are ready at your convenience."

"Thank you. I'll just finish breakfast."

"Of course, ma'am." Alex hoped that would be five minutes, not fifty, but they were paid either way. She should also know they'd need plenty of bracket time.

This time she acted appropriately, and came through only eight minutes later, with JessieM. Highland clearly had armor under her blazer and polo.

"Ma'am, may I ask about your armor?"

"Angelwear, Rating R Two."

"Okay," he said, and left it at that. Angelwear looked good, and he recalled they'd tried to use her for some contract leverage. It hadn't worked because the stuff fell apart under military tests. However, for what she was doing it was probably okay. The idea was for her not to get shot anyway.

"And you, Jessie?"

She shook her head. "I don't have armor."

Elke said, "I have a spare undervest. It won't stop armor punchers, but it will stop common civilian projectiles and fragments."

"Thanks, I'd like that."

"Back here, then." She indicated her room.

It took another thirty minutes of quiet but active bustle to get everything sorted and ready. They had their uniform and armor, weapons with ammo—Alex wasn't sure Highland realized that, and wasn't going to say anything, backup gear and the vehicle warmed.

Downstairs at the dock, Alex looked for the weapon testing barrel he'd been told would be provided. He glanced at Cady with raised eyebrows. She shrugged back a response he read as, "Yes, I ordered it."

Shaman said, "Over there in the corner." Yes, red drum, mounted on frame.

"Good. Bart, Aramis, drag it over here."

The two men jogged over, grabbed it and heaved. The only effective ways to trap a bullet for test or practice were water or sand. Sand was easier to maintain. This was a specific silica grade and particle shape. With some scraping and yanking, they maneuvered it into place near the exit.

Alex said, "I better contact the command post, just to make sure." He flicked his mic to phone, said, "Command Post" and waited.

It was only five seconds before he heard, "Command Post, Senior Sergeant Terkel, this is not a secure connection, how may I help you?"

"This is Marlow, Special Agent in Charge, Ripple Creek, escorting Ms. Highland on her approved itinerary."

"Yes, sir?"

"We need to test fire our weapons before departure. Please disregard the fire."

"Sir, we can't do that. All reports of fire must be responded to. Additionally, no firing is allowed inside the perimeter except while under direct attack, with logged evidence."

There was nothing to be gained by arguing the point.

"Then we'll do so as soon as we're outside the perimeter. Respond as you wish. Marlow out." He closed the connection at once.

As he expected, Terkel called back in seconds. "Sir, any fire will be considered a potential threat and investigated."

"Go right ahead," he said and disconnected again.

Shaman asked, "We're really going to piss them off like that?"

"Yes. They need to understand we do our thing our way and not according to their policies."

"I approve. I do wonder about repercussions."

"We'll play Highland against them. Two can run that game."

He chuckled heartily. "I approve."

Highland arrived moments later, with JessieM. Elke was with them, and one of Cady's females. Ridling? Amanda Ridling? Yes, that was it. Highland and Jessie wore long tan skirts, with tights underneath. Some cultural more they were complying with, no doubt.

Highland smiled, nodded, made her way past and stepped aboard the vehicle. They were still using the ARPAC.

Apparently, she felt safe enough on base. Well and good for now, but she really should let Alex make that decision. She obviously knew this, and obviously didn't care.

"Good morning, ma'am," he said. "We are ready with your itinerary."

"Very good," she said, seeming quite genial now. "Will you be adjusting the route and arrival?"

"Always, and at random. We will deliver you on time, but sometimes earlier or from an unexpected direction."

"Very well. Let's go." She took a seat and seemed comfortable enough, with a rollout computer on her lap. JessieM took a seat across from her.

The young woman then looked up. "I can't get a signal in here," she said in Alex's general direction.

He casually tapped Bart and they started rolling.

"It's one of the vehicle's reinforcements, against electromagnetic effects, including pain stimulators, directional energy weapons and electrical capacitance."

"I see," she said. She almost seemed to be in withdrawal, denied her outlet. Perhaps he was too hard on her. It was her livelihood she was being temporarily deprived of.

The vehicle swayed in maneuvers, though it had a tight turning radius.

"We're out the gate," Bart announced.

"Good. Function check. Ma'am, we're testing our weapons momentarily."

"Oh, yes," she nodded, looking up from her work. "I thought you had already."

"They don't want us to do it on base."

She rolled her eyes. At least they both agreed on that much.

From the top turret, Aramis said, "We have a clear radius."

"Bart, drop the hatch. Quickly, folks, with cover."

Highland and Jessie both seemed familiar with the process and covered their ears.

The rear hatch eased down a few centimeters, then dropped with a bang that shook up dust. Elke skipped down, fired her shotgun into the dirt, swung it and slung it, raised her carbine and shot, dropped it on its sling, drew pistol and shot. She reholstered, turned and came back, as Jason stepped back and did the same with his weapons. He swapped positions with Aramis as Elke swapped with Bart while he and Shaman shot, then Aramis and Alex brought up the rear.

"Done," he announced, and Bart, already back in the driver's cabin, ran the ramp up at maximum speed. Aramis fired one short burst up above. Sirens were already audible on base, as the military responded to the "threat."

Alex sighed. He'd hear about that later. There was always some territorial dispute between branches. Increasingly, the military was run by MilBu, emphasis on the Bu. All their patrols should be testing weapons before venturing outside the wire.

That wasn't his problem at present. His problem was keeping this woman alive, along with her tagalong.

"We will be at the first location, Maharin Square, in a few minutes. We will need a few moments to check the area, and the dignitaries."

"Keep your hands off them, please!"

"We will. They'll be scanned, and they won't even notice it."

"Good. Does this bulletproof vest show?" Highland asked, turning her torso. Obviously used to crowd noise, she spoke loudly and clearly, over the drivetrain noise.

"It doesn't show, but be aware some styles of modern bullets can penetrate it, and it doesn't cover extremities."

"Yes, I know," she said, though not as haughtily. "I am grateful for it."

She suddenly seemed quite a bit more personable. Some of that was likely stress reduction and familiarity, but some of it was most likely also part of her act. He didn't trust anything she said or did, and it wasn't paranoia; she'd not gotten where she was by being nice, and they already knew she'd waste them to get in a shorter line at the coffee counter.

The city had chaotic architecture. Unlike other troubled worlds, like Salin, Mtali had been colonized by groups with money. There were religious groups with tithe support, and corporate investment to boot.

Some of it showed.

They drove along a main thoroughfare with a median park between the ways, and the houses were a strange blend of Western U.S., Colonial French and Arabic. They were tall, with courtyards, and overhangs, the upper levels built out.

But just past that were classic government-architectured blocks of apartments, with laundry hung on balconies, and parted out vehicles in the dead areas below. Alex kept a scan up. It wasn't likely this vehicle stood out from any other military transport, but that alone might draw fire.

The commercial district next was typical of downtown. Deluxe shops and lodging in various styles from several eras spread across the blocks, but they weren't crowded. The colonies had space from the start, and decent levels of technology. Their cities started off roomier than those on Earth and kept spreading out instead of up.

Maharin Square was on their left, up ahead. Some of Cady's team plus their subcontractors, some Army troops, and local cops had the area ringed. They weren't sure the locals were safe, but that was the point. The hired goons were more reliable than the rabble, the cops more reliable than the goons, the Army better than the cops, and Ripple Creek had only to worry about any few who might manage to get within.

The press turned toward their vehicle, probably cued by JessieM, and started their feeds. Bart pulled past, took a turn and another, and came from the cross direction. That also put the primary hatch closest to where Highland would stand. Details like this had been worked out in advance for previous clients, but were largely instinctive now. Every location was a threat zone, every person a threat, and they all planned accordingly.

By radio, Cady said, "We're clear."

Alex gestured to Bart, who popped the side door. Aramis pushed it open and stepped through. Elke followed, being about the same size physically as Highland, with her uniform coded to similar colors. There was a swell in the crowd noise that tapered off as Highland and JessieM stepped through and down. The cheers climbed again. Jason and Shaman were next, with Bart following Alex.

Highland stepped up to the podium, waved in an arc, smiled for the vid crews, and launched into her speech.

Aramis tuned out the blather. She was a politician, so she could say nothing and say it very well. He kept track of Cady's men Lionel and Edge. They'd worked together before and he trusted them for backup. Or, if they led, he'd back them. It was reassuring.

Not everyone outside the cordon was thrilled. There was a group with signs, including one very sophisticated holographic imager, showing an aerial picture of Highland with horns. This was definitely a more sophisticated dump than Salin.

It was three minutes in when the action started.

Something flew in a high arc and he swung toward it, opened his mouth to sound a threat, and instead said, "Eggs incoming."

He sighed and stepped in front of Highland, as Elke and Jason pulled her back behind the podium and threw up its shield. The egg splatted harmlessly on his helmet and dripped down his ear and neck in a cold gooey trail. A second one splashed across the crown, and he dodged a third. Elke had taken one and several others flurried around.

Then the smell hit him. These had been left in the warm sun for a while, but not where they could actually cook, just rot.

In his earbuds, Alex said, "We're departing. Speech is over."

"Roger," he said, and backed under the vehicle to take the lower hatch. He scrambled up from the dust, and Shaman handed him a wad of rags to clean the slimy gunk.

Highland was seated, had a bottled cocktail, and said, "The Ripple Creek guards were attacked with hurled eggs, probably by some faction angered at their status as paid contractors."

JessieM pressed send, and Aramis seethed. *No, you bitch, they were throwing at you, because of your status. We took the hit. And fuck you very much.* It was understood that "security" could be used as an excuse for a lot of things, and the company, and the team would take the heat for missed appointments, delays, intrusions. This was a new level of contemptibility.

Highland didn't even inquire as to how he and Elke were. All she asked was of Alex, "Can we proceed to the next location?"

Alex kept his attention on her as he said, "I see no reason not to at this time. If the threats escalate it may be advisable to pull the plug."

The stench was mostly gone, or at least the egg stench. Aramis felt it get sticky and dry, then Shaman handed him a bleach wipe. A daub with that and he felt physically clean and emotionally dirtier. But he'd do his job.

They convoyed, Cady's team and the military in their own vehicles, split and rolled into the next location from three directions. They were a few minutes early.

Highland said, "Early is fine. We'll avoid some of the planned response. Is the press ready, Jessie?"

"They were when I churped before the hatch closed."

"Good."

And there went OPSEC again. Aramis almost wished someone

would shoot her, except he was contractually obligated to jump in front of the attempt.

So here I am, protecting our principal, her pet, exceeding the contract by working on her campaign rather than her officially requested mission, getting tired, sore, pelted with rotten eggs by her detractors and taking the blame for it because we do our job well for pay.

He'd had exciting missions and hated them at the time, but they were exhilarating, and even the roughing ups he'd taken were okay in hindsight. This, though, was dirty.

They bailed out three ways, waited for her to step daintily down the steps, smiling and waving as people gradually realized she was someone important, and then realized who she was, before her banners unfurled. So some group of supporters had been ready.

At no point did she mention a bid for SecGen. He'd give her that. It was blatantly obvious what she was doing, but she was sticking to the letter of that law, and only promoting her current task at this event.

He moved out to help keep a perimeter, and between the real and intimidating camouflage, armor and weapons, the crowd assumed he was some sort of ass kicker and pulled back.

There was no particular mood to the spectators. Some looked snarly, some thrilled, some showed that minor interest of seeing someone famous, or something different from the routine. They were probably here more to skip work than from any care about politics. He could see three types of turbans, two of keffiyeh and the bulbous knit caps that marked the Amala sect, along with the basic round caps favored generally. There were women in everything from hijab to slacks with bare midriffs. This area was mostly Muslim. He understood the Christian areas were less varied.

". . . what Mtali needs is a debate that treats each of its cultures with the appropriate respect . . ." Okay, that was off the environmental and trade path a bit, though certainly trade would be easier if they weren't constantly shooting at each other. Shooting at, not shooting, the incompetent tweets.

He kept an eye on the crowd. That man with the asymmetric beard was very interested, and looked hostile, but he seemed to be recording on a hat-mounted camera. He probably wasn't a direct threat, but it was entirely possible he was feeding someone else.

"Jason, I have a man with a cam." He pressed the button in his hand that let the image be shared.

"Got him," Jason replied. "He's recording nothing now." Directional jamming made him smile.

He saw that Elke had wandered several meters west and upwind. She was probably prepping smoke charges in case they had to extract in a hurry.

Still, there was movement within the mass, as people grew bored and left, and others migrated forward. Placards and signs in English, Arabic and Turkish proclaimed support or opposition.

Politicians, competent ones at least, always wanted to meet the public, and their guards always wanted them not to. In this case, it was even more risky. She'd had more expressed threats than the baseline, and was clearly angling for a SecGen position. There were people who'd try to preempt her.

Jason muttered back, "There are so many damned things that present as possible weapons I'm getting twitchy. 'Anything longer than it is wide' is a fine definition for a Freudian, but too broad for physical threats."

He chuckled back. "As long as we only have to look at weapons and not dicks."

"Depends on if they're pump action or single shot."

Aramis faked surprise and said, "Woah, that's between you and the goat, man."

The jokes broke the boredom, but they were on duty and resumed silence. The important message was that eyeballs would have to do more work than the electronics.

Right then, Shaman said, "Incoming." His voice was trained, and conversational. The team triggered on it and moved. Aramis jumped forward with Bart. He heard Elke tackle Highland, Jason open the door, and Alex call for backup as Elke stuffed the principal into the ARPAC.

He could see the projectile falling, and his sphincter puckered. From its trajectory, it was dense and brick-sized. Then he caught a slight reflection off a protrusion, probably a fuze. So it was more than a brick. It was a large grenade or small block charge.

Once the hatch closed he leapt over to the front wheel, rolled backward while tucking his carbine, and dropped behind the mass of the engine and wheel. Bart chewed up dust to his right with a thump of a landing.

Whatever the projectile was, it far overshot and went behind something, then popped with a cracking noise. Had it squibbed and failed? Or was it gas? There were two more in the air, and he'd IDed the point of origin, even as his goggles blinked a location. There was the dirtsucker.

That detached feeling hit him as he stood, clambered up the ladder and switched the cannon to manual. It was more important to take out the source than hide. Someone was starting to move the vehicle, so he swung the gun, splayed his legs, guessed at point of aim and cut loose a burst. It was high, he adjusted, and shot again.

The shooters realized he was targeting them and dodged, first back, then upon realizing the first burst was overhead, toward him, and right into the second spray. Three bodies tore, disconnected limbs flailing, and their launcher shattered.

Jason fired a long, stuttering string that crossed both remaining projectiles. They broke up and fell . . . oddly. Liquid? Green?

He kicked the hatch and dropped inside, as Bart shimmied up through the rear hatch, cursing in German. At least he presumed so. He didn't speak German, and he couldn't hear the man anyway, over Highland's total meltdown.

"You murderous fucking mercenary retards! You egotistical male jerkers! And you . . . AFRICAN! You worthless bunch of—"

She was cut off as Shaman slapped a contact patch on her throat. She turned and smacked, connected only with his armor and harness, and started to slur.

"You weren'th hiredh to dop me, youuu . . ." and trailed off. She was still awake, but very lethargic. It must be a fast-acting tranquilizer.

Jason said, "Jessie, I'll connect the external antenna to your MoodMod in a moment. What are you going to send?"

Her voice trembled and cracked as she said, "Uh, that we were attacked and had to defend ourselves, but no one is hurt."

"Very good. It's important that you send that message first."

"Okay," she agreed, sounding unsure. She waited for his nod of assent, and loaded the comment.

Aramis sweated and buzzed from adrenaline and leftover fear. It was always a rush to survive combat, even when it was one-sided. He looked quizzically at Jason, who signaled over to Alex, who looked around at everyone and replied.

"They were shooting paint canisters with bursting caps. Green paint."

Oh, shit.

"They were political agitators?" Aramis asked.

"Yes. And you opened fire with an autocannon."

In half a second, scenarios ran through his head. Jason or Elke had enough connections to get him out of the system fast. Caron would stand up for him. He wouldn't get brain wiped. He might do a decade in prison. He did have that stash of money for emergencies that they couldn't seize because he'd hidden it on Salin and Grainne. The company would back him up; he'd acted in good faith.

Alex said, "You acted in good faith, and fast. It'll take paperwork and lawyers. You're covered."

Under his breath, Bart muttered, "And maybe the stupid hippies won't do that again."

From the driver's compartment, Elke said, "Don't hurt my hopes."

Jessie at least seemed sympathetic.

"Oh, dear," she said. "Oh, my. This is not going to be good for . . . anyone. Was anyone hurt?"

Aramis decided he shouldn't answer that question. He was surprised to realize he really didn't give a shit about the fucking morons who'd put pyro charges on projectiles and thrown them at a cabinet member. Pyro. Projectiles. That's what he needed to ensure was in any statement. He'd feared for her life and acted to protect it. Damn the bitch for attracting such idiots, either for or against.

Jessie said, "I don't know what else to say."

"The Minister is unharmed. You can say that. Don't say where we're going next."

"I don't know where we're going," she protested.

Yeah, that was probably intentional, Aramis thought with an inward smirk.

Pyro. Projectiles. Potentially explosive threat.

Did Caron have that much political pull, and would she use it? She did owe him her life, but she'd paid in cash for that service. She didn't care what anyone thought of her, but was she willing to spend that kind of political capital for a boink buddy?

Could he egress the system alone if it went sour?

Jessie stuttered as she very quietly said, "I need to find a restroom. Is there . . . ?"

Alex said, "No, there is no bucket aboard. I can pick one up for next time. You'll need to hold it another ten minutes."

She nodded. Then they hit a bump and she flinched.

Alex pulled a hush hood. He was probably talking to the military, or relaying a message to Corporate first, to get the lawyers primed. There'd be an investigation. At least Elke would have video for his side of things.

Alex pulled the hood and said, "We're going straight back."

Elke said, "Understood."

"We will unload before the gate, and the guards will inspect our weapons. Drop me at Base Operations. I need to talk to them."

Aramis didn't like the sound of that.

The rest of the ride was smooth enough, but just the hammering dread he felt made it feel worse than actually getting wounded. Chills, shivers, flushes, roiling bloodflow in his ears—massive shock.

Politics was scarier than combat.

He followed Jason's lead and slipped out magazines, cycled the actions and locked them open. He carefully started to rise for the autocannon, but Bart reached up and took care of it for him.

At the gate, Elke lowered the ramp. The sentry was three steps up before it clattered on the ground.

"Show me clear weapons," he said, very firmly, very intently, with his right hand on the grip of his carbine and his finger twitching near the trigger. Aramis cautiously bent both weapons to show the open chambers.

"Do not load them again without orders," he said, and crabbed down the ramp sideways, keeping an eye on the team.

Through all this, Highland sat silently, but not tranked. It had obviously worn off.

Elke rolled up in front of Base Operations, and Alex slipped out the side hatch. Jessie looked very miserable and very uncomfortable. Highland looked furious.

Elke maintained exact base speed limit as she rolled into the diplomatic compound. Jessie looked almost nauseated as she staggered, body clutched tightly, toward the latrine. Aramis felt nauseated. He needed to drain, too, but that wasn't it.

⊚ CHAPTER 8 ⊚

ALEX STEPPED INTO THE OPS BUILDING. He had legality on his side, but that rarely mattered to military officers, especially Infantry officers or Staff officers, and this would involve both.

A master sergeant stood waiting, and said, "In there, sir," while pointing. He was polite enough, and didn't sound any more bothered than any NCO whose bosses were pissed, so this was probably just a staff matter. That helped, a little.

He knocked on the door twice, firmly, waited three seconds, and walked in.

Captain Das was seated there, and seemed neutral enough. With him were Colonel Stack, the Facility Commander, and Colonel Andronov, the Operations Officer. They both bore professionally blank expressions, the kind that presaged formal actions. Stack was barrel chested and clearly a bred soldier. Andronov lean and bald.

Stack said, "Agent Marlow, you had a rather interesting day. In fact, it became interesting for a lot of people."

That was a fair enough opening. He had not been asked to sit, though.

"It did, sir. The tactical situation differs from our original terms, and our client is making additional trips we had not counted on."

Andronov said, "I am not interested in justifications. I am interested in unauthorized weapons fire right outside the perimeter, and firefights with locals who are not armed."

Alex took a measured breath and said, "As to the latter, sir, they

87

made every attempt to appear armed, and that they were using deadly force. What appeared to be explosives required an armed response. Had it been a rushing crowd or such, we would have blocked physically and removed Ms. Highland, and we did that as well. My agent's response was appropriate at that moment, even if it seems otherwise in hindsight. I do not yet know BuState's position, but it is my company's position that he was fully in accordance with contract. That means everyone's legal teams will have to decide the ramifications, and it becomes a matter for our employer, which is BuState. The military will not legally be involved."

Andronov spoke sharply. "I don't give a damn for legalities. I care that the locals now perceive violence on the behalf of the UN. My soldiers will have to deal with that. Or is that not of concern to you?"

Alex could feel the prickliness. "Sir, anything that interacts with hosts, allies or opposition is of concern to me. I will say again that the circumstances were rushed, threatening in presentation, and that our original contract has been stretched. However, abiding by the strict letter of that agreement will create"—enemies *would be a bad word*, he thought, "—problems with BuState. I couldn't address it then. I'll do so as soon as feasible."

Andronov seemed about to reply so he added quickly, "As to the former, it is standard practice to test weapons before a mission or movement. It also used to be a standard practice in the military. I will not put my client at risk over a difference in policies. To that end, I informed your operations team that we would conduct that test, and that we would do so immediately upon leaving the wire."

"Is that true, Das?"

"I'm told it is, sir. They made the call, and informed Lieutenant Ghar."

"Ghar did not propagate this information to you?"

"Neither to Security Operations nor to Intel, no, sir."

Andronov looked at Stack. Stack didn't say anything.

Turning back to Alex, Andronov said, "There will be some discussions, then. I will accept, under protest, that your rules are different. I will discuss this with our people, and with BuState. I make the official request of a favor that you provide me with as much information as you can."

"I'll do so through Captain Das. And of course, anything we observe that might be of intelligence interest will be shared, including relevant footage." *After Elke scrubs what they don't need to see.*

Andronov didn't seem at all mollified, but it did appear he grasped the problems of a completely distinct chain of command he had no control over whatsoever.

"Very well. You may go."

Alex wasn't about to be dismissed like an errand boy. There was an issue of status, and that had to be covered at once.

"There is one matter you raise, sir."

Andronov leaned on the desk and said, "Yes?"

"While information on certain of our movements are necessary for cooperation, and I will do my best to improve that, we are an adjunct of BuState, operating at the highest level—the Minister is our personal responsibility. I must request that you not attempt to track anything without clearing it through me. State will not be happy with certain information, some of it personal, being furnished even to BuMil, and if it spreads sufficiently, of course, there is an OPSEC risk."

"Agent Marlow, as you have explained to some of my people, and to myself, I will explain to you. I will conduct my operations my way. If I need to discuss them with BuState, I have my own superiors and my own lawyers. It would be in both our interests to avoid that."

"Understood, sir. I'll do what I can. I'll start on it now."

He took the previous leave for granted, turned and left.

When he put his glasses back on, he had a message waiting. He scanned it.

Highland wants to see you ASAfP. J.

That was choice. He made use of the latrine in this building, washed his hands, opened his armor, and walked the half kilometer to the Dip compound.

Cady's people were on the gate, and recognized him.

"Chief Marlow, good to see you," the sentry said. "Check here, please."

He stepped over for a bio scan, waited for acknowledgement, and walked through the turnstile.

Their building was comfortable, if warm, and he felt a bit of burden release with his own people around him. Though they were a bit tense. He needed to deal with Highland first, then debrief them. He walked past with a nod, through the hallway door and down the corridor that served as one of several breaks against eavesdropping.

He knew this wasn't going to be pleasant. He braced himself inside while keeping a neutrally agreeable façade outside.

"You called, ma'am," he said as he stepped into the room. Highland was alone.

"I perfectly understand why people hate your outfit," she said.

That wasn't necessarily a preface to attack, he thought. Comprehension did not necessarily . . .

"What in the fucking hell are you . . . thugs . . . playing at?" She panted and flushed and looked incensed already, from merely irritated moments before.

He'd heard of her famous temper, and he wasn't going to interfere. Best to let her run out.

She stood, fists on desk. "You shot unarmed protesters, which makes me look bad. You pissed off the military, on purpose I gather. You unleashed weapons of mass destruction you knew were intended for deterrent appearance only."

He reflected that she really didn't know what "weapons of mass destruction" meant, and he'd be careful not to let Elke know, because she'd be too happy to demonstrate.

"Ma'am, our mission is to protect you. We have specific approaches and technique, and these were detailed in our contract addenda."

"Fuck that trash!" She turned and straight-arm heaved her glass at the wall. It shattered in a cascading rain of wine and crystal. "We all know that's just ass-covering. I'm not some rich-bitch schoolgirl or a third world babysitter. I am the Minister of State, and the next Secretary General! Your job is to look imposing, stay out of the way, and cover me in the rare case it happens to be necessary. You will not engage in any hostile action without specific permission from me. Is that clear?"

He wasn't going to argue the point. That's what lawyers were for.

"I understand, ma'am, and will so inform my people you said so personally." If she weren't so incensed, she'd realize he had not agreed to the demand, only acknowledged the statement.

"You had better," she said with a finger point. "In one day, *one day*, you've splashed me across every feed, page, stream and vue in the universe, as some kind of right-wing, uncompassionate kitten stomper."

If the shoe fits, he thought.

She seemed to have run down, and just glared at him.

"I'll work on improving things right now, ma'am," he said, and backed out under her stare.

That could have been better. It also could have been worse. He cooled off as he walked down the hall, and took the stairs rather than an elevator.

Back in their common room, he asked, "Where's Elke?"

From the couch, Jason said, "She said something about making friends with the engineer unit."

He started to ask, "Does that mean—" and Jason cut him off with, "Yes."

He sighed.

"Okay, I'll need to talk to her about that. In the meantime, everyone understand that we must hold the real weapons in reserve. We'll get fried if someone else gets it."

Bart said, "We will get fried if her hair gets parted, too."

"Yes. All I can say is, Meyer thinks this is worth doing, and has something planned. We're not doing this for us, or Highland, this is for the Company."

Elke walked through the door at that moment, and said, "They pay us well. I am not sure they pay us well enough."

"Did you catch the rest?"

"Yes, Jason had a channel open to me. I will comply, as always, under protest, as always."

"Please. I don't know what the endplan is, but we have to make it work. I get the impression it's a test of loyalty and discipline. That means more government contracts."

Aramis flared his eyebrows. He said nothing. Jason glanced at him, looked at Alex, and spoke.

"On the one hand, government money is as good as anyone's. On the other hand, they abused us the first time, did nothing to help in the interim, and clearly want us as a splatter guard this time. Miss Caron was aggravating to deal with, but she had good cause, and her money is freely given, with better behavior. The whole point of being a mercenary is not being tied to one master, especially a government."

"Then feel free to go independent," he snapped. Alex understood Jason's position. He also understood his own frustration. "This is us, and the Company, versus them. Choose your side."

"Oh, I'm here," Jason assured him. "I will back you all the way. I don't know that I have enough bleach wipes to get the politician shit off, though."

"Yeah. We're in this together, remember."

Elke said, "I will do what it takes for my team. The rest is just money."

"That's all we're asking."

Shaman asked, "Is there any clarification on JessieM?"

Alex sighed. "Yes, we cover her, too. A bill will be presented later. Then the lawyers will argue it. I gather Meyer is trying for leverage back against BuState. We're all looking for position."

"What is her status?"

"She's 'also protected.' Highland is primary. JessieM is secondary. She should be covered when possible, brought along when possible, reported and documented if needed. She is not disposable but she is expendable if Highland is in danger. In other words, she cannot be collateralized, but she can be triaged." He sighed. "Now I have to report my discussion with Highland and get an official guidance on that. In the meantime, we're carrying nonlethal weapons, but do not use them except against close, direct threats. We will respond to indirect weapons with evacuation and cover. Use distraction and pain first, disablement second. Only if there's a mob like we had on Salin do we use lethal force, when it's obvious we had no choice."

Aramis was the first to respond. "Understood." He seemed relieved to have clear guidance.

"Roger," Jason agreed. The rest nodded and confirmed the order.

Jason continued, "I'm going to check over the nonlethal stuff, and prep additional gear. Aramis, can you assist?"

"Yes."

Alex nodded, waved and went to compose a draft. He wondered if drinking heavily would help, though he couldn't do so.

Just then his phone beeped.

"Marlow."

"Alex, Captain Das."

"What can I do for you, Captain?"

"I must relay some bad news."

Alex sighed. "Go ahead."

"Ms. Highland requested military escort for her transport. That request has been categorically denied."

"I see. She won't like that at all. I can't say I'm thrilled with it myself."

"I understand. Can you guarantee Ms. Highland will not mention her campaign in her appearances?"

"What? No, she generally mentions it every time."

"Yes, which makes her 'candidate' Highland. 'Minister' Highland is an official representative of the government, and can have as much escort as we can spare. 'Candidate' Highland must provide her own support. She's certainly in violation of BuState regulations, too, but that's not an issue we have jurisdiction over. We cannot, however, allow a candidate to make use of our taxpayer resources."

"I completely understand. That's most unfortunate."

"We'll be letting her know, of course. I wanted to make sure you could plan accordingly."

"Thanks. I appreciate it."

It was Bart who brought up the next issue. "News," he said. "Churp from JessieM."

He let it scroll on his glasses, then scrolled it again.

Then he sighed. He talked to his phone.

"Cady, are you free? Priority Three."

"Sure, I'll be right there."

Turning to the others he said, "I'll use the armory for this discussion."

Jason said, "Go ahead, boss, I'll clean later."

Cady arrived at once, looking unbothered but concerned. She knew most of what had happened. He motioned her back into the room.

As soon as she closed the door he said, "I need to give you a status update. This is official, but personal."

"Oh?"

"Yeah, JessieM put the word out that you're trans. It's no one's business, but that's the business she's in. And Highland likes having 'diversity' to point to politically."

Cady looked confused rather than offended. "Are you saying I'm here because I'm trans?"

"No, you're here because you do damned good facilities. The principal wants you here because you're trans."

She nodded thoughtfully. "I see. Well, I don't like that, but I don't have much choice unless I want to leave, which defeats my moral purposes and affects the mission."

Alex said, "Yeah. Sorry you're getting caught up in it."

She looked a bit wistful as she said, "It's something we get from time to time even in modern societies. I expected trouble from the locals here if word got out. I had hoped our principal would be diplomatically savvy."

"She is, and she sees a benefit back home, among her potential voters."

Cady sighed. "Yes, the opposite of what works here. I could offer a comment on that."

Alex said, "It's been made."

She nodded. "Well, I'll do the best I can."

"The locals know now, of course."

"I understand." She looked sad. This couldn't be a new event, and had to be tiresome and irritating. "It doesn't affect what I do, unless you'd like me to leave to preserve order."

Yes, this had to be a tender subject for her.

"That's very professional of you. No. Even if it would help, I'd say no. You're not an interchangeable unit. You're our best facilities expert. They'll just have to deal with it."

"So will I."

"Yeah, that's the part I don't like."

She shrugged. "As I said, it's an old story. I'll manage. Thanks for the update."

"I think we both favor a free media," he said. "I know there's no real privacy. But some things shouldn't be dug out and promoted. No one should care about our names, backgrounds, locations."

"Except the enemy. We're not allowed to say that, though."

"There is no enemy. They're just misunderstood. Anyway, that's the brief, I'm back on duty." He started for the door.

Cady said, "I have a standard statement I can give her if she asks. You know why I transitioned, yes?"

He halted. "I never asked. It's not my business."

"Well, we need to work together and it's come up, so it's your business now. Genetic irregularity. XXY chromosomes, and at puberty I seemed to lean more toward female both mentally and physiologically. So they finished with modern science what nature got half-assed."

"Got it."

Truth be told, he found it uncomfortable, even if it was a fairly straightforward process anymore. She did good work, though, and there was no reason for personal details to be public.

In her quarters and well away from any military or contractors, Highland let out a tight sigh and asked Jessie, "Okay, give me the bad news on the numbers."

"Actually, it's not bad."

"Really?"

"It's polling well. Large numbers of rural and wealthy urban demographics support it being a legitimate return of fire."

Again, she said, "Really?"

"You lost eight percent of the lower income brackets, but gained twenty-three percent in the ones I mentioned, for a net gain, population adjusted, of three percent. That puts you back at thirty-one percent, and a credible threat to Cruk."

"I haven't heard anything good about Ripple Creek."

"Oh, they're widely hated. The bounce seems to be a perception of your strength."

"Well, then I supposed I need to spin it that way. I'm strong, not afraid, and these manipulated attacks aren't a credible threat. I can denounce the excessive violence."

"That's not very fair to our guards."

"This isn't fair. It's a campaign."

Elke paused the replay and looked around. This was a type of issue she didn't understand.

Jason was angry. His reply was moderate. That was scary.

"Well, we expected to get bent over. It's part of the job, and why we get paid so much. But she actually wants to use us not only as muscle, but to then decry our techniques, while sobbing about her compassion. That's an election strategy?"

Aramis of all people looked very calm.

"Sadly, I think it will work. She can play good cop/bad cop, blame the SecGen for our presence, play the victim and compassion cards, promise vague, undefined 'difference.'"

Elke asked, "How will the blame affect us?"

Alex said, "That is a good question. It can play out as more of the same, nobody cares. It could turn into nuisance suits that hurt the company. It could get very ugly with some kind of General Assembly investigation that has us being deposed, and charged with perjury for saying we had eggs for breakfast when the camera clearly shows turkey ham."

"I could persuade her to be nice," Bart said.

Alex looked around. "Are we positive we're not being scanned? Aerospace Force was able to hack us quite well the first time."

Elke said, "I am sure. I'm also not as worried about them as her."

Jason nodded in agreement. "Yeah, though she may have friends, and they may decide the info is worth money."

Aramis sat back and stared at the wall. "I guess we need to make sure Captain Das is on our side."

"He seems like a good man," Elke said.

Alex said, "I'll draw some materials. Jason can you work out a polite trade, so he's slightly beholden?"

"I can. No specific requests, just 'we heard you needed this'?"

"Exactly. We have the Golden Cargotainer. We're good people."

Elke said, "I guess I'm unhappy protecting someone who will use us so hypocritically. It's not that we're enemies, nor that we're con-spirators. She means to play us as fools."

Aramis said, "You're unhappy because she thinks we're that stupid."

"Yes, that's it."

Jason said, "It's common. You have to be something of a sociopath to get high in politics. You've seen it; she really has little compassion for anyone. It's not that she's mean. She's just not capable of empathizing with anyone. That makes narcissism that much easier. It's all about her, and she isn't even cognizant of us."

Shaman said, "It's not entirely like that, from a medical perspective, but I will forgive your irregularities for the rough summary."

"Yeah, I'm sure my terms are wrong. I'll clarify: she's a smug, self-centered bitch."

"Spot on," Shaman agreed.

Elke was learning from this, but it still wasn't clear. "How do such people make way? Get ahead?"

Aramis smirked, but it wasn't unkind. "They have lots of people along for the ride and the money and power, and others willing to back them for payoffs later."

"It seems a precarious way to get ahead."

"It is," Jason said. "It always collapses eventually. Which is why we get paid to protect them meantime. Remember how they tried to set up Bishwanath?"

Alex said, "They're being smarter this time. No deaths, just harassment. We can't really respond, but we have to treat every threat seriously."

"But they're improving her visibility and popularity."

Alex continued, "Could it be staged? Not by her, but by the party?"

"Possibly."

Very serious now, he said, "We have to assume there's some agency behind the nonlethal attacks. She admits to one. So, she set up the first one, but these could be either staged higher up, by some anonymous benefactor, or they could be legitimate protest by fucking idiots, or just harassment by someone wanting to embarrass her without risking actual jail."

"Or trying to entice us into killing someone so they can hold it against her, or us. Or trying to entice us into killing someone so they have an excuse to start another revolution."

Bart said, "It could be any of those. She fits profiles for celebrity, politician and important official."

Aramis asked, "Should we not return fire?"

Elke said, "I would return fire. In case they are trying to lull us so they can attack." She looked around at the others.

Alex said, "Yes. Our job is to protect her from threats. We do that, against every potential threat. Don't use more force than you have to, so avoid the autocannon. But by all means return fire. If she wants to spin it for her bravery and risk-taking, we'll allow it. That's even semi-legit as long as she's not orchestrating it herself. However, we need to find out what the strategy is. Shaman, research the history of this place for similar events. Elke, you get everything you can from her quarters. Spy on her however you have to. It's for her own safety, and ours. I'll get everything I can from Captain Das."

Bart said, "He is not in BuState."

"He's not, but he probably has some good leads anyway."

"I will get on it," Elke said, though she wasn't comfortable.

She did not deal well with most people, and had trouble with some cues. She knew that. This required determining how someone else would think, and that was uncomfortable. She also had no idea how it was done. It had taken two years to understand how most of the team thought. She'd been the last person to fit in, and still was very much outside them. If it weren't for Jason, she might not have made it this far.

However, it seemed it was something she needed to learn. In the meantime, she had sensors and bugs to place.

Now there was the matter of several explosive devices she needed to inventory, adapt, or strip for material. She'd need more caps at once, more explosive shortly, but she had a few kilograms to get her started. It was obvious to her that Highland was using them as every kind of shield, decoy and prison bitch possible. Otherwise Elke wouldn't be stealing what she needed.

At least the guns had ammunition. It likely hadn't occurred to the *kurvě* that they'd actually shoot at threats without her say so. Truly, the woman had far too much regard for the capabilities of government.

At some point during this mission, that would become apparent. Elke looked forward to *that* facial expression. It was quite perverse on her part, but she was comfortable with it.

Aramis stretched as they broke up and fell to. There were weapons to clean, routes to plan, exercise to take, food, rest, itineraries. He had more maps to plot, gear dumps to arrange, and Jason might need help with weapons.

They moved around and funneled out the door back into the common room. He twitched as Elke brushed past. Had that been a grope?

She turned slightly on her way to her own room, and her face wore a smirk.

That was disturbing.

Aramis was still trembling from the earlier incident. He had no idea how close he'd come to brain wiping, but that had to have been skirting it. From now on, everyone got a half second consideration, and nonlethal fire first. He understood protecting the principal. He also understood not letting her use him as bait, a taunt or a campaign slogan. He had no reason to care that much for her. He'd save the firepower for the team's safety. He would fire to protect his teammates, though.

It occurred to him the harassing attacks might be intended exactly as a confidence shaker for something bigger later. Or had they discussed that already?

Yes, he was shaken. Still, fire to save the team, and fuck the politicians.

That resolved in his mind, he went to see Jason. He found the man hunched over a sheet on the floor, working on weapons.

"Hey, Aramis, what do you need?"

He started with, "I want to make sure my carbine is as zeroed as you can get, and I want that scope set with all the bells and whistles. Show me what I need to know."

"Can do. I have a few minutes before I can catch up with Captain Das, who is certainly going to know something is up with all the bribery, so I need to make the bribe bigger but practical and not ridiculous."

"If you're busy . . ."

"Nope, I need to think, and handling guns helps me think. Let's do it." He pulled Aramis's carbine from the cabinet, and his own. He seemed to relax and calm down once he had a weapon in hand. That bothered a lot of people, but Aramis understood it. Much like Elke with her explosives, it gave him focus and control.

"Okay, you have frequency shift here, which can be done manually, or through the slide on your combat goggles. UV for smoke, IR for night, or thermal. Punch up the IR here to at least eight, given this wimpy star. In my system you'd dial down to three."

"Got it."

"You boresight here, and put a dot on the wall there, that's why I have that mark."

"It's a centimeter high."

"So it'll be smack on at a hundred meters."

"Yes."

"How's the grip?"

"Comfortable. I'd like more butt weight."

"Here," Jason said, took the weapon, and attached a small tube that held an extra capacitance pack for the optics. He handed it back.

"Yeah, that does it, and gives me a second spare."

"You'll never need it, but someone else might."

"Excellent. Got time for one more question then?"

"Yes, go ahead." Jason stood, stretched, and wiped his hands on a towel.

"It's about Elke."

"Okay."

He hesitated slightly. "Look, you've known her a long time."

"On and off, yes. She's an unusual character."

That was a sympathetic opening. Good.

"Yes, that's it. Previously, you know how she acted toward me. Distant, even condescending, and I deserved it when we first met. We got past that. Strictly professional, much the way she is with you."

"Yes, and that's good, I hope?"

"It was. She's a hell of a blaster, glad to have her around. Always reliable. She opened up just a tiny bit last year."

"Which is huge for her."

"Yeah, I got that," he said. Then he blurted, "So why is she hitting on me now? I think."

"Ahhhh," Jason said and smiled faintly.

The older man leaned back and said, "Well, that probably has to do with you banging the trillionaire."

Aramis cringed. He hated hearing it put that way, even if he thought that way himself.

"Jealousy?"

"Elke? No. More like 'challenge.' Or possibly 'curiosity.' If someone who can have anyone is interested in you, there must be a reason. Elke's rather poor at social cues. That is, she's very observant about others, but can't manage her own. So she's playing her own game."

"I really don't think that would turn out well."

"Yeah, ain't maturity a bitch? She probably knows that, too. She's seeing if she can mess with your mind."

"I'm afraid she's going to be insulted if I don't respond."

"Probably. I don't have much in the way of advice beyond this. It's a grudge match."

"Thanks. Really, thanks, though that last just doesn't help."

⦾ CHAPTER 9 ⦾

FRANKLIN LEZT WAS NERVOUS, and tense. Things like this risked more than one's job. His appointment arrived, and as soon as the door closed, he tapped on the security field. That and a random hotel should mean they were safe. The heavy drapes were closed, and there was a screen taped to the window as well.

"It's helping her ratings!" he said. They both knew which it and whom this was about.

Will Hepgard was not the man's real name. It would do for now. He was too calm as he said, "It's not an ideal result."

Lezt tried not to be too uncalm.

"Ideal? The idea was to either disgrace her with photos of her covered in Eco Party green paint or eggs, or have criminal charges against her or those thugs." They'd spent a lot of money on this. He needed results. He paced around the suite. Then he grabbed a beer. He'd be damned if he wasn't going to get something positive out of this. He pointed at the well. Hospitality helped.

Hepgard said, "And it didn't work."

What a revelation, he thought. "I fucking know it didn't work!"

"We still have time." Hepgard reached in, took a beer, thumbed off the lid.

The man was infuriatingly calm, but then, he had half the considerable money already.

Lezt said, "She's at twenty-three points. We have to peg her back down below twenty or we lose the advantage we paid for."

Did Hepgard know the significance of thirty points in the polls? Possibly not. So steer away from that.

Hepgard leaned against the wall, clearly wanting a chair. He wasn't large, but he was soft. He did all his work with terminals and phones.

"We will. We can do some promotion here on Earth, too. And another thought: Her trip splits both her office and her campaign. Can we arrange something embarrassing around her office?"

Lezt said, "Are you kidding? Jaekel's the real worker. All Highland offers is guidelines, and she can do that just fine from there. It's probably running smoother without her nitpicks." Was that useful info to share? Or too useful?

Hepgard nodded and leaned back. "Okay, so we need to focus on her campaign."

"And besides us, Hunter's people are about to jizz their pants over her being away. He's plowing money into ad loads to get a good lead now."

"A shame that's all going to fall apart when word gets out."

"A shame. The week before the election, too."

Hepgard shook his head. "You like that too much. I want to do it sooner. A month out. That gives time for him to try to justify it, and for all the inquiries to build. Then we have professional outrage people to be outraged. Unless your boss is set on the last minute?"

Lezt sighed. "Look, I'm telling you way too much on this. The SecGen is not the sharpest spoon on the rack. Nor is he the most determined. He'd probably object, and he'd certainly let word slip to someone. They might or might not reveal it, but we're not telling him. You know Ingo makes most of the decisions, yes?"

"I knew he made recommendations."

"That's the official story. No, he's the brains. Cruk is a pretty face, but too emotional."

"Is that why he has two types of speeches?"

"Yes, the ones that piss people off are his own cute creations. The ones that sway people are written by a professional Ingo hired. And we're not talking about this anymore. What can you arrange on embarrassment?"

"Some amusing ads. I can even pin them on Hunter. Then use her money."

That was interesting. "Hah. I like that a lot. Do it, and make sure this one works." Damn, he'd finished a beer already.

Hepgard nodded confidently. "It will. Even if she has a boost now, it'll all add up to a decline later."

It was dangerous to meet in person, but there was no way such an issue would ever get discussed over any kind of connection.

"Good. But we need both short term and long term. Trends."

"I'll be on it. Thanks for the beer." Hepgard took one healthy swallow and set the rest of the bottle down.

Lezt considered. Hepgard could probably pull it off. He'd done a good job with the Eisington campaign, if you measured good jobs by dismal failures that everyone followed in amusement. But just in case, there was another source.

"Yeah, those specialists. They are very good at keeping someone alive, yes?"

"Absolutely. They've never lost a patient."

"Good. Then I want them to proceed. There are going to be casualties, and I wouldn't want them to die."

"They're on site already, of course."

"Yes, get them in play. Someone's life is at stake."

Or would be, very soon.

Jason looked through the inventory to see what they could offer to Das as a diplomatic gift. They'd certainly share intel that would help the military if it wouldn't hinder them. Ammo or weapons wouldn't matter, nor most logistical items. Though they did have some sanitized handguns. Those could make useful dump guns for officially unarmed technicians or support troops. They could even be presented casually enough. Three of those, then.

What about staging their own fake attack and having Elke volunteer to help? But that was complicated, deceitful and risky. He had no qualms about cheating, but their position with Das was improved if Das could trust them more than others.

Unmarked bullion and cash. They could spare some, but it would have to clearly be "logistics" and not "cash bribe." He'd work on that.

Could they spare some tracking units? They had several, and planned to consume/abandon/destroy them as they went. If they could get more in a timely fashion, those would work. Good.

He was jarred from his planning by Elke's voice.

"We need to talk."

"Yes, what do you need?"

"My explosives. Did you not know they were canceling my request?" She was agitated, almost fidgeting.

"I put in the request. Alex put in the request. They said they were approving the weapons. They didn't specifically mention explosives."

"When did you know this?"

"I knew we didn't have them when we left Earth. They were supposed to catch up. At no point did they refuse." He'd gotten every indication the order was in process.

"And here?"

"Nothing in the crates, and no inventory or request mentioning them. Black hole."

She said, "You knew the ROE, though. That they weren't allowing explosives other than very small charges for demolition on the controlled range only."

"Elke, I did not know that, at all. I've heard nothing on limits."

She stared; he stared.

He wondered now. They'd both been given different stories. "So, they lied to us about the availability, or rather, deliberately concealed the information. And lied to me about rules of engagement. Just a moment." He thumbed his phone.

"Intel, Captain Das."

"Jason, Jason."

"Hi, Jason," Das replied, sounding cheerful enough.

"Can you confirm for me the military ROE with weapons?"

"Yeah, patrol commander key for nonlethal release. Lethal weapons require shift commander approval from here. Support weapons restrained for two minutes, then only by shift commander approval. The colonel can release earlier on personal authority. Explosive munitions restricted to artillery, Aerospace Force air assets, and Special Operating Units or allied equivalents, which we agree means you."

"Thanks. Just needed to confirm."

"Understood."

He clicked off.

Elke said, "So the military would allow us to do whatever BuState authorizes, as is proper. Meaning Highland's people blocked the shipment."

"Can we ask her to intercede?"

"Please don't," Elke said.

"No?"

"No. I and Aramis shall make a shopping expedition."

He thought that over. They needed Elke, but they also needed her with best gear. Aramis needed to stash more stuff, too. They'd fill in temporarily.

He said, "I'll clear it with Alex. Go."

Aramis was still a bit surprised that Elke trusted him that much. Serving together seemed to have smoothed out their differences. She was a disturbing flake, but incredibly good at her job, certainly courageous, and tough enough.

The vehicle they were in was a combination truck and passenger escort vehicle, with an improved chassis. It would handle rubble just fine. It wasn't a track, and it wasn't proof against anything above pistols. Still, they hoped to blend in enough. Their clothes were generic unless one looked closely at the armor thread, and no one should notice one vehicle of thousands. As war-torn as this hole was, it was still much richer than Celadon had been, or still was.

"I find religion useful," Elke said.

"Oh? Are you religious?"

"Not very. I am nominally Lutheran through my grandmother. I was christened, and I have been to a friend's church wedding."

"So what's useful?"

"Half of the people here are either rabidly worshiping today, or pretending to. The other half will worship on Sunday, or prepare to."

"Except for the ones on Earth's clock, who will worship at two random times next week."

"And those few extremists who will worship on Tuesday, and the splitters from them who will use Earth Tuesday."

"It's also near shift change for the military."

"Oh, how convenient," she said, failing to hide her smile.

"So how do you plan to do this?"

"The really old fashioned way," she said.

"Shoot someone and take it?"

She shook her head. "Sadly, no. We shall bribe them far too much. These Grainne coins and a small amount of gold will attract plenty of attention."

"That's potentially a problem."

"It is for the person attempting to cash them in, which will not be us."

"Ah, enough to get them to say 'yes,' not enough to point at us, but too much for them to easily dispose of."

"And unmarked to us."

He checked the map—printed map, so it couldn't be tracked by anyone, though there were still ways to follow the vehicle. Jason assured him the module on the dash would fuzz and distort their location so they'd be only very generally locatable.

"Left here," he said. He saw what lay ahead and added, "and forward." There were police set up near the building. He wasn't going to stop.

"It would make sense," she said, "that a warehouse selling precursor chemicals would have a police post, on this planet."

"What next?"

"Vehicle store, pharmacy, standard hardware store."

He looked around at the business signs. "This way seems to be lighter industrial and commercial."

Another five kilometers found all types of stores. Elke grabbed a paper pad, printed very rapidly, and handed him a list.

"You are working on a swimming pool for a wealthy client," she said.

"Understood."

Inside, he felt nervous about the amounts in question, but piled them on a dolly and nudged it into motion. It followed him.

"Hydrochloric acid," he said.

"Aisle Three R," it replied in passable English, though the accent was both simulated and British with an overlay of Turk.

"Chlorine pool shock."

"Aisle Five M."

"Heavy grease." And so it went.

He reached the exit and the dolly scanned, but a clerk checked the contents by hand against the screen as well.

"You are working on a pool?" the man asked with a smile.

Damn, Elke's good. "Yes," he said. "Wealthy client up north."

"Tessekur." *Thanks*, in some dialect of Turkish.

"And you," he said.

He loaded it into the truck, climbed in, and Elke asked, "Did you get it?"

"Yes. What's next?"

"I will take the vehicle and engine store."

He drove to it, she slipped out, and he sweated in tension. He stayed in the vehicle surreptitiously watching all angles. It was twenty minutes before she returned, and loaded more cartons in the bed.

Once in, she said, "I will not be able to fabricate at the compound. I will need a safehouse."

"Jason has two. I'll also be adding supplies."

"Better equipped, more private, closer, are my needs, in that order."

"Luckily one of them fits all that."

"Good. I badly want caps and detonators, but I will have to improvise."

"You aren't going to try to buy some?"

"They are too obvious and they are alert here."

She flipped open her phone and keyed it, voice only.

"Argonaut," was the answer.

"We're going to need a rest at the apartment. We'll catch up later," she said.

"Understood. Can you be back in fifteen hours?"

"Yes."

"Sleep well."

She keyed off.

"Resting?" he asked.

"Manufacturing," she said.

"I'll do what I can to help." Manufacturing explosives on a remote planet full of factional violence. That was a beer story.

It took several minutes to drive to the safehouse, and several more to find it, without being traced. Paper maps were secure, but often harder to read, especially in this poorly laid out ratmaze.

True to form, Highland didn't really notice two substitutions in her escort. Horace really wondered just how many issues the woman had. Her anger, introversion, smugness, ego and greed were all indicative of any number of dysfunctions or disorders.

He was sure the backfills were competent. He even knew them slightly. He still would rather have the regulars. However, there was a promise of actual explosives when they returned.

JessieM was clearly shaken and nervous. She was holding up, but likely due to being a subordinate to Highland. On her own she'd be a wreck. If they were to cover her in an engagement, she'd need hands-on escort, and possibly carried. Mass around sixty kilos, he estimated. Doable.

Still, this evening's mission was with limos. They'd roll from the compound, out the back gate guarded by a mixed force of Army and State with Cady monitoring both and gibbering in rightful paranoia at the potential risks. Once out, they would have an Army escort, this being one of the few official BuState meetings.

It went well enough. They'd tested weapons inside the garage, and the Army seemed to actually accept it, with grumbling. The gate was ahead, and he counted three Grumblies with mounted guns.

From the front, Bart said, "We have escort from respectable armies."

"Yes. I'm glad to see them."

Highland asked, "Who are they?"

"Brazilian troops in one, Finnish in the second, Kazakh in the third."

"I like the Finns. They have such an earnest, hardworking culture. The Brazilians are very mixed and equitable."

Alex said, "Yes. Though in this case, they're good soldiers first."

"Of course."

Then they rose over the first speed hump and stopped.

Bart swore in German, threw the vehicle into reverse and tried to work it back.

Alex said, "We're supposed to have sufficient clearance. What happened?"

Horace looked around. There were no apparent threats, but this was not good. He saw a camera crew outside the fence zooming in. They were exposed and stuck.

Bart said, "I believe the surface collapsed from the mass of heavy vehicles. The difference is enough, with our load, to cause this."

"Will debarking help?"

"It is worth a try."

"Right. Ms. Highland, please remain aboard."

"Of course I will," she said, sounding incredulous someone would expect her to walk.

"Lionel, stay with her. Everyone else out. Bart, I'll drive."

"Yes, sir."

Horace bounced out and took another survey while breathing the clean air, tinged with exhaust next to the car. Bart took his frame out, Alex slipped in, and tried again. The car scraped and dragged, but made it over the hump. It shrieked over the next two. That got them outside the gate, though.

Horace jogged forward. The gates locked behind them, Bart resumed his position, and they all slid back in.

Highland looked offended.

"It seems no one cares about the dignity of my office," she muttered loudly enough to be heard.

Alex had his phone out and was almost certainly demanding engineers fix those depressions at once. Whether military, BuState contract, local hires or several Company people with shovels, someone had to fix it fast. It was an accidental choke point, now revealed on camera.

"Shaman, radio link with the escort, please."

"Radio, roger." He grabbed the small encryption module and clicked it on. "Patent Three to Roller Six, over," he said. The call signs were good. There were neither three nor six vehicles in either contingent.

"This is Roller Six, go ahead Patent Three, over." If that was a Finnish accent, it was very interesting.

"Patent Three to Roller Six, please advise on weather, ongoing, over."

"Clear, visibility at five zero, no storms. Expect light precipitation throughout, over."

That translated as no current combat, no traffic snarls for five kilometers, but some traffic expected. They had a feed from State's traffic scanners, and their own, and now the military's.

"Understood, Roller Six. Patent Three listening, out."

"Roller Six listening, out."

Of course, all the OPSEC was for naught with JessieM churping away.

She spoke to Highland. "Ma'am, we're getting churpcades all along. The crowd should be drastic."

"Good."

Alex said, "I thought this was a private meeting?"

"The meeting, yes, but I always like to make time to greet the people who matter."

Horace watched his quarter. At this point, everyone with any kind of node access knew where she was. It was irritating. Could they arrange to exclude Jessie?

He was most nervous when they slowed, though they never quite stopped. The military vehicles used sirens and PA to keep the way clear. This was one of the more prosperous areas, only fifty years out of date, or three centuries ahead of Celadon. The buildings were extruded concrete with little variation save size, featureless overall. The people were apparently mostly of the conservative Muslim sects, in robes and headgear. Though as they traveled the peoples' appearance grew more western.

"Patent Three, this is Roller Six, over."

He raised the small box and said, "This is Patent Three, go ahead, Roller Six, over."

"Arriving in nine zero seconds, over."

"Understood, Roller Six. Thanks for the ride, out."

"Anytime, Patent. Roller Six out."

Horace was out first, followed by Lionel and Corcoran. Highland and Jessie stepped onto the walk, and Alex and Jason filled in the rear. Bart would stay in the vehicle.

There wasn't a lot of attendance outside. This was a basic, boring policy meeting, and there was no reason for it to be public, nor even face to face. Diplomats and politicians liked their formal traditions, though.

It was anticlimactic. They strode in through a cordon of guards, all with beards and bushy mustaches. A wave of cool, dry air washed over them as the doors opened. There was a receiving line, and they parted so Highland could shake hands with dignitaries. An usher appeared and led them to a waiting area with sandwiches, water and soft drinks, and they weren't even asked to disarm.

They had a choice of vids, and the locals and some of the other details seemed absorbed. The Ripple Creek team mostly stood, snacked lightly, and kept to themselves, while following news and updates. They could see Highland, though it was amusing to know that image was sent to a satellite and back even though they were perhaps a hundred meters away. JessieM sat back with other escorts, associates, factota and significant others. He caught a brief glimpse of her churping away.

Jason said, "I'd like to hear from our other contingent." He meant Aramis and Elke.

Alex nodded. "Babs pinged a note. They're still working."

"Good, that was my concern." He looked relieved.

Lionel said, "You guys operate seamlessly. You've been at this as long as we have, yes?"

Horace said, "About the same. We started when the company first got launched, when the military deployed to Salin and needed protection for diplomats."

"This is much more interesting than facilities. Apart from occasional device threats and rockets, we have a consistent routine, or else it means something's gone east."

"This is a quiet one so far. I'd like it to stay that way. You noticed the baggage we have?" He meant JessieM of course.

Lionel nodded. "Yes, that's inconvenient. We were advised to extend all courtesies."

"Yes. It'll get settled on the tab afterward."

Lionel sipped his drink and faked watching the screen. "That's hard for you to deal with, though, I presume."

"Hard enough. We have ROE to cover it."

"I'm interested in more of that."

Horace grinned. "It pays a little better, but it's not routine."

"Yes, I know. I don't particularly crave adventure, but it's something I want to pursue."

He wanted to offer something positive, even though this was just time-wasting chatter. "Well, good luck. We don't seem to want for business. You're steady and seem mature."

"Thanks. Any antics you can share?"

"We stayed in a cave off a mine once, on Govannon. Carved rock, shelf bunks, vacuum-evacuated toilet. It was big enough for one and we had seven. Porn on the walls, processed worm meat and stabilized rice to eat."

Lionel grinned. "Wow. That's something we don't get on the perimeter. The worms weren't optional?"

"No. Chewy, a bit like squid, but beefy tasting."

"And now I know." He chuckled, but seemed put off as well.

Two hours later they embarked, convoyed and returned. Lionel looked amused rather than bored, and still paid attention to his threat sector.

So far, this was mission was aggravating, but quiet.

⊚ CHAPTER 10 ⊚

"**WHAT NOW?**" Aramis asked.

"How are you at cooking?"

"Um . . ."

In minutes he was very carefully monitoring four double boilers heating over the induction coils of the range. Elke had several tubs full of goo, which seemed to be plasticizing. Aramis wasn't an expert on explosive, but he knew that hexamine, nitrates, phosphates, acids and ionized metals led to stuff that went boom.

"How is the soap and chlorate?" she asked.

He carefully drew a spatula from each and gauged the runoff. "Fully liquid," he said.

"Good, I'll take them."

One tub was a gray mess of ammonium nitrate and some liquid booster. One was a translucent greenish mess. One was white.

"Dare I ask?"

She indicated without flicking the gray stuff off her gloved hands. "Low-order plastique of potassium chlorate and petroleum gelatin. Improvised but unstable dynamite of nitroglycerin in ammonium nitrate base, which I will entube. The semi-crystalline stuff is RDX. You're going to help me take rifle cartridges apart and place them in the copper tubing, using the propellant and chlorate mix, as priming caps."

"How unstable is 'unstable'?"

"Just don't get in an accident on the way back, and don't inhale the fumes."

They'd shopped most of the day, and cooked most of the night, with the kitchen curtained off and the outside windows curtained as well. There was enough light leakage to indicate occupation, and Jason had set controllers to cycle the lights on a randomized but standard schedule to indicate habitation. There was not enough visibility for anyone to spy on them.

Aramis realized how tired he was.

"Money and determination," he muttered.

"What? Oh, yes," she said, obviously distracted. "I need explosives for my part of the mission. I will have them. These will suffice until I can find better materials. I'm quite sure a construction site will have what I need."

"Are we actually resting before we leave?"

"Do you need to?" she asked, quite seriously. "Return trip should be under an hour."

"I'll be fine," he said. He squinted through the curtains. "I just wanted to confirm. It looks dawnish out there."

"Yes, so it does," she said, and glanced at her watch. "Oh five twenty-seven. Highland has a movement in four hours. I suppose I have what I need for now. I'll destroy some of the partials and stow the rest, tragic as it is to waste material."

"You can buy more. Money's not an issue."

"Money is not the issue," she said as she carried the first tub into the kitchen and placed it in the sink. "Wasting material is the issue. Explosives are supposed to detonate, not flush down the drain." She sighed as she turned on a trickle of water.

In five minutes, she had a large box neatly filled with devices and claylike blocks, and a bag of the improvised caps, including some with electrical leads for remote or keyed detonation.

There was no traffic on the stairs, though sounds and smells indicated residents awake and preparing for work. Aramis smelled tea, coffee, pastries, some meat that was probably not pork, given the cultures here. There was occasional music and news chatter. All in all it was quite homey and reminiscent of a century long passed. Earth buildings had much tighter soundproofing and seals, and audio was always focused or through personal devices.

He led outside, since Elke was hindered with the box. A couple of backpacks would have been easier, but far less discreet.

Elke placed the box carefully in back, and slipped in with it. Aramis ignited the turbine and pulled slowly out into the rising traffic.

They were two kilometers down the road when his phone chimed.

"Musketeer," he said.

Alex said, "Are you carrying smelly stuff?"

"Uh, maybe?" he looked back at Elke, who said, "Fumes are outgassing, yes."

Jason cut in on the other end. "Their sniffers have it, reporting a threat, and they're responding."

"Who's 'they'?"

"The official mil types."

"Response?"

"We're calling Das. We'll try to clear it. Stand by and out."

"Will travel and stand by, out, waiting." He twitched his eyebrows, felt a flush and said, "That's not good," to Elke.

"They have better sensors than I anticipated. I should have triple wrapped and sealed."

"They'd find it sooner or later."

"Car coming up fast behind," she said. He heard her fumble with weapons.

"Pursuit? Police?" He glanced at the rear screen.

"Armored sedan, looks semi-official," she said. "I wonder if they're plugged into the milnet."

"Not good. Evading." He swung the wheel to send them straight down a side street, thankful there were no zone controls to worry about here.

However, that sedan braking hard in front of them wasn't in his plans.

"Entrapment," he said, amazed at how cool he sounded. There was an alley on the left just past. He flung the car into a turn, gunned it, fishtailed twice and went down what was apparently a service lane, slaloming through trash and pallets.

Elke said, "I'm loaded, tell me if you need support."

"I expect so, soon. Call for backup."

Mild precombat nausea gripped him, and fatigue didn't help. He was out the alley, back onto a street, but it was crowded and slow.

Elke said, "Hostiles attempting to herd us. Request backup soonest."

"Working. We have your location, keep your line open."

"Line open, roger."

No good. They were penned in by traffic, and there were men getting out of a car thirty meters back. He wasn't going to find an opening.

"Proceed on foot, we need a bughole," he said.

Elke was out the door in a second, wearing her backpack and with the box looking a bit lighter. Good woman. A moment later a sharp bang accompanied a brilliant flash and a directional cloud of smoke. She pulled alongside him.

"Did you secure the car?"

"I did not boobytrap it but it is locked. The burst was just distraction."

"Hostiles?"

"Delayed, but there are some ahead."

"I see them," he said. "Move into a building."

"This one."

It was a closed office that hopefully had a rear exit, or a roof, or some way to barricade themselves while backup arrived. Aramis reached the door at a sprint and kicked it. The latches shattered and they were in.

"That wouldn't work in a more modern world," he said, as they dodged between dividing walls.

"Two distractions behind us, set for vibration."

"Not lethal?"

"Allies may come."

"Roger. No upstairs access I can see. Out the back."

There was clattering behind them, then a *bang*, and another.

Elke stepped aside and let him take the lead. He flipped the latch, kicked the door open and slipped through, raising his pistol.

His brain exploded inside his skull and he went down.

Bart drove, though usually he was in a limo, not a Grumbly. The rotary-diesel was turning fast enough to have a smooth hum, not a grumbling lope. They were in a hurry.

As he understood it, they were also in violation of contract.

Their mission was Highland's safety. Cady's mission was

compound security. Recovery of missing personnel was properly the military's tasking. However, that would take time, and they knew Aramis's and Elke's location now.

Elke's voice came through the channel. "Musketeer is down, probably captured."

Bart felt chills. That was bad. Peripherally, he saw the others swapping glances.

Alex asked, "Understood. Are you covered?"

"I have created a safe zone."

That sounded bad, too.

"We're arriving in six minutes."

"I can hold—*BANG!*" her voice cut off with an explosion, but the signal was still live. "Do hurry, though."

Another voice came through, "Alex, this is Das."

Alex said, "Alex here, go."

"We have an extraction team en route. Fifteen minutes will get them there."

"That's ten minutes behind us."

"Understood. I must advise you that you are not on military contract and do not have engagement privileges."

"Meaning we will observe as long as feasible, or the lawyers will have lots of work to do."

Das sounded tense but sympathetic. "I understand your concern but there will be trouble if you breech status of forces."

Bart cursed. Yes, rules existed for a reason, but this was not a military engagement, it was a criminal incident. It was probably even harder to find a political agreement regarding that.

Before Alex could reply, Elke said, "Hostiles are gone."

"Retreated?"

"Yes. They have Musketeer, as far as I can tell."

"Shit."

Bart's chills turned to burns. This was unprecedented.

"Arriving in two minutes," he said, as calmly as he could.

Alex said, "Babs, can you meet at your reported location?"

"I am two hundred meters from there and prefer to meet at this location. Advise when you need directions."

Bart nodded, and said, "Tell me in twenty seconds, which turn to take."

Elke coolly guided him in to a stop next to an alley. She darted out with a box and ruck and was aboard at once.

She heaved for breath and there was a chemical stink of explosive over the perspiration. Her hair was greased with sweat, she was scuffed and dusty, but alive and intact.

"Reporting," she said. "We were corralled by four vehicles at the same time you reported notice of us. Either the military has a leak or the hostiles have similar sensors. We entered the building ahead, where the traffic jam and dust is. I left a distraction device outside, two inside. There was no good barricade or roof, and pursuers triggered the devices. We attempted to leave out the back. Aramis was hit with a combination of two heavy stunners and an impact projectile. I shot and hit two hostiles, outcome unknown, then shot and blasted through the wall into the crawl alley to the south. I made a short chimney ascent, entered a first floor window, exited the rear behind the hostiles. I covered in a trash abutment and held them with fire. I made my report, then they departed, presumably with Aramis."

That was so precise it was frightening, Bart thought, but not as much as Aramis's abduction.

"Can we trace him with that stuff?" Alex asked.

"He will have residue, yes. His clothes especially will be impregnated."

"They'll probably ditch those if they smell them. Channel, Das, sir, what's the recovery unit ETA?"

"Three minutes."

"This is our location," he said, and pinged it through. "We need to search the contact site."

"They see you and are arriving."

Aramis awoke nauseated, in throbbing pain, stripped to underwear, wrapped in cargo tape restraints at wrist and ankle, sitting on a cold floor. He could vaguely identify others. Two people were in front of him, well-built, probably military. One lurked behind. Two others were off to the left.

Ohshitohshitohshit. It kept tumbling through his brain.

No way out. Not a chance. The restraints wouldn't yield, and he was quite sure the one at the back would happily shoot anyone he tried to grab as a shield. Assuming he could see anything. He wasn't sure how he knew the man behind had a gun, but he knew.

His wrists ached, his head had that burning pain that felt as if it were bleeding from trauma, but often meant only a concussion.

A voice from the left said, "He's awake, get to it."

Another voice, in front, said, "I need her movements."

He understood that was addressed to him, and replied, "They're chosen at random, even when there is a schedule, and I am not told until we are en route."

A tremendous slap rocked his cheek and jaw, like fiery gravel. He'd been hit with some kind of heavy glove.

"Ridiculous. You have to know."

He sweated and teared up through the bursting pain, which was triggering his pulped skull again. "The Agent in Charge knows, or his deputy. The rest of us do as we're told."

He stood there. He knew what was coming, and it terrified him. Combat was one thing. To be bound helplessly and . . .

The blow felt as if a car hit him in the cheek. He grunted, convulsed and lay out on the floor, trying to get into a fetal position to protect himself. His ears rang, eyes blurred, he thought his cheek probably broken. The pain was a lance, and then a suffusing pulse of agony, fading slowly to a burning sting.

Someone hauled him to his feet, and he tried to clench his abs, just in time for a massive punch that paralyzed his diaphragm. He gaped like a fish and did nothing for what felt like hours while boots and sticks thudded and cracked his ear, shoulder, spine, all over. The pain was warm and sharp.

Then he was hauled to his feet again.

"What is tomorrow's schedule?"

He was angry and hurt. He cried and sobbed. "Dammit, I don't know. Even if I did, it would have changed by now. This is fucking stupid."

The pain, the disorientation, the fear were beyond anything he'd ever felt. Nausea collided with anger, terror, and he hyperventilated. They helped him with that, with plastic over his face until he passed out watching purple blotches as he surged against it in panic. He'd stayed still to conserve oxygen as long as he could, but there were limits, and his left cheek was stabbing agony . . .

He woke upright, his hands now bound on an overhead rail, helpless to protect his torso from crashing impacts. Blindfold off, he saw a stick line up and was too restrained and hurt to cringe. He watched in slow motion as it arced full force up toward his crotch.

He didn't pass out, but he did throw up. A heated rush flooded his brain as his panicking body tried to compensate.

It was terrifying and surreal, like falling off a cliff.

It didn't end with that, and he never got past it all feeling like a dream, an hallucination, an unreality that he couldn't wake up from and desperately wanted to.

He took a full look at each of the three attackers. They were local, muscular and southern European in ancestry. That might make them Christian or Muslim, no way to tell. He memorized their faces. Then . . .

Got to leave, he thought. Not physically. He couldn't. That sensation, though, that crazy, mind-warping sensation, he'd felt that before and it hadn't been bad.

Sticks smashed under his armpits and across his shoulders. He passed out again.

He woke slightly and heard, "Shit, I think this pervert enjoys it," accompanied by a thumping blow to his groin. He grunted out breath. Yeah, he actually was erect. Apparently the distraction worked.

I probably shouldn't tell Caron about that, he thought.

He settled for keeping his eyes closed, easy through the bruises, and breathing slowly and steadily, tough to do through his battered nose and painful as the air flowed over his wounded teeth. Apart from that, his whole body was a quivering nerve, aware of every current of air, every gradation of temperature, every bruise, fracture, laceration and contusion. He found he wasn't worried about getting hit again; that was just part of this reality. He'd ride the wave of pain and appreciate the surreal sensation, and let that take his brain back to Caron and Ayisha, their full, painted lips colliding around him, with each other, tongues swirling . . .

Yes, someone had hit him, he vaguely realized. He'd blacked out from the pain. Pain, shooting up his spine, just like that sensation when he looked over to see Caron, mouth open and tongue probing, curiously and nervously . . .

The intense jolt made him scream, the pain was in his hip, his muscles cramping up in gripping waves, tight under his balls, and . . .

"I swear this sick fucker is getting off on being hit. Either I kill him or we stop."

"He's not really of use. Hit harder."

The next blow broke his focus. Ohshitfuckmebitch that hurt. Shooting hand. Writing hand. Hand I used on Caron to . . . to . . .

A rain of blows with a hammer started at his feet, ankles and shins, working toward his knees. He could feel tears streaming down his face. He wanted release even if it meant death, because he knew he was crippled, probably going to be emasculated, and left in a heap in a gutter, probably set on fire to twitch and scream, and these fuckers called him a pervert. He was going beyond anything he'd ever imagined, and this wasn't real, except it was, and Caron's ass was amazingly toned and taut and . . .

✺ CHAPTER 11 ✺

TWO OTHER GRUMBLIES arrived mounting guns. They were followed momentarily by two armored hex-wheels. Four machine guns, a grenade launcher and a multicannon were not artillery, but were more than enough for this street. The civilians were surprisingly scarce, having cleared the outside entirely, and probably all hunkered down inside.

An officer swung out easily, in gray splinter camo. That was reassuring. Not only wasn't it the insane pink, it was private purchase. That meant they weren't too hung up on Military Instructions, hopefully.

"You're Marlow?" He was a captain, lean and fit, seemed competent and that scowl was probably permanent. He was an older careerist, face a bit craggy.

Alex said, "Yes."

"Captain Jay Roye."

"Glad to meet you; thanks for being fast."

"Yeah, we'll cover that later. You have one MIA?"

"Correct. Here's his info." He'd have to make sure to recover that later, under BuState privacy laws. For now, he needed to save Aramis.

"Any leads?"

"They didn't tell you? The same explosive trace you followed should continue."

"Stand by." The captain raised a hush hood and spoke to base. They spoke back. He spoke some more.

Alex clenched his jaw and took slow, measured breaths through the anger thudding through him. There was nothing he could do to speed up the process, and any complaints might hinder things. It was almost a full minute before the captain spoke.

"It goes north. Intersperse and follow."

Bart said, "I will take second position."

Roye agreed, "Good, do it."

They found a lieutenant suddenly holding the door for Shaman and Elke, and sliding in behind them. Or he tried to. Elke arranged for him to step in as she slid under, taking the door herself.

"Lieutenant Eranio," the man said. "I have a briefing summary for you."

"Go ahead, sir," Alex said, hoping he sounded polite and interested. Eranio came across as prior enlisted. He wore big glasses and had that scraggle that suggested he'd always be in need of a shave.

Eranio said, "For joint operations in the AO with contract personnel, Military Instructions are in force, and the on-scene military commander will determine operations within standard guidelines. All Law of Armed Conflict and Conventions Pursuant to Hostile Engagements are to be observed. Contractor personnel will limit their activities to observation and reporting, or noncombat support activities as described in MI Two-Five Dash Seven One Nine Bravo. End quote. The captain will not allow you to proceed without acknowledging this."

"Not only do I acknowledge it, I leave the engagement to you," he said. Would they take the bait?

"Oh? Why's that?"

"Our specialty is getting people into cover, and as you've said, there are Instructions that must be followed. There are undoubtedly multiple hostiles waiting."

Eranio said, "I understand what you mean." In moments, he had a hush hood up, and was talking to the captain. Alex was sure of that, because the model was cut rate and didn't have a shimmer screen. Alex could read lips. They thought it was a shameless attempt to pass casualties and possible blame onto the military.

The lieutenant dropped the hood and said, "Given the nature of the incident, and that it's your agent who's the captive, we've been instructed from higher up to have you conduct the raid."

Thank you, Captain Das.

Straight-faced, he said, "If you believe that's best."

"No, I'd rather we did it, but I have instructions. You will conduct the entry, we will support and observe, and document."

There were too many snide comments Alex wanted to make, so instead, he nodded and turned.

"Bart, you'll punch. Elke, can you make a hole?"

"Yes."

"Good. Jason takes gun position. Shaman and I follow."

Elke turned to face the lieutenant. "I need real explosives. Now," she said.

"That is beyond my authority to grant." He turned to his phone, but hesitated when the driver slowed.

Jason said, "This is as far as we could trace. We have to dismount and sniff now."

"You have a sniffer?"

Jason said, "One, yes."

Eranio twisted his mouth for a moment and said, "We'll use ours."

Elke opened the door and slid out; Eranio followed. His troops pulled up right behind and hopped out in a reasonably professional fashion. He immediately gave orders.

"I want one troop with each contractor. Moheng, with this guy, Franklin with the big German, Trinidad with the female, Barnes with the doctor. I'll stay with Marlow."

Alex nodded and bounced out the door. They could talk as they moved. "Do you have troops who can follow in our vehicle in case we need a quick departure?"

Eranio nodded, pointed at one troop and the Grumbly, and indicated the other driver was to remain aboard his vehicle.

Elke was alongside at once and said, "Lieutenant, I need explosives. I am certified all the way through nukes, and expect a dynamic entry. I will file all documents and our company will reimburse promptly."

The captain approached, and had obviously overheard. "I can't authorize that."

"Then I will use what I have—homebrewed RDX, aluminized AN-nitro dynamite and some rather smoky flash bangs. Unless you want to waste resources restraining me, and breach the door yourself?"

"Goddam you." He looked at Alex, not Elke, and said, "All right, I'll give her a couple of door poppers and they can each have a flash bang. Will that do it?"

She smiled thinly. "Crude and marginal, but I will make it work."

"I'm only doing this because I don't want the admin of a dead civilian. But you arrogant *contractors* need to abide by your own rules. We're cleaning up your mess."

Jason burned in rage, but calmly said, "We appreciate it, and will work out details later. Thank you for assisting in recovering our man."

"Don't thank me. You can take the risk and lead the way in. Remember the lawyers will have your balls for breakfast if you kill any civilians."

They were talking instead of acting, but they'd been given something they wanted. Was it a favor, or an error? Either way, Alex would take it. They were better at kicking in doors than most of the military, had motivation, and could let lawyers deal with the carnage. Meyer would back them as he had before.

"Then let's proceed. What intel do we have?"

Eranio consulted with a sergeant holding a chemical sniffer. "Traces are inconsistent. He's within two hundred meters or so."

Alex looked around.

"There's a lot of structure within two hundred meters. What can we rule out?"

The lieutenant was probably being helpful when he said, "You can rule out the law office and the UN aid office."

Alex avoided snorting, and he heard Jason cough. It wasn't really funny, but the surprise factor did it. Depending on what other evidence they found, those might be exactly where they'd start.

The Army's technical specialist said, "Definitely north."

"Concur," Jason said. "Map shows several storefronts. Some are substantial, but all have storage areas."

The sergeant, Tames, said, "That wind gust helped. Got the arc down to forty-three degrees."

"Overlay," Jason said. "I have forty-six, but the intersection is thirty-eight."

"That tall building is interfering."

"Yes, definitely beyond that."

Elke said, "Your area is approximately seven five zero zero square meters. Sergeant Tames, if you can move thirty meters north to the corner, check your density there."

The captain nodded, and the sergeant with two second classes moved that way, checking for threats.

Tames said, "Probably east of me here."

Jason moved down an alley, Alex and Bart covering him along with their escorts.

A burst of fire made Jason flinch and duck.

He said, "Contact right front," as someone else shouted, "Contact left!"

Whoever was shooting had bad aim and poor weapons. He recognized the muzzle cracks as Brasarms carbines. There were lots of them here, sold cheap for police use and stolen for factional fighting. They were cheap, and marginal, and cheap. However, they put bullets downrange, and he was downrange. He hunkered down against a building wall and crabbed around into an alley. He went across the alley. Bart backed into the opening, facing the street. Their troop escorts did stay close, and tensed with their weapons.

He spoke to his chaperone. "I want to suppress and advance."

The sergeant looked around nervously, then nodded. "Agreed."

"I'm moving." He swung, fired a burst, sprinted across the narrow alley, which had suddenly devoided of people. He reached the far wall, fired a burst straight up parallel to it, and another high around the corner, as the soldier sprinted over.

Heavy fire from a Grumbly's cannon echoed down the walls, booms turning tinny and hollow.

The troop said, "It's apparently some random potshots. Three locations, not coordinated, seem to be dispersed."

"What does the captain say?"

Right then, his earbuds spoke. "Argonaut, Playwright. Bars reports containment. Advise your movements."

"One square red." *South.* "I can advance."

"He's ready," Alex said to Rowe as he came up. "Unless you want to sweep and secure first?"

"What's your preference?"

"Hell with that, let's get in and get Aramis, then we can operate as a mass unit."

The captain nodded. "Yeah, since you fuckers are going to do that anyway. Lead, then."

There were no overt signs of previous combat in this area, which was probably why it had been chosen. Ground of the enemy's choosing was not ideal, but they should have the upper hand tactically.

"Do you have observation all around?"

"Cameras on three Grumblies, two Dragonfly drones at five hundred meters, and the evac bird three klicks north." Rowe gestured with a hand.

"We have the south approach. Do you have anything for containment?"

"Same Grumblies and crews."

"I would like to have them dismount and patrol, sir."

"Very well, stand by."

He'd give the captain this: the man took it seriously and was playing by the rules but with practicality.

"They're dismounted and advancing slowly," Rowe said.

Alex spoke on his voicemitter. "Team, we want to be dynamic and watch for collaterals. I'm quite sure they've got buddy berms. Approach orders from the captain. Sir?" he said as he turned.

Rowe said, "Thank you, by my orders, advance in leapfrog."

Alex waited for the first movement, then he and the captain jogged forward. There was no fire, and people left the streets as soon as they saw troops with guns. Of course, that meant a good chance the enemy knew they were approaching.

Then it was time to advance again, past doorways, alleys and enclosures locked or barred or full of pedestrians. Vehicles traveling by accelerated to clear the area. Passing a woman and three kids huddled into an entryway, he gave a short, quick wave. Hopefully they'd grasp that they weren't of military interest.

This was an actual military assault, and he sweated and shook. Aramis had experience doing this. On paper, Alex had no actual combat experience. All his was escorting principals to safety, and the only rule of engagement was "keep them alive." Here, he was very much accountable, easier to predict, and the principal was not under his control. Getting that control risked Aramis's death.

Still, there was nothing to do but go forward.

Then they were across the street and huddled themselves, trying not to present targets or recognizable military appearances.

Elke came alongside and he asked, "Are we positive it's this building?"

She waved a scanner. "Yes, I can pick up a second trace, of a secondary chemical. This building." She nodded.

"What's in there, officially?"

The captain said, "Paradise Clothing. They seem to make garb for Muslims and Christians both, middle class."

"Track the owner later. What do we have on intel?"

"Right now it looks like people sewing. I'm reluctant to deploy drones. They'll be obvious in this environment."

They'd also be subject to damage and loss, which he'd have to account for. Though that might not be fair. They would be easy to spot. There was little airborne traffic of any kind.

Elke said, "Let me take a scan." She unslung her shotgun and fired a recon round up past the windows. She scrolled the images on her glasses.

"The quality is not good, and the frame is small, as well as blurred from speed. There are occupants, several, male. There is a lot of debris. I note rags and cloths and possible bloodstains."

Alex said, "Good enough for me. We'll kick it and try. We have lawyers if we're wrong." He looked at the captain.

Rowe sighed and twisted his mouth. "I don't like the potential collaterals, but I don't see how it can get better if we wait. Go ahead and tell your people. We'll lead."

Elke rose and sprinted fearlessly, with everyone else playing catch up. She obviously took her buddy's safety personally.

One nice thing about the shots outside, they offered distraction. The team might be compromised already, or the engagement might be taken as some random interplay. Either way, though, it was noisy. They were quiet. Anyone looking for them should be looking in the wrong place.

They ran to the entrance, and Elke pressed the door switch. It slid, they swarmed through into a very obvious sewing shop. There were gasps but no outright shouts or screams, and several troops raised fingers to lips then held calming hands out. Alex headed up the broad stairs with Elke and Jason each a half step behind, Shaman and Bart flowing through the door and falling in. They moved in practiced, gliding steps that minimized noise. There was still quite a bit of shuffling and clattering and some yelps from the workers. If they hadn't been compromised already, they were now.

Jason rose up the stairs. There was a bare landing about a meter square, a featureless metal door, needing some kind of signal or having a hidden touchplate for access.

Jason was not minded to be picky. They stacked, Elke slapped a charge against the door, gave a thumbs up. Shaman goosed Jason, he goosed Elke, she fired the charge. Smoke and sparks fled in an arc. Bart managed to fit his bulk into the available space, and kicked the door off the tattered remnants of its hinges. He went right, Elke went left, Jason stepped right across the downed door, hearing a muffled grunt from someone trapped underneath it when it fell. Behind him, a shot indicated Alex had stopped the man's pain permanently. Yes, there was a weapon next to the corpse. Good kill. Eddying dust roiled up in light from the windows. The hostiles should probably have covered those, but it might have drawn attention. This place was long abandoned.

Elke and Bart were shooting, and he had targets ahead of him. He fluttered his finger on the trigger, pointing as he moved, treating them as moving targets to his subjective stillness. He shot four before any of them could fall. He got the last one right under his raised weapon and high on the chest.

Bart called, "Right blue clear." Elke said, "Left blue clear," very calmly. Alex said, "Left red clear."

That left one man behind a bloody sack that was Aramis, raising a pistol toward Aramis's head. Jason put a bullet right through the hand and gun, and a second two centimeters past Aramis's ear, directly into the thug's right eye. He convulsed with a gurgle and collapsed, his hooked left arm half-hanging on Aramis's restrained body until he slipped free. Aramis gurgled too, and moaned.

"Right red clear. Babs sweep, Bart run a patrol, Playwright we need evac."

Then the Recon team burst right in behind them, and stopped.

The captain stuttered for a moment, then said, "Well done, contractors. Barnes, help with their casualty."

The combat medic was already three steps forward, his ruck unslung as he reached for gear.

Jason tried not to look at the ruined mess that was his young friend. Elke looked greenish behind her ears and around her mouth, but swallowed, squinted and stayed with it. Shaman ran forward with his pack. Jason decided he'd better at least look and see if he could serve backup.

The man was a beaten mess, though most of his insides still seemed to be inside, and intact. He might have died from trauma, but not from hypovolemic shock. If he'd died. Jason wasn't sure if surviving this was positive. Gingerly, three people supported him, while one drew a knife and cut the tape restraints. They kicked debris aside and laid him down.

"Alive," Shaman said. "Pulse weak but steady, breathing labored but adequate, no major head trauma." He spoke all this as he helped handle the naked body. Aramis had great muscle tone, but it didn't show now. He was just a flesh-colored mannequin, lacking any vitality.

There might not be major head trauma, but his jaw and cheeks were ugly. It looked like a slightly reduced form of the ancient Hawaiian execution, with most of the bones broken, to be followed by eye gouging and eventually shattering blows to the clavicles.

He had no idea why that had suddenly come to mind, except that . . . ah, right. Shaman now lived in Hawaii. The brain was capable of the most fucked up connections.

But they had him down and in a basket, with monitors. Sergeant Barnes was solidly professional, running an IV line at Shaman's direction and checking for critical trauma or bleeding in the legs, then for spine damage. Shaman did the rest. Elke and Bart mumbled ill comments and pulled back to maintain a perimeter.

It stank. Aramis had leaked from all ends, sweated, bled. The building hadn't been too clean to start with. There was now the stench of smoke and explosive debris, and he felt a tickle of dust catch in his throat.

Shaman sprinkled something, said, "He's stable enough. Let's depart."

They backed out, with Elke screening them with smoke against any prying cameras. They left the bodies for the military to deal with. They could claim or blame as they wished.

Jason decided they would find out who was behind this. He'd make calls to acquaintances if need be. Then he'd pay a visit.

Outside, Bart watched with concern as they loaded Aramis into a military ambulance under dim red sunlight. Shaman jumped aboard and said, "I'll see you on base." Two troops slapped the doors closed and it rolled, joined in the convoy by two Grumblies and an ARPAC.

Without waiting for clearance, Bart slid into their vehicle, as Elke dove straight through the window. Marlow and Vaughn used the doors, but weren't much slower. He counted four heads, then accelerated before the captain could complain about anything.

They drove back at race speeds, Bart slaloming through traffic, using horn and attitude to clear a route. They had an appointment with Highland, but also to make sure Aramis arrived safely.

Pedestrians here fell into two classes. Those who were very cautious and polite, and those who seemed suicidal. They would ignore the vehicle until it was on them, then skip aside barely enough that Bart felt the fenders brush their clothes. It would be bad to kill any. It would mean admin and delays.

Behind him, he heard Alex speaking into his phone. "Cady, we're coming in the back. I want to avoid any military debrief, and get out fast with Highland. I need two people to fill in. Thanks."

He spoke louder. "We're changing to suits fast—just clean up with alcohol gel. Lionel and Corcoran are filling in."

"When is departure time?"

"This says she moved it up on us. Fifteen minutes from now. How far are we from the gate?"

"At this speed, about ten minutes."

"Go faster."

"I need a clearer path."

Elke said, "Turn left up here, and I'll take the top." She slipped restraints, braced her feet and stood behind him.

He heard Marlow curse. Elke fired a short burst. Marlow fumbled with his phone. "Warning shots, we're firing warning shots. No engagement. I understand policy. Circumstances dictate threats but not engagement."

He clicked off the connection and said, "We may as well call the lawyers now. This is going to be a nightmare."

The city thinned out and the route became narrower, but less busy. Bart rolled onto the fused shoulder to pass a driver who had a dopy look and was picking his nose.

At last he came to the outer perimeter that IDed the vehicle and let him past, the first slalom barricade, the scanners the military didn't know they knew about.

"Cady's waiting."

"Understood."

Even out here there was a military post, and patrols, but it was officially BuState jurisdiction. The troops on duty were lesser paid contractors who did a reasonably professional job. Cady waited at the third ring, and waved.

Bart slowed but didn't quite stop. Cady vaulted onto the hood and grabbed a tiedown ring. He accelerated slightly. In moments they reached the berm, wire, tanglers and stunners that protected the fence, along with the manned machine gun and auto cannon that officially didn't. Cady waved again, the outer gate opened, and they locked through to the inner berm.

There was Highland and Jessie, fidgeting and waiting. He slowed and turned. He pulled up on the next side of the building so as not to be seen.

The others debarked and he followed, all of them at a run. Cady spoke into her phone, "Lionel, Corcoran, go." She pressed off and said, "They'll meet her and calm her. We need to roll in four minutes."

Jason zipped out of the blouse, kicked off his boots, dropped trousers and grabbed the alcohol gel, the soldier's best friend when water wasn't available, or not in time. It cooled the exertion he felt, and most of his sweat evaporated with it. Someone had laid their suits out. He grabbed shirt, threw on jacket, pulled on pants and used the thoughtfully placed shoehorn to slip into his already tied shoes. He could adjust everything in the vehicle.

They made it down in three minutes, stuffing shirts into waistbands in the elevator, and checking stunners and handguns. Cady and her men were outside, ushering Highland into the ARPAC. They followed her, and the four sprinted out.

Once aboard the vehicle, they were subjected to Highland's random seething rage. Lionel and Corcoran had managed to get her seated. She half rose and stood in an uncomfortable crouch as she railed against them.

"I don't know what you were playing at, sightseeing when I have a schedule to keep. I will be communicating with your headquarters to note a very unsatisfactory attention to the job."

Jason kept a close eye on everyone. Elke had a faint expression of annoyance, which was bad. However, she was controlled, not fixed in place. Jason's jaw worked. He was quite angry, but seemed to have tuned her out.

Highland, though, was managing to escalate herself. Jason wasn't sure if there was any approach that wouldn't piss her off.

"It's fine to sit there pretending I don't exist. It's an admission of unprofessionalism . . ."

He checked his contact sedatives. She really might need one, judging from her vitals. Her pulse was over 120, and oscillating moment to moment. Her BP was edging into unhealthy territory. She was visibly agitated and trembling from hormonal overload. He wished Shaman were here. This was much more his tasking.

Perhaps a tranquilizer would be better. If she missed her speech, she'd only be that much more incensed.

However, she gradually tapered off, seeming to run out of things to say. As she did so, her vitals lowered. It would be a tense speech, but that might work to her favor. If, of course, she realized that.

She did eventually wind down, and upon arriving at the destination debarked and was gracious, at least to the press and her supporters, in public.

Twice Jason checked his phone with a surreptitious sweep of his glasses. Both messages were that Aramis was stable, and had improving vitals. Shaman mentioned various nano and pharmaceutical treatments. Beyond the cursory level, they were past Jason's medical knowledge.

Otherwise, the event was without incident and they all traveled back in silence. Highland didn't seem to be aware of Aramis's and

Shaman's absence and no one seemed inclined to mention it. Elke for one napped leaning against the bulkhead of the ARPAC, her head rocking and swaying as the vehicle shifted.

They were all agitated on return. Cady had more people waiting, who immediately took charge of the ARPAC. Bart ran to the vehicle park and returned at once in a standard staff car. They checked out at the gate and headed straight to the military clinic.

Everyone seemed to know who they were, which had both bad and good connotations. Any semblance of anonymity was gone. For now, though, it got them through protocol quickly.

Shaman met them outside the Major Care Unit. That was a positive sign.

Shaman said, "Yes, he's stable. He will certainly survive. He will almost certainly be fit to resume duties after treatment. There was quite an argument about the ground ebony powder I sprinkled on his pillow. I had to assure the doctor it was both a religious necessity for Aramis, and fully sterilized for medical purposes. I did not mention the garlic cloves in three locations. They are dry and should not present a problem."

Jason still didn't know if the witch doctory Shaman insisted upon was done seriously, in gleeful mockery of modern medicine, or as a cultural practice for his own comfort. It might be all of them. Or he just might figure it couldn't hurt to toss the stuff in. Regardless of that, the man was a hell of a cutter in the field and a first class surgeon in the clinic. If he said Aramis was going to recover, that was the end of it.

After they had a collective sigh and swapped guarded smiles, he continued. "Whoever did this was very experienced. It's large scale damage, but none of it is traumatic enough for lethality. My guess is they planned to leave him to rest a bit after this, possibly even treat the contusions and use anesthetics. After they wore off, the pain would be that much more palpable, but they'd only need to prod him to trigger it."

"Sick fuckers," Elke said.

"Very. However, that's part of why he's still alive."

Alex asked, "When are you transporting off planet?"

Shaman almost smiled. "Oh, that shouldn't be necessary. The damage is substantial, but superficial. The jaw and cheek repair will be complete in a week. The rest is just muscle bruising with some bone bruising. It will remain painful, but is entirely repairable."

"That's not the only issue. How is his mental state and is it fair to keep him in place after that?" Alex looked tense again.

Horace asked, "Is it fair to send him home?"

Alex paused, then nodded slowly. "I hadn't considered that. Well, we need a substitute until he's better either way. We can reassess then."

"Most certainly. I will want his input, and to assess his emotional state before concluding a decision."

"When will he wake?"

"I expect to bring him out of induced coma in about eight hours."

"We'd like to be back then. Highland isn't scheduled for anything else today."

"Yes. In the meantime, my medical advice is for all of us to rest. We are approaching reduced functionality."

Jason had something he needed to do, but he understood the advice. With a glance back at his wired and intubated friend, he turned to ride back to their lodging and rest.

⊚ CHAPTER 12 ⊚

"HE SHOULD BE CONSCIOUS. Aramis, are you there?"

He croaked. His mouth was full of . . . splints? He was splinted all over. Tubes, wires, stents that would be painful if he didn't feel as if he'd been rolled under a tank.

That voice. It was Shaman.

"I . . ." He couldn't get "am" out.

"You're going to live. You are in a military hospital, so I'm using powders and potions to supplement their care."

He could hear all around. Shaman. That was Elke shifting in a seat. Some troop in armor and weapon, the rubbing sound was clear, near the door. Just outside, someone said, "—Bed Nine, and fifty milligrams for, good God what happened to him? Um, fifty milligrams—"

So, I look dead, or worse. I'm alive, though, and not sedated on a transport off this rock.

"Ima sleep," he muttered. He didn't know if they could hear him. He was alive, though. If he hurt it meant he could be healed. He felt tears well up and run hotly from the corners of his eyes.

It meant what he and Caron had was complicated. He could never tell her about this. Or could he? He knew he felt fuzzy and was falling asleep.

Alex had a coded message waiting. He downloaded it to his connectionless module, ran it through three decryptions, and read it.

"I support you, but there's a lot of press. Lawyer arriving tomorrow. Try not to frag any officers before then—Meyer."

That was expected, but reassuring. Was the lawyer from Earth, or someone they'd tagged locally? Actually, for future reference that was something they should plan for. They really did need legal intervention regularly.

At least they had that. The military were simply hogtied by laws, regulations, instructions, policies, guidances . . . he felt sorry for them. That captain had trod a very delicate line in Aramis's recovery.

He wiped the read message and sent back, "Need further leads on potential hostiles to principal. No significant leads, all speculation."

In the meantime, they'd hold their own war council and discuss that issue.

But first, the next message said Highland wanted to talk again. He took several deep breaths, reminded himself how much money he made and that Aramis was alive, then walked through to her apartment.

Without preamble, she shouted, "Marlow, you will fucking explain what happened this morning. Why was I delayed, then stalled, then hindered from my transport? Why were you late?"

She really doesn't know, he thought. That did mean they'd been discreet.

"Ma'am, Agent Anderson was kidnapped while on assignment. We took a few hours to locate and recover him, in a joint mission with the military. Our intelligence indicated he was likely to be murdered if we didn't respond at once."

She seemed taken aback, and at a loss for words. It was an entire ten seconds before she said, "Okay, then I will excuse you. However, I expect you will inform me before any of these missions take place."

Not a chance in hell, but I'll smile and nod, he thought, as he said, "I understand, ma'am."

"Exactly what assignment was he working on?" she asked.

"He is tasked with mapping, which includes reviewing escape routes to determine their quality. In addition, he stockpiles gear where we can reach it in a hurry while traveling."

"You mean 'weapons'?" She looked suspicious and angry again.

"Not generally. Food, water, local cash and clothes. We are usually carrying weapons, but if a vehicle gets damaged or otherwise compromised and must be abandoned, we need to have support logistics."

"Very well. You can go."

"Thank you, ma'am," he said, turned and left.

At no point had she either asked how Aramis was doing or expressed concern about him. There was no point in being angry. She probably wasn't aware of him as a human being. People were just numbers to her, or potential votes, or exploitable counters.

He didn't have to like her, but it would help if she wasn't actively antagonistic to them.

Once he got back to their quarters he said so.

Bart said, "Perhaps you should treat her as an obstacle. Assume she will hinder at every turn."

He twitched his eyebrows and said, "You know, that's very logical. I hadn't thought of it, but it makes sense."

Elke said, "You will have to juggle the diplomacy of not calling her a self-aggrandizing, hatchet-faced narcissist, while working around her, but I am sure you can do it."

"Indeed. She really can't hear in here, right?" he said, looking at Elke.

"She cannot, nor can anyone else. It is possible Intel has snuck something past me and Jason, but I can't see them sharing with her." She stretched, hands in her hair, then working her shoulders gently. She was a bit bruised and battered from the day's events.

Jason said, "Unless there's a profit in it for them."

Alex cocked his head. "We can't rule that out, though there's no existing pattern of it, that I know of."

"That, and you can see how the BuState rep reacts."

He checked the time. "Yeah, he's coming up now. Can we clear this room?"

Jason said, "I'll go check on Aramis and relieve Shaman." He grabbed a day pack and left the room.

Two minutes later, Mr. Gillette, with BuState intel arrived. Bart let him in, and Alex decided against any searches for now. They wanted the man as comfortable and agreeable as possible. Alex would have Jason and Elke sweep it again later, just in case. The table had a well with water, sodas and snacks.

"Good to see you, sir," he offered.

"And you." Gillette took the offered seat and grabbed a water gratefully. "Thanks for this," he said with a nod.

"Long day?"

"Yes, I forget to drink, or I drink too much coffee. Ice water is refreshing. So what can I do for you?"

"Before we start, let me say this is in person for confidentiality. We should be secure in here, and welcome any additional precautions you wish to take."

Gillette nodded. "I'll keep that in mind. I'm fine for now."

"Very well. We're trying to build a threat matrix for Ms. Highland. Any hostile or potentially hostile groups or significant individuals."

"Ah, 'significant individuals.' Well, that's the complication."

"Go ahead."

Gillette leaned back and said, "Well, obviously, in her duties, she does things that help or hinder any number of companies, to the detriment or benefit of others. Their interests, though, are limited to financial. Some will donate to her campaign, some to her opponents, this will change as the platforms and odds stabilize closer to the election, and some will split their bets and contribute to more than one."

"Of course. Do you think any of them would contribute to a physical response? Whether intended to harm, scare, or attract notice."

He considered for a moment, then shook his head. "It's not impossible, but none have done so in previous elections."

"Right. Though there was speculation about Mr. Crindi's death."

"There's always speculation. He died, his wife ran in his stead, and she was dumped by the electorate on the next cycle. She accomplished little. Hardly a worthwhile endeavor."

Alex nodded. That was mostly how he took it. However, that had helped swing party numbers. He wasn't sure how much benefit that had been, but if it suggested to him it was a potentially viable method, it might suggest it to others. And Gillette was readily aware of the incident.

"Then what about well-trained or financed kooks without economic interests?"

"It's impossible to rule out, of course, but hundreds of anonymous threats come in weekly. A handful are deemed credible. Every few weeks one turns up someone violating the law. Twice they'd actually started overt action."

"And groups here?"

"Yes, here is the interesting part," Gillette said, running a hand through his hair. "The Amala don't like her at all. She's female, powerful, publicly called her husband out over that waste disposal vote last year. However, they're generally not wealthy enough to do anything, and have poor access to communication, due to cultural factors."

Alex heard that as, *They're backward savages who hate technology.*

"Go on, please," he said.

"There are certainly members and subfactions who'd like to harm her. We expect that to be more along the lines you've seen—rocks, sticks. They might consider an explosive device."

"Okay. We can monitor that."

"The Sunni like her, generally. The Shia perceive her as favoring the Sunni and don't like that. Some have been very vocal about it. The Mowahidoon, the Baha'i and Sufis have nothing against her. They're very modern and productive. The Coalition Christians run on a spectrum from disliking any woman in office, to disliking her policies. They aren't friendly but are no more actively hostile than anyone else. A few outliers."

"That leaves the Faithful group."

"Yes, those people. Actively hostile, though they tend to seek to instigate incidents so they can sue."

"Which has happened already over our response."

"Expect more of that. They'll do anything to get attention."

"What about credible threats, though? Not them?"

"No. We're at a loss. Obviously, there is at least one element. We don't know who. You were brought in to offer protection while we devote resources to observation and deduction," he said.

Interesting. That was pretty much an admission they were being spied on. They'd need to review their procedures and make ongoing checks for surveillance.

"So you're pointing at the Amala as potential physical threats, and the Faithful as hostile distractions."

"That's how we interpret it, yes."

"So who tracked, kidnapped and tortured my man?"

"We don't know," Gillette said. He seemed genuinely troubled and embarrassed.

"All right," Alex said. "We'll coordinate with other agencies and share what we find." *Pursuant to massaging it ourselves first, and not sharing details we need.* "Can you do the same?"

"We will," Gillette agreed.

And no doubt with the same provisos, he thought.

Alex said, "And these harassment attacks. What are those about?"

"We presume those are to goad a response. It's essential you not overreact to those."

"We try not to, but it's impossible to tell a paint balloon from a grenade in the time it takes someone to throw one."

"I understand," he said, though Alex got the impression he only understood as a mental exercise, not as the recipient of something potentially hot, fast and lethal. "But that's the officially suggested response."

"I concur. It's just hard to implement in a fraction of a second, while guaranteeing Ms. Highland's safety. Are you able to tell me if she's planned more demonstrations to promote her stability under fire?" *Damn, and I said that with a straight face, too.*

Gillette shook his head. "Not that we can tell, and we officially advised her against doing so, as it opens up a potential window and leak."

Okay, so the guy was a chair-warmer, but at least he was an astute and educated chair-warmer.

"All right, then we'll do what we can," Alex said. "And swap what information comes our way." *After we use it first.* Ripple Creek understood allies. It just didn't have many, and fewer that were reliable.

Jason noted when Aramis shifted again. The rebuilding nanos had some effect. Swelling was down considerably. He now looked like a broken human rather than a bloated roadkill.

"Aramis, it's Jason, I'm here."

"Yes," the man mumbled. Jason was surprised he could talk with his jaw in that shape. Sonofabitch. That had to redefine pain.

"No need to talk if you don't want to. We're taking turns watching." He didn't mention losing sleep or being worried. They all volunteered for this and stood shift as well.

Aramis managed actual speech. "I'ng conshus. Hurd like heww. Goan ngake ih, tho."

"Good. I know you are." Now, yes. Yesterday, thirty percent. Damned good medical work, and the man had a serious constitution.

"Had do figh through fain."

"Yeah, you mentioned Caron a lot in that context," he advised. In detail. Though it didn't sound like a fair trade.

"Ah, shid."

"Don't worry. The docs don't know who she is, and we won't talk. If that got you through it, good. You're unreal. Anyone else would be dead, but you're just too brutal for it." He wanted to keep the man's morale up, and keep him tracking on anything real.

Aramis sounded a bit strained, but said, "Ih had this insane, flyne, crazy feeln. The indenzdy. Ih uz aww I could think of. I ngus ve a ferverd."

It took Jason a moment to translate "I must be a pervert."

He said, "You're alive, it worked, no need to be ashamed at all. You probably shouldn't tell her, though."

"Yeah. I'ng goan ve quie for a whi. Ngusic? Case or cuve."

"Probably not at the moment. I'll call and ask. Alex and Shaman will hear my notes and recordings. They'll be destroyed soonest, per policy." Actually, policy said any communication related to a government operation should be kept, and he was fucked if his friend's personal issues were going to be archived.

He was just glad, and amazed the man was alive.

On his glasses, Shaman's image hand signed approval, and sent a text confirmation for record. "Shaman says okay. I'll look for a music load," he said. Also, a second blanket to cover the man's groin.

It was possible his brain had completely rewired pain as arousal. Was it important enough to discuss with Shaman? Maybe.

Bart arrived, and he rose and stretched. They didn't need to sit watch, but they wanted to, and Aramis should appreciate it.

Back at the billet, Alex met him at the door.

"Jason, I have a specific instruction for you, which is not an order."

"Oh?"

"I have no authority to require this, but as your boss and your friend, I am telling you not to look at any news or comments regarding the attack on Aramis. Best case, you'll want to smash things."

Jason sighed deeply. "Yeah, I can imagine. That's good advice, and I'll give it a few days to age off the list. We're all mercenary scum and deserve anything that happens to us, yes?"

"If that was all, I'd be happy. The depths that 'tolerant' people will sink to never cease to amaze me."

"Okay, then I'm already pissed enough and will avoid it further. Thanks."

There was an emotional toll to being an unemotional mercenary scum.

Alex was drained. Lionel and Corcoran were reliable, but they weren't part of the regular team. Shaman was back most of the time, but still checked Aramis twice a day. They'd been painted and egged again, and now he had another brief with Captain Das.

"Good morning, Captain," he said as he arrived. He wanted to be polite, but he didn't want to call anyone in the military "sir." It was too easy for them to take it as subordination.

"Good morning, Agent Marlow," Das returned. He probably had the same guideline in mind. They were polite, courteous and supportive of each other, while recognizing that they might have to diverge on strategy at any moment.

He asked, "Were you able to get the packet from BuState intel?"

"No, I was not. They won't release it."

"What? That's ridiculous. I was briefed in person and there wasn't even a recording or a release."

"Therefore that briefing never took place."

Alex took a moment to ponder that. Shit. He'd missed that.

"Okay, so why would they do us a favor and not the military?"

"It could be some territorial issue. It could also be unofficial, but sanctioned because you're protecting their boss."

"They generally stay well out of our way. But I appreciate the heads up they gave."

"They didn't ask for a classification statement?"

"No," Alex said. "I'm not officially held, and he didn't say not to share it with allies, but if I'm going to do that, I need your personal assurance you'll be discreet on what gets released among your people."

Das said, "I can do that. Will you have the room swept?"

"I don't need to. I'll accept your word."

Das blinked and stared at him for a moment, and Alex realized it had been a request.

"However, if Agent Vaughn is handy, it might not be a bad idea, just in case of outside sources."

Das nodded.

Alex called, and Jason came in, swept the place quickly, and set a small device on the table. It hummed something that wasn't quite white noise, and shifted in modulation.

"Go ahead, that's as clear as I can make it. There's the captain's official mics over there, and one in the corner behind the shelf."

Das's eyebrows flared. "Interesting. I wasn't aware of that one."

"I can try to track it later."

"Delicately, please."

"Absolutely." Jason waited a half second for any potential invite or followup orders, then nodded and left.

Alex said, "That's why I have these people. Okay, Gillette gave me a rundown on threats." He rattled off as best he could, from memory at the time and his compiled notes, which were not here, being in a safe that was set to char all contents and churn them to powder if tampered with.

When he finished, Das looked quizzical.

Das leaned back and said, "There was a substantive threat with seizure and arrest two weeks ago."

"Amala?"

"No, Coalition. The man seems to be a freelancer. He's suspected in three bombings."

That made Alex jolt alert. "Still in custody?"

"No, he was released on two million bond. He made the bond."

And Gillette hadn't considered that important enough to mention.

"How was the threat worded?"

"I'll bring up a copy. It was directed at 'enemies of the God of Heaven, and the idolaters and gamblers polluting even His chosen new world.' That's this place, and it refers to the stock market that opened up three months back, and any loan agency."

"So, not directly at her, then." Had Gillette not mentioned it because he didn't think it was relevant?

Alex never trusted anyone without proof, but at this point, BuState itself moved onto the "not trusted with any significant information" list.

To Das he said, "Thanks, sir. I'll follow up on that."

"You're welcome. By the way, I forwarded your generous donation to several officers. It was well-received, and the derision seems to have lessened slightly."

"Good. Glad to hear it." Though he didn't think it would please Jason much.

He shook hands and he turned to leave.

On the way back he considered their position. Their own contractee was potentially the enemy. That could lead to all kinds of fun.

They'd need to have two levels of prep at this point.

Aramis crossed the line from sleeping to awake with a snap. He felt rested, but there was that confusion from the medication, and dread of the pending pain, though it was substantially lessened.

Elke was next to him.

"Morning," he said.

"I am not allowed to tell you you'll be on your feet in a week."

"Oh, sorry I didn't hear that." Good. He wanted out of here. Doing nothing sucked.

"You did well," she said. "I am very impressed."

"Thanks," he said. If Elke said that, she meant it.

"You've been here a week. Probably another week. You are bored?"

"You wouldn't believe. The pain I can handle . . . yeah, let's say so. I hate vid and can't move to do anything."

"I will bring more books."

His eyes suddenly felt tired. "I appreciate it, but I'm burned out staring at the screen for books or vid. I've had enough music. I just need to get on my feet."

"You can't move now, though," she said, while looking him over.

He flexed against the bonds. They were to prevent injury. He could undo them if he chose, he just couldn't thrash and tear anything.

"No, I'm pretty much restrained between shifts."

"Well, good. You can't strain anything, or interfere with therapy."

"I don't get therapy here," he said. "It's all . . ."

Elke's hand was under the covers from the side, snaking slowly toward him. He lit up with goose bumps all over.

"Elke," he said, "I—"

"Last time you earned a kiss. This time, you're unable to manage alone."

Her position meant no one passing by the door would see anything untoward, as long as he didn't trip any biometric alarms.

Those were the fingers she used to fabricate those incredible bombs, from firecracker to ground shaker. They were amazingly delicate, just feathery touches.

"So we just hold a conversation?" he said. It felt like *that* again. He wondered if he'd ever enjoy normal sex again, or if it would all have to be violent, edgy and extreme.

"If you like," she said. That look of concentration. She was intent on this, and he could feel it.

"This isn't going to take long."

"Not if I know what I'm doing, no." A long caress along his nerves threw his endorphins for a loop again.

He closed his eyes, tightened his breath and rode out the thudding waves in his brain.

When he looked, she was sitting in the chair, a calm expression on her face and a towel stuffed into her harness.

"Oh, damn. I really did need that," he said, as waves of tension thudded through him and ebbed away.

"Only while incapacitated. That is not an offer," she said, with a quirky smile.

He nodded slightly. "Understood, and thank you most sincerely. I'll try to stay in one piece."

"Bart will be along in ten minutes, and I will revert to bitch. You will respect that, of course." Her face was professional, but behind her eyes, just a hint of something he recognized.

"Unquestionably," he said. Yup, never mention it again. And no, it wasn't worth getting chewed up, as much as he did appreciate it.

He hoped Bart would smuggle in some liquor, though, because his brain wanted to match Elke and Caron.

Goddamit, not again.

◎ CHAPTER 13 ◎

ALEX WAS GLAD to have Aramis back in one piece. That was his primary concern. Officially, not losing the principal was primary. In actuality, he cared more for his people than the job. Stopping bullets was their mission, but that was just it—the principal was a job. Aramis was a friend and valued subordinate.

So, whether Aramis was mentally fit for duty or not, he was alive, safe, healed. That was first.

Das was with them in their own conference room in the BuState compound. Aramis had been debriefed several times in various levels of consciousness. This was to confirm the intel and have him sign off on it, and decide if he would remain on mission.

"Before we call him in, I need to know if he'll be fit for the trip next week." It was a long trip, too, visiting two other cities and several smaller towns. The argument for Highland's visit as minister was incredibly tenuous. It was obviously an election junket.

Shaman said, "Yes. He will be fit, if a bit weak, and he's eager to resume operating."

"Good, then. I'll still keep Lionel on call as backup for anyone who might go down."

Jason said, "That's a reasonable precaution. We can also cycle Aramis back with Cady's group as he spools back up, as an interim."

"Yes, we discussed that. It's possible." He turned and asked, "Captain Das, are you ready?"

Das said, "Quite, and relaxed. Please don't let me hinder you, and

I appreciate your hospitality and cooperation." He still had that faint smile. It was nice to deal with a professional.

"Well, we appreciate thirty kilos of Composition G. But you can bet Elke will want more."

He grinned for just a moment. "I'll allow it, if we can find it."

Jason said, "Here he is."

Shaman escorted Aramis in. His limp was mostly gone, and he seemed to be fatigued and battered at this point. That was a significant improvement over the sack of meat he'd resembled a few days before.

Alex offered, "Morning."

"Yes it is," he said, in mock disgust over the cheerfulness he couldn't hide. "I should have been drinking to feel like this."

"Well, you can do that in a few days, too. I'll allow one evening of relaxation, if Shaman agrees, regardless of Army rules."

"Thanks."

He indicated the tablet and hard copy notes on the table. "Here's the audio debriefs you had, though you're not coherent in some. You'll need to go through them again and see if you can decipher your mumbles. We don't expect additional data, but have to check."

"I'll check. I don't remember those at all, so it's going to be a formality."

"That's what we expect. Then you'll need to review the written notes and sign off. This here is just a release form," he passed it over, "so Captain Das can officially use your intel. I took the liberty of extending him courtesy on that."

"By all means," Aramis said. He glanced over the page easily enough, printed the thumb block and signed over it in pen.

Das said, "Thanks. Before anything else, I'm very glad you're alive and recovering. And I do appreciate the intel. Everything we can get is not enough. You know this and I'll spare you the breakdown, but do know I'm grateful."

"No problem, sir. Thanks for cutting the resources loose to recover me."

Das nodded and moved on. "So, we're still trying to narrow down who might have targeted you as a means of targeting her. They asked about one specific schedule. Anything else you remember at all?"

"No," Aramis said and shook his head firmly. "They asked lots of questions, but I only remember that they wanted Highland's itinerary, accused me of lying for not knowing, disputed that it would be changed if there was a problem. Then they made personal comments about my resistance."

Alex pondered, "So the question remains, were they stupid enough to think the schedule couldn't change, or connected enough to believe she wouldn't let that affect her?"

Jason said, "The question may remain a while longer. However, I'm tending toward the latter. They had good intel and surveillance practice to get Aramis, their interrogation was brutal but effective at its purpose of causing extreme pain with minimal critical damage—not even fractures. They understood the potential for embolism, aneurysm, internal hemorrhage and other complications, and avoided them."

Alex said, "Except they died quickly. They might know intel, but they don't know combat."

Jason said, "The ones interrogating didn't know combat. They may not have been the only ones."

"We also know they're local, from genotype and environmental cues."

Aramis started and flared his eyebrows.

"Shit."

"What?"

"The ones who interrogated me were speaking English. North American. Neutral accent."

Captain Das said, "You know, I could have used that information the day you were brought in here."

Jason looked at the man and said, "Yeah, well he was a bit distracted at the time. One tends to notice the unusual. I suspect being beaten with boat oars was more unusual than hearing someone talk."

"Sorry." Das had the grace to look sheepish.

Alex said, "Significant. So the brains had vacated the scene when we arrived and left flunkies to die in their place."

Das said, "This would tend to indicate we are dealing with seasoned professionals. The MO does not fit the Amala or Shia. It might fit the Coalition or the Sufis, though I can't find any motives for them. It also suggests it might be an Earth-based faction."

"Not necessarily," Jason said. "Grainneans have several accents, and lots of us sound North American because we were. They could also be hirelings, including possibly suborned military. No offense, sir."

Das shook his head. "None taken. I have to consider that, too."

"Could the Isolationist groups have hired outside contractors?"

Das said, "Shia most definitely would not, ever, do that. It would be beneath them. Amala might, but probably can't afford to."

"Are we missing any potentially hostile groups?"

Aramis said, "Random pissed off rich dude? I know you said we were told it was unlikely, but it is possible. Caron . . . Miss Prescot, might have ideas on who'd be willing to throw money away for that."

"I would expect not random, and well-concealed, but it's worth asking the question."

Jason said, "I'll send that inquiry ASAP."

Das said, "I appreciate your cooperation. This would be so much easier if we had control of the mission."

"Yeah, and the reverse is true, of course. Any interaction leads to delays and inconsistencies. I'm also still wondering why BuState wanted us when they have a good security force, and easy access to the military."

"They didn't tell you?" Das asked.

"Uh, no?" Alex replied. Was this something known?

"She's campaigning. BuState can't use their resources for private escort, just as we can't."

"I knew a bit of that, but they still have some personnel, and they're paying for it."

"They are? Because officially it should be her campaign's money."

"I doubt they can afford us. I will confirm, but I understood they were paying."

"Well, that's a potential discrepancy you may wish to investigate."

"Yes. Very. Thanks." That would fit a lot of things in, but it also compounded the potential number of threats. Did anyone like this woman?

"Useful. We need to talk more, Captain," he said.

"Obviously, I welcome that."

Alex said, "Good. So, with that covered, we have a unit issue to discuss." That was a hint for Das.

Das said, "I'll step out for a moment. I'll come back for the documents shortly. I must secure them before you leave the premises. Official copies will be forthcoming." He rose and walked out the door.

Aramis looked at Alex, and then the others.

"What's up?" he asked.

Alex said, "First, how do you feel about returning to duty? Are you ready now, or do you need more time?" That left it open for "more time" to be "past the mission" and then indefinite.

Aramis sat a little straighter and said, "Personally, I'm ready now. I'll accept your assessment on whether you think I'm ready. But I feel prepared. If need be, I'd be okay swapping out with one of Cady's people for a few days."

Alex grinned. "I'd considered that, too. Well, then, Shaman?"

Shaman said, "I'll want to keep checking him, but he seems sound on the whole. Endurance could be an issue, and that limp might slow him slightly, and, of course, we have had actual engagements."

"So yes or no?"

"Yes. With the proviso I may need to pull him back if he shows signs of fatigue or injury."

"Of course," Aramis said. "But yes, I'm ready and eager to serve."

"Jason?"

Jason extended a hand to Aramis and said, "Glad to have you back."

Aramis smiled, so Alex did.

"Good, then let's clear stuff up for Captain Das and get back to it."

When they got back to their quarters, Elke was waiting, standing.

"Aramis, welcome back, my friend," she said with a grin and a brief hug, standing a foot away. For her, that was close.

Alex caught her eye and said, "You look alert, what's going on?"

"Our principal has friends."

That was interesting. "What is special about these specific friends?"

"She talks to them. A lot. Too much, in my opinion."

"Movements and meetings?"

"Yes."

"So, we should suspect this is a potential leak."

Jason said, "It breaks down into analyzing which information goes to whom, and cross-referencing to any incidents. Then to attempting to divert schedules further than we do to hinder attacks."

Alex said, "Sure, but since we suspect elements in the military, local forces, local groups and BuState are toxic, who do we tell? I trust Das, but he has to forward intel to people we don't trust."

"Well, what do you have exactly, Elke?"

Elke took out her secure phone and played a recording.

Highland's voice said, ". . . Yes, Wally, I'll be speaking at the Mayor's Forum, then trying to catch lunch with Mr. Huble. If you want to catch up here, fifteen hundred should be good. I'll tell them to admit you."

"Wally?"

Elke said, "Walton Blanding, former state senator for Maryland, North America, then lobbyist for Breeze Power, then advisor to the current SecGen's Energy Minister."

"What's his connection to Highland?"

"He was state senator when she was on the Governor's Council on Trade."

Aramis said, "So this guy's from the windfarm lobby, and she's an orbital power proponent?"

Alex said, "Okay, Mr. Blanding just earned an investigation. I'll also caution Highland about releasing information like that. I'm sure she'll take it in the spirit in which it's intended."

Jason said, "In the meantime, just in case, I'll plan to vary our routes more. That means not using the military assets we tried so hard to get."

Bart said, "We will still use them, but only as decoys. A task they are well-suited for."

Alex nodded, "We can improve safety en route any number of ways, but we'll be fixed in place at the events."

Jason said, "Also, just because, or even if, rather, he turns out to be the leak, doesn't mean he's a conspirator. He may be a patsy talking to someone else, or they may have him bugged."

"Yes, but he's certainly a likely source."

"She'll never believe you."

"Of course not, but I'm required to try."

"There's more," Jason said.

"Yes?"

"I've done some research."

"Oh?"

"Yes. More that their rep didn't offer, though he might not have had a reference, given what you asked of him, or he may not have thought it relevant."

"Tell me."

"She has two vocal opposition groups, and they do have records of violence, but most of it is petty and direct, not sophisticated and indirect. About ten years back, Power to the People tried to plant a bomb and got caught. You know them—exploit every resource and damn the environment. Then, Friends of the Environment has managed to hack her personal files twice."

Alex said, "Amateurs then. Professional intel gathering isn't that direct. And obviously we're being observed, given what's occurred."

"Yes. Aramis and Elke were softer targets than the whole team. Also, it may have been intended as much as a psychological attack on us as an intel effort."

He nodded. "Yes, if they can sow fear, they can exploit it."

"We know what they can do. I really wish the hostiles had survived."

"I know, Jason. But I don't trust nonlethal force, they did present first, there wasn't much time, and realistically, neither MilBu nor BuState was going to let us even question them. They'd have a moral win since they'd be jailed at best, walk most likely."

"Yes, we sent a message and counted score. I support you completely. I'm just idly looking for better outcomes for next time."

"You expect a next time?"

"Don't you?"

"I definitely do."

"Okay, we need to know who they have here, and try to follow assets, though we're not placed for that. Do we risk asking Das?"

"I can take over the intel we have and ask."

"Do it. We don't need to keep it close."

Jason said, "Just so we're clear, we're concerned about protecting her for the duration of the contract, not proactively being belligerents against anyone."

"Right. If they bag her the day after we're gone, that's BuState's problem. If we can scare them off meantime, that's fine. Better, in fact, since any actual shootings will be used to build her up and attack us. If the word leaks we know who it is, the job gets done easier."

"I see two problems," Elke said.

"Yes?"

"First, we must be very sure we leak the right name, or we risk making things worse."

"Yes. Second?"

"'Easier' means I don't get to blow anyone into goo." She frowned slightly.

"It's a sacrifice you may have to make."

"You are aware of my standard protest on this matter."

"I am. Noted."

He wasn't sure if she actually liked killing people, or just liked explosions. She didn't seem to have any qualms about either. She did limit collateral damage, though. Usually.

She added, "While it would be good to know who is behind each MO, all we really need to know is what the MOs are. We defend against those. We are only six, and not investigators."

"Correct, but as we've found out previously, it's useful to know who the threats are. Mr. Prescot was the only principal the company has lost, and we lost four friends with him."

Aramis said, "So, much as I hate to know, what is the agenda for tomorrow?"

Alex figured that related to his captivity. He really didn't want more info than he critically needed. That was reasonable, but not necessarily compatible with their mission.

"Third round of the environmental summit."

"Am I the only one who sees a dichotomy in traveling several light years to discuss energy expenditures?"

Elke said, "They are saving Earth's environment. The sacrifices here are just necessary."

"Back on subject, please," Alex said. Yes, their principal was a politician and acted like one. That was only peripheral.

Elke said, "Sorry. Go ahead."

"Okay, this is in Shia territory, but it's on the edge of Amala territory. There's no fighting there currently, because there are lots of troops and cops on patrol. There's a protest planned, and a zone blocked off for it, and a counterprotest zone."

"Two groups?"

"No, about six groups, which is what scares me. The government, meaning BuState, has decided to have pro- and anti- camps."

"Can Highland change that?"

"I suppose I need to ask."

Elke said, "Better you than me."

"Thanks." Still, it was his job.

Alex called Jessie first.

"I have a question about venue and transport. I'd like to cover it in person with Ms. Highland, to maintain privacy."

After a moment's mute, Jessie said, "Ms. Highland can see you."

"Thanks. I'll be right down."

One of Cady's women had the door, and after saying, "Hello, sir," confirmed with Cady, and with Highland, before admitting him. He was glad that his own people didn't take anything on face or assumption.

Highland had a professional mask of cheer on. Or was it a mask? She had no trouble telling him off generally.

"What do we need to discuss, Agent Marlow?"

"Thanks for seeing me on short notice, ma'am," he said. "I have a concern about the venue, in that it's near a faction boundary. Also, there's a protest area, and a counterprotest area, but the multiple factions don't fall into simple for and against you positions. Is there a way to diffuse the protests with other areas? Spread them out farther?"

She said, "That has to do with budget and scheduling. They coordinate with our contract security here."

"Meaning Rosen Event Services."

"Yes."

"Can you issue instructions to them?"

She looked mildly irritated. "Only through Earth."

"I'd recommend it."

"I did," she said, looking embarrassed. "BuState have a guide-book with policies. There's an office for Mtali Cultural Affairs. They have to approve it."

"Do you think they will?"

"Probably eventually."

"Is this just normal process? Or do you think there's hostile intent from someone along the chain?" This was a delicate, but necessary discussion.

She seemed to take it seriously. She paused a moment, and replied, "Certainly the former is a matter of consideration. The latter may be, too. Any agency has factions within, and then there are party affiliations, too."

He said, "Then we'll do what we can. Hopefully there won't be any issues. But I'm not comfortable with pigeonholing groups badly, then consolidating them. I'll suggest to Rosen that they should watch for internal violence. The press would love to attach that to you."

He didn't want to go very far in that direction. It wasn't their concern, and he wasn't supposed to help with her career, nor did he want to.

"I appreciate that," she said.

He could tell she didn't mean it.

"We would rather not have an incident, or see any incidents. And of course, they present a PR . . . complication."

"Jessie will handle that," she said with an encouraging smile. "I'm glad you've decided to avoid any incidents." As if it was their doing.

"We'll keep an eye out for brewing problems, and change profile as needed to minimize it," he said.

"That will be fine."

"Very well. I'll take care of our end. Do please call if you hear of anything affecting it."

"Thank you." She turned back to her screens.

Yeah, that was a dismissal.

Twenty minutes later, though, Highland came through. "Let me in," she demanded through the door screen.

She was within their contract to demand, but it would have been nice to phrase it as a request. Alex nodded and Bart buzzed her in.

"I wanted to catch you before you got too far on tomorrow's preparations," she said.

"Yes, ma'am?"

"We're meeting with several contingents, and we've agreed to show respect to the host nation."

"Of course. What do you need from us?"

"For this, women need to wear traditional garb."

Elke asked, "What do you mean by 'traditional'?"

"A basic hijab or long skirt with long tunic, and head scarf."

Elke raised her eyebrows slightly and said, "I'm sorry, I will not be able to."

Highland seemed flabbergasted that anyone would refuse her orders. "But you must! They'll be insulted if they see a woman in Earth Western dress."

"I am unable to perform my functions in such clothing. If you wish, I will style my hair back and present as male. If a swap can be arranged with Cady's demolition technician, Adam Helas, I am agreeable if Alex is."

"I am not," Alex said. "I have a team that works and no need nor desire to break it."

"This isn't subject to debate," Highland said haughtily. "It's a polite order."

Well, this was getting tense.

"Unfortunately, ma'am, our contract and policy states that I decide operations and have override if I feel our capabilities are hindered. That mode of dress will hinder Agent Sykora. That hinders the team, and our ability to protect you. Additionally, while you may identify the level of dress, you may not dictate specific outfits. You are describing an informal public event. Sykora's garb will meet that standard, as will all of ours."

The woman flushed deeper and deeper purple in rage as he spoke. Her voice was only snappish, but it seemed to rise as she replied.

"Listen, you, I am the minister. I am the candidate. This mission is about me. You're paid well and we all know what for. So don't give me that letter of contract bullshit." She paused and heaved for a breath.

Alex said, "Elke, can you do the weekly inventory on our batteries and cells, please?" He pointed at the storeroom while doing so.

"Of course," she said, and walked that way. There was no such inventory. He just figured she'd appreciate the escape. Jason was in the armory already. Aramis wandered off, looking ill. It was probably an act, but Shaman went with him. Bart waited silently at the door.

Highland continued, "You can expect I'll have a call out at once. The response will be after this event, but you can expect it will support me. What you think as a contractor means little enough, and it's about time you egotistical strokeoffs got that through your skulls."

"I will await that reply, ma'am. In the meantime, I will need to review routes. You have my codes if you need to relay details."

He nodded politely, letting it be an abbreviated bow by way of diplomacy, then turned and left the room himself.

Behind him, Highland kept talking, to the air. That was just a little bit creepy.

She tried to follow him, but he'd latched the security bar and it beeped and tingled as she approached. She apparently then turned her attention on Bart. He deserved some kind of bonus for that. It took five minutes before she ran out of steam and left.

⊚ CHAPTER 14 ⊚

ARAMIS LEFT THE ROOM faking a headache. Shaman followed him.

"Are you all right, Aramis?"

"Yes. Faking. It didn't seem healthy to stick around."

"Indeed. She is hard on my blood pressure. As long as you're okay."

"I am," he lied. His head wasn't going to explode, but it was aching at every impact site. That meant ongoing healing, he hoped.

Shaman nodded and checked out the door. Highland was facing Bart and berating him, and with a shift of feet, the surgeon danced between doorways. Aramis barely heard that door close.

Aramis didn't sleep well, from a combination of pain, nightmares, worry and anxiety. That, and not taking his prescribed medication, but dammit, it made him groggy and hungover, and he had work to do. He wasn't going to admit it to anyone, though Shaman probably could read him, and it wasn't as if they didn't all know each other very well by now.

The escort mission started badly and decayed rapidly. Alex didn't seem to have slept much, either. Elke seemed a bit more relaxed. She had explosives, because nothing else would make her jacket that lumpy. She had pockets sewn to her armor, full of a variety of nasties. He was glad to see that.

Bart seemed fit enough, and Shaman. Aramis was worried

because Alex was ragged, and would probably take lead for most of the mission.

Sure enough, he did.

"Aramis, how's your range of motion?"

"Good."

"Pain?"

"Some, but it won't slow me."

"Good. The military finally relented, so we can test weapons as we leave."

"Oh. Excellent." Wow. What had accomplished that? Had enough shooting changed their moods?

He felt as if he was the new guy all over again. What had gone on in those two weeks? He'd seen the after action reviews, but they didn't suggest any real problems. He'd have to read between the lines, or ask once they were back. But no one had said anything to him.

This was an indoor appearance in a "Safe" area, so they wore light armor under suits. Elke always looked a few kilos bulkier from her vest full of toys. He wished he could do that, only it would all be armor.

They carried carbines and Elke's shotgun, which would stay stowed in the limo. They wore easy to access holsters for their pistols, which looked intact, even though Jason had very carefully disabled every safety circuit in them. Lionel, from Cady's team, was designated driver. Aramis gladly took right wing position as they formed up, fired one test round into the clearing drum, then waited for Highland and Jessie.

They were prompt, dressed in long skirts and high collars, and made a point of not looking at Elke's suit. Yes, it might piss off certain factions to be aware that she had legs. That wasn't his concern, or hers. Doing their job right was their concern. He was also surprised that such a vocal proponent of female superiority would deign to dress to suit the locals, whose culture was diametrical to one another.

It might be one of those diplomacy things. Or it might just be true that politicians were whores.

It wasn't his problem. All he had to do was keep her safe.

They boxed around her, Alex and Shaman first, Elke and he on the flanks, and Bart and Jason bringing up the rear. Alex got the door, and they climbed in. Jason closed it behind them and took shotgun seat.

They only had the one limo, which was disturbing, though they were supposed to have a military escort. That gray area Highland lived in was very annoying.

It wasn't nearly as annoying as what happened next.

They rolled forward, around the compound, while they stowed their carbines. Aramis propped his behind him and left, in a thoughtfully provided clip added by the manufacturer. In moments they all looked like suited assistants, though that would only fool the lower half of society. Anyone with a brain knew they were muscle.

They made a final turn onto the exit road out the BuState gate, and grated to a stop.

Aramis clutched at his pistol, then realized they were still inside, and that it was a blockage. He looked at Alex, wondering if they were safer where they were, or needed to unass with the principal and sprint back to cover.

Lionel said, "We're caught on the goddam speed bump. They built it up to meet the new standards, and it's taller than ground clearance on this beast."

"Didn't we do this once already?"

"Yes. New standards, poor communication."

"I'll clear it," Elke said.

Bart made a point of looking through the window before opening the door. Elke slipped through, bent down and did something. She walked around to the other side and repeated the motion. She stood up with a detonator.

Highland said, "Are you sure that's saf—" and was drowned out as Elke hit the button and whatever charge she planted made a rumbling pop. She motioned for the door, and Bart reopened it.

Alex muttered. "I don't care what the standards are, they will be made to fit Ms. Highland's transport, at once, and they can install an extra triggered barrier instead. These things are outdated and simplistic."

Aramis agreed. Simple was often better, but a barricade that defaulted to positive would work as well. If it failed to retract, they'd just detour, rather than being turtled.

Whatever Elke had done had crumbled the rise. Lionel eased

forward, and after a scrape and rattle, they proceeded normally. She'd also apparently cut wipes for the tires.

Alex spoke into his phone. "I want that gone when we get back. That's per me, Ms. Highland," he glanced at her for assent, and she nodded, tight-lipped and flushed, "and Agent in Charge Cady . . . Well, right now, I'm speaking as District Agent in Charge. That's the contract equivalent of Chief of Mission, Security." There was a pause, then he said, "I appreciate it."

To Alex, Highland said, "Thank you." She said it smoothly and without rancor, and Aramis knew she was pissed.

As this was an official function, at least officially, the military escort pulled in front and behind. Two Grumblies, ten troops, two machine guns, except they were crowd control machine guns shooting rubber pellets and mild incapacitance agents. It was Aramis's experience, on five planets so far, that nonlethal weapons didn't deter threats, didn't end threats, and often just irritated the threats or let them claim martyr status without the actual risk of being a real martyr. Still, it was better than nothing.

Lionel took a slightly convoluted route, but Aramis was easily able to follow it. He noted that.

"Alex, this route is too direct to suit me."

"Understood. Got a suggestion?"

"Pull two blocks north and resume."

"Sounds good. Lionel, did you get that?"

"Yes, sir, will do." The man was strictly professional. He might not agree, but he'd accept the guidance without debate.

Of course, their terminus was known. There was only one gate in big enough to handle the limo. Alex said nothing, but Aramis noticed everyone shift slightly to make weapon access easier, so he stretched and did the same. Highland might disapprove, so they weren't going to mention it.

The protest zones were a block shy of the forum, and weren't supposed to be on the approach route. It was clear they were. Situated in vacant lots, they faced each other across the street. Whoever had set this up was an idiot.

Of course, there were several entourages in limos of different types. A convoy of three was just ahead of them, and one group pelted it with garbage.

Lionel said, "This traffic is too slow for safety. Should I divert?"

Alex said, "Yes," as Highland said, "No!"

He diverted, pulling from between the escort vehicles, cutting obliquely across traffic, taking the left turn and accelerating. They went right past the protesters, who seemed to have brought all their kitchen trash with them.

Aramis observed. The crowd split in age between the very old and the quite young. It split between those in traditional Arab dress, and those in conservative younger dress. They would have religious or moral objections to some of Highland's many policies, or those of the government.

Highland shouted, "This is my vehicle, my meeting and my mission, and you will do as I say!"

Alex was on the phone, hush hood up, talking to someone. Highland turned to Elke, who was carefully looking out the window and writing notes. She faced Shaman, who was checking his response bag for something. She faced Aramis.

He hadn't moved fast enough, so he said, "Ma'am, this group knows who you are and doesn't like you."

She paused for a moment.

"Look at their makeup as we go," he said. They were a block away by now. "They're religious, mostly Amala, composed of quite young and quite old. That means they're swinging back to the conservative side."

Alex finished and said, "Lionel, go ahead and swing around. We should have an unobstructed approach. From now on, we'll do our own staging."

"Understood."

Highland asked, "So what are you saying?"

"I'm merely observing that the two military vehicles marked us, they knew who you were, and we were unable to move."

"I'm late, and it will show up as cowardice, with us pulling away."

Alex said, "I can state we perceived your safety was improved by the diversion."

"You'd better," she said crossly.

"I'd rather do that than have to fight," he said.

They were back around, as Aramis wondered at the insecurity or narcissism of someone who, with that much power, was concerned about being late. It seemed there was nothing to her but appearance.

Alex said, "The military escort will meet us as we turn back onto Amadi Street."

The troops were waiting, and pulled in as they turned north again.

Which was just as the two groups of protesters started hurling debris at each other.

Lionel asked, "Alex, what do I do?"

"We've already been pelted. May as well go through."

"Understood."

Yeah, what was more garbage? Except it looked as if there might be rocks. Then fistfights broke out in both groups. The limo drew between them and took impacts, though it was doubtful even the larger rocks would damage the surface.

Then someone started shooting.

Alex said, "Get us out of here." Everyone had hands under coats, resting on guns. Lionel threw them in reverse and sounded the horn for the follow vehicle to move.

Highland said, "I have to get to the forum. It is far more important than safety, and I thought this car was bulletproof?"

"Ma'am, it is, but they've escalated from protest to garbage to firearms. I'm not comfortable with the escalation. I'm diverting, we can reassess, and reapproach."

"No. We're continuing."

Alex sighed. "It is your prerogative to continue at this point, ma'am. I will override you if we actually get engaged. I comply, under protest. Lionel, proceed."

"Forward," he said, and they accelerated.

Then stopped.

The crowd had broken through the barricades on one side, had swarmed the street toward the other group, but were now milling in the roadway, blocking movement.

Elke muttered, "How familiar." She fumbled with something, which Aramis assumed was explosive.

He was amazed at how calm he felt. Apparently, enough firefights, a combat wound and a torture session had acclimated him to stuff like this.

The crowd realized the limo contained someone of note, then someone deduced that military escort implied a high-ranking Earth dignitary. In moments, people were shouting her name and rocking the massive vehicle on its suspension. Others were fighting them, pulling them away. They were presumably supporters of her.

The wrestling turned to punching, knifing, broken bottles and gunfire.

Alex said, "Lionel, disperse them."

He nodded and hit a button. One of the new stench gases farted out from under the car. It was fascinating to see it work. It was so overpowering that everyone stopped their activity and ran aimlessly, smacking into vehicles, curbs, each other, crawling, stumbling to feet and running more. In twelve seconds the entire street was clear forty meters each way. Aramis smelled nothing. The same control had buttoned them up and they were now on canned oxygen.

The military, however, hadn't had notice, and clutched for gas masks, shaking and retching, faces in gruesome masks. Aramis had had a bare whiff in training, for familiarization. He felt sorry for the poor bastards.

One debarked from the vehicle ahead and ran straight across the road into a building wall. After a few seconds, three of his buddies advanced to him, forced his mask on while he thrashed and panicked, then ferried him back. Even through their masks, Aramis could see the mean looks.

Elke kept the grin off her face. It was always delightful to see a weapon work to best effect, especially an invisible one. Half of those primitives had no idea what had happened.

She hoped the troop was well. The chaos of engagement led to such things, but the participants never found them funny at the time.

Alex was on phone. "Yes, I understand. Stand by, please." He looked up at Highland, and said, "Ma'am, the road is completely blocked by rioters. I recommend we back out slowly, to avoid injuring anyone. We can speed up if our safety dictates. This is why I was hesitant earlier. I'm less worried about us than the outcome of dealing with civilians. Alternately, we can attempt to push forward."

"It sounds as if you'll be pushing either way, so forward."

"Very good," he said to her, then resumed on the radio. "We're going forward. Slow and steady. Yes, stick with masks. I apologize for that. It came up suddenly."

From the other side of Highland, Jessie said, "I can't get any signal. Are you blocking me?"

Elke said, "I am not, but it would not surprise me if the locals have set up signal jamming and spoofing. Alex's phone uses tough algorithms, but it isn't impenetrable."

Alex stiffened, said, "Thanks," and called back to the forward vehicle. "This is Playwright. There's a strong possibility our signals may be jammed. If so, proceed on last . . . hello? Lieutenant? I am unable to receive, but will continue with my instruction. Proceed as discussed, and look for hand signals from driver. Playwright out." He looked up. "Well, this is going to be interesting. I want to get Ms. Highland and Jessie in unharmed. I want to minimize harm to the locals. Is that clear, Elke?"

"Of course," she agreed. That's what he always wanted. She'd do so if she deemed it advisable, but this was a riot, and riots generally deserved to be put down.

Alex continued, "Dump guns can be used for distraction. Elke, be ready with nonlethal smoke and bangs, please. Reserve hands-on force for Ms. Highland's safety only. Ms. Highland, we are attempting to drive into the conference. We may need to debark and walk a short distance, probably not over one hundred meters. You may need your protective mask."

"I understand," she said, and smirked. She actually liked the idea of getting into a fight. Elke decided she wasn't all bad after all. Though of course, Highland's goal was PR. Elke's goal was hurting people who needed hurt.

She watched her principal peripherally, and gave most of her attention out the window. The windows were high-quality one-way transparencies, so the crowd had no idea how their antics were perceived. On Celadon, they'd escalated to urination and very disgusting gestures. Here, they settled for childish faces, hand signs, and waving placards. It was so sweet that they thought anyone cared.

Still, they increased in number and density. Elke revised her estimates on everything from smoke to concussion charges, and waited.

Lionel called back, "They're swarming in close. If I continue, I'll be pushing people aside, and some may fall. If I stop, we won't be able to proceed. They'll probably lie down in front of us."

Jason said, "Given the cultures, I expect some of them are quite willing to be martyrs for visibility."

Alex said, "Move until you have to stop. We'll repeat the gas then. I don't want to overuse it."

That was why he was in charge, Elke reflected. Her reality did not match the illusion created by governments and media. She'd simply escalate violence until everyone left or was dead. Few people, and no governments, had the moral strength to do so. Still, she'd hope for her small part to play.

Jessie shivered, and Highland twitched now and then, seeming quite nervous. Façade aside, she obviously saw the real world threat here.

Lionel said, "I'm blocked. Solidly penned by bodies."

"Pop gas," Alex ordered.

Once again the crowd shrieked and ran. However, thumping noises indicated people collapsed against the vehicle.

Lionel said, "Front wheels are blocked. The subjects are persistent and seem to have restrained themselves."

That was a very calm report for an incident that was about to get exciting.

Alex said, "We're proceeding on foot. Nonlethal force only. Elke, note that."

"Nonlethal," she repeated. That was frustrating, but she had nonlethal toys she wanted to bring into play.

"Ma'am, Elke will lead you. Hold onto her jacket. Jessie, hold onto Shaman's. Bart and Aramis lead. Jason right wing. Lionel, proceed when you can. If they refuse to yield, call me and the military."

Everyone shuffled around, bracing, clutching and ready. They all held stun batons and Elke had her fingers on a fun gadget she hoped to use.

Alex said, "Report if not ready . . . go."

Aramis raised the door and sprang out to the rear. Bart shoved his way out and around forward. Elke followed, feeling Highland's hands on the tail of her coat. *I bet the bitch is glad of the suit now, rather than some stupid robe*, she thought.

Behind her, Alex went out the other door.

The crowd was well-distant, and the humid air still bore a whiff of . . . ugly. There was no way to describe that manufactured smell, but even parts per billion were awful. They moved forward as Aramis zapped one of the bodies at the front of the car. Yes, the *blázen* had wedged himself in tight, so he couldn't disperse when the gas hit.

Elke zapped him again, just to make sure, then joined the formation as they jogged forward. It should take only a half minute to reach the gate. The security guards there were locals, and made no effort to extend a safe corridor. Elke had expected them to be useless.

The crowd started to collapse back in, shouting angrily. It was probable some of Highland's fans had taken badly to being stink-gassed.

Alex had said nonlethal, and Elke complied. She tossed one disk left and behind, the other right and behind.

"Watch eyes," she said, a half second before they ignited.

They lit, and behind her, Alex swore. They were visible even in daylight, thought granted it was overcast.

The hundred bulbs in each ignited over the span of two seconds in a chain of reports. They sounded a lot like automatic weapon fire. However, they were mere noisemakers, plus zirconium dust with some enhancements. Anyone looking at that should be flash-blind for several minutes, because the output was close to 5000 lumens. There was also a strong chance of epileptic response.

In fact, as they passed the leading Grumbly, one of the troops swayed and collapsed. They were certainly taking a beating on this simple convoy trip.

Still, the team reached the gate unharmed, which was the point.

"Open, please," Alex said. Yes, they'd actually kept the gate locked and closed. Elke turned to keep herself between principal and crowd, and they huddled around their two charges. The mob seemed well-cowed at this point, refusing to approach, but settling for hurling gestures, epithets and the occasional chunk of garbage.

Eventually, the simpering monkeys rolled the gate just enough to allow the party to back through individually. Elke squeezed her shoulders past the polymer columns, and they were in, surrounded by media. While she appreciated their ability to ablate explosive threats, she had no other use for them.

The gate slid shut again as Alex came in last.

Highland, of course, was immediately in front of the cameras.

". . . it is a privilege to be here today, despite certain elements harassing my loyal supporters and attempting to deter me. This just confirms my support and determination to see all these processes— the environmental summit, the cultural divide, and my own service to humanity—through to what some would call the end, but what I like to think of as a new beginning."

Very pretty, Elke thought. Now can we get inside? Some of the protesters were trying to push closer, and some looked to have a giant slingshot ready. Yes, they did, with paint.

Fortunately, a transparent shield moved into place behind the gate. Highland had been last to arrive.

Elke heard someone ask, "Why was your motorcade singled out for harassment?"

"We were last to arrive, due to some scheduling matters, so we were easy to place. Please note I have many more supporters than detractors, and I appreciate their peaceful presence in the face of rudeness."

"Is that 'rudeness' why your security detail used dispersal gas?"

"I always prefer a peaceful response. In this case, there were elements presenting a risk to my supporters, and the military women and men escorting me. Gunfire was involved. My security contractors took unpleasant but necessary steps, the minimum necessary, to ensure the safety of all. Even after this response, my vehicle was blocked by extremists, so we left the vehicle despite the threat and proceeded on foot. I of course am sorry the incident happened."

She hadn't actually blamed them, but she'd certainly deflected all focus to them. The bitch.

With that, Highland gave a regal nod and started walking. They fell in around her, as contract and professionalism required, though Elke wished to be elsewhere.

No luck. As the female present she was required, for visibility. Gender didn't matter, so Highland made as much of it as possible. On the other hand, both Christian and Muslim extremists disliked that, so Elke decided going along with it wasn't entirely bad. She could sit, stay awake and watch for threats while ignoring diplophrasing if that's what was called for.

They made their way directly into the main hall, which had been dressed up to make it look less like a gymnasium and more like a dressed up gymnasium. Highland's box was the only one left, with seats for three. That was because no one had mentioned the Ripple Creek detail, which was a good thing, but it meant one of them standing.

Elke decided she'd stand. Even the glee of her new device working as planned might not keep her awake through hours of speeches. Besides, she'd be more visible for Highland that way.

Aramis hurt after twenty minutes of sitting in a chair. The seats were stiff, hard and apparently designed for appearance only. He made a gesture and swapped out with Elke. That would let him stretch and shift. It would be imperceptible to most people, but would be more comfortable. His shoulders hated him for those armrests. They were half numb, but only half, the other half a burning ache.

Standing, though, made him wonder if any of his kidnappers and antagonists recognized him. That caused enough fear, anger and introspection to completely wipe out any attention to Highland's speeches, or that of others. That was the good part. The bad part was that after a half hour, he ached again, this time his heels and ankles.

Shaman apparently read it in his posture or tremors, and stepped in to replace him, letting him take a turn outside. The steady rotation also helped with alertness, made them less predictable, and let them do a partial patrol of the hall, though everyone else's escorts tensed in professional paranoia as they passed.

Nothing substantive was done that day, and Aramis expected one of BuState's staff experts would take over. Highland had been present to pretend Earth cared what any other planet thought, and to get face time for election.

As the forum closed, Alex had his phone out, and looked concerned. Aramis interrogated him by look.

Alex said, "We're flying out. It's not safe. The protests are now riots and turning into brawls. Battles will be next."

Highland refused to hear it. "I must travel in dignity," she said. "If I drove in, I must drive out. I won't acknowledge a few protesters by diverting."

"Ma'am, militarily I agree with you. Diplomatically I agree with you. As your security operations chief, I must insist on aircraft. We can blame a mechanical problem, or you can blame me."

"Of course I would. But we're driving."

She probably saw Alex say, "Yes, ma'am," nod and turn to comply. Aramis saw the unsaid, *you egotistical bitch*, and the twitch in his boss's jaw.

So they trooped down to the vehicle apron, led fore and aft by local security, furnished by Emir Mudassir. They kept their distance. It was all a juggling act. Everyone here, of course, was trusted not to try to assassinate their peers, except that some few of them might, so everyone had guards in case of collateral casualties, and then the guards became a necessary status symbol.

The emir's detail seemed quite happy to depart as they reached the broad vehicle park, which was ringed by wall, umbrella'd by transparent shield, and patrolled by three agencies, plus the Army. Lionel rolled up in the limo, and Aramis knew the man had not stepped foot out, unless he'd had a company relief. They'd learned not to trust anyone in this game—family, assistant, doctor, even bureau chief.

Aramis got the door, Highland and Jessie slid in, as Jessie tagged a churp about leaving the conference. He'd enjoy using that device for target practice, but she probably had a spare and possibly an implanted backup. They just had to deal with it.

Highland would have to deal with not taking the car.

The rioting had reached what they called Level Two. It was a plateau of random shouting, hurling, speechmakers and sheer mass of bodies that made progress impossible. Three vehicles ahead were stopped and not proceeding.

Alex dutifully and professionally had his phone out, but Aramis knew it was largely for Highland's benefit.

". . . That's the assessment? Yes, I concur. Any response is likely to become violent. Letting them play themselves out is best . . . No, I expect any advance will result in casualties, both accidental, and planned by activists. It's best not to play the game . . . Yes, I will so inform Ms. Highland. Stand by." He turned from the phone and said, "Ma'am, they are scheduling or recommending aircraft travel for all participants. The Aerospace Force detachment has a Hummingbird transport lifter waiting. It can be here in ten minutes and will get priority."

Aramis could see her teeth grind.

"I abhor this turn of events."

"I would drive if we could, ma'am, but if the vehicles ahead of us won't, then we'd be leading the way into a riot. It's almost certain someone would get hurt, and you get blamed. I'm not willing to take a fall against my advice. I'm perfectly willing to take it for diverting. I'll issue a statement accordingly."

She spoke with icy clarity. "That won't be necessary. Proceed."

"By air?"

"Yes, as you advise."

Aramis suspected it didn't matter what Alex would take the blame for. She'd do as she pleased. Of course, that would lead to a grudge match. That could escalate . . .

Yeah, he wanted to be done with this mission, fast.

Highland did not like Ripple Creek. She'd been wary from the beginning, with good reason. When that incompetent but scheming snake in New York had assigned them—and she had no doubt it was the SecGen's office that assigned them—she'd known it was to embarrass her, either by saddling her with their disregard for bystanders, or the bad press that followed them, or the way they'd choke down on her movements. So far, the smarmy fucker was three for three.

They were certainly competent at keeping threats away, even when they lost a man. Still, the Army had gotten him back for them. It hadn't softened their attitude. Minor protesters were not a threat. She half expected the goons to follow her to the bathroom. In the meantime, they used stink gas, gunfire, explosives and vehicles, and had killed a newsworthy number of nobodies who'd follow Highland's career like zombies. She was quite sure that had been the reason they'd been sent. The Special Service knew to intercept bullets and keep quiet. These trigger-happy clowns seemed to enjoy shooting people, and she was fairly sure their weapons did not have biometric locks. Not working ones, at least.

She would be in need of a new biosculp when this was over, and that before taking office. They even saw Jessie as a potential threat, not to mention Huble.

So it was time to pull in some favors, have the mercenary

bastards marked as what they were. She could then separate herself, be magnanimous and fair, and regret it as they went down.

She just had to keep Cruk's publicity people from covering them against her. So perhaps a call to Blanding was in order, to find some nonprofit group who could sue on behalf of the low-class rabble they'd blithely shot.

The next load that flashed made her grit her teeth and growl. She wanted something to bite, to chew, to rip with her jaw.

People wondered why she hated the common morons the Equality Party attracted. It was because they were morons. Enthusiasm didn't equate to competence or even usefulness.

The slogan was, "Let's position Joy on top!"

It was on flash buttons, on shirts, on hats and pennants.

Even worse, at a rally in Bangladesh, a crowd was chanting. The reporter waxed eloquent about the turnout numbers, but behind her it was easy to hear, "Joy on top! Assume the position!"

It might be enthusiasm and lack of familiarity with English idiom. It might be unintentional idiocy. Or, it might be the work of some shill from Cruk's camp or even Hunter's. And yes, his name was most certainly part of why she wouldn't team with him. "Joy/Hunter" would have made this even worse.

It had to be stopped. Morons would ignore spelling errors, or even inadvertent insults. But a catchy phrase with innuendous potential would linger for years. She screened a quick message.

> Huble: Cease and desist these moronic fuckers at once.
> I want those signs gone within the hour.
> Spend the money to make sure they are destroyed.

Then she moderated it slightly, because it just might get cracked in transit. Polite in all matters, she reminded herself.

She understood why so many of her . . . well, no, they weren't peers, but competitors, took offers from the multinationals. The power was less visible, but that gave leeway to behave more casually.

But she would beat that classless buffoon. It would take a few phone calls . . . which she couldn't make from here. That twelve-hour delay was infuriating.

◎ CHAPTER 15 ◎

ALEX KNEW THIS WAS A GOAT ROPE. All he could do was keep roping.

He entered their quarters, which were covered by two of Cady's people.

Marlin said, "You're secure inside, sir."

"Thanks. Outside?"

Roger Edge said, "Nothing that we can discern."

Jason said, "I'll check," as he unshouldered his coat, slipped arms through his harness, cleared his pistol before reaching the door to his quarters, and tossed the whole ensemble on the bed.

Alex likewise took his coat off, unsnapped the armor, and said, "Elke, I'll want whatever feeds you have. In an hour."

It could be done faster, but they all needed to hydrate after a sweaty ride, standing for hours in a hall and a flight back. Then they needed bathroom breaks, to reconstitute gear, and save files, make notes, debrief themselves. There were several reasons they got paid as well as they did, and the long hours were part of it.

Jason reported secure. Everyone summarized their notes.

"Elke, what do you have for us?"

"She's angry," Elke said. "Just as she told us, she thinks it will be seen as weak. Here."

She started a playback from a video feed in Highland's quarters. It wasn't good video, but even the BuState intel people hadn't found the devices. Nor was he sure what Elke used. If found, he'd deny it, she'd get "counseled," the lawyers would apologize, and they'd go right back to doing what they'd been doing.

Highland said, "Cruk is going to be the cause of my breakdown. Or rather, his handlers are. That retarded African buffoon is beyond a puppet." She strode around, distorted slightly from the correction algorithm on the near spherical lens. She had a glass of something, half-drained already, and her biometrics seemed to indicate some sort of tranquilizer.

JessieM sat on the couch, looking a bit tense but unafraid. She said, "It hasn't affected you negatively yet. They're reporting that the unrest caused the entire conference to divert to air."

"Yes, so I personally am okay, but BuState looks like bumbling idiots. That's why we got rid of leMieure. I can't be seen in any comparison to him."

"Of course not. But you present better. Your intro went over well, and your followup release says you regret that further progress couldn't be made through intransigence and the stress of the civil unrest. I noted the unrest was due to economic and societal inequality, and that you wanted peace for all groups to pursue their joint destiny."

Interesting. JessieM wasn't just a lackey. That was a pretty well-phrased release, done on the fly. He looked at the others, they looked back and nodded. It was understood.

"Good. I need to distance myself from Ripple Creek before they take a fall."

"I've been churping that you would rather have BuState security. This change is due to the administration."

"We can't blame them! They'll come back on us."

"I haven't. It's stated as due to necessity, and I blamed the Liberty Party for refusing to accede to a reasonable budget, thus forcing this on us."

"Good. We're all friends here, and I greatly respect our faithless and fearful leader. Once we've cleared decks and are ready for the caucus, then we'll pile on."

"He's going to expect that."

"Of course. The trick is not to come across as too competent. If he has to throw resources at it, he looks like a bully. Passive aggressive strategy."

"Ma'am, should we be discussing this out loud?"

"Huh? Oh, it's fine. Mr. Gillette swept this place right before we came in. Didn't you get the churp?"

"I did not." JessieM looked somewhat nonplussed at being left out of that discussion.

"Yes, he's got us covered."

That was interesting, Alex thought. Had he done a half-assed job? A good job, but not good enough? Or was he a mole for someone?

"Elke, are you sure no one else has a feed from there?"

"I am."

Jason said, "So am I. Aerospace Force was able to check on Bishwanath as a colonial power. BuState has made it very clear they won't allow outside agencies, and I've checked. If the military got anything, it would mean someone's neck. So if someone is even trying, it's without permission and a hostile act. Then they'd have to go through Cady to do so. Nor did we find anything. Probability, then, is very low."

"Understood, but low is not zero."

"Of course. All a matter of odds."

They stopped as Highland said, ". . . will need to get moving on Ripple Creek. They are going to save me, just not the way those bloodthirsty retards imagine."

Very interesting, and unnerving. If she'd toss out the R word, and planned to take them down, then this was very interesting.

"I'm glad she underestimates us."

Aramis said, "I know the military does. We're deemed second raters. Hell, I used to think so, until that first mission. I suppose civilians have even less grasp of what we do."

"She's been around the track, though. She should know better."

Shaman said, "BuState security are very much expected to take fire, and to not hurt bystanders. It's not hard to do that among a largely disarmed population that isn't minded to cause major violence. We come in when there is major violence in the paradigm. Then, she's been shuffled out here for a reason."

"So, is this possibly a deliberate assassination attempt?"

"Setup, perhaps. It could be a combination of things. Comply with letter of the law regarding security. Arrange to embarrass each of us—Ripple Creek and Highland, and take out either one if opportunity presents."

Alex felt a chill.

"Yes, that does fit. Not only does everyone in the equation hate her, they also hate us."

Bart said, "And now we know."

"Indeed. Well, our tasking is to keep her alive. I am not bothered at the concept of pissing her off to do so. Whether she gets elected or not is not our concern. I would enjoy aggravating whoever comes after her. And if we confirm who's after us, we do as we need to."

Elke smiled that warm, creepy smile and said, "I love you at times like this."

"Yes, well, let's see what message she sends, if we can."

The next morning, it was necessary to sit in conference with Ms. Highland, Mr. Gillette and Captain Das to discuss threats. Das came up to see Alex first.

"Are you ready, Agent Marlow?"

"I am," he agreed. "I'm eager to swap intel."

"Same here, though it often seems we provide them more than they do us."

Alex took that as a suggestion that Das wanted more from him, too.

"It can seem that way, though circumstances do change."

"Certainly. Some agencies like to receive more than they give, especially at budget time."

Yes, that was a hint that Das didn't trust Gillette either.

Das continued, "Though of course, the military's relationship with BuState is quite solid."

But not Ripple Creek's. Yes, they were always an outsider, to everyone. Alex knew that.

"We'll make it work," he said.

When they entered Highland's office, she fairly cooed.

"Captain Das, so good to see you."

Was she trying to score with him? Enjoying the view? Genuinely pleased? Or trying to frazzle Alex? Who knew? It might be relevant later, so he filed it.

Gillette said, "Captain Das, Agent Marlow, how are you this morning?"

Ah, pleasantries. They didn't really want to know, so Alex said, "Good enough," and left it at that.

JessieM was an accomplished press flak, but her duties apparently included coffee. He accepted a cup, though he wasn't likely to drink it. He was also quite wary of her presence. She was not cleared, that he knew of, but was a personally hired shill, and he knew she couldn't be trusted with any modicum of privacy.

As they sat, he looked at Gillette, who gave the barest nod of acknowledgment. So, no one trusted Highland, but he couldn't officially say anything about his boss.

Highland sat down and said, "I wanted to say I do understand the necessities of flying yesterday, and bear no hard feelings."

"Thank you, ma'am," he said simply. If she wanted to accept an apology he hadn't made and wasn't going to, fine. As long as the bank transfer cleared.

Das said, "While the situation was unfortunate, we hoped it would offer an opportunity to identify either individuals of interest, or refine our understanding of groups."

"And what did you find?" Gillette asked.

"Not much that is conclusive, but we are building a database. Eventually it will yield results."

Unspoken was whether or not he'd share those results with BuState, contractors, or even his own people. Sometimes, intel served best by not being released.

Gillette asked, "There's nothing you can share at this point?"

Das spread his hands and said, "We have identified two groups friendly to Ms. Highland who may have, through an excess of enthusiasm, presented so as to alarm others."

Highland said, "Ah, the Mtali Women's Conference and the Justice League."

"You're familiar with them?" Alex asked.

"Of course!" she said, cheerfully. "Such enthusiasm. They're creating a future for us."

Gillette's expression indicated he didn't appreciate being blindsided by his own superior. Alex made a note to see if Elke had any other conversations of interest.

"Well, that's good to know," he said. "Can you suggest they limit their enthusiasm out of respect for you, to help things move more swiftly? You can arrange a personal meeting with them later." He intended such a meeting never take place, and he'd juggle schedule and create threats as needed to ensure that.

"I can try," she said, shrugging slightly. "But these are a simple people."

What a condescending bitch. Worse, she seemed to delight in "simple people" as her support. She must assume most people were "simple." Beyond that, many of them seemed proud of the fact.

He brought his attention back to security. There were still items of note.

Gillette said, "I do note there are ongoing discussions between you and Mr. Blanding. My concern is that his communications may not be secure."

"That's ridiculous!" she snapped. "He's been a confidant and trusted friend for decades. You may remember he formerly had your job, among others."

"I am not questioning his loyalty, ma'am," Gillette said with a tone that Alex interpreted to mean he certainly was. "But his phone and feeds are no longer subject to shielding through our system. They could be hacked from outside."

"He's very knowledgeable. He'd never let that happen."

"Knowingly, no, but some of the modern techniques are very discreet. I stress constantly over your own quarters here, in case someone is pulling conversations and other data."

"You assured me they aren't."

"That I'm aware of, they aren't. That doesn't mean they can't."

Thanks for that confirmation, Alex thought.

"I need his counsel. This is a critical time, and will continue to be so for the rest of the election cycle."

"Of course. I only suggest you be careful what issues you phrase."

Well, this had easily turned to protecting her campaign rather than herself. Still, if she paid attention, it would help.

Das apparently took a cue to keep her busy and not argumentative.

"Ripple Creek furnished us with their video and EM records. We are searching it for evidence. So far, there were at least three encrypted networks operating in that area. One was for your supporters.

Regretfully, some of them were well-intentioned, but seem unclear of where the line should be drawn. They actively agitated for action against your opponents."

"While regrettable, that's entirely understandable, given the cruel and false accusations leveled at me, along with threats and actual violence."

Really, was she unable to not make a campaign speech? No one here cared, all knew the score, and this was about a real issue. She seemed to think talking could fix anything.

Das ignored it and continued, "Well, we're still trying to crack the other two networks. The encryption was good. Very good. Good enough military experts are fighting with it. This suggests your opposition has serious resources."

She came out of politician long enough to be bitch. "It's taken you this long to figure that out?"

"We are determining details, ma'am. The method of encryption should lead to a source, and from there we can learn who is involved."

"Very well. Inform me at once. The voters must know this."

Das apparently didn't know how to refuse without risking her ire. Alex stepped up.

"I will also be using that information to determine best routes and appearances for you, ma'am. My job is to ensure your safety during high-visibility appearances."

"Yes, with safety that is very high visibility, and excessive," she snarled.

"Ma'am, you instigated events to create an impression, and neglected to tell us—" The expressions of the others indicated they hadn't known that.

"I did not! I—"

He cut her off with a steady, firm voice. "Had we known, we'd have helped you arrange it so we wouldn't respond in a fashion meant to hurt people. I'd have advised against it entirely. You may have now created the meme that it would be clever, amusing or some kind of score to attack you. Now we have to deal with it. My agents respond as the threat appears. If someone tries to look lethal, we respond accordingly. If we don't, you wind up dead sooner or later and we get the blame. You can have our security, or arrange your own."

He hadn't intended to tell her off, but the woman was beyond irritating.

"Yes, your job, your company comes first." Her tone was belittling.

"Word indeed," he said. "They do."

Everyone looked at each other, embarrassed, though she'd apparently forgotten her rising argument with Das.

"I see there is nothing further to accomplish here. Good day," she said and rose.

Alex realized the other two now considered him a hindrance. He'd had that intel, and not shared it.

He shrugged, nodded and stood himself.

Elke found it amusing to listen in that morning.

Highland was cursing up a storm to JessieM and the walls.

"Those mercenary assholes! That loose-lipped bastard, telling everyone we staged an attack. They can't be trusted with anything."

JessieM sounded timid as she said, "It's always best to keep information inside, ma'am."

Yes, Highland had told them of the fact herself. She seemed to have missed that. Interesting that she didn't trust her own intel people, or the military's. What a terrible world she lived in.

Highland said, "Well, we're safe here. Das admitted he can't spy on us, and Gillette said he detected nothing. As long as our phones are off, we're okay."

That was amusing, and even more so as her monitors picked up two phones handshaking the nodes and logging out. They'd both had active systems.

So, Elke must assume someone else with similar gear was monitoring Highland, too. It wasn't certain, but it was eminently possible. That was the nature of their world. Still, their principal assumed she had secrecy. It was a good thing she didn't know about Shaman's monitors, also.

JessieM said, "Ma'am, you present well. You are still perceived as strong, courageous and honest in the face of adversity."

"Hmmph. And what is being said about my security detail?"

"You're seen as a victim of the administration, with them as its contract muscle."

"Close enough to the truth. You say it's reading well?"

"Quite. Even the Neo-Stalinists are sympathetic. They're talking it against Cruk."

"Interesting. Then we need to keep playing that. There are just so many issues here. Showing position over him is as important as the opposition proper."

"Yes. They're all opposition."

"Exactly. I can have no friends."

"You do have me, ma'am."

"Of course. You're trusted and paid, and so is Erickson."

If Elke recalled correctly, Erickson was her campaign manager on Earth. She had quite a small personal staff, considering all things.

Jessie sounded timid when she said, "What about paying Ripple Creek a bonus?"

"What?"

A bit more firmly, she said, "You could offer a bonus for their support so far. That might swing them more your way, and amenable to promotion."

"No. They'd let it leak eventually, and then I'd be the one contracting mercenaries. That has to be played right, too."

"I understand. It was a thought."

"Not a bad one, but not right for this circumstance. But I'll call Mogreb."

Elke perked up at that. Mogreb . . . oh . . . *kurva drat.*

Mogreb was a Serbian thug disguised as a lawyer, who'd been Highland's employer before she went into politics. Interestingly, it seemed she'd taught him more than she'd learned from him.

Still, he was an ugly man. Intimidation and coercion were typical of him, though never proven in court. He'd been on her payroll early on, handling interventions for constituents in her district. If she took an interest in a case, Mogreb showed up to "express concern." Most of the time, the problem then resolved amicably.

Certainly it saved court costs. It was also certainly unfair.

So he was either still on payroll, or was a consultant. So why call him? And where was he?

"Zoltan, hello again."

He was on planet, then, if she spoke to him directly.

"Did you see the broadcast? Yes, Ms. Landinger's comments were rather unkind."

They spoke for several minutes, but Elke gained all she needed from that opening. Highland wasn't happy with the press, and was arranging for muscles to mix it up. That was useful to know, and the team would need to be prepared for that if she ever went nasty. More than she already was.

When she briefed Alex and rolled the file for him, he nodded.

"For two reasons we can't get involved. First, it's none of our business what she does to others, except as it affects potential threats. Also, we can't let her know we have that feed."

"She also might escalate against us," Elke added.

"Yes. Still, I'd like to find a way to dissuade her."

"Without mentioning it?"

"It was an encrypted signal, yes?"

"Yes."

"Can someone 'discover' the signal and report it to us as a security issue? Meaning to Cady's people?"

"Everyone knows she has secure and personal communication."

"Yes, but can we pretend we didn't know? Then hint contents to encourage her to shut up?"

She flared her eyes slightly. "Probably not. I'll think on it."

Highland had what she needed. Keeping it discreet across light years had taken money, patience, effort, and a good rapport with people who could read between the lines.

Huble was good at that. It had cost money, though. The question was if the payoff would be worth it.

The newsload should be coming through this system any time now. There was the lightspeed delay from Earth, the wait for a ship to carry the signal through, for it to clear UN BuSec at this end, which should be a formality but could take time. More lightspeed delay. It should be now, dammit.

She sighed and poured a champagne and vodka cooler. It would happen.

There.

Oh, that was brilliantly done, she thought, feeling a rush that was almost naughty. It was even more spiteful than she'd hoped for. She brought the volume up so as to catch all the details.

—essman Hunter's wife. According to the release, she caught him

in an 'inappropriate embrace' with a junior staffer. She reiterates her belief in his campaign, and vows to stand by him despite this personal trouble.

The payoff would come shortly, because Amelia Hunter had made no such statement. They'd be days sorting it out, and Highland would have time to regain points.

But it got better. So much better.

The staffer was not identified, but came forward as Angela Soruto. Ms. Soruto asked for Whistleblower protection, and CNNBC News is discussing the release of further details from her.

Had he really been nailing the little whore? Or was she an opportunistic bitch making up stories to cash in?

Either way, that was a one-two punch to the guts of that condescending cunt Amelia. This, right after Huble's operatives had promised she'd ride out the trouble. She was a spoiled, frigid, diamond-digging cunt, and this should wreck her to more sleeping pills and sedatives. In two weeks, they could claim that was an ongoing problem, and that should be the end of that campaign.

It was back down to her and Cruk.

Damon Huble appreciated Highland's employ. She paid promptly from her not insubstantial personal accounts, her campaign funds from her legion of jabbering idiots, and occasionally, from money shifted from her position accounts. She always repaid that promptly, which would help in any kind of political dispute, but he had warned her once that it was illegal to pierce that veil, regardless of repayment. Official funds were official. He'd warned her. Once. Highland didn't like being told things she didn't want to hear, regardless of legality, but for several reasons he needed to cover his own ass. No campaign or administration lasted forever, and any number of suits and charges were possible. Any smart staffer covered all angles.

Really, it was a delight to perform these tasks for her. They were a challenge, a puzzle, and their resolution always satisfying. They were more satisfying the more artistic the result. He was especially proud of this one.

She'd covered all costs from a discreet, completely legal account filled with donations from her special fans. He'd kept it thirty percent under his original estimate to her, fifteen percent under his own private estimate. The payments were all tagged for perfectly legal processes and promotions to three companies neither of them owned. They had total deniability of any impropriety.

In addition, he'd been able to tell another client that he'd accomplished their task at the same time, and pocketed only a consultancy fee, no operations costs. Completely legal, and they were more than happy to make that payment by anonymous transfer through Sealand, Ceres and Breakout Station Bank in the Grainnean system into his anonymous account groundside.

Politics was the one game where every player wanted to leverage every other player. And if he could use the funds of an inevitable loser—Highland—to support the campaign of a certain winner— Cruk, the Secretary General, then so much the better for all involved. Except for Highland, of course, once the campaign folded. Or if not, once the legal charges started.

But he had warned her. Once.

Hepgard would be very happy. No doubt the bonus he was paying would also be reflected in Hepgard's own account. There was plenty to go around. On Earth, he was sure the SecGen benefited, but wasn't going to ask. The end result was to soften up Highland so he could get that position. It would probably be a decade, but he'd get the appointment. And if she did win, she might appoint him anyway, with plenty of dirt to use on her in return. Thuggery on Mtali, dishonesty with government money in her campaign. A good start, but it would take more.

Franklin Lezt sat in another hotel, awaiting Hepgard for followup. He'd had two stiff grape vodkas already. He really wasn't sure if the man got it.

He watched the scrolling news feed. It was almost at that critical point, and that meant playing the trump.

A knock on the door indicated Hepgard, and he buzzed the man in, set the interference and did not offer him a drink.

"So now she's at twenty-eight percent and climbing," he said at once.

Hepgard said, "That's just reaction to Hunter being effectively quashed." He looked around for a seat for himself. There wasn't one, on purpose. He sat on the bed instead.

Lezt said, "Yes, but she keeps climbing." He gripped his drink and the arm of the chair.

"Guy, my techniques are proven. She's just molecularly coated against shit."

"It seems like it." He wanted to be angry, but Hepgard was right. It should be working. Just nothing stuck to her. That little twitch personal she had, JessieM, was both a brilliant spinster and very popular. How could anyone hate a college girl turned promoter, who had no perversions, drinking problems, whatever? It seemed her only purpose in life was to ping inane messages around the nodes, and she was brilliant at it, and now getting paid.

He said, "The first thing is, *do not touch JessieM*. No matter what. She's a favorite pet and it will only be seen negatively."

Hepgard nodded. "Agreed. Do you have something specific in mind for the other?"

"It's time she made a personal sacrifice for her party."

"Guy . . ." Hepgard stopped.

"Yes, that's what we're down to. *She cannot break thirty percent!*"

"What is it with you and that number?"

The man didn't know, and he'd have to be told. Lezt took another heavy swallow, winced and looked up. "At thirty-two percent, it's established by the election commission that she can have Special Service security freely as a campaigner. She'd only have to pay transport costs for her own people. No Ripple Creek, still with BuState security, free military resources on request, all government. If she goes down for anything in front of the SecGen's personal guard, he takes the hit."

"I thought that didn't take effect until ninety days out?"

"That's for anyone over five percent. It's twenty percent at a hundred and twenty days, thirty-two percent at one eighty, which is next week."

"You don't want much, do you?" Hepgard was wide-eyed at the implied but not directly stated subject of assassination.

"My boss has agreed to the same elements used for that . . . apprehension."

Hepgard snorted. "Which doesn't seem to have worked. They didn't kill the man, and he's back at work. Highland benefitted by ignoring it. They've demanded more money and got it."

"In this case they'll be available to encourage her into an area where some very bad people will be outraged at civil society and very violent. So sad, but she tried so hard, let us remember her as we move on. Your job is to find that location, prep it, ensure everyone is in the right state of mind, and let me know. Keep in mind there's about twenty-six hours of delay round trip."

"And you want this in a week?" Hepgard looked very unsure. That was a nice score, but he better get sure in a hurry.

"I do. Why are you still here?"

Hepgard turned and walked to the door. As he closed it behind himself, Lezt heard him mutter, "Fucker."

And Franklin Lezt had just enough of a recording to ensure that any claims against him would take down the SecGen, as well as BuInt.

⚙ **CHAPTER 16** ⚙

JASON STRETCHED IN HIS CHAIR. He needed more exercise. He didn't like exercise, but he disliked not exercising more. However, as assistant team leader, he had administrative stuff to handle, and some specifics to follow up on. He was worried about Aramis, but the man did seem to be recovering properly. Still, the intimate details were going to be a problem for the man, and he wanted to do what he could to help.

Which was what the first tagged message was about. He opened it, let it decrypt, then decrypted the decrypt.

Aramis sat across the room, occupied with some kind of work of his own—charts, maps, something. He wasn't going to come see the screen, was what mattered. That established, Jason screened the message.

Dear Jason,

Thank you so much for keeping me informed. Aramis is a good friend, and yes, I was worried about him, about all of you, in fact, after you treated me so well during a very trying time.

"I have no specific information on who might be the threat to you or your charge. These things are generally discussed in private, completely off record, and the government responds to my ignoring most of its actions by ignoring me in return.

"I can very much suggest that you look inside for threats. I know that's what happened to me, but it's not uncommon. However, from all I can tell, she is actually on very good terms with her family and

immediate friends. They do well from her existence, and her will calls for most of her money to go to several causes, not personal inheritors. I would look for anyone who might have connected recently and has influence, and also anyone who profits from her demise. Not her family, but certain competitors, or businesses who stand to improve their position if she's out of the way. It's also possible for agencies to act that way, though she's mainstream enough I can't see her threatening enough cuts or profile changes to trigger that. Of course, someone scheming enough could manipulate others into setting up a complicated trap. I'm confident you'll hinder that, but it could get messy and I want you all to be safe. Cocktails here when you return.

I've taken the liberty of informing Aramis's recent paramour of his safety first, incident second, with most details redacted.

"Thank you again, my trusted associate.

C.

He hadn't expected Caron would have much, but she'd certainly be looking now, and she deserved to know Aramis was okay.

The list of people who'd be happy with Highland out of the way, though, was huge. Most were not able to connect here, but enough were that was a fruitless pursuit. It would take a graph that could weight each of them on several factors, several locations, timeframes, all in several dimensional arrays. There certainly were ways to set that up. He had no idea how. Elke might.

Nor was it certain only one group was targeting her. In fact, it was certainly more than that, even if some hurled nothing but invective and the occasional piss-filled water balloon.

In the meantime, they had another escort for another speech. He did have to respect Highland on that point. There weren't a lot of votes here, but she was angling for every one she could get, and she did hold up against threats. She probably figured enough small blocs of votes could swing the election, and it was entirely possible she was too self-centered and snobbish to really grasp threats.

"Ready, Aramis?"

"Yes." The man seemed calm, prepared and relieved to be back at work. Good. Though Shaman indicated he had occasional nightmares and was taking medication for sleep. Still, work was good therapy, and they worked best as a team.

The military had relented on the test-firing issue. The team had their own clearing barrel in their wing, in a well-insulated and deadened alcove, with extra fill to trap bullets. Officially, there was a ventilation system for toxic gases, because Cady, Alex and the BuState facilities engineer said so.

They approached the drum, Alex said, "Escort Team, performing function check," and waited for the computer to acknowledge and flash green.

"Please proceed," the waveform voice said.

Alex pointed his pistol and fired, checked the cycle, then repeated with his carbine. He stepped aside for Jason.

Jason never flinched when shooting, but in these quarters, even with earbuds and deadening panels, the volume was painful. Still, it was good prep and practice for combat. He let the anticipatory tension build, then drain, slipped the muzzle into the tube, and fired. The shockwave rolled over him. He reholstered, slung the carbine around, pointed, and fired.

Yes, that got the adrenaline rushing, just enough to heighten senses. He was well-primed for the mission. Not for the first time, he thought that the test fire served to check the shooter as well as the weapon.

Fergus Hendry from Facilities arrived as Bart checked his weapons. They trooped to Highland's apartment, and Alex knocked.

"Minister Highland, we're ready," he said.

As always, he was polite. They worked well as a team. Alex was always polite. Jason could defuse trouble with humor. Of course, he could also exacerbate it when that served better.

Highland and Jessie stepped out to join them.

"Good morning, gentlemen, lady," she said, also polite. They all pretended.

Hendry walked into the room to keep it occupied and secure, and coincidentally to sweep for bugs other than theirs. Jason had no idea if he planted more, or even knew about their own. He didn't need to know.

Minutes later they were in the ARPAC and rolling.

It was likely an easy mission. She wanted to meet with some factory workers, have lunch, ask their opinions on climate, as if they were likely to have useful input, or she cared, or any other politician cared, or would do anything about it if they did. Or if they could. It was a camouflaged campaign stop.

For Highland, the ARPAC was so she could play the hero. For the team, it was an easy security improvement. It was a harder barrier. It also now had a honey pot next to the rear ramp, with a rudimentary curtain.

If it were up to them, they'd use the ARPAC for every mission. The limo looked political, but even its armored bulk wasn't close to this beast. Politicians lived by image, though, and Highland was a slave to that unless and until she won SecGen, and probably after that.

Elke was glad to have actual weapons and not just nonlethal. More and more, society sank into decadence and avoided the practicality of just killing people who caused problems. Nonlethal force took repeated applications, and often failed to sufficiently terrify those who needed kept in place.

Highland was annoying. It was obvious to Elke she was the kind of woman who actually would like to use force when needed, but was afraid of the political repercussions. Still, she might be a better option than the effete soft-skin now occupying the Earth Mansion. On the other hand, Cruk certainly liked throwing troops around, and had at least signed off on the team's presence, at least by proxy.

In the meantime, she had a job to do, and hopefully to enjoy.

As tough as an ARPAC was, rolling around the city in it made them a slow target. The two Grumblies on detail made it obvious it was a VIP mission, not a combat mission. That changed the profile of the threats. There were always threats.

The trip was short enough, since most of the industry was near the ports. The airport, river port and railhead all ran together on the west side, connecting to the rest of the continent. It scared her, because she knew what she could do to that infrastructure with a carful of explosive. They really needed better security, given the factional disputes. It was certain every group had a blaster good enough to accomplish that task.

They pulled up streetside, where local cops had marked a clear zone. She watched Alex for cues, nodded to his point, and dropped the hatch just slow enough not to slam it on the road. Bart led the entourage, she took tail end after the rest, as the troops and local police formed a cordon around the vehicle. That didn't thrill her, but she'd planned accordingly. The device she left on the bench would be harmless unless someone entered the cabin, and the rear-facing camera she'd mounted up front would give her notice.

The engagement was well familiar to Bart. He led the way down the ramp, through the pathway left by police, and into the building. One of the BuState protocol people was just inside, next to the president of Wataniya Engines, Arul al-Harun Bawani, which didn't sound like an Earth Arabic name. They fought over silly things here, and that was after leaving Earth because they couldn't get along there.

Bawani had one assistant and one guard, both male, in Western suits but with keffiyeh. The atrium was mostly clear. Building security, and three of the military detail, plus two of Cady's people, strode around the upper balcony. Everything was near-transparent crystal, supported by black stone a bit like marble. The floor tiles were pale gray of similar material, with gold veining. Yet if he remembered Aramis's map correctly, a kilometer away were slum shacks of left-over wheels and packing materials.

Highland stepped forward, and he noticed she was wearing a glove. She wasn't going to actually touch his hand.

"Mr. Bawani, thank you for meeting me," she said as she offered her hand.

He reached out and shook it long enough for the photographer to get a grip and grin shot, then said, "Madam Minister, you honor us with your presence."

"I'm glad to be able to visit such a forward-looking facility . . ." she said, and Bart tuned it out. He would listen for keywords relevant to her safety. The political talking was not of interest.

An honest assessment of the factory was that it was decades out of date. Colony worlds either had substantial investment backing, or lacked. This one lacked. There were still advantages to being off Earth, but they faded against the negatives.

In this case, JessieM's constant feed of content probably helped. Highland's supporters and fans, for she had both, could see the equipment, see her interaction, and the small scatterers they all wore now should prevent anyone seeing them clearly. The major risk would be a disgruntled employee, probably easy to stop, since the details of this event had not been promoted. It was unlikely anyone would blow up others to get her, though anything was possible.

"If you will all come this way," the production manager said in reasonable English, "we can show Minister Highland the production floor. You will all need protective wear."

Jason tapped his ear and said, "That's covered, but we would appreciate head protection."

"Of course."

The hats were bump caps only, and Bart had to completely unfasten the tensioner to fit it on his head. He suspected most of the safety, and likely the security, was similar. Visible, but not substantive. That was notable.

As they walked along the floor, the workers paused and looked to see who the VIP was. Most of them wore basic coveralls; a few supervisors wore robes. It was probably as caste-ridden here as anywhere else they'd been, but it was harder to tell, except for the management in suits.

Most line workers seemed happy enough for either the distraction of the visit or the presence of the Minister. He didn't foresee any serious threat.

A tiny window opened on his glasses. He reached up and made the slight adjustment that broadened it. It was a note from Jason and a news load that showed a crowd gathering outside. It probably wasn't JessieM's fault. The word would have gotten out anyway. Still, crowds were problematic at best. He wondered what their instructions would be, when Highland said to the work group, "It's been very nice to talk to you, and I welcome your inputs. But I must reluctantly beg your indulgence for another meeting."

Some of them understood the English, others waited for the interpreter.

They formed back around her, as much to protect her from adoration and delay as potential threats. He and Aramis took point, both as meat shields, and because Aramis had his own map, in case of any issues.

Roger Edge and the NCOIC of the military detail stood near the front door.

Edge said, "There's a sizeable crowd out there. A hundred or more. Some are friendly, some antagonistic."

"I'll talk to them," Highland said.

Bart thought that completely stupid. He glanced back at Alex.

Alex said, "Ma'am, that isn't necessarily going to be positive. It depends on—"

"—on demographics," she cut in. "I have some experience with this, Agent Marlow."

"'—so we'll give you some space and be prepared if you need us,' I was going to say," he said.

"Very well."

That established, Bart waited for the door, then led the entourage outside.

The exit was greeted with cheers and calls. The banners were mostly Arabic, though a couple looked Turkish, and one in English read, "Back to Earth with the Harlot of Babylon." He had no idea what that was about. The crowd didn't seem violent, but there were surges and ripples, and clutching hands from those closest to the police line. Three press people had cameras in a prime location, clearly having prepared for this eventuality, and Highland approached them. It might be okay. It certainly seemed routine to her and them.

"Thank you for coming out today," she said into an offered mic, which was wired into a PA. "I'm glad to see my supporters, but I am also glad to see those with concerns and issues. This is the type of interest and activism we need, if we are to progress . . ."

This speech sounded much more earnest and productive than the canned platitudes inside. She might pull this off. He waited and watched his sector, though the police seemed to have most of the eager crowd controlled and restrained. Some of these people were aggravated, but none of them seemed violent enough for an immediate threat.

Then he heard a pistol shot.

Yes, one never could predict.

Elke heard the report. This time it was real gunfire. She identified it as a pistol, and swung her shotgun up as Shaman and Alex shoved a gawking Highland down the sidewalk and under the vehicle skirt.

The principal was covered, so she dialed for recon, shot a round over the crowd, and ducked and rolled.

Three rounds had been fired so far. Bart was in the vehicle and sparking it. Aramis and Jason flanked Elke behind the shield, close together and spilling out. She drew back a bit so they could get friendlier, trusting on her earbuds to have correctly reported direction.

The crowd was in chaos, running in all directions. That was mostly good. They'd disrupt a gunman. However, they would also conceal him if he ran, as he probably was.

The image flashed up on her glasses and showed nothing useful in that small format. It did, however, show the local police well-mixed with the crowd and subduing apparently at random. Clicking off the image, she could see it live. They had stunners, obviously scaled up to maximum, old-fashioned batons, and boots. There were a lot of them.

A faint smile crossed her face while she scanned for active threats. This wouldn't do Highland's image any good at all. She wondered, in fact, if it were deliberate.

It had been an entire nine seconds since the shooting started, and Alex's voice said, "Withdraw."

She replied, "Babs moving," and skittered back, with the shield between her and the last known threat direction.

She reached the skirt, swung behind the ladder's plate and said, "Babs covering." Jason acknowledged, rose to a crouch without using his hands, then did that silly-looking dance step to slip back, feet never leaving contact with the ground. Silly looking, but very effective.

"Argo covering."

"Musketeer moving," Aramis said, and bounded back holding the shield. They scurried up the ramp in turn, though Elke found herself very clumsy moving backward. The steps were serrated for traction, and caught on her boot sole pattern. She noted that for followup.

They boxed around Highland and coaxed her into the vehicle. As soon as they were inside, Bart engaged the drive and they rolled away, as another platoon of police arrived to break heads.

Elke shrugged to herself. She'd seen it in so many places she couldn't keep track. The only difference was how the power was applied. In some places they used hands, fists, sticks and stunners. Some used incapacitance gas and blinding lights. If need be, they had stun fields and pain stimulators. In the nicest societies, it was all done with money and political power without the need for violence.

But the peasants were always kept in line.

As hirelings, they had many of the advantages of the upper castes, without most of the ties. It was a system that worked for her.

The cops here popped some kind of clear gas that emanated in shimmery waves. Ahead of it, people clutched at their faces. It seemed to be some kind of sulfide thiol that carried a tremendous stench, similar though less potent than their own variety. Then the cops waded in swinging sjambok-style whips, using the stinging, flicking tips to herd people, slowly at first, but faster. A second echelon had stunners set to a strong tingle. They did seem trying to avoid actual injury.

Highland looked amused for just a moment, then started to protest, accompanied by mild histrionics. She obviously had no concern about troublemakers getting smacked. She only cared that she be seen as compassionate. There were truly two complete sides to her, and one was a pure façade.

Still, so far Ripple Creek wasn't taking the blame, and Elke didn't see a need to use any significant force.

Once seated, the woman took a breath and said, "Well, that was positive."

Jessie said, "They weren't a friendly crowd."

"Not at all, but the imagery is good."

That confirmed it for Elke. The woman craved headlines, and would manufacture them if there weren't enough. However, that suggested a possibility.

"Ma'am, regarding the harassment incidents."

Highland looked up, and looked curious. "Yes?"

"If we are able to completely destroy incoming devices, then there's no way for the press to scale them. They will be reported only as potential explosive devices in our log."

Alex was paying attention, but letting her take the discussion.

"That's true," Highland said. "Would you be able to report for my releases as to the level of danger?"

Yes, she would want to claim the points. "I can report the range of possibilities to your staff," she said, indicating JessieM. "Our own files are kept secure unless officially requested."

Highland twisted her brow and thought. Elke was offering the opportunity for them to exaggerate to the limits of feasibility, unhindered.

"That sounds worthwhile. If we only report the information, it's up to the media how they interpret it. I know one or two who'd enjoy having their own experts comment."

She looked over at Alex, who nodded.

"We can give you a properly phrased release after each mission. Please understand we will not be confirming it officially. It will be 'based on information provided by her detail.'"

"That's fair enough," she said.

Alex gritted his teeth and Elke knew he was angry. To protect themselves, they were assisting this woman in her campaign, by fabricating a myth of her being heroic in stature, and an underdog in a power struggle. Somewhere between professionalism and duty to the team, detachment had gone for a raft trip down the rapids. Still, the compromise helped them do their jobs with less hindrance. And all politicians lied.

Jason was frazzled when they delivered Highland back to the compound. It had been a long, bathroom-short day with little food, some borderline combat, and the media circus was in full swing. "Shots fired" had turned into "major battle around the Minister's investigation," though it was hard to tell if she'd exaggerated or the press had, and if the latter, from incompetence or bias. She certainly wasn't going to dial them down, though, when she derived benefit.

To be fair, the team wasn't going to issue any corrections either. They had no intention of giving intel to the enemy, and if it was perceived as a more dangerous event, that was good for their PR. Two could play that game.

In the armory, everyone cleared weapons, ran basic cleaning, and parked them. They slid off their file cards and Jason logged them into their secure archive. It was as uncrackable as they could make it, shielded, and never connected outside. Those records were for intel, legal protection, and, hypothetically, counter for anyone trying to blackmail them.

He counted weapons easily enough, accepted the tallies on rounds fired—recon and smoke for Elke, none for the rest. That was something else they had different from the troops. While their rules of engagement allowed looser fire, their discipline kept them down. Even the six of them were out-heavied by a mob. Never out-classed, though.

"When this is done we should hit the rec center. Fresh air without armor, and hot food among people will be good for us."

"Concur," Alex said.

Aramis said, "Yeah, as crappy as those pocket pastries are, I could use one right now."

"There is no beer," Bart lamented.

"Yeah, we'll take the bad with the worse."

Elke asked, "Casual uniform?" She had her blouse halfway off. She didn't like being touched, but she was perfectly comfortable disrobing among her teammates. She had not a bad figure at all, too.

"Yes," Alex agreed.

Twenty minutes later, they trooped to the rec center. He figured that despite the friction with the troops, a change of scenery was good, and perhaps they could plug into a game or two. In the meantime, someone might let slip some intel.

The new push for "equality" meant there were no distinct areas for officers, NCOs and enlisted members. Tradition maintained, though. The enlisted troops gathered near game pads. The NCOs sat in groups to talk and drink dealcoholized beer, though Jason was quite sure some of them had found ways to doctor the beverages. The officers had trivia and logic puzzles, though honestly, most of the problems weren't that hard, and only a handful of the officers seemed to actually care or be any good. They had definitely doctored their drinks.

The team found an alcove off the main lounge, so they could soak up some noise, ambience and hints of music. It wasn't Jason's thing, but it was an escape from their apartment. He might suggest trips to the chapel and theater as well. Anything to break the rut. He took a chair with his left side to the room, back to the wall. Aramis faced into the room. Elke faced Jason. At an angle, the other three took a couch. It gave them good view and some distance.

While others might be violating regs on intoxicants, and they could claim immunity under BuState, though not officially on this side of the base, Jason agreed with Alex that to do so was to invite trouble. He had a ginger ale. Elke actually took a Coke. Caffeine was as rarely her thing as it was his. They shortly were all gathered around a drink table, slumped in chairs and soaking up atmosphere.

Aramis said, "Thanks. I needed this." Jason followed his eyes to see a very shapely Malaysian woman in snug workout clothes. Yes, that was nice.

A clean young man walked past and asked, "What's the uniform?"

It took Jason a moment to realize it was addressed to them, in their basic pants and company shirt. It had the logo on the chest. Theoretically, they'd prefer blank clothes, but uniforms were required over here, for a combination of security and international agreement.

"Hey, what's the uniform?" the kid repeated. He wore the new camo, and it looked brand new. He hadn't been around much.

"We're Minister Highland's personal security detail."

"Ah, them," was the snide response.

Some troops really respected them, or at least had a case of hero worship. Some just treated them as any other contingent that wasn't their own. Some of the young ones, though, believed too much propaganda.

"Yup. Them," was all he said.

"I sure wouldn't mind making ten times what I'm earning to slouch around in chairs."

"Well, put in an application."

"Huh?"

"Yup. We're always hiring."

The kid wanted an argument. "You make it sound like I won't make it."

Jason gave him a neutral, interested look and said, "We prefer Recon veterans, or those with two years executive protection experience. Special skillsets like paramedic, demolition or encryption help. So if you're not one of those, your odds are reduced, but it never hurts to apply."

The kid snorted derisively.

Aramis said, "We might be the best."

That didn't help, but it was pretty clear this kid was looking for escalation.

Aramis put his drink down and rested his hands on the chair

arms. Jason knew it was so he could be on his feet and at a sprint in under a second. Shaman, Alex and Bart stayed back on the couch, not commenting.

It was clear the troop was young enough to have been impressed by his instructors, and to not pick up on social cues from anyone outside his narrow peer group.

"And I'm the guy fighting this war so you have the right to say stupid things like that, civilian."

It took a moment for Jason to process that. It was ridiculous in so many levels.

His brain decided to ignore the comment, to defuse things. His sense of the bizarre responded faster, and he laughed hysterically.

"Thanks," he said, and turned back to the conversation. "So," he said to Aramis, "when you get a chance, you really need to try the new mods on the autocannon."

Then the kid clamped a hand down on his shoulder.

There were still ways to defuse this, but Jason was getting pissed. He glanced sideways, saw the kid opening his yap to talk, and went for the object lesson.

He reached over with his right hand, gripped the kid's wrist and twisted, followed it with an elbow bar, and pushed him grunting down to the ground. He placed one foot casually on the kid's shoulder blade, leaned into the wrist, and bent the elbow back against his left knee.

The kid's voice was muffled with his mouth against the ground and pink fabric against his chin.

"Let me go, cocksucker."

"Not until you learn some manners around your betters, son," he replied, while putting just a little pressure on the wrist, until the troop squirmed and grunted.

However, he was not at all fazed. Through the carpet, the kid said, "I'll fucking pound your ass when I get up."

"Well, I guess I shouldn't let you up then, if I know that's your strategy. Aramis, will you please find someone to take charge of this?" He pointed down. The only direct pressure he had on the kid at this point was two fingers. The rest was all leverage.

Aramis was still smirking, and said, "Sure, just a moment. Would you like a soda while I'm up?"

"That would be great. Ginger ale with vanilla, please." A beer would be nice, but while the ban was annoying, it wasn't nearly as troublesome as some other issues.

The kid seemed to finally deduce he was out-classed, and lay still. Jason wasn't injuring him, they were at least semi-public, and while a crowd wasn't forming, several snickering gawkers gathered across the lounge. They didn't act offended.

A familiar voice spoke a little too loudly.

"What the hell are you doing to my troop?"

"Well, Lieutenant, let's say I don't like having a hand on my shoulder unless it's a proctologist or a close friend. Then he threatened violence. Now, I'm sure there's a record on one of our monitors." He tapped his glasses meaningfully, though they weren't set to record right then. "However, I really don't have time to argue the point, and would simply like to add some separation. Can we do that?"

The lieutenant looked very irritated, though whether at Jason or his recruit who had instigated the incident was hard to say.

"We can. Come with me, soldier."

Jason relaxed his grip and pulled his foot free. The kid scrambled up and tried to put on a show.

"That's once. I give anyone once. Next time, you and me—"

"Private!" the lieutenant snapped, and the kid jerked. He'd probably just realized that regardless of who the officer blamed, he'd be the one downhill from the shit.

Very quickly, the team had the alcove to themselves. Jason sighed. Sure, that was good tactically, but long term, it sure would be nice to get along with allied forces.

Elke said, "Let's not do this again."

Aramis said, "We're just not the diplomatic type."

◎ CHAPTER 17 ◎

ALEX WOKE, wondering if there'd be any complaints about an almost fight in an almost bar. It seemed the lieutenant was wise enough to realize he didn't want the attention. There would be propagating rumors, though, some positive, some negative. There was nothing to be done about that. Some personalities just clashed. Ripple Creek had press visibility and a certain amount of notoriety. That led to fallout.

He and Jason had an appointment with Captain Das, then Highland had another promotional run later.

The whole point of zones on base was to hinder infiltrations and threats. They signed out of State, who were finally taking such things seriously under Cady's management, but the military side waved them in. It seemed to vary on which troops had the detail. Aerospace Force was by the book. Marines was firm but polite. Army varied by nationality. The more troubled nations took it seriously. America, China and Europe, less so. At least there weren't any locals this far in. MilBu was resistant to suggestions from BuCulture.

Not being stopped and cleared made things faster, but he'd rather be delayed and secure. The drive was short, but his brain ran through a lot of comments in that time.

At the Operations Building, they were expected, and a sergeant led them straight into Das's office.

"Gentlemen, good morning," he said.

"Hello. Thanks for seeing us."

Das didn't mention the rec center, and he would have, so it was a nonissue officially. Good.

"You're welcome. I'm hoping you can offer some input."

Jason said, "What do you have?"

Das said, "Here's the weapon. It contains four unfired cartridges. They're old style, with metal cases."

Jason took it and Alex let him. He was the expert. He opened the breech as a precaution, then started examining it.

"It's a shame I can never keep these things for my collection," Jason said as he turned the weapon in his hands, rubbing, manipulating. "They're always so interesting. This is a century old, give or take, a Bridemore Pocket Lion, and someone has stippled the grip by hand, filled it and grooved it. Then it's worn mostly smooth. The barrel's been replaced, and it was an aftermarket job. Someone milled the outside themselves, and the rifling looks electrochemically etched after a pantographic stencil laid it out. Cheap, but not very durable compared to forge-rifling or beam cutting." He seemed to finally notice Das's grin, and finished with, "Sorry. You were saying?"

Das said, "That's farther than we'd got, and I'll add that information in, with thanks. We also found the empty cartridges. The interesting thing is there is no residue in the barrel to indicate bullets."

Jason nodded slowly.

"They'd definitely leave debris in this material. So it was fired with blanks?"

"It was fired with sintered polymer alloy of some kind I don't remember." He flipped up his desk screen. "Here, 'Duralon particle-cast densiform.' It's about half the mass of lead, which is more than enough to cycle the weapon, but it would fragment to dust within a meter from twist rate."

Alex said, "So someone was instigating a riot for the purpose of getting police brutality involved."

"Have you seen the alleged wounds? Quite a few are self-inflicted. The cops were not gentle, but they didn't do some of the stuff we've seen. There are razor slashes, bruises, chemical burns and the latter two had to be done ahead of time. So some group of masochists showed up with the intent of getting roughed up."

Alex said, "We have the twofold problem of protecting Ms. Highland and not reacting in a fashion that can cause bad publicity when any attack might be real. That could easily have been real bullets. The odds of a hit are remote like that, but obviously the threat of worse exists."

Das said, "She refuses to allow us to scan the crowds. Cultural sensitivity issues to their religious beliefs."

She also may be hiding further instigations for PR, but this probably wasn't one, because it backfired if so, he thought. "It's also not practical to search that many people when she wants a large crowd, and it would work against her stated policies, and the diplomatic issues. Of course, ideally she'd do everything only inside this compound surrounded by us. In the real world, however, she has to meet people."

Das nodded back. "Well, I have to both investigate these, attempt to prevent them, and and try to get the locals to work with us. That's more than a 'both.'"

"I appreciate the information, Captain. We'll do our own digging."

Back at their quarters, the team discussed the updates, with drinks and snacks at hand.

Jason said, "We have her admission of instigation action for PR purposes. She knows we disapprove. We'd also play along, but it's better if we're deniable. 'Better' from her point of view, of course. So that's one element that won't directly be a real threat, but could be infiltrated." In front of him was a timeline and chart of events they'd dealt with.

Alex said, "There are just too many factions. It could be her own employees' union. Unlikely, but possible. There are three factions here who could afford those pros, who apparently weren't that pro. Skilled wannabes."

Aramis said, "There are enough groups who outright hate her. Some of the religious factions have declared moral war based on her visible support of Cady, and the rumors of her being gay."

Alex said, "Yes, and Cady knows the score and is holding up. She's more of a pawn than we are."

Elke said, "I would assume that the actual hostiles will try very hard to get into her confidences, and would find out about the staged attacks. They'll try to use those as cover."

"Yes," Alex said. "Which is why I want Aramis to keep treating

210 *Michael Z. Williamson*

every threat like an invasion force and responding with violence. It will have a deterrent effect."

The man grinned and said, "I cherish my role as a preemptive violence technician." He grabbed a handful of cookies and started munching. He seemed to be recovering well.

Jason said, "Yeah, it keeps her safer and us safer. Nail any and all threats first, then ask questions if there's anyone left."

Bart said, "So we have friendly idiots, and unfriendly schemers who will make use of them. What about other groups?"

Shaman said, "I've seen some of this before. You must understand now you will never get inside information from the groups, especially as to how they ally. But, they will attack her so they can blame another group, or to claim credit and show their mettle. They'll do so against her influence, or Earth's influence, or because they don't like some group she spoke with. That glove of hers was nauseating, but brilliant, I'm ashamed to say." He slumped a bit and reached for his tea.

Elke said, "So any group who hates any other group might attack her for or against them."

"If they think the cops will rough up their competition, yes. Then there are the gangs and their smuggling operations." Alex sighed.

Aramis said, "Translation: no chart we can put together is going to help."

"The idiotic thing," Shaman said through tight lips with a tense face, "is that many of these groups had these same petty squabbles on Earth, and moved here to separate, but all moved here. Then they found the planet isn't as conducive as they'd hoped, and are all stuck here in the temperate zone on one continent."

"What is our approach, then?" Bart asked.

Jason said, "Attack all threats; try to coordinate with Das for intel from interrogations. If we can catch a live one without undue breakage, we ask the best questions we can then turn them in, undamaged, for the military to question further."

"We can monitor residue," Elke said. "Also, some of these incidents might take money. We can narrow down the focus on which groups would be willing to spend it, and have it available."

"I want to follow up on her 'dear friends' and 'former employees.'

They might have reason to hate her, or might be plants. Or just suborned, as happened with Caron and her servants."

"That's the ongoing problem in this business. We can keep someone safe locked in our dungeon with no contact. Beyond that, there are threats."

Bart said, "I would also watch current events. Any large swings in the economy, or to any nations or groups, will affect her presence."

"This is why BuState has its own security and its own intel."

Aramis asked, "How is the intel from intelguy? Any good?"

"It's not bad, but not great. I don't know if that's par for the course, par for him, incompetence, brilliance or deceit. We're getting more from Das. Obviously, though, that's directly military."

"And her friend?"

"Yes, I will have to talk to her about him. Let me cue up standard spiel about how enemies may use friends for intel."

"Do you think that's going to work?"

"No, but I am required to try."

He pinged a link to Jessie's private line.

"JessieM."

"Miss Jessie, it's Agent Marlow."

"Yes, sir, how may I help you?"

"I need to discuss a communication security matter with Ms. Highland. It should be in person, at her convenience."

"Stand by, please."

It was only a few moments before she came back on. "Ms. Highland says she can see you now."

"Thanks, I'll be right over."

Cady's people checked him in, and she was waiting at the desk she'd had installed in her parlor. Really, he wished she'd stop with the fake smile. Though it was probably both automatic and a matter of constant practice for her.

"Chief Marlow, what can I do for you?"

"Thanks for seeing me on short notice, ma'am. This is a secondary security concern, regarding communications."

"Should Jessie be here for this, too?"

"She can be, but it's not a technical concern."

"Go ahead, then, what do you have?"

"This concerns Mr. Huble."

"You can't be serious!" she said with a half laugh, half protest.

"I have no reason to suspect him directly," he said, to get that in there. "The concern is that any consistent, predictable communication outside can be compromised, either en route or at the far end."

"We use PrivatProtocol."

"I'm told that's very good. I also know it can be compromised. That's the first concern."

"There's more?" She seemed derisively amused, which wasn't the worst possible response, but certainly not good.

"Mr. Blanding is connected to certain groups that would enjoy information about you."

She laughed more nervously. "He would never offer information like that."

"I wouldn't suggest so, without knowing him. But, it's entirely possible for someone to look for messages from you to him, and crack those. Especially while you are here."

She looked thoughtful. "But it's encrypted . . ."

"Anything can be cracked. Then, there's what's called traffic analysis. Knowing the volume and timing of messages offers keys, as does the sender and recipient."

"I could send a lot more messages, about inane matters."

"That is an excellent idea," he said. It was a partial win against other threats, but it all helped. Deescalate one threat enough, you could focus on others.

He concluded with, "Do please add as much variety and randomness to those communiqués as possible. That will help all over."

Meanwhile, he had another PR meeting to prepare for.

Elke's position was that interaction with locals was always problematic. Factions made it worse. She hadn't considered this day's mission could top all that. They were flying to the event, which she was never very much in favor of. She liked control, and flying meant surrendering control to someone else.

In this case, the pilot was a local, of one of the factions.

Elke never screamed. She did, however, get roiling guts and sweats, and this did it.

They boarded at the military field, around Highland, into the cabin of a Emirates Aircraft EA6 Djinn. That was a so-so aircraft at best, outdated and at least half-used up, if it was here, and now piloted by a local.

She did everything as required, watching her sector, keeping position and distance from Highland, and putting a visual void over that aircraft.

Once aboard, she took a seat facing aft, fastened her restraints and donned helmet. She made a cursory visual check for any threats, then gave her attention to her sniffers and scanners. Jason would check also, and the military had done so when it landed. It was also politically inadvisable for their host to stage an attack, so he'd have made his own checks. Between them, the only threat that should remain was pilot error and shoddy maintenance. She shivered again.

Alex had a familiar expression on his face, and was looking at Jason. Jason gave a nod and a thumbs up. She translated in her mind.

If need be, can you toss this yokel out the hatch and land us intact?

Yes, no problem.

Somehow it didn't reassure her.

"Intercom check. Playwright."

"Argonaut."

"Julien."

"Babs," she said in turn.

"Pirate."

"Musketeer."

"Witch and Black Cat accounted for. Pilot reports ready to lift."

And they did, as Elke stared straight at the bulkhead.

Ten minutes into the flight she unfastened two suit buttons for ventilation. It was crowded and warm, faintly chemical, and not in the sweet way Comp G smelled, and the vibration hit a frequency that irritated her bladder and stomach. She was glad she'd not eaten or drunk yet today.

"A bit turbulent," Jason said.

It was more than a bit, in her view. Of course, she didn't like heights, altitude or movement anyway. The engine tone shifted periodically. That was perfectly normal, she knew intellectually. It still made her flinch.

It was only five minutes later that Alex announced, "Landing." Though it took over 200 seconds to make the approach, gauge the winds and reflections, and put the beast down.

They were in a large compound ringed with low, but multiple walls and fences at comfortable distances, each in overlapping fields of fire. She could even draw the range markers. At least someone here understood basic tactics. Now as long as they respected Highland, or Ripple Creek, enough to not start trouble.

Bart and Aramis debarked first, she was last, being female and not the principal. She knew some women who'd be incensed over that. It was Alex's order, and how things were done here, so she did it.

The Most Beneficent Mohammed Saliman al-Khazra actually greeted Highland in person. His own entourage was clearly a factotum and six guards in silly uniforms, with pompoms on their boots, pointy hats with neck cloths, and pink piping on white tunics and shorts. At that, it was better camouflage than the army issued.

He even spoke respectable English.

"Madam Minister, you grace my humble abode with your presence," he said with a nod that wasn't quite a bow, combined with an extended hand.

Highland reached between Bart and Aramis, who stepped obliquely back.

"Effendi, I greet you."

With that in progress, Elke eyed their opposites, who were probably very respectable infantry, from the gear and muscles under those ridiculous outfits. She had no doubt that if Bart and Aramis couldn't smash four of them, Jason could drop the rest with one bullet each, and she could shred their legs with a disc explosive.

Shortly, all the guards sat in a ring, six on each side, sipping from sealed bottles of juice, while the two politicians and their aids sat at a table and chatted, under a hush hood, over a doc screen. Elke's only significant activity was to escort Highland and JessieM to the toilet, and take a turn herself, while Aramis and Shaman stood guard outside.

After that, it was another grueling flight back. She'd rather have a firefight than a decrepit aircraft, but at least it was objectively brief, even if it felt like hours.

Alex appreciated the casual event. If only more could be like that, but then of course, they'd not be employed.

Nothing. Not even a handful of protesters with signs outside the gate, and it was obvious who'd be on that flight, given its departure point.

In several ways, that was more disturbing than the violence. It implied both an outside agent, and that a single one, or one that had significant influence over the others.

The pattern continued.

Tuesday was a summit on "Environmental Compassion" at the conference center. That afternoon, they met with interest groups to answer questions. Highland spoke like a politician, and gave vague answers. She was professionally competent at raising morale and causing smiles, though how long those lasted after the event he couldn't gauge.

Wednesday was a forum debate in the National Parliament, which all groups sent representatives to, but it seemed to be a contest to see who could send the least important flunky with the most impressive name.

After a week with no threats, Alex was more disturbed than ever.

"It's an indication of something, but what?"

The team was in their armory, being the most secure room. He had a chart up on their secure system, showing the events, locations and which groups were involved, incidents, her running popularity figures, and whether or not they'd had military support. They gathered around in an arc. This was a war council.

Elke said, "Her popularity increased after each unsuccessful attack."

"Yes, which makes me anticipate a successful one."

Aramis said, "That, or obscurity as a tactic."

From behind a tall glass of raspberry juice, Bart said, "Have her supporters also reduced their actions? There have been no low-level attacks as they do. Those boost her popularity."

"They ran out of money," Aramis said.

Jason said, "No, I suspect collusion."

"Sure, but how?"

"Okay, let's go through it. She's arranged some low-level harassment for PR. Some of her fans picked up on the riff. She's refused to coordinate that with us, but gets upset at our response. She may have asked them to back off, fearing we'd actually kill someone. Again."

"Yes," Alex said. "Her conflict was between coverage for bravery and headlines, and the risk of us being stuck to her."

"But she managed to stick us on Cruk."

"Right. So she was benefiting anyway."

"Which suggests her random fanbody activist attacks were coordinated by one of her people."

Elke said, "It would make sense. They all had the same goal in mind, and were all relatively low-scale, and similar. Random attacks with nonlethal stuff."

Aramis said, "And this recent attack, again, not enough to be lethal, but certainly to look so."

"That's aimed at us," Jason said. "They want us to overreact, to try to bring her ratings down. So that is hostile activity, not propagandist."

"Hostile against us, but dialed back against her," Bart commented.

"Yes," Jason agreed, looking thoughtful. "So, all her propaganda seems to have one source. Attacks against us seem to be a second."

Alex said, "Which leaves the rioting that increased, then stopped suddenly."

Aramis said, "Hostile attempt to either intimidate her, or provoke over-reaction from us—meaning overreaction from a press perspective, not reality."

Jason said, "I understood you. So that's a possible third source."

Alex said, "Which leaves a potential fourth aspect or source, if ignoring her doesn't lower her popularity, which it seems to not be doing."

"You expect a bonafide professional hit."

"That's why we're hired. Someone is spending a lot of money on us, from both her campaign and the administration, to keep her away from her regular security. Part of that is political. She can't use them while campaigning. But they're splitting the cost due to some accounting method. So who insisted on us?"

Jason said, "It comes back to Huble, her adviser."

"Is it that simple? He's a plant trying to drag her down?"

"I'd say all the promotional attacks are through him."

"So why wouldn't he tell her of the others?"

It was Bart who said, "Because they're intended as intimidation against her. They're more embarrassing, less heroic, and act to work against her campaign."

"He's a double agent then. Strong suspect. But so far, nonlethal."

Elke pondered, "The administration runs him? They get benefit in close, and intel. Which explains how he can have the inside information, and manipulate her."

Aramis said, "Wait, she orchestrated some propaganda against Hunter, yes?"

"Yes."

"And Cruk likewise benefits from that, out of her campaign, without anything attachable to him."

Jason said, "So he backs off to let her wreck the opposition, and himself."

Alex said, "That all adds up. So the attacks aimed at us are likely from the left—factions who want us out of the way. No logical reason, they just hate us generally."

Elke said, "They hate anything with a profit motive. Wars are bad, if for assets, like Salin. But this war is pure and clean and ideological, for peace, except for filthy mercenaries like us."

"If they hurt some of us, they win. If they get us sanctioned, they win."

"Are we ruling out local threats?"

Alex chuckled. "No, I suspect every faction here would like to take us out. We're either filthy mercs, or guards of the harlot, or poisoning her purity."

Elke asked, "And attacks against her?"

"Amala definitely, when they have the money and capability. They will continue to be third raters. Sufis don't like her, but aren't antagonistic to us other than we're her shield. They've hired their own contractors at times. Shia hate her guts. The Faithful whatever Christians hate her for talking to Muslims."

Aramis said, "You know, I was disgusted that she wore a glove to shake hands with Bawani. But that gave her some deniable distance from the Muslims."

"She still had a riot outside."

"Yes, and that's just par for this place. We'll go crazy trying to sort that out, then it will change."

"So, unscripted local attacks, scripted harassment for PR and intimidation, from the administration. Attacks against us by opposition to hurt us and discredit her, and potential nuke if and when they decide she's too popular."

"The result of that is a wave of sympathy for the incumbent who's worked so hard, and the party, and without any internal opposition, he goes up five to ten points and wins regardless of any issues."

Bart asked, "When do we need to pull her out?"

Aramis snickered. "The question is 'can we without tranking her?'"

"I am prepared either way," Shaman said, with a nod to his medical pack.

"So, we watch the news, her ratings, major events, and gauge the ongoing lack of attacks and any resumption."

Alex said, "I assume we're past this stage. The next attack will be a killer."

⚙ CHAPTER 18 ⚙

JOY HIGHLAND HATED THIS PLANET. It had little scenery anywhere inhabited, lots of savage religious nuts whom she had to publicly pretend to respect, was far too distant from her campaign, and she was saddled with too few staff and too many bloodthirsty mercenaries, especially that bitch Sykora, who wouldn't shut up about "her" explosives.

Now they were questioning her friends and communication. She'd smiled and laughed, but the sheer gall of that man. Marlow's job was to stop threats, not intrude on her private life.

Which brought up the question of how he'd found that out anyway. Had they been cracking her communications? PrivatProtocol was one of the best encryptions out there, updated weekly, and she used a nineteen-digit key. The key was secure, unless someone knew as much about twenty-second-century beers and twenty-third-century legal decisions. Though there were ways to derive keys, of course.

She did send extraneous messages to Huble, but she had to keep real communication up, too.

Dear Damon, I'm about to head out to the Peace Wall dedication. Thanks for arranging this. It's visibility I can use, and presents as both official and campaign. The military didn't even twitch, just authorized the escort. So I will make sure to use it to best effect. Thanks, dear.

That done, she checked on Jessie.

"How are we looking?"

Jessie damped her screens and looked through the transparencies

219

at Joy. "Ma'am, things are trending well, though the violence actually boosted your headlines and perception. It's leveled off. You're still fifteen points behind Cruk, but that's up from thirty behind, and we've not yet had the official challenge statement."

"Yes, once I announce there's an alternative, the no-confidence people will pile on him. But we're stagnant, still?"

"Not stagnant, but the curve has flattened. It's still positive, though."

"And if the economy is in a state, I can blame him, using Ripple Creek as an example, when I have perfectly good escorts available from the military and BuState."

"That seems to be the way to play it, ma'am." Jessie almost never smiled. She was strictly business, though relaxed and not stiff.

"So let's get out on the road. If we're early, we can stop and talk to people on the way, and put a soft face on some of this military stuff. That might deescalate things, and of course I'll claim credit if it does."

Bart sweated in suit over armor in hot sun. It might be dim, but they orbited closer and the heat built up over time. Add in the clothing and it was uncomfortable. He could ignore the talking, and the slowness, but not the environment. Eventually, it became uncomfortable, and it was there now.

Ripple Creek got these jobs because someone or someones wanted to kill the principal. They didn't have to like the principal, though that was never a bad thing. It did help to have some empathy for the person for whom you contracted to jump in front of a bullet. However, in this case, none of them could claim to be a fan of Highland, and little about her gave them reason to change their positions.

That didn't make the job harder of itself, but it made it unpleasant at times. On the other hand, empathy with the enemy did make it easier to counter some threats.

She is very brave with us, Bart thought. The woman kept making appearances, despite the threats, and yes, it seemed to help her political popularity. He didn't like her, but she could manipulate. Anything that happened she pushed to her own advantage. She would probably make a competent SecGen in that regard.

This memorial, though, was a wall. It was low at present, would be ten meters tall when finished, and a featureless extrusion. It was being sold as a fence between neighbors, but it was a wall. He wasn't keen on standing against it, either. She had her mic and the cameras. They had Elke and Anderson behind the camera crew, Marlow and Vaughn on either side, he and Mbuto just barely in view, with glasses and hats to provide a little concealment, though Bart still felt very exposed in all ways. Outside of their line were some Marines, who had armor and helmets and were in much better kit for combat, even if their weapons weren't lethal. That, and the awful camouflage that would almost blend in with some of the rubbish and graffiti. He was amused.

It was one of the hazards of the job, wearing a marginally reinforced suit and hoping nothing big enough to defeat it came in. On the other hand, Marlow and Vaughn were even farther in and more exposed, if someone decided to go for the principal. Or if a riot started, as had been known to happen.

Highland at least had a good speech writer, and was a decent presenter. If Bart could appreciate it through the language barrier, it must be effective in English.

". . . we should not see this as a wall dividing people, but as a joint effort in architecture, an agreement on boundaries, from which we can move forward . . ."

Something fell, and his mind said it was tossed from over the wall. His glasses flashed a trajectory, but it was hand tossed, not projected. The laser hadn't stopped it because it was not a balloon, too massive. It was a real threat.

Bart stared down. It was a grenade, equidistant between Highland and himself. He was going to die, unless . . .

The Marine on his left outside was a head shorter, and in reach. Bart grabbed the pull handle on the front of the man's armor, swung and threw while jumping. In his peripheral vision, he saw Jason and Alex hurl Highland right and rear.

The Marine landed on his back on the grenade, there was a crash . . .

. . . and Bart woke up in hospital.

It seems I survived, he thought to himself.

He did a quick check. He could feel all his limbs, and feel the pressure of the bed and sheets against them, so nothing was missing. His entire body burned and stung, but it all seemed to be functional. He was thirsty and hungry. A glance at the monitor proved his neck still worked, and that his vital signs were normal.

Alex said, "Well done." He sat across the room on a chair. He rose and approached. Mbuto was with him.

"Is everyone okay?" Bart asked. Then he said in English, "Is everyone okay?"

Alex smiled and nodded. "Everyone is fine. That was inspired. You got the kid over the grenade and his back plate damped the blast into the ground. He took a little grazing frag to feet and scalp, as it rattled through his helmet, and severe bruising as he landed. You both went about four meters straight up."

Mbuto said, "You're stung and flash burned but intact and in observation. They let the sedative wear off because there's nothing wrong with you beyond the stun. Not even a severe concussion."

It confused him for a moment when the talking continued, and he realized it was Alex again. He looked that way.

Alex said, "I'm reporting it up the chain because it was brilliant. We couldn't have run far enough, had no cover to dive behind, and you got that Marine over it in under a second. Everyone survived with no more than minor scrapes, Highland has a heroic story for her followers, and we're all alive. Thanks for saving my life, and everyone else's." He extended a hand.

Bart took it carefully, shook, and glanced around as well as his position allowed. He made sure they were alone, and whispered, "Alex, I didn't know he had a back plate."

Marlow's eyebrows flared slightly. Mbuto choked back a laugh.

"Yeah, we probably shouldn't mention that," he said.

Alex left the clinic in a bit of shock. Certainly, they knew there was a risk of casualties. Aramis had taken fire before, and Elke had an arm beat up pretty bad in a fight. They'd risked toxic atmosphere, been too close to explosions, and of course, been shot at any number of times, as well as being gassed with everything from irritants to incapacitants. But this was the first time he'd had two men down in a mission. Aramis was lucky to be alive, and so was Bart, really.

But that paled next to what Bart had just admitted. Yes, it was their job to save the principal. Yes, they'd do whatever it took to accomplish that. But had Bart actually admitted to using an allied troop as a meat shield? Had the man died, there'd be hell to pay. Though perhaps he thought it would get spun as heroism on the Marine's part. Or perhaps Highland would spin it as an attack on her greatness and it would all get lost in the howling.

Otherwise, Bart was a callous, calculating killer. Jokes aside, he wasn't sure if he wanted that trait among his people.

Still, they were all unhurt, the principal was unharmed, and the worst case would have been one dead Marine.

The math still bothered him.

Maybe it should.

For now, he'd assume tactical brilliance on Bart's part, and quick thinking over callousness.

As they went out into ruddy overcast, Shaman seemed to pick up on the thought.

"There isn't time to be more than practical, sometimes."

"It's better than the alternative," he said.

As he entered their quarters, everyone came through and looked up, including Cady.

Shaman said, "He's fine. They'll release him tomorrow."

Aramis asked, "And the Marine?"

"Yes, he's a little worse for wear, but all superficial."

Jason said, "Report on Highland: hearing loss, almost certainly temporary, minor disorientation, no gratitude."

"Of course. And JessieM? The frag?"

Shaman said, "It was a thrown pebble. Easily extracted with ultrasound and vacuum. The bone was treated with Ossifix. Next time she should wear boots."

"Good all around, then."

Aramis said, "And we were correct on the lethal escalation."

"Yes. But, we still don't know either the local actor or the power behind it. I'd like at least one."

Cady said, "They're conducting an investigation to try to find the local. It was a hand grenade, but thrown from a rifle with a blank cartridge, so they have that to work with."

"Archaic," he frowned. "And someone who was good at ballistics.

That does narrow it down, if they have any leads on who fits those criteria."

Elke said, "Highland asked me personal questions about fitting armor to her figure. So she'll be better protected after this."

Jason said, "And she'll blab that to the press to show how brave she is, so the next real threat knows they need a bigger bomb or a sniper."

Elke said, "That's my assessment also."

Cady asked, "Did you get the news load?"

"No."

"Stand by." She cycled her phone and slid up the volume.

". . . Ms. Highland's popularity is reaching giddy proportions as she fearlessly tackles Mtali. What started as a summit meeting has become a classic battle of courage that hints of a great strength of character. Could this be a hint of executive power?"

She turned off the feed.

Jason shrugged. "Like it or not, we're helping her career."

Aramis said, "She's helping her career. She could bow out any time. We're just the muscle."

"It seems like we do more than that."

Alex shouldn't be frustrated by now, but it happened with boring regularity. "Yes, we get blown up and abused, and blamed for it because we were asking for it, by protecting the target. But if we let her down, we'll get blamed for that, too."

Aramis said, "I do love the size of those checks, though."

Jason said, "So do I, but there are easier taskings, and I can roll this experience into those, and my land is paid for. Nor am I young anymore."

Aramis said, "Hell, I'm not young after that."

Jason looked serious again as he said, "I'm glad we got you, brother."

Alex said, "Are we concluding three threats?"

"I think so," Jason said. "One seeking harassment. The MO was different on the ones she staged. One is seeking to kill her as efficiently as possible, and one is very sophisticated, still largely not identified."

Alex sighed. "Well, we're going to earn our pay from here out."

⊚ CHAPTER 19 ⊚

A LIMO WAS NOT JASON'S PREFERRED VEHICLE, even for a trip to the Colonial Liaison Office. Anymore, he wanted the ARPAC every time, even if it was less comfortable.

Highland's visit covered personal business relative to the election, making official interviews with several press outfits. They weren't allowed in any military or BuState location, and Alex had refused to certify any private location. The CLO was acceptable to everyone, so all that remained was to track the mileage and time for charging back to her campaign. How many accountants did it take to do all this?

They were out in a light but chill rain, on their way back. The trip out wasn't eventful, but that wasn't unexpected. The trip back was when everyone would have had time to learn her location, set up OPs and be in position for anything.

Highland and Jessie actually talked in front of them at this point. Though of course, the limo was quieter than the ARPAC.

"So, just about thirty percent, with Cruk down to forty-eight, Hunter at ten and I'm not even going to dignify the rest with recognition," she said.

Jessie said, "One of the trends has you at thirty-two by week's end."

"I can call in at once then," she said, "or give it time to stabilize and for the public to demand so."

"I like that better," Jessie said. "You respond to the electorate."

"Yes. We'll need to leak it. Can you do that," she looked up at

Jason, who kept looking out the window, "through one of your secondary feeds?"

"Of course! Angela DuMont is an ardent supporter."

Jason wondered when Special Service took over. At some point, a candidate becomes "viable" and protection was extended to them. That should be soon.

Right then Bart braked hard and swerved slightly.

Jason looked forward in a hurry. Alex was shotgun, but he wanted eyes on target. There were three men blocking the street after apparently having jumped out in the rain. He watched as the leftmost one disappeared under the limo.

Bart swore, swerved and braked, though he was taught not to. He was also under orders to protect the stupid to some extent.

The man went under the front of the limo in a double thump, then a bump, and a rev of lost traction.

Highland asked, "What was that?"

Bart said, "The wheelspin? Probably his face. Brains are pretty slippery."

In the rear inside screen, Highland gagged and Jason grinned. Bart kept his smile very tight.

Jason said, "I really don't like limos and this is why. We're obvious as a stripper in church, but not as armored as we should be. Firing angles are limited."

The car accelerated quickly, and Bart wove between vehicles, first with wide margins, then with near misses, then close enough to catch on protruding edges. Brushing scrapes sounded every few seconds.

Highland screeched, "Slow down! Each of those hits is a vote lost and money that will have to be paid out!"

Bart ignored her totally. His job was to move and maneuver. He took a turn and kept going. He slowed a little, scanning the rear to see if there was pursuit. Alex caught his eye, but gave no indication of objection. He kept driving.

He felt the rumble, then heard it. He kept his eyes ahead, but let them draw images from the screens.

They were being chased by a tank.

More accurately, it appeared to be an old Mod 46 Assault

Vehicle, with the articulated plate wheels, but as he was driving a car, that was effectively a tank.

WHAM!

Especially with the 35mm gun on top. He leaned into an evasive turn as the shock wave and projectile cracked overhead.

Alex shouted, "Aramis, up top, target the mechanicals! Elke, we need a disabler! Jason, do we have any rockets?"

"On it."

"Working."

"No, BuState operations refused to allow it."

Alex replied, "Then snipe the vision ports."

"When I can."

The passengers said nothing, just whimpered a bit. He couldn't blame them. Bart accelerated right to the intersection ahead, then brake-turned hard into it. The AV had to scrape to a stop on the pavement, pivot and resume. That slowed it a lot, but Bart had pedestrians and cluttered traffic to deal with. He'd run someone over if he had to, but he'd rather not have to.

Out the roof, Aramis hammered away with the autocannon. It was a big enough gun to need actual cases, and they clattered over the shell of the car, a few bounced inside to ping against each other.

"I'm not going to do anything to him with this," Aramis said. "The armor's too heavy."

Bart took them between two cars, scraping and bumping both aside. Pedestrians jumped, screamed and cursed, but the shrieks spread the message to others, who cleared the route. Except, of course, for rubberneckers. Two, just ahead.

He leaned on the siren, and one jumped back. The other craned in closer, then stood defiantly, and finally jumped, as the car clipped him.

Behind, a car moved to fill the gap in traffic, the driver oblivious, and the AV rolled right over it. Plastic splintered and crushed, and the driver's arm thrashed out the window before hanging limply from the wreckage.

Someone really wanted the bitch dead.

Elke said, "There will be collaterals."

"There already are. The AV is crushing its way."

Alex said, "Do it."

"Aramis, take this and hit the driver compartment."

"Got it," he said, hefted it for weight and stood.

"Fire in the hole," she said in a lovely voice, as Aramis stood and threw.

It was one of her rugby-ball things. Bart watched it arc back in a perfect spiral, impact right over the compartment, and erupt. If he guessed right, it squashed enough to be a platter charge, and shattered the hatch.

The AV veered to the left, high-centered over another car, and stopped.

Alex said, "Keep moving, evade and evacuate this area."

"Rolling," he agreed, the tension in him easing a little. There were more bodies to deal with now.

Alex said, "Good thing we're on our way home."

Aramis said, "The events seem to be providing intel to people, and it's usually prescheduled events."

Alex said, "Discuss later. Roll, eyes open." He sounded forceful.

"Rolling," Bart reiterated.

Behind, Alex spoke into his phone. "Captain Das, we were attacked by what looks like a Mod 46 . . . Yes, I am serious. Driver tried to run us down, ran over several civilian vehicles and pedestrians in the meantime . . . that's about our grid, so yes, that would be it . . . You should move fast. There could be evidence and we don't want it to go missing. Excellent. Sorry to bear bad news. Marlow out."

Jason wasn't sure if he wanted to keep doing this. At some level, people should figure out Ripple Creek would stomp on any opposition. But, they kept getting bigger, more dangerous taskings. There wasn't much room for error.

Alex was tied up with lawyers, BuState, the military and the ambassador.

It was interesting that the ambassador had no problems with them. He was technically under Highland, and then under the SecGen. His word would have them off planet at once. But either Highland wanted them for deniable cover, or she approved, or the SecGen was insisting they stay there.

Was her boss worried about her, worried about what would happen if she died, or trying to embarrass her?

That was one set of questions of many.

Two minutes later, Alex burst into the suite with Das.

"Jackpot," he said.

"Yes?"

"Got this from the remains of the driver that Elke and Aramis liquefied." He held up an armored data stick.

Jason took it carefully. It appeared to be intact.

"Anything on it you've found?"

"Just the arrival time written on the outside."

"Yeah, that narrows it down to a few people. Let's see what's on it."

"I'll help," Elke said.

"Absolutely."

He stuck it into his system, let Elke remote in, and they went at it.

Everyone stared at them, but in a few minutes, Elke snorted in disgust and said, "This isn't even grammar school encryption."

"No?" prompted Aramis.

"Oh, some of the files are better than others, but I'm getting partial hits already. Sloppy."

"Here's tables," Jason said.

"Not just tables," Elke said in wonder. "Let me throw this up. Hold on."

A moment later an image scrolled on the screens.

Jason said, "Wow."

Alex agreed, "Wow."

Jason pointed with a finger. "This actually has her movements, all past, known future, and a grid. It has summaries of ranges and timeframes. I can't think of any way to look at this except as intent to assassinate."

Alex said, "Okay. Elke?"

"I concur. There's no other way to consider it. This graph is drawn up as a predictive syllogism. When they fill in one of these boxes, they can move to be in the same place and get a free shot, and likely not even hurt us in the process."

"Yeah, that would eliminate her and destroy us professionally. We've never lost one. But lose the wrong one . . ."

"Or," Elke muttered, "if they miss her, they can try for us."

"That depends. Do they want to embarrass us or kill us?"

"Some would go for either."

Alex held up a hand, and said, "Captain Das, I need to politely evict you at this point. Elke, cut him a copy of the stick."

Das said, "I really need to take the original."

"I know you do, sir, but we need to cover our legal ass. I'm holding onto it. Do please file with your legal office. That will help track its existence, and then we can let you have it in a day or so."

Das looked uncomfortable.

"I officially have to refuse your request, take it with me, and I'm afraid I can't leave without it." He looked sad, stubborn and irritated.

"I understand your position perfectly, sir," Alex said. "Bart, carefully throw him out." He clicked his phone. "Cady, Captain Das must be escorted off the premises. Gently."

Das let Bart drag him to the door and shove him into the waiting arms of two of the Facilities detail.

Once it was closed and Bart sat back down, Elke and Jason both ran scans again, nodded, and continued.

Jason said, "The point is, this is clear evidence of a current lethal threat, in process, against our principal, at any event off this installation or not in a facility we control. Even on the latter, I'd be wary."

"Yes. So we need to pull the plug."

"Where? We can't take her back to Earth. That's obviously a nonstarter. She won't hear it, and any threat will be ready for it. We can't hide out until the election's over."

"Can we hide out until she can't win?"

Shaman said, "That would mean entire days. We'd have to kidnap her. In which case, we face criminal charges ourselves, and of course, that would boost her popularity, in which case they'd want to arrange an Elke-sized accident for her."

"So what options do we have? Face known threats? Admit we know about the threats and hope to evade them, with the added danger of them knowing our awareness?"

Aramis said, "I have a suggestion, but it's extreme."

"So are the circumstances. Go."

"We take her, skip out, leave some hints, make some calls, and try to orchestrate everyone to dogpile. Once they're all coming down on us, we take out the internal threats, evade the minor ones, and return here triumphantly."

Jason said, "Hell, man, that gives her the election." Is that what they had to do?

Bart said, "That is what her opponents are trying to stop."

"True."

Elke said, "It also exposes us to a lot of fire."

Alex looked at her and replied, "If we pursue that tactic, you may of course use all the explosive you need."

She smiled faintly. "Then I approve of it."

Jason said, "Do we need to move now? Let's get this clear."

Alex pulled up a connection.

"Cady here."

"Jace, Alex. Come down. We need advice and may need backup."

"Arriving."

She was at the door thirty seconds later.

Once it was closed, Alex said, "We're discussing Plan E." *Evasion.*

Jason said, "So, this Huble character is a friend of hers. He knows all her official movements, and he knows some of the campaign ones, but not the most random ones."

"The random ones get nuisance attacks. The scheduled ones get more serious attacks."

Cady said, "That is to be expected anyway." She seated herself on the edge of a table.

"Yes, but these are significant attacks, escalating. They're not massive enough to take her out, but are major enough to provoke a response from us."

"Embarrassment?"

Alex said, "It fits. And Huble is a known bastard. This is not a surprise."

"But he's in her party," Cady observed, and stared at her fingers.

"And she's a questionable candidate—it's very up in the air as to who might win, and she's got a lot of baggage. But Cruk has little background. That means no dirt as well, and he's photogenic and a good speaker, and has the incumbent edge."

"You think they're trying to off her to push him?"

"Sympathy vote. Remember Champion died in a ship crash a

decade ago, and his son took the vote? Reginald, the son, was trailing by thirty points, but sympathy and a clean slate pushed him over the top."

"So you think they're deliberately looking for that?"

Aramis said, "It fits. She's talking to a friend and relaying her movements, and they have that damned JessieM for fire correction once they're close."

Alex said, "I think they're trying to either get a lucky kill or cause us to hurt her and ourselves politically."

Jason said, "And they get to try to blame us if they set it up right, or at least decry our 'incompetence.' Or even eliminate us in the process, if they get lucky enough."

Bart asked, "Do you think any of our past enemies are involved?"

Alex said, "Who knows? There are so many. None of them would mourn us. Would many of them invest money or time in it? Likely not. It's bad for existing business. A couple of them are completely out of the field, too, and not players."

Alex sighed.

Shaman spoke up. "The problem is, we aren't investigators and have limited resources. We can't depose anyone or go digging too deeply. So we're doing this based on available raw intelligence and our own problem-solving ability. We're good, but this is not our field. What we need to stick to is how urgent and significant we think a threat is, and go from there."

That was a clear summation.

Jason said, "It's clear the threats and tactics are escalating. It's not a case of if they'll reach critical, but when. We need to pull her out before then." He stared at the screened charts, hoping for enlightenment.

Bart said, "I'd do so now. It registers as unholdable. What is the word?"

"Untenable," Aramis said. "Whether or not we can, I agree we certainly should. I have my own reasons, of course." His jaw clenched as he spoke.

Shaman asked, "What else can we tell, though? Who? Who have they hired?"

Jason said, "They're increasingly good. My guess is they're not amateurs, but are playing it. An obvious pro hit would be bad. An accident or faction split would be beneficial to the campaign."

Aramis said, "Wait, there could be some interest in a faction, too."

Alex nodded. "Yes, but I don't think we have time to figure out all those connections. We should try, of course, but that's secondary to the power behind it."

"Still, they escalate until they succeed, and blame whichever group is nearest, most likely, most interested at that moment, had a previous interest, doesn't really matter."

Elke said, "They are going to try to take us out, too. They can either then play the 'We're all allies' card or the 'mercenary bastards had it coming' card. Which means they'll be better placed for any followup against her."

Cady offered, "They might also try for us as a secondary target, getting them closer to her."

Alex grinned. "That sounds almost vid. Would any of their people trust them?"

"They'd bring in second stringers," Aramis said. "Other agents borrowed under the exigencies of the situation, from some bureau they don't like as well."

Jason remembered something from a year past and said, "Like the Nutrition and Medication people caught in that payoff scandal."

Alex sounded unimpressed. "That would almost be obvious."

Aramis shrugged. "Not to the typical vid watcher."

"Yeah, I think you're right. But it doesn't matter who at this point. They're not our concern, and in that particular case, the bastards have it coming."

Cady said, "Right. Our concern is keeping us alive, her alive, and disabling their attack. That's all tied for first. Anything else is second."

Shaman said, "Assuming we do positively ID the threat, we cannot tell her. Nor discuss it meantime. Between her and her friend, and JessieM, we might as well flash a bulletin to the enemy directly."

"Concur."

"So we're going to string along until almost the last minute, and try to bail before the hit happens, close enough that the attempt is made so we're proven right."

Elke said, "What could possibly go wrong?"

Alex said, "She'll refuse to believe me. I'll put fifty on it."

"No bet," she said, sounding sad.

⦿ CHAPTER 20 ⦿

ALEX WAS QUITE SURE his logical appeals to Highland would be a waste of time, but he was required to make an attempt. He looked at Cady.

"Highland is probably going to resist the idea. I'll need backup from you later. For now, I need you to let us go."

Cady said, "It would be better if you didn't tell me this and just did it. But I understand. I'll delay my people as long as possible. I'll prep for interception later. Are we telling Corporate?"

"Eventually, by coded message. The one I sent today just tells them I'm about to go to Earth. Meyer trusts me."

Cady said, "He trusts you, while he swallows handfuls of stress relievers."

"Yeah, well he has that luxury."

"I'll be ready. Good luck, Alex." She smiled and offered a hand.

"Thanks," he said, and shook.

Cady turned and left. He waited three minutes, then walked to Highland's section. Aramis went with him, with a nod.

Leitelt and Branson were on duty, checked his name as a formality, and waved him in. He knew them by sight only. Cady had twenty-eight people now, in three teams.

JessieM received him first.

"Chief Marlow, how are you today?"

"Very good, Jessie, thank you. Is Ms. Highland busy?"

Jessie nodded her head toward the inner office. "She's conducting a recorded interview. It should be done in a few minutes."

"I have a security issue to discuss. We can wait."

"I'll ping her screen," Jessie said, and swiped across her own interface.

Two minutes later, Elke, Jason and Shaman came in, looking relaxed and casual in sport shirts for local daywear. It was disarming camouflage for what they were about to do.

JessieM looked at them a bit quizzically, but monitored her screen and after a couple of minutes said, "You can go in now."

"Thank you."

He took one deep breath, knocked as a courtesy and pushed the door in.

"Good morning, ma'am. Thank you for seeing me again."

"What can I do for you, Chief Marlow? I'm afraid I only have about ten minutes before my next call."

"That's plenty, ma'am," he said. He stayed standing as he said, "The first item is that we know why the threats are escalating. They make you popular. The original intents seem to have been to embarrass you out of the race. Then they attempted to make you afraid. Then to make you look incompetent. At each level, though, your visibility and popularity increase. You're the underdog. So now they're concertedly trying to kill you."

"That's what you're for, isn't it?" She looked dismissive and almost gratified.

"It is. That is exactly what we are for. Which is the point of the second item." He watched. She didn't notice Aramis sidling back along the wall.

"What's that?"

"We need to vacate this area now." His voice was calm, but had that professional urgency to it.

"We seem to be perfectly safe and comfortable here," she said, holding up her open arms. She seemed reasonable, but he expected that would change as soon as he took the next step.

"We may seem to be, but given the progression of attacks, I must consider more explosives to be a credible and expected threat."

"Then deal with it. That's what you're paid for."

"Yes, ma'am, we are, and my recommendation is to leave."

She shook her head and turned to her screens, dismissing him with a flutter of fingers.

He tried again while motioning discreetly for the others. "Ma'am, whoever is trying to assassinate you are professionals."

"That's ridiculous, it's some group of backward peasants."

"No, they want it to look that way. Right now, we need to move, and we have to accept collateral damage."

She looked up again. "I can't have that with my poll numbers! It will end my campaign!"

"Ma'am, either you walk or Aramis stuns and carries you."

She turned to see Aramis holding the baton centimeters from her.

"This is felony kidnapping!"

"Yes it is. Aramis."

Aramis zapped her, she twitched, her eyes rolled back and fluttered, and she slumped into his grasp.

"That's a nice perk," he said, as he heaved her into a fire carry. Shaman reached over and sedated her. They both looked at JessieM, standing in the doorway, who shrugged.

"I will come along without being stunned," she said, sounding very nervous and fragile.

Jason said, "Jessie, you're probably safe if you stay here. You're not Ms. Highland. On the other hand, they might decide to make you a sacrifice."

"I'd like to come along," she said. "I expect it to be scary, but my place is with Ms. Highland." She trembled as she spoke, but her voice was firm.

Alex still didn't know why anyone was loyal to this bitch, but he respected her for it anyway.

He nodded, then said, "Jason, Elke, get us to the ARPAC. I much prefer any real allies be left alive."

Jason kicked the door, Elke went through grabbing for something off her harness, and they all followed.

Jason ran as Elke did something. It was loud and pyrotechnic, but probably not actually lethal. Jason wasn't sure if she enjoyed the hell out of that or hated it for not being potent enough. Still, they were unmolested to the vehicle. There had been some sentries and personnel around, but whatever Elke did had them all behind cover. He jumped into the driver's hatch and hesitated.

It was good transport, and obvious transport, and that made him scared.

Elke apparently had read his mind.

"I did a multifrequency burn for detonators or links, no hits. I'm checking latches and seals now. Stand by."

Oh, good.

"Safe to start," she said, as Alex said, "We're in, Elke on ramp, ramp up, roll." There were thumping noises of gear. A glance back showed rucks and a crate, which probably had the jump harness.

Alex hit the igniter and nothing happened. That is, nothing bad happened. It fired as it should.

He heard and felt movement, and Elke's hand thrust something past him.

"They won't be needing this." It was small and flat and looked like some kind of wire harness fastener.

"Explosive?"

"No, tracker. When we get a moment, I'll stick it on some other vehicle."

"Understood." said Jason, "how's the fighting?"

"I have only intermittent access, since we don't want to be tracked," said Alex. "What I saw on the way out was clear in this area, but we should avoid the northeast and south."

"West it is, then. There's a lot of clutter that way, though, if I recall the map." Jason looked up at the tracking screen.

"There is," Elke said as she disconnected the unit. That was another hindrance. While it provided fantastic data, and was theoretically proof against enemy cracking, their putative friends could easily get into it—that's what it was meant for. They'd travel buy the seat of the pants.

Well, it wasn't the first time. It felt good to be all together, well-armed and with decent protection for once.

"Status," Jason asked.

Alex said, "Aramis on top gun, I've got the rear, Shaman has witch, Bart monitoring engines, Elke on support."

"Direction?"

"North for now."

"Excellent. Rolling."

It was good to be running a proper military vehicle. The best armored limos were not close to this. That it had largely been for Highland's image didn't matter. It was serendipitous functionality.

He also wasn't concerned about cosmetic wear and tear on the vehicle, nor collateral damage. That let him drive much more aggressively.

Damn, it felt good.

He exploded through the gate-warning barricades, plowed through the movable blocks, which were just sand-filled drums, and slalomed around the sunken bollards.

"Aramis, I may need obstacle removal," he shouted back.

Aramis replied clearly, "Can you connect? If not, say the word."

"Elke, do we have internal commo?"

"We will in a moment. I'll plug you in."

He rolled over the curb and didn't notice until afterward, then cleared the bump the stupid limo had hung up on. This was how to travel.

Then Elke shoved ear muffs at him, bulky, but hard wired directly into the vehicle's system. He yanked them over his head. "Test."

Aramis replied, "I hear you."

Alex said, "I'll direct if needed." He was at the commander's console, with screens slaved to Jason's.

"Understood. We're in traffic. I'll try not to kill anyone."

Alex said, "That would be best. We'll be hard to hide as is."

"Do you want to debark for alternate transportation?"

Alex said, "Not yet. Right now, the armor and speed are useful. I'm hearing chatter about pursuit. They're trying to figure out whose vehicle it is. They've just now figured out it's ours. My phone is ringing. I may as well decoy before I disable it."

"Agreed."

Intercom went dead as Alex played stupid and innocent. Seconds of delay there could provide minutes of leeway here. He was back in less than ten seconds, though.

"They didn't buy it. I don't think they can scramble aircraft fast enough, but they can get one up for recon soon enough, or even satellite will help once they locate us. They will pursue on ground at once."

"And shit," Jason said, looking forward. "Homebound convoy about to pass us."

"I see them. They're wondering where we're going in a hurry."

Aramis said, "I'm smiling and waving. We're all friends and there's no threat."

"They seem to be buying it. We're rolling."

They passed out of view, and Alex said, "Thank god for bureaucracy. They still haven't figured out who's where, and of course, they dare not shoot at us with Ms. Highland aboard."

"Do they know that?"

"Yes, I made sure to tell them it was an urgent need on her part."

Jason smashed into a vehicle that strayed across the road.

"Very urgent. I just crushed a Mercedes."

"Casualties?"

"I don't think so, just the nose and part of the side. Occupants should be fine."

"Cady has a location picked out. She's stashing a car for us. We'll debark nearby, hoof it, load up, relocate."

"Understood. Though I'd much rather fight from this platform."

Aramis said, "We'll steal another."

"Or more."

Elke had managed to plug herself in, and said, "I can offer distractions if need be."

"I'm sure you'll get a chance soon."

"That will be good for our relationship," she said brightly.

He took another turn and found the way blocked. There was heavy construction here.

"I can't turn, going through," he said, as he swerved around a small crane. It looked as if they were doing sub-road drainage repair.

He hit the trench at speed and bounced over, causing slumps and collapses along that width. The excavated fill slowed them slightly, and he felt the vehicle rise, then flatten the pipe section awaiting installation.

Beyond that was a man with a multiwindow camera setup, leaning against his car and shooting video of the scene. The ARPAC was unmarked, so it wouldn't immediately tag to Ms. Highland, which was a good thing, because he slammed into the man, smashed him into a broken bag of cold cuts against the car, which he crushed under the wheels in a popping, rolling, bumping, grinding crunch. Well, if you stood in traffic, you were liable to get hurt. Jason told himself he didn't care, but didn't believe it. Stupid or not, the man had been a human being, and not actively hostile.

His introspection stopped when Bart quipped, "I believe it's crush hour."

He stifled a response, and instead asked, "Where to?"

Aramis shouted, "Take any left, three squares lateral, then north again."

"Left three, resume north, roger."

It was easy to tell who was who in traffic. Extreme Muslims didn't dodge. Insh Allah—as God wills. Sufis swerved, then cursed and threatened. There weren't many Baha'i or Christians in this neighborhood, but they cleared the way and pulled back afterward, shrugging it off without public commentary. Local police dodged faster than anyone, and might even go onto the sidewalk. Mercenaries went over any obstacle or threat, and if it came down to it, might back up for a second try.

Highland was not only well-tranked, she was weeping. He assumed it was for her career, not from any real compassion. Still, alive she might pull it off. Dead she'd be only a footnote.

Alex said, "You have alarmed the locals. There are gathering groups and I predict armed response."

"Yeah, that was not my intent." He thought for a moment and added, "But I guess it was inevitable. Do we FIDO, unass or split up to do more damage?"

Alex said, "Right now, FIDO. Follow Aramis's directions."

"Fuck It, Drive On," he muttered loudly. They might get that fight Aramis suggested, right now.

He reported, "The road is getting clogged. They're less willing and able to clear a hole."

Highland was functional enough to bawl, "How many poor people do you plan to kill?"

At least one more, he thought. JessieM's transmissions were completely squelched, he hoped. Otherwise there'd be military force en route to them as well.

"Aramis, advise me."

"Keep going north. How far out do we want to abandon ship?"

"How hot is it?"

Elke said, "Very. Milnet full of talk. Local police being brought in."

Alex said, "They probably won't shoot us with Ms. Highland in the vehicle, but mistakes happen. We need to unass soon."

Aramis said, "Miss Jessie, are you agreeable to churping some misdirection? Which can also leak out the intel we need known?"

"I can. You'll . . . have to tell me what to say." She flushed and blushed at that.

Alex said, "Damn, what do we say?"

Aramis said, "I have an idea. Jessie, churp that we're heading west to seek shelter with the Right Baptists."

"Okay. Just like that?"

"Yes."

"Jason, where's your safehouse? We'll divert there."

"It's a safe room. Northwest."

"'Safe room'?" Highland asked. "As in an emergency retreat?"

"Not very secure, but no one should know it exists and we can keep jamming against scans. We can gear up there. I have some extra funds stashed."

Jessie asked, "What are you going to do?"

"You'll see. In the meantime, we're heading through an area controlled by the Pure Shia. They're looking at our lone vehicle rather angrily."

Alex said, "I think it's more hungrily. They have quite a few veterans who know how to operate one."

"Good point. In either case, there's no way around and I expect some trouble."

"How's the traffic?"

"Starting to get very tight. I can plow or crush light scooters. Actual cars will stop me."

"Detour as needed, keep moving. We'll need to swap out and abandon this. Elke, we don't want them to get hold of it."

"Fireworks it is," she said, clearly cheerful.

Jason said, "It's going to be soon. I'm on a secondary now, if I have to turn again we're going to be hosed."

"Roads aren't wide enough?"

"No, they seem not to have taken advantage of the modern grid layout other than the main thoroughfares. They balkanized their neighborhoods on arrival and made a mess."

Alex called, "Everyone ready for transfer?"

There were nods and rattles.

"Ms. Highland, Jessie, we are about to abandon this vehicle and commandeer another. It will be noisy. It may be a bit rough. Grab onto Elke's pack, and Jessie, you onto Aramis's. Keep hold as much as possible. There could be some bruising. Do you understand?"

"Yes."

"Yes."

"What do you have, Jason?"

He took in the surroundings and reported. "I think we have a half a block. I see several good Mercedes we can use. I have a coder that should work on most of them. They're common enough to get us farther out before another swap."

"Sounds good. Do it."

"They're in front of a hotel. Elke, you'll need to distract people."

Elke stood swaying and took broad steps to the rear. "I have smoke, squibs and mild irritant." It was about time she got to do her job. She gestured to Highland, who nodded a bit vacantly but did grab Elke's harness.

He braked hard and she clutched a rail to avoid sliding forward.

"In five, four, three, two, one. Drop the ramp."

Aramis hit the ramp release; it clanged to the ground. Shaman went first. Elke followed, skipping down the angle with Highland hanging on through a near stumble. Once in sunlight, she took station still half on the ramp, her body and the side armor protecting the principal.

Bart was right behind her, and went past at a brisk walk.

Shaman knew his stuff. He casually opened the car's gullwing door, reached in before the driver could respond coherently, and dragged the man out by his collar. Bart slid into the driver's seat and dropped the door. Elke shoved Highland loose, next to the passenger door.

The driver's expression went from confused to irritated to angry, and he started jabbering in Arabic or Turkish or something, as Shaman zapped him with a stun baton. It was all still relatively quiet, but some bystanders had passed the surprise stage and were in the alarm stage. That was Elke's cue. She thumbed a code, slid a package tab into it, then tossed it on the sidewalk. It whuffed into a cloud of smoke that obscured them from anyone on that side. She followed with a second thrown behind the car and in the middle of traffic.

Aramis came through with Jessie clinging to his back, bent over and making *meep*ing noises. Aramis dove in the back easily, Shaman helped shove Jessie in. Jason made a quick check, assumed the package in the ARPAC was Elke's parting gift, and rolled in himself.

Alex grunted, "Elke, go."

"Moving," she announced for Highland's benefit. At least the woman was trained well at this aspect. She moved well enough.

The crowd was starting to panic and point, though. Elke tossed squibs in two directions as Shaman steered Highland into the rear. She waited a moment for the squibs to start cracking in loud, echoey reports, and slid in, using her arse to shove Highland further back.

Alex came last. He rolled rather nimbly for a man of his age, over the quarter panel, and slid into the shotgun seat. He hadn't finished closing the door before Bart had them in traffic with the throttle nailed.

"Your coder works," he said to Jason.

"I thought the engine was already running."

"The driver had a disconnect. He pressed it and looked smug. Then he looked concerned. Then he ceased looking anything when Shaman dropped him."

Alex said, "Well done. Get us lost first."

"Moving," Bart agreed and took a turn.

Elke scrolled through her feeds, didn't see something, and said, "Alex, we have a problem."

"Talk to me."

"Jessie's update is not showing on the churp feed. I am seeing other feeds that look like her style. Did you say something about a trip to the Eastern Forest Reserve?"

Jessie looked confused. "No?"

Alex shouted, "The receivers. Jessie, give your phone to Elke right now!"

Jessie stuttered and said, "Uh, okay. Hacked?" She handed her phone over reluctantly.

Elke flipped it, popped the back, pulled the power cell, pulled the card and fumbled for a case. She had one in a thigh pocket she used to isolate circuits, but she was squashed next to the door and Jessie.

It took considerable wiggling and arching, but she got it and placed the card inside.

"Yes, hacked," she said. "None of this is going on local or system feed. Someone has control of the service, which is run by the Lezt family. They are either corrupted or conspirators. And oh, yes." She clicked her detonator. There should be two warning pops to reduce casualties, a shame that, and then . . .

BANG, flash, thump.

She did love overpressure.

Highland seemed to come around to something at the mention of Lezt. She didn't notice the explosion.

"It would take someone in UN Security Agency or Intelligence to order the nodes locked, even that minimal amount. It must be Lezt doing it for some third party."

Jason said, "And that third party is UNSA or UNBI, working under orders from someone in your party."

She shook her head. "I'm not convinced of that at all. You're being dangerously paranoid."

Alex said, "That's my job. I'm paranoid so you don't have to be. Regardless of who it is, they've set it up so they can get signals and you can't communicate. We have spare phones, but we can't waste them for Miss Jessie to churp notes. If they accomplish nothing else, they've cut your communications, and are masquerading as you."

"I agree with that. How do we stop them and get control back?"

Jason said, "That depends on how they approach it. This just became an intel fight."

Aramis said, "As I see it, and I've done publicity, they can play this at least three ways." He ticked off on his fingers. "They can simply post reports, and compile B roll video, to show you having meaningless PR meetings with small groups. The locations will be vague, so you can't be positively pinned down. That gets you out of the campaign eye. Or, they could have you say some odd, malicious or incriminating things to wreck your campaign. At the far end, they'll try to locate and kill you."

Alex said, "It depends on if they think slowing you will do the job, sabotaging you, or if they need you as a martyr."

"We don't martyr people in the Egalitarian Party," Highland snapped.

Elke said, "Except for trigger-happy mercenary bodyguards, and potentially silly but useful hangers on."

Color drained from Highland's face, then flushed back. That had hit her hard.

Elke did enjoy being able to love her work.

Bart said, "Cruk's ratings are low and sinking. He needs a substantial boost, and less competition. The Party specifically said they were 'looking at all options for candidates,' when I saw the German feed. They are not confident of his popularity even in your own party."

Highland snorted. "It's not that I think he wouldn't do it. He'd readily do it. He's just too fucking stupid. He's a pretty face and a soothing voice, and never ran even a Third World constituency. He wins elections by handing out largesse and manipulating people."

"This would manipulate you, yes?"

"He couldn't do it, though."

"So who got him in?"

She was silent. Bart drove, maneuvering constantly.

Eventually she spoke. "I have to trust you with my life. That's much easier than trusting you with party dirt."

"Ma'am, unless you want to be a martyr, I'd suggest you relay us information. Have you heard anything ugly about our previous principals, from us?"

"No. But it's not that simple." She sighed. "I suppose I must. You're seen as a threat."

She left it hanging as if it were a revelation.

Elke said, "We deduced that before we left Earth."

Jason said, "We'll continue this inside. We're here. Alex, how do you want to do it?"

Alex never hesitated. Elke appreciated that.

"Jason, you'll lead Elke in with Ms. Highland. Bart will get out with Aramis. Shaman will take over driving. Around the block, I'll get out with Jessie. Shaman ditches it and comes last."

Bart pulled over and they started debarking, onto a sidewalk lightly traveled by only a few matrons with wheeled baskets if poor, or humming floaters if a little less so.

After two stops, Horace slid over to drive. JessieM was still stunned silent, and debarked with Alex. That left him alone to park a stolen vehicle, and of course, that's when he drove past a parked police vehicle.

He made no funny moves, just drove as a limo driver would. In the rear screen, he saw them frown slightly. The vehicle was out of place in this area. It wasn't out of place enough for them to risk the wrath of whichever mucky-muck was aboard. He took a side street, then another, keeping direction and distance in mind. It was quiet and dusky, so he pulled over, raised his scarf to a hood, checked his pistol, parked and stepped out.

All his gear was already inside, or should be. He shouldered a small cross-pack that held emergency sundries, and kept a clear path between hand and pistol. No one molested him; indeed, he saw almost no one until he reached the thoroughfare, where he seemed to blend in well enough. Three minutes of steady but unhurried walking got him to the saferoom.

Horace hadn't expected any particular apartment. Location and discretion were primary, then cost always played a role. Too pricey would raise inquiries. Too cheap affected reliability of the landlord and neighbors. He was surprised when he walked in the door.

Furnished, it would be a very nice place. Seven plastic chairs and seven basic cots filled a nicely laid out common room. This was probably considered a studio, but it was a large studio. The bathroom was back there, with a frosted one-way pane. The kitchenette was modern, and quite a few cans, instant packages and beverages sat waiting.

"New phone," Jason said, and underhanded one. Horace caught it.

Elke stood in the middle observing. She said to Jason, "You already set the bathroom window with a line and a breaking charge."

"Yes."

"Not a bad job. Should I tune it?"

"I assume you can do better, so yes."

Elke seemed happy and relaxed with explosive in hand. For most people, that would be insane. For her, it was comfortably normal. Good.

Alex said, "I hadn't planned on Jessie, so we're short a cot. However, we'll need someone on watch."

"I am on now," Bart said. He had a tub of soup open, steaming, and sipped it like a drink.

"We won't be here long," Alex said. "We'll be planning an offensive and moving. Ms. Highland, Jessie, while this location is probably safe, nothing is guaranteed. Remain dressed. Keep all property immediately at hand. We may move on a moment's notice. Do not make any communications. That is an order."

Horace examined Highland as she flared her eyebrows and said nothing. She at least understood the practicalities of the situation. Jessie just nodded.

Highland said, "I'll try to rest then."

"Good idea. I want half down, half up for now. Eat, rest, rearm. How's our stock?"

Jason said, "We've hardly shot anything. I have spare ammo here so we can take full loadouts, but that's mass."

"Juggle it on a personal basis. Ammo first, then water, then food, then sundries."

Jason said, "I'd like to see about finding a deeper hole, cruder and more remote. We can spend a little money and do things discreetly."

"How fast can you get a vehicle?"

"Fast isn't the problem. If I stick down a wad of cash and shiny metal, someone is going to know it's questionable and word will get out. I have no way to justify financing. So I need to find a private party and make it worth their while, but we still don't know we can trust them."

Aramis asked, "Would they rat us out, knowing they might lose their payoff?"

"They might be that stupid, or they might just lie about how much it was."

"Oh."

"Yes."

"So I can get transport, but we must then move at once."

"At the risk of sounding prejudiced, we want to stick to Christian groups."

"Or the Turks, or one of the rare Bahá'i."

"Possibly."

"I really hate trying to sound as if I give a damn about religion. It's dishonest of me, and I feel worse because it matters to them."

Highland said, "But you're fine with shooting people."

He faced her and said, "Mercenaries have morals, too."

"I can do it," Elke said. "I'm not particularly religious, but I can accept a blessing and offer friendliness in return."

"You and Aramis. Go." As they left, he dimmed the lights to ten percent.

Since they'd picked up JessieM much like a stray dog, Horace considered her one of his patients and charges. She looked very wrung out at the moment, and her breathing indicated a borderline panic reaction.

"Jessie, let me check you for injuries quickly."

"Oh, if you need to," she said, snapping alert and looking worried, growing a shade paler.

"It's just a precaution," he said. "Have a seat here." He indicated the corner away from the plotting and scheming, and kept his voice low. Highland took no notice. Though to be fair, the stress was affecting her, too.

"You seem a little out of sorts, so I want to make sure it's not trauma." There were no marks on her.

"Oh, it's stress," she admitted readily. "I've been through a battle. I don't know how you can do that more than once. There were bullets . . . explosions . . . things fell. I saw bodies blown apar . . ." she turned greenish and paused for a moment.

She sobbed and continued. "I hate this. Publicity and presence is my job, and I can't do it here. Not only can't I do it here, it's deadly if I do. I never learned the details of politics. I just rented out to promote in clear, short phrases. I've been with Joy for ten years now. I don't have any useful skills."

Horace said, "If I may professionally and discreetly inquire, is there more to your relationship?"

Jessie looked quizzical for a moment and then said, "Oh. No. I wish there were. She's so powerful and exciting." Horace said nothing, shivered slightly, and considered that everyone had at least one unique taste. "I think she knows that, but she really is a very dedicated wife."

It was hard to believe, but if even a close confidant thought so, and there were no rumors from reliable sources, it must be true. That aside, however, there was another point.

"That's fine. But you are a close acquaintance. She can confide in you, and it will do her good to have close contact with someone."

Jessie shook her head sadly. "I suggested that. She's always been very much alone. Even at home, they sleep, actually sleep, in separate rooms. She's almost pathological about her privacy."

"We noticed. Well, I can talk. Have you considered a stuffed toy?"

She stared at nothing and shook her head. "No."

"It does help. Quite a few of the soldiers here have them."

She looked up and said, "I'll try it. I don't regard it as immature."

It occurred to Horace that with the background she was getting here and now, the young woman might be a serious contender for politics herself in a couple of decades. It disturbed him to realize he'd be more likely to vote for her than any of the current thieves.

Of course, in two decades, this young lady might be a jaded political whore herself.

"Go rest," he told her, and took a look around at the others. She nodded and went to a cot, curled up and closed her eyes. She actually did sleep as exhaustion overcame stress.

Horace didn't sleep. He'd have to be more wrung out. He wished he could, though.

He saw Highland shifting, fidgeting, and eventually, she sat up.

"I can't sleep," she said.

"I understand, but you should keep trying if you can."

"It's not going to happen." She swung off the cot and stood up.

"As you wish. I wouldn't recommend a sedative anyway."

"Due to the need to move?"

"Exactly that. When you are tired enough, you will sleep."

"Or go insane," she said with an honest smile.

"We deal with fatigue a lot."

"Why do you do it?" she asked quietly.

"The fatigue?"

"No, the mercenary work."

"We're not precisely mercenaries. We don't take just any money, and we do stick to missions that are legal and ethical."

"Really? Are you saying that?"

"Exigencies can force us to be violent, but we engage very little, preferring to use evasion. We rarely act except in response."

She looked quizzical, probably considering their actions over the past few weeks.

"But, in answer to your question, ma'am, it's a challenge, it's well-paid, and it's rewarding to keep someone alive. Doubly so for me."

She nodded. "I suppose that makes sense. But why not a regular detail with someone?"

He had to think about that. "This is more honest, really. We don't have to like or pretend to like our principal, just do our job. That gives us more freedom than staff security have."

"You don't like me."

"I didn't say that, ma'am, only that we don't have to."

"You don't need to say it. None of you like me."

"There are numerous issues of personality and politics."

"And I'm a whore for taking practicality, compromise and yes, money, over ideology." She sighed. "When I first ran for local judge, I was so earnest and clean myself. I accomplished nothing, but I felt very good about myself."

She sighed again. "As time went on, I accomplished more and felt worse. Constituents and now the public at large vote for me, so regardless of anyone's thoughts about integrity, the Charter of Freedoms or equality, I represent what people want."

"It bothers you, ma'am?"

"Oh, yes it does. Look, I personally have nothing against you, and yes, I think of the resource potential of anyone, any group, any business. I was not in BuState when you rescued Mr. Bishwanath. But it most certainly annoyed certain factions. Ironically, in the same Traditionalist party that your CEO favors. They'd planned on parting out the system as 'recolonies,' with ownership of resources passing to them."

"Predictable enough," Horace said.

"Then, most recently, you protected and made friends with Caron Prescot. Very close friends, I'm led to understand."

Horace reflected it was a good thing Aramis was out shopping. The man would be flushing and stuttering at this point.

He offered, "So the ability to do our job well threatens certain elements, yes. However, if they're in the opposition party, that doesn't explain how your party ties in. It reinforces what some people say, that there's no real difference."

She looked up. "We have weird supporters. Jankin is worth a tenth what Prescot is worth. He's more into politics, though. She has no need to be. No one can touch her, and she's not petty, I have to say. He is. He purports to support the liberals because it's advantageous. You also may have noticed that a lot of our supporters are . . . below average. That's our appeal, to the common person. He milks that, and profits from it, and he gets a perverse glee out of it. But I can't see him killing over it."

"Is there some deal pending that you oppose him on?"

"Everyone winds up opposing and supporting him on many issues. He has fingers in everything."

"That's hardly what I'd call liberal."

"Of course not. He wants what's best for him. You don't get to that position by caring about anyone except yourself. It's a constant struggle for me—where's the line between protecting myself so I can do the right thing, and being a petty elitist?"

Horace twitched his eyebrows slightly, but she didn't see it.

◎ CHAPTER 21 ◎

ALEX WOKE AS ELKE RETURNED, carrying a canvas bag. He'd had twenty minutes of nap. It would have to do. It was probably a good thing. His spine didn't like cots. He rolled off gingerly and stood.

She said, "I have a basic, reliable Road Cruiser."

"Not bad. How did you get that?"

"I found an ad for a widow needing to sell property for living expenses. I was able to play the pity card and didn't haggle over price, and also bought two pairs of work boots and some shirts. They may be a bit large for the ladies, but should make it easier to travel." She tumbled them out of the bag. The boots were spattered with paint and grease, well broken in and wearing cracks. The shirts were sweat-stained and distressed.

Highland wrinkled her nose in distaste. "Those cannot be sanitary," she said.

"We have disinfectant spray."

JessieM slipped her shoes off, waited for Shaman to spray a pair, and slipped them on. Her expression was a neutral mask. She didn't like this, but wasn't going to complain. She pulled a khaki shirt over her blouse and became much less noticeable, even here.

Highland wasn't disposed to argue. She shook her head and shrugged, and followed suit.

"What's that?" Aramis asked, and pointed. It was a small wooden carving of a penguin.

"She graciously included that as a gift for my son."

"Son?"

"She assumed I had offspring and I saw no point in correcting her, for either time constraints or camouflage."

"Very good. It's a cute figure."

"He's our mascot for now. The Evil Penguin."

Shaman said, "Jessie, carry the penguin."

"Okay," she agreed.

What was that about?

Alex asked, "Does anyone have a reason to remain here?"

There were negatives all around.

"Then let's take the valuables and the gear and vacate. Jason, Aramis, what do we have?"

Aramis said, "We have a choice of nice hotel, flophouse, apartment or rental. There's a poor working neighborhood I've identified where no one will question us. We can pretend to be three married couples and three singles, though Bart's size is a bit distinctive. Local garb will help."

"Demographic?"

"Primitive Christian. Hats, scarves, coats. Women don't normally wear pants, but jobs can require it."

Highland said, "Agent Sykora refuses to wear a scarf."

"I will not wear one for political purposes. I have no objection to wearing camouflage."

Highland's jaw clenched. Alex figured Elke was really enjoying herself, now that she had explosive, someone to taunt, and the rule book sailing through the air.

He said, "That sounds like our neighborhood. Do we have a reservation?"

"No. We'll need to sneak, peek and drop."

"Is anyone good with the appropriate scripture for this subculture?"

"I am," Shaman said, "though I may stand out. The African émigrés were few."

Elke said, "I can do it. My family was nominally Lutheran. I'll just stick to basic references and invoke Christ."

"Are you okay with that?"

"I feel no animosity to their faith. What some of the more insane have chosen to do with it is a separate issue."

"True. The majority of them are still nice people. The whackos just make up for it in volume and violence."

"I will go ahead, and take Aramis with me. We can pass as a couple."

"They'll probably expect me to talk," he said.

"Yes, and you can be gruff, I'll be pleasant."

"We need to record that. No one will believe it."

Elke said, "We must hope they do."

They slipped out.

Quiet could be aggravating. No one was shooting at them, there were no rioters, things were quite calm. That left all kinds of time to fret over being found, or Elke and Aramis being traced, a sudden missile, anything.

Alex needed to discuss issues with Highland, but he wanted to wait until he had the whole team regrouped and they were ready to roll. In the meantime . . .

"Bart, keep an eye out to the east. Jason, you have south." He kept his voice soft. Highland was actually dozing. Not only did that make her easier to deal with, she did need rest, and her health was their concern.

Eventually his phone beeped. It showed as Elke, and he opened voice.

"Coming in," she said, and was gone. He pointed at the door while pulling capacitor and circuit again. They would need more backups for future use.

Aramis and Elke arrived moments later. Jason glanced down the hall, Bart closed the door behind them.

"We have space," Aramis said. "A small strip condo."

Alex asked, "How long do we plan to do this? We're just relocating as we go." At one level it made sense, at another, they'd be spinning wheels, wasting assets and risk being seen.

Aramis said, "Long enough for the news to settle down and see how it's spun. Whoever gets blamed will indicate potential sources."

Bart said, "We'll get blamed."

Alex grinned. "Of course, but on whose behalf?"

"Good point."

"So let's share coordinates, address, the works." He docked his phone to Aramis's and snagged the data.

After sharing the info around, Alex turned to Highland to try again.

"Ma'am, I . . . we need to discuss the threat status and be sure we're in agreement on the best course of action. We are temporarily, and I stress temporarily, safe here, but we are at risk if we are identified, and need to work around that."

"I actually get a choice?" she asked. "I rather thought I was a prisoner of my own security."

"It was necessary to vacate the area fast against potential threats. If you so order, we will go where you wish, but it will be recorded and noted so as to cover us. It's one of the ironies of this business that we'll catch bullets for you, but we will not enable you to get shot yourself."

"Very well. What leads you to believe there's an immediate threat?"

"Other than a grenade and someone trying to crush you under an armored vehicle?" he asked. He didn't think she was that clueless, but she might be that convinced of her own credibility.

"Look, the SecGen has been so completely clueless even his own party, your party, doesn't want him. How often do they allow a caucus before a sitting SecGen steps down? But, if he can orchestrate your death, he'll eliminate the main contender in his own party, and play the other four for sympathy. He only needs a plurality to pull a runoff and eliminate the Randites. They're certainly not going to vote for the Neo-Stalinists in the next round. The Neo-Stalinists are not going to vote Islamic Conservative. They're not going to vote Liberal-Labour. The tertiary parties don't count at all. That means the Equality Party wins, meaning him."

Jason stepped in to help.

"If she runs, what happens?"

He looked back at her as he said, "Polls are split on you winning, bad for him, or you losing to Liberal-Labour, worse for him. Also worse for the party as a whole. They could play this the other way, too, and have him iced. Except that he's much harder to hit with the Special Service around him, and that would look suspicious. You being here lets them blame some faction or other, like Celadon only moreso, then come in and stomp as they wish. They then have territory they can parcel out to supporters as concessions."

Bart said, "They can also give us as a company bad press."

"That, and I wouldn't put it past any of several of them to want us personally dead after saving President Bishwanath. They put together a scam on that, and we gutshot it."

Highland said, "That fits. We're a hundred and eighty-three days out."

"Yes?"

"I'm over thirty percent. At thirty-two and one eighty, I can call for Special Service protection details."

"Oh, shit. How the fuck did we miss that?" Really, that was . . .

Jason said, "That was it! I heard the conversation and it didn't click."

Aramis said, "Hell, that's easy. We stay hidden for three days, then call ahead and hand her off."

"As long as she has the percentage."

"We can fix that," he said confidently. Son of a bitch, they were about to help this narcissistic cunt win the election.

"How?" she asked.

"First, escape, evade and hide."

"But where? We can't get off planet."

"We have before."

Jason said, "Ms. Highland has an emergency transponder chip. They'll only find it here with a tight directional scan, but any port will show it."

"It's deep, too," she said. "When I had my gall bladder worked on, it was set then."

And at that moment, her expression changed, to that of a person who knew she was being hunted to death, regarded as a trophy and convenience, and who'd been completely betrayed.

Elke felt the tickle run up her spine, and kept her smirk hidden behind sleeve and glasses. That was the intangible she wanted out of this, and it was very sweet.

Shaman said, "I would be reluctant to go digging, without a modern clinic."

Jason said, "Which we're not going to have access to."

"How long can we lie low?" Bart asked.

Alex said, "If we can't pull this off, it would have to be until after the election. At that point, they'll shrug and look embarrassed, accuse us of paranoia and kidnapping, and wait for it to fade in the loads."

Highland said, "I am not missing the election!"

Jason looked at her. "Nor are we going to be accused of kidnapping, again."

She didn't even look sheepish. The woman was an uncaring sociopath. Elke might be herself, but at least her suggestions were practical.

Aramis said, "I don't see what other options we have. Delay, escape, or fight are the three courses."

"Well, I guess we fight," Jason said. "We stir up enough noise, they have to see us, see the threat against Ms. Highland, then they either give her the protection as her due, or take it from us and make the same jokes about us everyone does, pay our fee, and she's alive, mission accomplished. We're Ripple Creek's best team, and we don't care about cover stories, or looking good in the press."

Shaman said, "We'll be outnumbered."

"Likely not. I expect the unofficial government agents on planet are under ten, possibly as few as two."

"Based on?"

Elke said, "Based on what we both know about BuIntel paramilitary teams. We've both considered applying."

Aramis said, "Paramils?"

Jason said, "Who do you think snatched you, knew enough to keep you alive, and had locals do the dirty work so there was no connection? That was meant to deliberately scare us into either leaving, doing something foolish, or embarrassing Ms. Highland enough we got dropped. Now that the lethal force is out, we had a very well-thrown grenade, using primitive tactics, and someone able to steal an armored vehicle and get it to our location. Even with foreknowledge, that's an expert."

"Shit," Aramis said. "Yeah, that makes sense, but . . . aren't all those guys former Recon?"

"Or before it was Recon," Jason said. "Spetznaz, SAS, Kopassus. All professionals, with extra training."

"What do we do about them?"

Alex said, "We'd have to kill them. Ms. Highland?"

Slowly, she said, "If they ally against the government, which is me, then they're enemies." At least moral decisions were easy for her, as long as they benefited her.

"Elke?"

"I could use the practice." This would mean some nice overpressure.

Bart said, "We can get allies too."

Aramis said, "We could get dead, too, though that or mindwiping seem to be the choices."

"We've faced that before."

"So, you're seriously proposing attacking the paramilitary arm of BuInt?" He looked shaken, but then he had been captured by the bastards and tortured. She'd have to add in a factor for that, when she built her charges.

"I don't see what choice we have."

"Alex, we're good. We're really good. But jokes about 'we might be the best' aside, those skullbangers are the wrath of the gods themselves."

"They're also few in number, don't want to be discovered, and aren't likely to risk their lives for a campaign."

"Possibly. It's not like we can call a truce and ask them, though."

"We can maneuver around them and hint, and let them tell us how they're playing it."

Highland cut in with, "Are you discussing abandoning me?"

Elke got another thrill. The woman knew she could be a bargaining chip, or just ballast in a sack.

With that score, Elke decided she needed one of Jason's cigars, and a bottle of eiswein.

Jason said, "Not at all, ma'am. We've never done so and won't start now. We are discussing, however, the best way to keep everyone alive. I think in this case, we have an extra asset."

"Yes?"

"JessieM can misdirect for us."

Elke looked at her and said, "I opened a new churp for you. It won't stay open long unless your followers can secure a pipe and mirror it."

"They can! And they will!"

"Assume someone will try to hack as soon as you make your first churp."

She nodded. "What do I need to say, then?"

Aramis said, "Keep it simple. Your communications are compromised and you need your followers to hold the channel and relay. You won't be able to churp often, they need to be alert. Ms. Highland is battling subversive elements. They'll want to hear that. Leave it there, pull the card for Elke to secure, and after that you'll be sending leading messages to get people where we want them."

"What are you going to do then?"

"Kill them by the fucking thousands."

Jessie whimpered.

Aramis grinned.

"These fuckers dismembered me, tried to kill you, tried to kill my friends. They need to be taught not to do that. Then, there's this thing about killing Ms. Highland, who is under our protection. That's a professional issue, and it's also a marketing issue. If you screw with Ripple Creek, we will turn you into a goo sack."

"Ready, then, Aramis?"

"Yes." He looked much more himself, now that he had an enemy to aim at. That was all he'd needed, Elke realized.

"Lead the way. Elke, you drive."

They loaded the car as they'd unloaded, in three groups. Aramis went with Elke. Highland went with Bart, overwatched by Jason, and boarded at the next corner. Shaman took Jessie down. Alex and Jason went last, locking and securing as they went. It was unlikely they'd return to this apartment during this mission, but if they could recover supplies afterward they would. In the meantime, even a poor safehouse was better than none.

They moved quickly and quietly, each carrying a basic box, bag or case with supplies. They had field rations, bottled water, lots of ammo, basic weapons and two big support weapons. It didn't seem like enough to start a battle with, much less win one.

That's why Elke had her toys ready.

Shaman was already curbside, climbing into the van in the cool morning air. Elke checked conditions. It should remain dry.

There was a momentary but tense mixup, since Highland had to be in the middle for best protection and bailout. She was flanked by Bart and Jason. Aramis and Elke were up front. That left Alex and Shaman to squeeze into a rear already stuffed with gear.

Elke pulled smoothly into traffic, got onto the thoroughfare, crossed one major intersection and turned into another quiet area.

"Aramis and I are to be seen as a couple. Jason, switch with me and drive. Aramis has directions."

"Understood."

They got out, walked rather than ran, and were still back inside in under three seconds. Jason pulled out faster than Elke had, and nodded as Aramis pointed.

"You will come back here afterward," she said and pointed. "At the house, we can all load stuff inside, then most of you will leave with the van, and return with a load of furniture."

"Perfect."

"That's very clever," Highland said.

Alex said, "Thank you. We've had a lot of practice at evasion."

"I can see where a lot of incidental expenses go."

"Yes. We're more flexible than official agencies. That costs money at times."

Bart and Shaman remained because of their distinctive appearances. Alex stayed with the principal. The rest went out to get furniture. They chattered a bit as they left, to keep attention on themselves.

Bart moved quickly, placing blinds and curtains. Alex laid out weapons and ammo where they could be reached in a hurry, in several locations. Any intrusion would mean a retreat to the hard center of the domicile, and hopefully Elke would be on hand at that point, to dissuade people.

Highland actually sat quietly. She fidgeted and twitched, but didn't interfere. Nor did she offer to help.

When the "movers" returned, they also brought food. Jason took a box into the kitchen and started tossing stuff onto the counter.

"We have fresh ingredients. Salad and fruit and sautéed beef to follow."

To Highland's glance, Alex said, "Jason believes he's the best cook here. He believes that because he's demonstrated it repeatedly. We just help with cleanup and perimeter security while he does."

In three clunky trips, furniture came through the door and was set to barricade and cordon the rear and one of the windows. Out of the drawers came clothes, weapons, ammo and assorted supplies. That done, Jason went back to the kitchen.

Shortly, he came out with bowls of salad, two at a time. It was an interesting dish, Alex thought. Romaine hearts supported wedges of tomato and apple, and were surrounded by cucumber, goat cheese, chicken and scallions. Fat olives stuffed with garlic, and pepperoncinis garnished it, under grated ginger, ground pepper and a drizzle of oil and vinegar.

Alex wasn't a salad person, but it was refreshing, especially after field rats and the scavenged canned stuff they'd had the last day.

By the time he'd finished, Jason had placed a thick roll of pita in front of him stuffed with sautéed shaved paper-thin sirloin with mushrooms, onions and slivered almonds. There were eight liters of raspberry juice to sluice it down with.

"Ah, that's good. I'm ready to sleep or fight. What's our status?"

Shaman said, "Ms. Highland is reported kidnapped, speculation pointing at us or some 'right wing faction.' There's lots of human interest stories by her supporters." He turned to face her. "So, ma'am, your popularity is benefiting from this."

"Excellent," she said. "I'm glad their plot is working against them."

Alex said, "Unfortunately, it makes it more worthwhile for them to find a way to eliminate you and blame either us or some faction. As we've been portrayed as several kinds of puppy-abusing sociopath, if they can hit you, they can blame us. Our lawyers can probably save us, at a cost of tens of millions, but you'd still be dead. By then, of course, it will no longer be news and no one will care."

Highland looked shocked, and attentive. She finally seemed to be grasping her actual place in things, far below the lofty station she'd assigned herself. She wanted to be SecGen, but that carried a huge tag in risk and outlay. She probably had the outlay. She had to pay the risk.

Next to him, Elke sighed slightly. It sounded creepily sexual. She must be thinking of explosive again.

Highland almost shivered.

"I hadn't expected this level of treachery. I'm loyal to the party. I'd hoped they'd be loyal to me."

Given her own backstabbing tendencies to anyone and everyone in her path, it hardly seemed surprising she'd be regarded as a threat. No doubt she thought her own goals those of the party, and they might even intersect, but she wasn't the Equality Party Committee. They'd probably even tried polite measures, and found her oblivious.

Well, people had tried to kill them before. Though usually, not multiple professional and freelance factions combined.

Alex didn't think he was going to rest well.

Shaman continued, "The search continues for Minister Highland. All the latest gear is being used, and it is hoped her biometrics or personal gear will be traced soon."

Alex felt a shiver.

"Can we do anything about that transponder?" he asked. "Lead vest, Faraday cage?"

Jason said, "We can make a mesh vest easily enough, for her to wear under her coat. It won't be a hundred percent, but it will certainly help. I don't think we have time to figure out how to spoof it."

"Do it. Even if it only reduces detectable range."

Elke said, "I'm going to reconfigure some charges as well. I'll do her vest first."

"Ms. Highland, you need to try to rest. So do you, Jessie. Everyone else on shift rotations."

He was going to enforce it, too, even on himself. They were all wired, tense and determined to hardball it, but they needed rest or they'd be ineffective.

Jason looked at him, and said, "You first. I'm up."

He nodded. Jason's schedule was all messed up with having a different clock at home than Earth, and that different from here. There was some sense to the military staying on Earth's clock. Unfortunately, they couldn't.

He sprawled in the corner on a pile of crushed boxes. They were reasonably comfortable, he placed his carbine over his lap, and closed his eyes.

CHAPTER 22

HORACE TOOK WATCH WITH JASON. He'd rest, but he wanted to be sure of the others first.

Aramis presented functional. The man was resilient, and action kept him busy, which seemed to help. He had paper maps and scales, saved files of routes from street and air, drawing implements in hands, and a carbine across his knees.

Elke and Jason each took a piece of mesh and sewed wire along seams. Then Jason finished while Elke prepped charges in the kitchen, turning the stove and sink into an explosive lab. Her mental health was not in doubt. Intensely focused, asocial, very high functioning sociopath.

"Ms. Highland, I need to measure you."

"Oh, yes."

Highland was a bundle of live wires. This was far outside her experience and background, which was common for them, and anticipated. He wasn't going to tranquilize her unless necessary, because it would be necessary, and he neither wanted to overdo it, mess up her metabolism, or create paranoia.

Jason held up the vest, and said, "Arms apart, stand straight." It fit against her well enough.

"You'll need to try it on, please. Be careful, it's not strong, and it may be a bit scratchy."

She nodded. Her expression was blank but showed comprehension. He held it as she skinned into it. It was loose, but covered her from collar to waist.

"You need to leave it on. You can wear clothing under or over or both, but that will offer shielding from scans."

"How effective?" she asked.

"I can't say. Better than nothing, but not perfect."

Alex was asleep, sprawled but with a faint tension of readiness. That should be addressed. The stress was getting to him.

Bart looked relaxed enough, though that sleeping angle was going to lead to muscle spasms. He was half on a chair, half leaned over the table, jaw in hand, gun in other hand.

Jason said, "We're done, ma'am, go rest. Just keep it on."

Highland nodded and said, "Bathroom first. Excuse me." She moved tight-legged. Yes, it had been several hours for all of them.

JessieM spent a few minutes rolling up the hidden hood of her knitted brynj, and adjusting pillows. She made two spots, one for her, one for Highland. The location put a chair directly between them and the back door. That was either tactically smart or cautious.

Horace felt a wave of fatigue wash over him. He was reaching his own limit. Elke came through, very carefully laid out her weapons and kit for fast recovery, leaned into the wall with her knees up, and passed out. Highland came back through, crawled down next to JessieM in a most undignified fashion, and tossed a bit while going to sleep.

His own fatigue crushed him down as Jason said, "You're down. I'll wake Aramis for a bit."

"Thanks," he muttered, and leaned against the couch.

Jason's taskings kept him in the house, without a window for fresh air. They needed to minimize traceable pheromones.

Elke and Aramis made several forays for food, clothing and general supplies.

"We have enough weapons for now," Alex said. "We need support gear, rations and camouflage."

The news loads were all about Highland's "disappearance and suspected abduction." Jason followed several threads and compiled a chart. The next morning he had a good cross section.

"I actually like what I see here," he said.

"So do I," Alex said behind him. "Please elaborate."

"Certainly. First, we're only one possible suspect. There are also respected authorities, and commentators who shouldn't be respected but are anyway, blaming the administration, the military, Huble and the Amala, as well as some of the Shia and the Faithful of The One True God sect of Christians. It appears Ms. Highland's Mtali Assistant for Development is following all leads at once."

She muttered loudly, "Ferin never could find his ass with both hands. He just does what he's told and smiles vacuously. He's also not my assistant, he's a third-tier functionary. At least Jaekel is on Earth, keeping things stable."

Jason continued, "The good news for Ms. Highland is that this is creating a surge in popularity, over the needed mark. Of course, that also means at this point, any hostiles will simply go for her demise, and try to blame anyone, probably us, for it."

Alex said, "We need to identify who, and we don't have the intel resources we need to do so."

"So we get them all fighting and see who issues what releases first, or who tips their hand."

Alex said, "Ms. Highland?"

She raised her eyebrows. "Obviously, I'm thrilled at the boost in numbers. Without any political talk, it shows that I do have a good image, and yes, I can see why that would be a threat. Hunter wouldn't have the means to stop me. That idiot Cruk is both slimy and vicious enough to do so. He's really not very bright himself, but his cabinet and many of the ambassadors put him in so they could get their positions, junkets and graft. That's been covered in the news, and no one with a brain disputes it."

She paused. "I won't say I've never taken favors. It's part of politics. But this man's a petty Czech thug who's been set up to be nothing but a graft nexus. They want him in place."

Jason was bemused. "And you didn't think they'd kill over that?"

"No," she said. "I didn't think they'd kill *me* over that. I do have a large following, visibility, and security."

"They set us up so they could take us down with you."

Bart asked, "I would like to know why Corporate let us take this mission."

Alex said, "Because if we pull it off we'll be untouchable. If we die, we die protecting a major persona, and I expect there are ways to expose the source. I have all our recordings, for example."

Meyer may also have planned to use that information as blackmail. He wasn't going to say that in public. It was easy enough to figure out, however. Highland had been in BuState since the debacle with Bishwanath. She'd just taken over the reins about that time. So she very well might have been involved in trying to off him, or at least in profiting from it. Dirt over her would be very useful if she were elected.

Jason said, "Well, we know where everyone stands. The local threats are no longer significant. Bart?"

"I concur," he said. "We can easily avoid or overwhelm the locals. The relevant threat is some agency under orders from New York."

"Agency?" Highland asked.

Bart said, "I have trouble with English at times. I mean an agent, an actor, under their orders. It may or may not be an actual agency."

Aramis said, "I suspect it would be. It's much easier for them to bring gear in."

Elke said, "Didn't someone bring in that crate of gear two weeks ago? It was immediately out the gate and we were told not to worry about it."

Alex said, "That was BuIntel . . . who have all kinds of shady connections."

"Equipping local hires?" Shaman asked. "Or doing it themselves?"

"Too obvious themselves," Alex said. "But just in case, we'll plan accordingly."

He addressed them all.

"Is everyone rested? Cleaned? Latrined? Fed? Stocked with ammo, batteries, fresh phones?" He pointed and said, "JessieM has two units prepped. We have maps," he nodded to Aramis. "We're going to create a riot, and . . ."

It suddenly came to him.

"Jessie, we want Ms. Highland's *supporters* to demand she have Special Service protection, that her electability has reached that point. It doesn't matter that she has BuState personnel and us merc types, she deserves and must have official escorts."

Jason grinned. "I like it." If the SpecServ had control, they'd have to take the bite on anything happening to her. It would be too obvious it was action from within. It also meant acknowledging she was a challenge at caucus for the serving SecGen. So Cruk would be admitting her status and protecting her.

Hypothetically, it was possible to arrange a hit then try to spread the blame around to other agencies, since during the transition, SpecServ, Ripple Creek, BuState Security Directorate and the military would all be milling about. But it would still generate suspicion, and it would be much safer to run an actual election, no matter how crooked.

God, I'm glad I moved off Earth, he thought to himself. There was corruption everywhere, but even Salin had nothing on Earth.

Alex concluded, "And we pass off the ball amid a massive scrum, bow politely, and leave the hostiles wondering."

Elke said, "Does this mean I can blow things up?"

"Anything hostile, obstructing us, or that makes a nice video for the news."

"Always with the restrictions," she sighed. "But I'm in."

Shaman said, "You didn't ask me, but I have a full trauma bag and enough painkillers to turn a hippopotamus's toes up. I suspect we may need it."

Highland was wide-eyed again, but give her credit, the trembles didn't show in her face, nor did she object. She was a world-class bitch, but she did have guts.

After a moment's pause, Alex said, "Okay, we're out of here," and pointed to the door.

Highland moved okay for a civilian. JessieM was faster. They were still the lag factor on the rest of the team.

"Elke," he said, "this building is not to conveniently explode after we leave."

"It's not full of hostiles," she said. "Why would I waste explosive?"

"Just so we're clear. Everyone has water, food bars, a small pack, and we have two rucks of big stuff for backup, plus medical, the jump harness and extra guns." He checked off and pointed as he counted.

Probably someone noticed them all piling into the car, meant for five, jammed with eight plus gear. It wasn't likely anyone would tag them as Highland's contingent, but only as one more factional group of many. Without knowing whom they represented, most people would leave them entirely alone.

Aramis navigated by memory. He really did excel at it. When they first formed the team, he'd been just an expendable grunt with an attitude. Brave, tough, but irritating and just muscle. He'd matured, improved and become a crack pathfinder.

"Destination is fifteen kilometers generally northeast," he said. "Take any route north to Peace of the Prophet Way, then west. Yes, I said west. We have to go around one of those stupid peace walls." The glance he shot over his shoulder seemed to be a dare to Highland to argue. She didn't.

Bart drove, partly because he was the best in civilian vehicles, partly because he wouldn't fit anywhere else, nor could anyone sit on his lap without being crushed. He was laconic as always, but took Aramis's directions and moved them smoothly. It was still most of a half hour before they neared the coordinates Aramis provided. The roads were that messed up. This hole wasn't colonial. It was a dump.

Aramis said, "This is the right area. We're going to need to debark, get seen, then depart before we get too much attention. Do we want to keep this same vehicle?"

Alex said, "If it works, we'll use it. If we see something better we'll take it."

Shaman said, "I see a very nice church van. On the one hand, opposition groups will be more likely to shoot at it. On the other hand, they can't shoot very well, and the allied groups will avoid shooting at it, and will act to defend it."

Alex said, "On yet the other hand, it's fine transport and I don't care what the locals think. Jason, steal the church bus."

"On it. Elke, I need a distraction."

Bart braked to a stop right alongside the van. Jason kicked the door, Elke bounced off his lap, he followed. She jammed something into her detonator coder and tossed it, and it erupted in a drumroll of squibs.

The locals didn't stick around to determine if it was actual gunfire or not. A woman in a long black robe and hood, with four kids in tow, snatched up two and shuffled quickly for a doorway as the other two kids hung onto her robe, just as Ripple Creek taught its principals to do. In moments the area was clear.

Jason jammed a wedging bar into the door and heaved. Since they didn't care if the vehicle survived the ordeal, they didn't worry about cosmetic damage, and a sheet plastic door was cosmetic. It wouldn't stop any fire, so it wasn't a concern.

Once he had the door open, Alex shoved Highland off Shaman's lap.

"Move, ma'am, now!" he said. Aramis unassed from the front, tossing JessieM ahead of him. Bart kicked out of his door and Alex came last.

Elke's ass protruded from under the dash, but in moments she'd completely bypassed the control module with a universal one of her own. Most of the instruments probably wouldn't read, but all they cared about were wheels and motor.

Or in this case, engine. Diesel engines were easier than most modern electric drives, and that's what it had. Still, it rumbled and farted to life and Jason looked for instructions.

". . . six, seven, eight, roll," Alex ordered. Eight including Jessie? Yes, eight. Good.

Aramis said, "As we head south, we want to draw some attention to ourselves."

Alex said, "Everyone loves a parade. Let's wake them up."

Elke fumbled with her window, it didn't open; she raised her carbine butt and cracked the plastic out of the frame, then she reversed it, fired a burst across a building, and tossed out something that flared incendiary bright for a few seconds, then screamed and banged.

"Drive slowly," she suggested.

Nothing happened for two minutes, but just as they hit that tick, two vehicles fell in behind and the occupants started shooting at them, badly of course. A pedestrian fell clutching at his leg, and one round punched obliquely through the roof.

"Don't stop them," Alex said. "We want to be followed."

"Just roll the dice," Shaman said.

He grunted. Enough bullets in the air meant someone getting hit sooner or later.

"Jessie, now churp the location we left."

"The condo?"

"Yes."

"Found condo on west central side, but must leave soon. All supporters meet us . . . where?"

"Where we stole the van would work fine."

Highland asked, "Are you trying to kill my supporters?"

"No, ma'am. Any threats will beat them to that location and anyone smart will avoid the resultant firefight."

She said, "While most of my supporters run the median, some are . . . not too bright."

I'm not surprised, and we might be better off without them, Alex thought.

"They should be fine," he said. "No more at risk than anyone else here. Elke, do you have a spare feed handy?"

"I do."

"You churp 'Ms. Highland returning to the BuState gate.'"

"Understood." Her fingers fluttered for a very few moments.

"That ties them up in two places. Next, since we can't hide entirely, I want to bring them closer to us, still split by some margin, so they create multiple trouble zones behind us and near each other."

Aramis said, "I can word a press release from us that we're doing something."

"Such as?"

"I'm not sure. Possibly that we're vacating the city due to the growing violence? This would be aimed at mass release, not to just the tagged observers."

"Do it." That was rather slick.

JessieM was getting into it, too.

"I can do a release either endorsing or denouncing you," she said.

"Make it denounced. You've left our vehicle and are on foot. Jason, find her a place to transmit it from."

"Will do. This is going to be all kinds of entertaining."

He bumped his phone, said, "Cady, now's the time to work on that conference," then handed it to Elke. "Make this go away."

She looped something around it and threw it out the window toward a cluster of adults with guns. They departed, the device banged, and the phone turned into plastic confetti.

Bart said, "Traffic is blocked ahead. Divert or debark?"

"We better debark. We wanted a blockage, we have it."

Bart pulled to the side and stopped. They rolled out into a square around Highland, with Alex next to her, standing close.

"We need to present as a social group," he said.

"You're kidding," Highland said.

"Watch."

Aramis and Elke took the lead, weapons slung behind them, moving slightly closer and suddenly appearing as a couple. Bart got next to JessieM. Shaman pulled back with Jason.

"I see what you mean," Highland said with a fake but friendly smile. At first glance, they did look like three couples and a pair of friends. Anyone glancing at them would be unlikely to look again.

Alex kept multiple views up. Jason had a news feed running on his glasses. He tapped Alex's arm and spoke.

"Boss, it's working. They're tangling up with each other and it's spreading. If they're in a hurry to get Highland, they're going to wind up fanning it into a brushfire battle."

"That serves our purpose, as long as it doesn't get out of hand for us."

Jason said, "It might. Do you hear it?"

"The gunfire? Yes, distant, but regular."

"It's been getting closer and there are now reports in six locations. Das says we didn't get that from him."

"Very good. You have him on phone?"

"No, he gave me access codes for their threat feed. I believe we can trust him, and I'm only on receive."

Someone IDed them as a threat, there were shouts, and a couple of half-hearted shots not really aimed in their direction.

"Do we need transport?"

Aramis said, "It might be an idea. If we keep changing, they won't know where our final destination is. Right now, any reports will make them think we're going to ground. So changing would confuse them more."

Bart said, "There is a market a block that way. There are lots of parked cars."

"Then we'll take one."

Bart led the way with Jessie, who had to stride fast but kept up with him.

They found a microbus with a roll-off roof, rolled off. It was secured by recognition software, but Jason worked around that by shooting into the module as Elke clipped her bypass unit in place underneath. They jumped in, exposed but with lots of visibility as a tradeoff, and Bart slid into the driver's seat as Jason took shotgun again.

"Elke, how's recon?"

"I can't do this very often," she said with a flare of her eyebrows, but she leaned back and shot a cam straight up. She lowered the shotgun, touched a button and sent the scrolled image to Alex.

He reported, "Running gunfight north of us, small arms with light support weapons, seems to be a handful of machine guns. The army is west. It looks like they don't want to engage the existing battle—"

"Probably politics," Jason said.

"—I assume so, and is trying to coordinate counterfire against that incoming rocketry."

Shaman said, "That leaves us here with two very hostile snipers and two unknowns with local help."

"Do we want to stick it out, fight the mob, or try to meet up with the army?"

Jason said, "Army is not our friend. They'll have orders to detain us, probably phrased as 'coordinate with.' Staying here means being sniped at their leisure. The local conflict is something we have practice with. Ma'am, we're going to need to go through that local battle. We'll be going fast, attempting not to engage, but if we do get engaged, we'll need to fight very violently to break contact and continue."

"I would like a weapon," she said. "For my own protection."

"I don't have a moral objection. However, what is your training level?"

"I've shot guns on the range. I handled the M Ninety once on a military reaction range."

He raised his eyebrows. "Tell me honestly, was that mostly for show?"

"Yes," she nodded, "but I know which end to point."

"Very well," he nodded, and Jason handed back a spare carbine. Highland checked the chamber and flipped the safety off without much fumbling. "Keep it pointed away from any of us, and do not fire unless one of us fires first. Jessie, what about you?"

"I'll sit in the corner of the seat and be very small." She seemed too scared to be embarrassed.

"That's a good tactic. We may need to debark and run, though. Can you do that?"

"Yes," she said firmly.

"I need you to remember that we have to cover Ms. Highland first, and can only cover you if circumstances permit."

"Yes," she said again, her lips trembling a bit.

"Let's move. We find new transport, Bart drives, Jason shotgun, Aramis tailgunner, Elke clears the route as needed, and the rest of us cover Ms. Highland and Jessie."

Jason said, "An open truck is not my first choice, but we can get that one right there."

The truck contained six fighters in mixed camouflage and keffiyeh, with a mounted machine gun and rifles. There was a gunner in the passenger seat and a driver wearing a helmet and looking almost professional.

"Do it. Elke, chase them off." Aramis vaulted out and took off at a sprint at that command. Bart led Jason.

Instantly, Elke grabbed a softball-sized something from her harness and flung it in a high arc. It dropped accurately, popped a tiny chute, and started exploding in a string of vigorous reports. They were not firecrackers, but probably blasting caps. The crew in the bed fled, taking their weapons and leaving the rest of their gear. The passenger unassed, but the driver fumbled as if to shift gears and move.

Aramis reached him right then, punched him solidly in the side of the head, pulled the door and unceremoniously yanked the unconscious form out. He swung his legs up into the bed, tangled and tumbled over his cannon, then got positioned. Bart scooped up the driver's dislodged helmet and squeezed in, cursing in German. Jason rolled across the hood. His entry around the door in a twist and leap was far too gymnastic for a man in his forties.

Elke tossed another distraction and some smoke. It was thick, yellow and smelly, but probably proof against IR and UV frequencies.

Alex had one of Highland's shoulders, Shaman had her backpack, and they ran, with Jessie sprinting behind while shrieking in a whimper.

Shaman jumped and pressed himself over the bed side, reached down and pulled Highland up by her armpits as Alex shoved her rump. He then turned and grabbed Jessie between her legs and by one shoulder and handed her up to Shaman, then jumped, pressed and rolled in himself.

"Go!" he shouted, and looked around to get organized.

Aramis had just passed his cannon forward to Jason, who laid it across the battered panel and hood. There were no windows left in the vehicle. Aramis looked quite comfortable in a reclining lounge chair, even if it was half-mildewed, sun-bleached and torn. He did a quick function check of the AA-tripod mounted machine gun in the middle, and leaned back, letting the gun sweep buildings as Bart nailed the throttle. It was a fine sunny day for a drive around the park in a truck full of weapons.

Aramis said, "Shaman, you take the gun for threats in front. Jason has my cannon."

Elke said, "And I have Jason's squad weapon." She grabbed a folding carbine one of the occupants had abandoned and handed it to Highland, who had taken a seat between wheel well and cab, legs around one of the tripod supports, leaning against Aramis's seat. "Spare," she said.

Jessie was on the other side, hunched down but apparently still functional. She kept an eye out her side, with occasional nervous glances around.

Alex said, "Make sure you can debark in a hurry when we have to."

Right then, Jason fired a round from the cannon, to clear the route ahead of them. Elke fired a burst in a rearward sweep across the road, because the former occupants had noticed the theft of their transport. They were probably fairly elite by local standards, Alex thought. They all wore new Blackwing work boots.

Aramis shouted, "Four hostiles on Springblades, rear!" and pointed.

Alex followed his finger and saw them, or tried to. They were in distortion suits, but the rucks, weapons and Springblade boots were clearly visible.

"That's different," he said.

Aramis fired a burst, but the range was too great, and moving platform to moving target made it an impossible shot.

Highland shouted, "What is it?"

"Springblades, ma'am. They're those boots parkeur traceurs use for rooftop chases, only in this case, I'm assuming they're hostiles."

Aramis fired a second burst as Elke twitched. She wasn't in front of the muzzle, but she was close enough to get hit with the pressure wave. Shaman was half-prone, leaning over the side like the gunwale of a boat, head under the tripod.

"Scared one," Aramis said.

The truck stopped suddenly, as Jason shouted, "Cover, all around!" He was sitting on the console, facing rear, resting his arms on the roof.

Alex turned to cover the right, Elke had rear, Shaman left, and Aramis swung the machine gun around, holding it at an odd angle where it would eject links into his face, but would cover forward, if Jason ducked in time.

But Jason stared for a moment, eyes tracking, then raised his carbine almost casually and burped off a burst of five.

"Got one. Drive!" he said, and everyone gripped hard as Bart took them back to speed.

Jason shimmied back through and resumed his seat. Over his shoulder he yelled, "If you're in trajectory, you have no cover, and no maneuverability."

Alex nodded, but he was considering that they'd just shot one of the government's best assassins. Nothing good was going to come of that.

They turned a corner, and Bart called, "Contact front!"

They were in the midst of a huge mob, who seemed to be spectators to a small engagement between two rival gangs of ten or so each.

Then the crowd noticed the truck, and half of them turned toward it.

Aramis fired a descending burst toward the crowd, Elke dropped another string of squibs, Jason shot a round from the cannon low over the fight ahead, and Shaman casually punched someone in the face with the muzzle of his carbine. He didn't hit hard enough to knock the man down, but it was enough to raise a bloody welt and dissuade him from climbing into the truck. The rest of the mob suddenly vacated a clear area a good twenty meters in diameter.

Bart prodded the truck forward, just as a round from one of the rooftop pursuers meteored into the dirt behind them. That caused the crowd to dissipate further, right at the moment they needed all the bodies they could get. There was no expectation that the local presence would dissuade attack, but the mob might soak up a few bullets at least.

Aramis swung back and fired another burst up and to his left—vehicle right. Bart turned the vehicle left and tried to put a street gap between them and pursuit. The surrounding mob broke up into several little cliques and brawls, but stayed thin enough that Bart was able to weave slightly. He certainly wasn't the type to swerve for hostile idiots, and he wouldn't use the horn, either, assuming it still worked.

About half a block down, Aramis said, "Gun's empty, no spare belts. Clear me a path."

Alex stood and stepped toward the cab, using the gun mount for a handle, then gripped the cab. Elke and Shaman moved aside. Aramis heaved, and gun and tripod tumbled over the back of the bed to crash on the ground. It might still be functional, but wasn't likely to come into play against them, and they needed the room and mass reduction.

Alex said, "We need to change vehicles, get to cover or otherwise well-clear the area. Those fuckers on the Springblades are insane, but obviously competent."

Jason said, "Let's make a couple more turns and persuade someone else to take this vehicle."

"That fits our psychology so well. Do it." He faced Highland and said, "We once paid someone to be hijacked by us. It's weird, but it works."

"Start now," Jason said, as they rounded another corner.

Highland nodded. It seemed to be acknowledgment of being spoken to. She looked to be in shock. If she'd thought them trigger happy before . . .

Elke slipped over the side in a crouching sprint, straightened and entered what looked like a vacant building. Aramis hoisted Jessie over, who crouched and scampered through the doorway after her. He rolled over and down, and caught Highland by the chest and shoulders as she followed. The woman wasn't in bad shape, but was not young or athletic. Parts of her anatomy, however, were probably deliberately built to fake it. He shuddered.

Four people ran out of the building with Elke behind, prodding with her carbine. Shaman took the rear of the vehicle, Jason the front, and corralled them into it. Bart shouted "Drive, *habla, sürücü!*" Apparently he knew a little Arabic and Turkish, too.

The whole process took twenty seconds, and the evictees drove madly, lest they disturb the crazy Earthies.

"We can't stay here too long," Jason said. "They'll do some kind of scan, or DNA sweep."

"Where do we need to get?"

"I would like to get to this area here," Elke said, and projected a map on a mostly clean section of floor, while pointing.

"Why there?"

"Because I have enough explosives in the area I can simulate my own battle, and tie everyone up for hours."

"Fantastic. So we should get there."

Highland said, "I'm very impressed. I'd call it paranoid, but it seems to be very forward thinking."

Elke looked at her coldly and said, "Next time a professional tells you she needs explosive, or even network keys, or a doccase full of cash, please believe her."

"I will." She nodded vigorously. This time she actually blushed a bit.

Shaman asked, "Are we going on foot?"

Aramis said, "Yes, but do we want to pretend to be locals?"

Alex said, "I don't see that working long enough to bother with. Shoulder up, let's move. How far can you jog, ma'am?"

"I can handle five kilometers at a normal pace."

"Good. This will be shorter but a bit faster. Jessie?"

"I did track in school, but it was some years ago. I don't do as much as I should."

"Can you run a couple of kilometers?"

"Yes," she agreed, sounding positive.

"Then let's go."

They went out the door, formed loosely around her and let her set the pace as Aramis led.

✺ CHAPTER 23 ✺

ELKE HAD TO KEEP CRANING to watch her rear quarter. They were unmolested across the street, and reached the alley. That felt less exposed, but the terrain was terrible, with uncollected rubbish heaped and piled. It wasn't that it was filthy. It was that it was filthy, unstable and prone to shift and outgas methane, ammonia and rot smells as they clambered around and over. Above them, windows were dark caves that looked threatening even without hostiles.

Highland might be an obnoxious bitch, but she didn't complain about rough conditions. No doubt boasting of it would be part of her next level of campaigning.

Then they were through, and onto another street. Traffic seemed normal enough here, though civilians drew back in the face of what was obviously a small military unit. Then someone recognized Highland.

Elke sighed for a moment and grabbed a stink gas grenade. She yanked the cord and rolled it left, then rolled another right, and one straight ahead.

The crowd screamed and drew away, except those closest, who tried to get closer. While not quite as potent as the vehicle mounted dispensers, the stench was so strong it was palpable, as slight whiffs drifted by.

Alex caught what she did before she said anything, and ordered, "Deep breath, sprint forward."

She dragged in a breath tinged with that awful sulfur smell, and put a hand on Jessie's shoulder to keep her moving briskly. Her eyes teared up as they passed through the fumes in front, but she felt it clear in the slight breeze, and they were soon in another alley, this one less disgusting but narrower, dodging between bins and tubs, piled debris and stacks of crates. It turned to the left and they followed it, then right again.

Aramis said, "We should be coming out onto the Plaza of the Caliph in a moment and . . . wait . . ."

Everyone ahead stopped and Elke moved up close in case she was needed. She checked behind again, hand on a device just in case.

Jason said, "And now we find out just how effective a wall between sectors is."

Ahead was the broad, glistening curve of the Peace Wall. More trash leaned against it, including abandoned cars and boxes. Above that, it really did look like marble, but that featureless concrete extrusion was impenetrable to anything she carried. She could divot it, but . . .

"Move," she said, and the team cleared her path, yanking Highland and Jessie aside.

She turned her back to Jason and said, "Spare cassette." She indicated with her thumb.

"This isn't a mine is it?" She had on occasion rigged an ammo cassette as a claymore.

"No, it's loaded with spalling charges." She took it as he pulled it out, swapped for the one in the weapon, then handed the shotgun to him. "You're the best shot, make us steps."

"Understood," he said. He hefted the shotgun, chose a spot just over an abandoned van, and started shooting.

The charges were designed to punch through block. She'd had in mind opening a large hole by perforating a wall, or creating loops he could snipe through. In this case, the first shot impacted the wall seventy centimeters above the van's roof, and blew a crater several centimeters deep and roughly conical. It would support a hand or foot. His next shot moved up the wall, then again. By the time he emptied the cassette there were steps within a meter and a half of the top.

"I can't climb that," Jessie said.

Aramis said, "Sure you can. Take it one step at a time, don't look down, and try to ignore the bullets peppering the wall under your heels." He had the harness from the bag Bart carried, and was stepping into it.

It was impressive how fast the locals had abandoned the area and turned it into a dump. The team was unmolested as they crossed the street, which served as a ring road, as in a walled town in Europe. It was quite clear to within five meters of the wall, then the debris started. The van was a shell, stripped of engine, wheels and seats. The windows were gone, reused no doubt, and likely someone would be along soon for either body panels, sections of them, or to salvage the polymer plate for some other use. In the meantime, it got them three meters off the ground, leaving only five meters above Bart's head.

"First," Elke said. It wasn't that she liked heights. She didn't want to think about heights, and going first left less time to fret.

The craters were deep enough, though tight on her boots. That could be a problem for Bart and Shaman, with the boats they wore. She shrugged and kept climbing, reaching in with gloved hands, gripping hard and placing each foot carefully. It was like climbing a very narrow ladder with no gaps between rungs.

Also, with incoming fire. She flinched as she heard it. It wasn't well aimed, nor was it in volume, but she had no cover.

With that distraction, though, she made it to the top of the wall, oozed over and clung there. It was just over a meter wide, it was ten meters down the other side, and there was less debris. The government had insisted there were no spikes atop the wall. Technically, that might be true, but it was very rough and jagged where the polymix had stretched and shifted inside the mold as it set. The nearest buildings were a hundred meters away, and the terrain in between was razed urban rubble. An entire street of buildings was gone.

With a loud hiss of gas jets, Aramis bounced up, facing her.

"This is why they pay us those big dollars," he said with a grin, as he rolled onto the ledge.

"Yes," she agreed tightly.

From out of his ruck he drew line, swore as it partly uncoiled and tangled, then got it laid neatly in front of him. He pulled out a clamp that looked specifically made for the corner, and clipped it on the near side. It came loose when he tugged, but after two more sets, it remained in place.

"Down fast," he said. "The rest are coming."

She nodded, took the line, wove it over her shoulder, hip and crotch into an improvised abseil, and shimmied over the coarse, abrasive edge. Her brain buzzed and thudded because of that single clamp holding her, but she started walking down. The rope cut into her flesh through the fabric, she desperately wanted to dump the ruck, fearing its mass might push her total past some limit and dismount the clamp. She also needed to pee worse than ever, and the shotgun kept jabbing her heel.

Ten seconds later she was on the ground. She crabbed sideways two meters, hunched down and unslung her shotgun.

This area was a bombed-out mess. There were few people, and fewer as those people realized armed troops were encroaching.

There was no cover, though. This had been the other byway of a large road, and the crumbled remains of a curb were nine meters ahead. Another ten meters or so led to shorn foundations and infilled basements, with some structural steel projecting upward. Clumps of weeds were reclaiming the land. The hundred-meter gap to the nearest buildings didn't reassure her. That was a short range for rifles, but a long range to run.

She felt better once Jason zipped down next to her. Highland was lowered but managed to walk herself rather than drag. Jessie kicked a bit but came down, though her expression indicated complete terror. Horace dropped a bit too fast and grunted as he landed. Bart landed hard enough to create seismic waves, but seemed unbothered. Aramis looked graceful.

"Lowering," Alex said in her ears. She looked up to see the rucks. They still had them? Good, but still.

Then Alex slid down last. He stretched until his feet reached shoulder height for Bart, who stood underneath to support him. Then, reaching far up, he cut the line. He hopped free, Bart caught him and slowed his descent in a squat, and they were all down, with hard cover behind.

He said, "This won't stop the springblades, if they're determined."

"No, but it will stop that round of allies, temporarily."

"Aramis?"

Aramis said, "Twelve degrees from magnetic north, we'll shelter in that building for a quick reassessment. Move in three teams."

※ ※ ※ ※

Aramis always got a bit of thrill from the chase. It was probably a bad habit, but he preferred it to the alternative of crippling fear.

This, though, was a bit more than a chase. They were in the middle of three angry groups who'd shoot even if they didn't know who Highland was, and especially if they did, with at least one group of assassins following. They were using the battling factions as a shield against the hit team, who were using the factions as concealment to get closer. All in all, this would be hilarious to watch happen to someone else. Aramis had a starring role, though.

He shivered briefly. Death was no longer the worst thing that could happen. If it came down to it, though, he'd kill as many as he could and save one round. It was for damned sure the army wouldn't save him without political prodding, which Alex couldn't do anymore, Highland was unlikely to, and Corporate was unable to. This was some serious shit.

Still, gloves off meant he could shoot back, and the threat level wasn't any greater than before. He, they were just aware of it now. That was the difference.

Elke and Jason went first, coaxing Jessie with them. He and Bart took Highland, and he had to admit, she bore up reasonably well. She wasn't Bishwanath, who'd been an actual veteran. She wasn't Caron Prescot, who could have been a spoiled brat but turned out to be a very courageous woman. She was far better than most politicians or celebrities, though.

The building was structurally sound, and had a few panes of well-crazed polycarbonate left in it. There were even small sections of carpet and a couple of chairs inside the lobby. It had been some kind of small office building, probably rather high in rent, in its past.

The rest came over in a dodging, shifting rush, and they had cover and concealment again.

Alex said, "Aramis, map."

He laid down his phone and pulled out the plastic roll.

"We're here," he said, pointing.

"This is a less nice neighborhood."

"That's understating it, but we're separated by the wall and by culture. This is an Amala area."

Highland said, "We're in Amala territory? They're very antagonistic to me. Why did you do this?"

"They won't look for you here, and it was the safest physical location under the circumstances. We'll be moving constantly." He said. He did want to keep her involved and mentally busy.

Shaman asked, "How are we going to maneuver the hostiles into place?"

Aramis said, "I've thought of that. Look here." He pointed at the map.

"We're here. The Amala are hostile. If we flee east we wind up in moderate Sunni territory—fairly safe. They hate the Amala. North is Sufi. They don't like her but won't go out of their way to attack. Northeast, at that point just a kilometer away, is Covenant of the Lord, and they are crazy and will try to attack both us and the Amala, if we can goad them into it. That will draw the Sufi in to keep their border secure if nothing else, which yields a three-way fight, which means the military has to show up to break it up. While that's going on, we can be active against those Security Agency guys."

Highland said, "You are seriously proposing to start a war?"

It was fun to tell her, "The war has been going on here for fifty years. I just propose to escalate it."

She was definitely insecure now, completely out of her comfort zones.

Alex said, "If we can tie them all up, they'll prefer each other to you. That's the survival strategy. And now it's time to move."

"But—" she sputtered in protest as he took her elbow and "suggested" she move. She was on her feet and walking before her brain shifted gears.

Alex said, "Elke, Jason, find us transport."

The two strode faster and pulled ahead.

The building filled a block. Their route through it was circuitous, due to rubble from collapse. It also had a complicated floor plan, having been refitted several times since its original construction. Owners changed, uses changed, factions changed . . . he stepped over the remains of a block wall, then through a framed doorway in an extruded wall barely in evidence. At least they'd have cover, concealment and distraction if attacked here.

Ahead, Elke and Jason walked out into sunlight. The red glow resembled that of a perpetual sunset.

The rest of them reached the door a few moments later, to find the two had acquired a box van. A man hurried away, and Aramis was fairly sure he was pocketing a large wad of scrip as he did so. Likely some bullion was involved, too.

They clambered aboard through the side hatch of the cargo box, and the stench hit them. This was a trash hauler of some description. It smelled of rot, piss, moldy socks and putrefying something. He gagged, and sat Highland down on a seat. It was quite literally a wooden dining chair, old style, well-scarred, stuffed into the corner.

The one opposite was a dilapidated office chair, unpowered. Both might clean up as valuable antiques, if anyone bothered, and if any potential buyers would care.

They all gasped for breath. The box was enclosed, hot, humid and some of those fumes had to be toxic.

Bart said, "I will open the back enough to kick trash out."

Alex said, "I'm not sure on doing that."

Bart said, "I am. The vapors are not safe. I smell mercaptan, sulfides, some alkynes. It must go."

Alkynes? Really? Or was he lying just to make sure they could clear some out, because it smelled that bad? Either way, Alex didn't protest.

Aramis clutched at Highland's chair as Jason took a corner fast. He didn't complain because there must be a reason, but Highland almost slid off the chair into a bag of goo.

Bart and Shaman kicked and shoved stuff out, using boots and carbine muzzles. No one wanted to touch anything.

Then a round came through the box, up high, downward angle from the rear.

Alex shouted, "Unass and take cover!" as Aramis grabbed Highland's arm and moved for the rear, or tried to. Jason braked hard, and he was pinned in place. Then braking stopped and he bounded toward the rear, tangling, dancing, and just avoiding a leaking puddle of diapers, canned peas and something really nasty.

Shot from high rear had to be the BuInt assholes on the Springblades. They were really pissing him off, and it was personal.

"Someone take Highland," Aramis said, and grabbed the bag slung over Bart's shoulder. "Keep the vehicle moving. I'm going up to delay those chasers. I'll catch up on that." He pointed at the bag.

"How?"

"I did go to the Mountain School."

Highland said, "Thank you for that," with a somber expression.

It took him a moment to figure out her meaning.

"Huh? Lady, I don't plan to die. I'm going to tangle up at least one of them, and they're more interested in pursuing you than me." He clutched the bag and bailed out the side.

Aramis lit out at a sprint, amused and revolted that Highland thought he'd risk himself as a decoy for her. He had clear orders on what he was required to do, and deliberately hunting BuInt Paramils wasn't on that list.

He was doing it for fun.

He realized it was cocky and potentially lethal, but it was necessary, and he was up to it. Yes, it was grandstanding, but the payoff would be huge.

Yes, those black dots were them, and if they could make small arms shots at this range . . . shit. They were Jason's quality. Though it could have been luck. Or it could have been a piloted shot. Or massively processed.

The rest hustled off, and that feeling of being a bug on a plate hit him. No one here was a friendly, and faces poked out of windows as they realized he was alone.

So much for donning the gear here. He shouldered the bag and sprinted in a crouch. He turned the corner, found the door, yanked and it came off its hinges. He shrugged, shoved and kept moving. The stairs were nothing but debris-covered concrete, and he found the best way to ascend was to just move his feet flat and kick stuff out of the way. He heard glass tinkle and crunch and was glad for the armored soles on his boots.

The top landing was secure enough. There were no signs of occupation, and he'd hear anyone below. Time was short. He had to get on the roof, and luckily the hatch was half askew anyway. He paused just below to catch his rasping breath. He had time if he was fast, so he stepped into the harness, then yanked straps around until it fit, hoping he had it correct.

In the shotgun seat, with a shotgun, Elke realized Aramis was correct. It was getting violent, and almost certainly propagating. She wanted to fire a recon round, but unless someone else shot first, she was reluctant to draw attention to herself. They had no drones.

At the corner, Jason stopped again, shouted, "Now!" and the rest bailed out of the back with Highland and Jessie. As soon as they were clear, he drove off again.

Then someone did shoot, and she realized she couldn't fire a recon round. The remaining shells were all cratering charges, because she hadn't swapped cassettes.

No problem, then. That man over there was about to get a lesson in potshots. She raised the gun, got the arc, snapped the trigger. The report struck her earbuds and was dissipated, but was unfiltered as a shock wave against her face. As the recoil bit her shoulder, the charge blew a perfect ten-centimeter hole through his midsection. He looked surprised as he sat down, slumped at an odd angle because his spine was gone, along with his heart, then collapsed in convulsions above the hole, while his lower two thirds remained limp and meat-like.

That would teach the fucker.

More shots sounded, and she grinned. Now she would get to teach lots of lessons. *That* was exciting.

Ahead of them a squad of irregulars deployed on the sidewalk. They must have been waiting for some kind of action, and as eager as she. Now, where were those tubes? There. She pulled one from her harness, slid it over the muzzle, and carefully fed the gun back through the window.

"Don't start a war if you can't take a joke," she mumbled, chose her target, thumbed the selector and clicked the trigger.

Her chosen cartridge was an overpowered blank to act as a launcher and igniter. The large muzzle charge elevated the recoil to a sharp jab, but that meant it was working. If she'd called it right, they were eighteen meters away. The projectile arced deeply, being several times more massive than a standard shell. At fifteen meters, it fuzed.

She was quite proud of that piece of improvisation. The tail fuze hit a triple charge that ignited, split the case and dispersed in a cone.

The powder puffed before deflagrating, like a beautiful flower petaling open. The cloud was a dark gray with perfect twisting swirls, then a flash that coned and roiled so as to form a perfect base ring. It reached about three meters wide, imperfect due to the ground, the building, and four bodies inside the fireball, convulsing then screaming. One ran like a chopped chicken, his robe billowing into smoky flames. The others just rolled around in a tangled, darkening mess.

Jason said, "Pocket thermobaric?"

"Yes."

"Damn, woman. That's sexy." He glanced and grinned between steering around obstacles.

"I knew you'd care."

She loaded a second one, and paused. Much as she'd like to torch a few, they were retreating. She didn't want to waste ammunition.

However, that group over there, with what looked like a machine gun . . . she swung, snapped and felt the shoulder sting. This one upset her. The charge was a bit asymmetric and favored the lower arc. They all still burned, but thrashed around clutching and beating at their shins.

"Impact," Jason said calmly, and someone thumped off the left quarter.

She saw others, and there were too many. His last turn had taken them out of sight of her previous targets, so the thickening crowd had nothing to judge the situation.

"We're going to get swarmed," she said.

"Yes. We need to get back to the others. We've done enough distraction. Hold on."

Bart was probably a better limo driver, but Jason did just fine with heavy vehicles. He swung violently left, and the truck leaned crazily, but didn't roll. There were multiple thumps of bodies being hit and thrown, and much more gunfire. One cracked through the open window, and punched a hole just above Jason's head.

"Shit, that was from street level," he said. He was observant.

"Stand by," she replied, while digging in the front of her vest. Somewhere there . . . got it. She held it out the window, snapped loose the lanyard, snapped the lanyard free, and tossed.

"Faster," she said.

He clenched and stomped and they accelerated at the best rate the lugging old vehicle could manage.

"What is it?" he asked.

"Distraction. Check behind."

She couldn't see much from where she sat, but she knew what it was doing. It was flammable gel with a surfactant to disperse it. It wouldn't burn for long, but it would cover most of the width of the street while it did, and of course, lead to injuries and possible ignition of other items. The popping of ammunition cooking off seemed to suggest so.

"Very nice," he said. "Revolting, even."

"Thank you."

"You're welcome. I'll slow at this corner. You bail out, cover me as I bail out, we'll proceed across and down that alley."

"Understood. I have an alley load ready."

"Good. Hopefully we won't need it."

"Well, you hope so." She most certainly wanted to use it. It might be unnecessary, or even a bad idea, but she hoped otherwise.

"Turning, braking," he said.

She popped the door latch as he came out of the turn, and brake momentum threw the door forward to slam against its detents. She hopped out at a sprint, dug her heels in to slow, and swung in an arc checking for threats.

He jumped out, stumbled, cracked his chin on his knee, stumbled again, rolled and recovered. She charged out, snagged him by an elbow and guided him at a full combat run.

"Thanks," he mumbled.

In the alley, she sought a nice pile of debris and pulled him down next to it. She twisted and sat hard, put a hand under his thigh, and let him fall almost to the ground before snatching her arm out. He grunted and starred with glassy eyes. He had a bad abrasion on his right cheek, blood seeping around grit. There was bruising underneath.

"Will you be okay?"

"Yes, I can move now," he said.

"We're fine for a few seconds. The crashed truck is drawing attention."

"How far do we have to go?"

"A few blocks, depending on where they took cover."

"Then let's at least walk. I want distance from our last known location."

"Good." She helped him to his feet and they started a brisk stride.

☺ CHAPTER 24 ☺

JOY HIGHLAND SHOULD NOT BE IN THIS POSITION. Here she was, dependent on armed thugs who enjoyed violence, and considered her voters expendable.

What was frustrating, aggravating, irritating was that they had been, and were, right. Her own party had turned on her. Her choices were to be a martyr physically and politically, just politically if she wanted to throw herself in front of the train, or trust these contemptuous troglodytes to drag her through a developing nation hellhole, and hope their body count was low enough, and the headlines big enough, to give her the edge. They represented corporate excess, the uncooperation of outsiders, smug elitism, everything her platform stood against. And she was dependent upon them to save her life and her career.

Poor Jessie was cut off from all her resources, and that directly affected Joy's campaign, too. They were going to take Jessie's career down with her. Joy didn't mind playing off against Ripple Creek. That's what they were for. But her own party, Cruk that slimy fucker, planned to not only take them down, but kill them in the process, and make her a shill.

It couldn't be Cruk. It had to be Lezt. She'd always suspected Champion's flyer crash was no accident. If she won this, she'd have him taken behind the Mansion and shot. No, she'd arrange a flyer accident. Perhaps that scary, flaky Sykora could be persuaded to stage it.

She should not be wading through rubble and trash, pulled by the arm like a detainee or child, and cowering from rioting underclasses. She was their savior.

Gunfire made her flinch and whimper. Jessie tried to grip her hand, but she shook it off.

I will not show fear in front of rabble, she thought. Except she was. The German, Bart, pushed ahead with Marlow. That doctor they called Shaman was right behind. The others were somewhere. She wanted all six around her.

She realized she'd completely forgotten her gun. Had they anticipated that? Were they snickering at the politician who wanted to play soldier? Did they know she'd served slop in a mine and minced fish guts to pay for school promotions? Everyone focused on the fact she'd had to pay, rather than earning her schooling on scores, but she'd earned it as much as anyone, with real work.

Another shot jarred her senses, and she realized she had a blister on her left foot. The ball stung and felt wet where it had burst.

She growled and pushed faster. She'd be damned if she'd give up now.

Jason was right, Aramis thought. Once they were in trajectory, they had no way to maneuver. The first one sailed cleanly overhead, about ten degrees down from his view. He raised the web gun, angled it for a good lead, and waited.

A moment later the second came into view, higher up but at the same speed. He shifted, snapped the trigger, realized the slow speed weapon needed more lead, and tried to shift.

The figure hissed out of sight, and the third one arched over before he could make ready.

He sighed, snarled and grumbled, poked his pistol over the ledge and fired, stood, fired again, jumped right, fired again, just to keep their heads down if they'd decided to pause for him.

Two of them kept right on bounding across the roofs. He didn't see the middle one, and from the spacing of the two remaining, he just might have gotten that one.

He took a wide arc toward the building's edge, raising his carbine, slinging the web gun, then holstering his pistol. He kept a good point in case of threat, and eased up to the edge.

The shot had caught the man on one of his Springblades, and he'd tumbled over the side while the goo caught on the roof and guttering. It appeared he'd smacked into the wall, but was conscious if a bit disoriented. Hanging upside down by one foot couldn't help.

The man had dropped any weapon he might have in hand, though appeared to have other stuff harnessed or packed. He was attempting to maneuver a foot into place, probably to try to bounce back up. He might even have a counter agent for the goo, but while hanging over the edge was not the time to use it.

His gyrations brought him eye to eye with Aramis, and he froze. Then he seemed to realize there were spectators below as well. Some of them pointed and cheered, or jeered, and a few small pebbles flew up to rattle against the wall.

"Help me up," the man asked.

"I don't think so." Dammit, why couldn't he have just fallen and finished it?

"I'm out of the fight and I'm your prisoner."

"I'm not a combatant and have no way to deal with prisoners." He really was in an awkward legal position. He was a bodyguard, so armed, but not a combatant, so the Law of Armed Conflict only applied in certain ways. He couldn't take a prisoner, but killing the man now would probably constitute a war crime.

That voice. Could he . . . ?

"Then just cut me free. I'll take my chances."

This . . . person . . . was probably one of the ones who'd had him tortured. His voice was familiar, but Aramis had been barely conscious. False memory? Real?

It wasn't Aramis's problem and he wasn't going to shoot the man in cold blood. What the spectators below might do was not his concern.

He turned, located a window on the floor below, and jumped in a dizzying arc, praying the window was open or of breakable paning. The jets did cut in for just a moment, flattening his trajectory.

The window was gone, the frame was not. He crashed through and felt splinters, but it wasn't critical and he slammed stingingly onto the balls of his feet, tumbled, rolled over his pack, came up with more abrasions and ran for the stairs. He did feel some of the splinters dragging on the fabric of his pants. They must have been heavy pieces to do that.

He went through the outside door fast, weapon ready, right into a group of six locals. He fired bursts right, forward and left, sprinted across the line of the alley, and heard the sound of rocks smacking into walls. They were trying to stone the guy to death ten meters in the air. It might have been kinder to shoot him. They most likely couldn't touch the goo, but it would weaken in a few hours, if he hadn't succumbed to cranial pressure by then.

Well, that wasn't his problem either. However, he wasn't sure even Caron's pull could prevent a brain wiping if word of this leaked out. They had to eliminate every one of these fuckers, without a lot of credible or even not so credible witnesses, and play stupid.

He had at least one jump left in the harness, and now was the time to use it. The bladers had correctly decided Aramis was less relevant than whatever they planned to do to Highland.

Stupid fuckers. Had they asked, there was a good chance he'd give them five minutes with her. Actually, no there wasn't. She might be a sociopathic bitch, but she hadn't directly tried to kill him, just to use him as a tool.

Still, both of them thought of him as something they could use and discard. That had to be discouraged.

The window ahead was open, or rather, missing, save for a couple of dull shards, and how long had they been here for that weak sun to dull that plastic? He adjusted his run, leapt through, dropped free, and felt the jets engage. He landed in a crouch, stood and ran.

With those damnable peace walls, they should have all had these things from the start. It would have made scaling unnecessary.

Ahead was the waypoint, and between him and it, a crowd. He hoped for one last thrust, sprinted toward them and clutched for the trigger.

One saw him, then ten, then all of them, pointing and shouting and milling about, then moving. He judged the distance, waited until he was sure they were going to tackle him, a half second longer, and punched it while leaping.

Close. Fingers plucked at his boot as he rose, then a cacophony of small arms fire crashed in his ears. He clenched in on himself, knowing they were untrained and incompetent and the odds of them hitting him were astronomical, while his hindbrain feared it anyway. He clutched at something on his harness and dropped it. A stink gas grenade. He underhanded it ahead of himself.

He was starting to arc down, and hoped to make that window. He snapped down the aiming ring, pointed that way and pressed the button again. He raised his carbine, shattered the glass with three shots, and slung it back down.

The jets burped, coughed, sputtered and hissed, and he was in free trajectory.

The wall came toward him and up dizzyingly fast, and he knew he was going to miss the window, but if he was lucky . . .

Aramis slammed ribs first into the frame, cracking his chin and knees, and his elbows as they hooked the frame. Crying and tearing and with shocks of pain burning nausea into him, he scrambled up, every touch of his elbows causing him to clench. He thought his sphincters were going to release, and he almost hoped they would. Perhaps that would reduce the nausea.

He tumbled over the sill as more fire was directed his way, some few rounds of hundreds actually making it through the outline of the window.

Inside, eyes peeked from behind a couch, and an elderly couple rose, hands up.

"You're safe," he said. From him they were.

Aramis slowed for a moment, took deep drafts of air, swallowed two "instant" analgesics with two swallows of water, and limp-sprinted for the far side, waving to the seniors as he passed through their door. With amusement, he noted the prayer box on the door sill, meant to keep threats out. So much for that myth.

There were certainly a confusing number of these standard pattern colonial buildings around. The locals would know their way, however. He needed speed. He unsnapped the harness and pulled his pack off, too. What was in his pockets would have to do.

He staggered down stairs, ignoring people who ignored him. It seemed all the violent-minded were outside, and the ones inside were meek and fearful.

However, the violent ones were on the far side, so for now he was safe, and the team should be meeting a klick away.

Those apartment blocks made great cover and boundaries. There was no fighting or rioting on this side. People noticed his gear and guns and shied away, but it was unlikely any of them would either start trouble or say anything. He walked briskly but without racing, kept his ears open for any pursuit but deliberately did not look back. He tried to blend in, as best he could in battle gear. The Catafract camo would help with that, since it had no color of its own.

He avoided shoving, stepped aside when possible, and most people were surprised to encounter him, which meant he was doing his job right. He knew he was close when the crowd thinned rapidly and disappeared, while the buildings turned drab, damaged, cratered. Just like that. This was an abandoned zone.

He got a very faint ping from Elke. She had power dialed way down, which meant they still expected active threats. The Bladers were somewhere nearby, and were both a direct threat and an intel leak.

He saw Elke ahead, just peeking from a corner. He made the hand signal that he was not under duress, and went past. It didn't matter much; the next doorway entered the same space, but it was habit. You never went straight to your cover.

"Got one," Aramis said as he dodged in.

"At least two left then," Shaman said.

"How are we doing?"

Jason said, "How are you doing? You're as much of a mess as I am." Jason was bandaged and sprayed. Wow. It looked like impact trauma and rock rash, though. A fall, probably.

"Ran out of fuel, crashed into building. On with the show."

Alex said, "We plan to stage from here, and get to that point you noted, three blocks from here. Shoot a lot, hard cover, wait for fight. What's the plan after that?"

"Kill them all," Elke said.

"Who are we staging with?" he asked.

Right then, a voice came through his headset on company freq.

"Welcome, welcome, Playwright, to the show that never ends."

Alex breathed relief. That was good news.

"Jacqueline, where are you?"

She giggled in his ears. "Really? I can see you. We'll be over in a few moments."

From outside he heard a hum, and looked out the window, startled. Cady and her team zipped around the corner in a beat up Mercedes. She waved with her left hand out the passenger window, while her right held a machine pistol, probably an iOrd.

The odds were still ridiculous, but with backup, he felt better. Though he blushed at not having tagged them as they came into the area. The locals might be incompetent, but Highland's foes were not. They had to know everything that went down.

Cady bounced out like a dancer, followed by two of her team, Lionel and Marlin.

"Okay, so now we have twelve. That's only half as pathetic."

Aramis said, "There are only two of the Agency guys on Springblades now."

She raised her eyebrows and said, "That doesn't mean there aren't others somewhere, on or off Springblades. And where did they come from?"

Alex said, "True, but those were a fantastic recon advantage, and intended to corral us. Now we are corralling the opposition, or will be shortly. As to where, we figure the administration sent them."

She looked surprised. "That's fascinating, and a bit disturbing. What do you have in mind?"

"How good is your driver? Bart and Jason are both excellent."

"As is Lionel, you know. Do you mind local hostile casualties?"

Highland snapped, "Yes!" as Alex said, "No. Hostiles are fair game." Inside he grinned. Active combat meant she no longer gave orders. It was almost a fair trade.

Cady said, "Well, we have one vehicle. We're going to be a clown car with guns."

Aramis said, "I'm okay with that. Get me there and we'll make it happen."

Alex said, "Slow down. Aramis, details."

The man turned and looked a bit surprised, probably still groggy from his impact.

"Oh, sorry. Okay, we'll be between three warring factions. There's lots of cover. We stir up shit, throw it in all directions, then duck. We see who shows up to take care of the Minister, and our best people," he pointed at Elke and Jason, "ice them."

Alex said, "That's your plan?" as Highland said, "That's your plan? To use me as bait?"

Aramis turned to her and said, "Ma'am, you're what they want. There isn't any other bait to use. If we wait, they get you. If we step out, they arrange an accident or incident, and then blame that faction—you can bet it will be one you favor—and move on."

That was it concisely, and Alex saw no reason to offer additional comment.

She stared, though, and he saw her façade crumble. Her lips trembled, and while she didn't cry, the fight went out of her.

She spoke, but it was inaudible. He could read her lips. "I can't do this anymore."

He said, "Our job is to keep you alive, ma'am. We can do it. Just stay with us."

She shook her head, trembled more, and didn't even protest when Shaman slipped over and slapped a patch on her neck.

There was uncomfortable silence for a moment. Principals had hesitated before, but Highland projected such bravado it was odd to see it shatter. JessieM looked stunned herself. Even she'd never seen this type of dissemblance.

"And now it's time to make that call. Who am I calling? Ms. Highland?"

"Oh . . . call the Liaison switchboard," she said.

He unshielded his phone, pulled the contact, waited for connection.

"Colonial Liaison Office, how may I help you?"

"Official request for Special Service protection for Candidate Highland, effective today, with a rating of thirty-two percent in three polls."

"That's . . . I'm not sure who handles that."

"Chief of mission will work. Put him on, please."

"Stand by."

Alex pointed at JessieM. "Announce we're doing it."

She nodded and pulled her own phone.

Alex wondered if they were stalling to trace. They'd have to move again quickly, but they did have the vehicle.

A voice came on, "Consul Beaumont. To whom am I speaking?"

"This is District Agent in Charge Alex Marlow, Chief of security, contract, for Minister Highland. We are officially requesting Special Service escort and security for her, as of one hundred eighty days from caucus, with multiple polls showing her above the thirty-two percent level."

"I see. I can relay that to the Executive Office."

"Please do so quickly. We're also publicly announcing the request from both her campaign and our official contacts. I need to disconnect. I will be in touch. Out." He closed the connection and shielded the phone fast.

"Now we wait."

Cady stepped in and said, "Well, we can't wait here. They're moving and closing as we speak, and we need to be at ground zero, not in a bombed-out ruin three hundred meters away."

Elke and Bart stepped up, gently took Highland's arms, and guided her. JessieM followed.

Cady said, "Marlin, get the door. Lionel drives, double up in all seats. It's going to be a party. We brought you a couple of toys."

They formed up and moved to the car, which had attracted some attention, and their movement attracted more. Highland went along, somewhat numb even before Shaman dosed her with whatever he'd dosed her with. She seemed lucid, but strangely compliant.

It was more than crowded in the car. The front section had driver and Helas and Edge crammed into one passenger seat, almost making out, with guns pointing across each other. That was nothing on the back, though.

Shaman had one side, with Jessie on his lap. Aramis had the middle, with Highland on his, and he did not look amused. Jason had the outside, with Cady on his lap. He looked a bit uncomfortable. Yeah, all of them found a transsexual a bit odd.

That left the open cargo hatch for Cady's other three, Bart, Elke and Alex, and a large crate already in place. Elke hung back as others boarded, obviously reluctant to be that close to that many people. She really didn't like people. It took surprisingly little time to get everyone crammed in, and Lionel drove off mildly, but brought speed up fast. Still, five seconds could seem like an eternity, and could be in an actual fight. The whipping air felt good to Alex as they drove in to what they hoped was an ugly melee all around them.

Wow, phrased like that, it sounded insane.

"Open the crate," Cady ordered.

Alex and Cady's man Marlin popped the catches and flipped the lid up.

A Medusa Weapons System, and ten kilos of Composition G for Elke.

"Merry Christmas!" he shouted. "Bart, can you possibly skin into this while moving?"

"If you get friendly together, yes."

Elke leaned far over Alex, snatched the blocks of explosive in a bundle just like a kid with candy, and drew into a ball against Jason's seat. Alex moved back against her. It wasn't an ideal spot, but she'd be more comfortable with him than strangers. Cady's troops scooted right to the hatch lip, leaving Bart an area about a meter cubical for his bulk and the Medusa. There was just no way that was going to work.

Lionel's voice came from the cabin, "We have potential contacts left, closing."

"Also right," said one of the pair crammed into the passenger seat.

"As long as we're still moving, we're good," he said.

Cady leaned back past Jason's head and said, "If or when the crowd stops us, you work perimeter."

"Yeah, switch. Until we're in cover. Do we have cover? Aramis?"

Aramis said, "That corner has a rebuilt booth arrangement."

"Good. Everyone understand we are not taking a squat hole. Once pinned down, anyone could hit us with a charge and blame others. Movement is our friend." He turned. "Elke, do you have your special loads and some jubilee fireworks?"

"Not enough for this crowd, but I can make a hole."

It all gelled.

"That's the plan. Once blocked, we make a large hole very fast and move into opposite territory, play the escaping victim card, then repeat, then find a dodge while they're all killing each other."

Aramis asked, "And the Paramils?"

"Kill them on sight if you can. That's my interpretation of Ms. Highland's orders. If they target her, they are enemies of the state."

It was disturbing to come to that. Certainly, that was a crime. It wasn't one he approved of. It was too easy to declare someone outlaw and go after them, but in this case, it did seem to fit. Assassination and power struggles from the administration level to bypass elections and courts were certainly not legitimate.

Bart said, "Here they come, the crowd." Somehow he was half into the gear. The new generation was lighter and smaller than the predecessor, but still a thirty-kilo load. His other gear was stuffed under the seats.

Elke seemed to have distributed the explosive, including giving blocks to Jason and Aramis. She handed one to Alex, then twisted and bent to retrieve Bart's abandoned gear.

Alex turned back to the street. Yes, it was getting packed, and there were thumps as Lionel hit a few, then bumps as he rolled over a few more, and stopped steering. He was going straight forward to use car mass against crowd mass.

That crowd also had taken to running to catch up with them. They were armed with everything from bricks to machine guns, though only two of those so far. He scrunched tighter inside the vehicle's frame, as the mob started striking the body. A club came close by his foot, but missed.

Across from him, Elke asked, "Now?"

The car jolted over what turned out to be two bodies, the men crippled and dying but thrashing in agony from crushed limbs and torsos.

"Not yet. As soon as we're slow enough we're at risk of boarding, take point."

She nodded calmly. Good. Bad for anyone else of course, but good for them.

A gruesome red smear appeared on the road and grew in proportion. Someone had been hit, stuck underneath and was being dragged and ground away. The volume reached enough the blood started bubbling and trickling.

Bart muttered, "*Scheisse,*" and adjusted his weapon grip. Elke fingered something and nodded. Cady's two men thumbed up and tensed.

Alex judged the speed and the crowd. Clutching hands brushed him as they rolled, and one caught the fabric on his shoulder enough to be noticed.

"It's now," he said.

Elke shouted, "FIREINTHEHOLE!" she raised her carbine, dropped her hand to the launcher underneath, snapped the trigger, and the world exploded. Alex's earbuds attenuated the blast, but did nothing for the shockwave. It seemed to blow through him, punching his guts.

What the hell did she just fire? His head rang, his eyes blurred and refocused, and he twisted out to the street. He caught a glimpse of her unloading an expended . . . something.

To his left, what had been behind him was a pile of mangled bodies with gaping wounds. Then his brain put it all together. Inside the launcher, she'd fired a block of large bore hunting rounds simultaneously. It was like a machine gun burst, in one concentrated rush. *Shit, that had to hurt. Her I mean.*

The crowd around the hamburger were in various stages of terror, and so in fact were all those in quite a radius. They'd thought it was a bomb.

"Smoke, distractions," Elke said in his ringing ears, and huge clouds of thick yellow puked out from several small scattered capsules. That was followed by a string of reports that sounded exactly like a small-caliber automatic weapon.

He came around the side to find the door open, Jason and Cady out, dragging out Highland.

"Proceed now," he ordered, and Jason grabbed Highland's hand, put it on his ruck and said, "Hold on, ma'am."

She nodded and followed, clenching one of the straps. She was well-practiced with the procedure and went along as she should. Jason looked back, half-nodded and accelerated to a brisk pace. Cady took right, the others filled in in a large block, and they walked.

The mob didn't seem sure what to do, but as always, some brave started the infall, and they closed.

Elke tossed another string of squibs, switched from carbine to shotgun with a fling of the slings, and fired low overhead. The bird bomb banged loudly and that part of the wave broke and scattered.

They walked around a couple of bodies. Fighting had been ongoing here for some time, or it might never have really stopped, just shifted from place to place.

They came past the front of the car as Elke fired again. This was some kind of incendiary that slammed into a guy's chest, erupted in white flame, and filled the air with the fried bologna stink of burning flesh.

Aramis fired left, a short burst. That cleared space for Lionel to slip into formation. Alex heard one burst to the rear, probably from Bart, and one more to right from one of Cady's men, and he needed to remember their names. Also, everyone was showing fantastic fire discipline, but that wasn't what they needed.

"Aramis, what's the route and rendezvous?"

"We hit a wall two blocks ahead. It's partially finished. We can work around to the east."

"Straight for the wall then, and left. Don't run out of ammo, but don't be frugal if we get crushed."

For now, though, this crowd wanted distance. They had respectable clear space, but there was a mostly hidden rifle, poking from between two kids, held by the man behind them. That was disgusting.

"Jason, fix that," he said and pointed.

Jason swung his weapon as if at some sport shoot, came into line, fired one shot, and the man's head split. He collapsed dead. The kids jumped back, stared wide-eyed, then ran. Good. Some of these savages trusted in God to keep them dead or alive. It was a convenient excuse to be violent shitbags. Did God tell you to stop? Then he must approve.

A large eruption behind them was the car exploding. Metal, plastic and body parts of looters tumbled and fluttered through the air. It was company policy, military policy and good tactics not to leave assets for the enemy. Elke really enjoyed asset denial.

There was sporadic fire here and there, though little seemed aimed their way. Occasional cracks indicated someone in one of those buildings was shooting at them, but not actually shooting them. Still, sooner or later he'd get lucky, though.

There were abandoned construction tools here, from both the wall and a new block of ugly being built to the west. If the troops wanted to complain about overpaid contractors, they could start with these, who were apparently owned by the SecGen's brother, and building all kinds of stuff that wouldn't be needed, appreciated, or allowed to stand long. Generators, a mix truck, several extruders, brace erectors, pumps. The breakage was awful, and the government's response was to send more.

Eh. Less interesting than the approaching wall.

Aramis spoke over net. "Hit the wall, turn east, we'll have right side hard cover, sporadic on the left. About a kilometer."

Alex said, "Cady, I want someone to drop those repeater phones as we go. Flank out about two hundred meters, toss one in a gutter or other convenient place. If they wind up wandering around due to local action, so much the better."

"Got it. Give five each to Roger and Adam."

Jason handed the sack over to Roger Edge, who dug in, handed some over to Adam Helas, then dodged out of the loose formation and headed west.

The rest kept running. Alex was in decent shape, and not that much older than the others, he told himself, but dodging through debris, obstacles and potential threats had him well-winded. A rest was in order, but firefights tended to interfere.

They reached the wall, found an unfinished ditch from construction, and piled in, Bart reaching up to handle Highland and Jessie down. The Medusa wasn't powered, so he was carrying its weight plus theirs. Once they were down he went back to function checks.

"Take a brief break," he gasped. "Water, breathe, check ammo and gear. Jason and Lionel keep watch. Rotate. Reports?"

Cady said, "All accounted for. I'm getting some tingles of scans."

Jason said, "So am I. We won't be hidden for long. Ma'am, are you still wearing your vest?"

Highland, bent with hands on knees, twitched and said, "That? Yes . . . and the body . . . armor. God, I itch." She belched, not quite a dry heave. The day was getting hot, too. Add in the haze around the construction, normal city dust and propellant gases, and everyone was going to have trouble breathing.

Alex said, "Catch your breath, ma'am; we'll be moving again in moments. It's going to be intense and hectic, but we'll have everyone tied up shortly."

She sounded a bit better as she said, "Tell me again . . . what we're doing."

"We're going to tie as many hostiles as possible up fighting each other. Then we only have to deal with ones who make a concerted effort to come for you. We're going to kill them."

She nodded while drawing in breaths.

"Jessie, how are you doing?"

"Scared," she said, and the trembles gave it away. She seemed recovered from the running and ready for more. Young, light, unencumbered by gear. Must be nice. And yes, scary.

"Good. Time to move," he said. "Bart, Aramis assist Ms. Highland. Lionel assist Jessie. Elke and Jason on point."

Jason said, "Always a punishment for being best. Let's do it."

⊚ CHAPTER 25 ⊚

ARAMIS FELT GOOD, with occasional tingles of fear. These trogs loved their random gunfire, and relied on prayer for hits. Prayer and hits had about the same likelihood of success, but enough millions of rounds meant someone would hit the jackpot. He'd been fragged once in a previous mission, tortured this time . . . he felt mortal. Not good.

Highland was in that state of mind where she'd try to lag for rest. It wasn't conscious, and military training taught you to get past that, but she hadn't had that, so he grabbed an arm with Bart and hurried her along. She was courageous enough. Again he wondered why she bothered posing. He didn't like the bitch, but she had enough guts if she'd just show those.

Jessie ran alongside, offering encouragement.

"Come on, ma'am. We're doing it. We're with you."

Aramis would have preferred to get Military Trainer on her, but it wouldn't help. She was working hard.

The route was as it should be. This wall was farther along than he'd expected, though. Trust the government to get something right at the wrong time.

"We turn in two hundred meters," he said.

Cady sounded angry. "The devil we do. Those crabherders got the berm built."

"Aw, shit."

Yes, he could see it, past the debris, tools and remains of buildings.

The wall was still being built, but the berm used to set it was steep, high and had that cut in the middle, where the wall would go. Some eager crew had run ahead of schedule, probably to wangle for budget.

"Now I hate contractors," he muttered.

"We'll have to cross it," Jason said. "Not quite my field of engineering, but if I can find some poly sheets or lumber, we can do it."

It was then that a targeted drone zipped over the berm and dove for them with an angry buzz.

Even Highland remembered her gun, and eleven weapons swung that way.

Aramis was just behind Jason. Jason was slightly in the lead, and grinned as he got the gun lined up. Then the drone spit itself to pieces, as he heard rapidfire from the Medusa. Bart had beat him.

"Well done," he acknowledged. That put him back to the event at hand—combat construction of a bridge while at the top of a berm between hostiles. Aramis wondered how the hell you did that.

Cady said, "I don't wish to alarm anyone, but the angry mob is about three minutes behind us and closing."

Some sort of projectile wooshed and crashed not far away, and they all dove for cover amidst cable drums and re-rod boxes.

Elke said, "Recon" and swung her shotgun. The dull sound gave away what she'd fired. The tiny camera snapped photos as it flew, and the computer in her visor stripped away the worthless ones that showed sky. She thumbed a control, clicked for several, and a moment later they popped up on his goggles.

Neither resolution, aperture nor size were good, but it was clear enough there was a missile mortar support element on the far side. They seemed to be some local army, but it was hard to tell which and didn't matter.

Aramis tried hard to chill the frustration. It wouldn't help, and they needed clear thinking right now. Active hostiles over the berm/wall. Others closing. Exactly what they wanted, except for being stuck in the middle. Engineering was Jason's job. They had light support weapons in the Medusa. They had a reinforced squad. Alex was a good leader, what could he do to help?

Alex said, "We could really use some mortar fire. Elke, any ideas? Charges we can toss?"

She looked at him, looked at Jason, Jason looked at her, and the two of them took off at a low sprint.

"I'll take that as a yes," Alex muttered. "Aramis, Bart, keep Witch covered."

"Yes, sir," Aramis nodded.

For now, all they could do was bunker down. That berm was very solid, and they lacked anything with the required punch.

Aramis was embarrassed. This new army was not as capable as his had been. In less than five years, the entire philosophy had changed with the leadership. They were more geared toward fighting lightly armed rebels than real threats. That came from consensus building rather than competent central authority.

Still, they were keeping the rebels here well tied up. Though at some point soon, someone higher up would order a heavier engagement, he was sure.

Some kind of engine roared behind the building. It was a turbine, and sounded military. He got ready to shoot at the driver if he had to.

It could also be an industrial engine, he realized, as a cement mixer barreled around the corner, leaving tire compound in tracks and throwing debris. Jason and Elke were in the cab, he driving, she on shotgun. Jason braked hard but kept it straight, which threw the doors open to crack hinges against the detents. They bailed out in leaping rolls as it reached zero speed, and took cover as it sped up again, the engine revving in an insane whine. Jason had jammed it in gear, pinned the steering and let the engine run.

It almost reached the berm when Elke rose enough to key something on her box, and the explosions started.

The first one lifted the rear of the vehicle two meters off the ground in a dusty slam. The second ripped the drum from its mounts and angled it up and forward while throwing the damaged chassis back down. The third one blew as the truck smashed into the berm.

As the drum stood upright, a dull whump rippled it, then peeled it into petals from the mouth, turning it into a bizarre metal flower. The contents erupted out the mouth in a volcanic splash of gray ooze, looking like ten cubic meters of fantasy lava, in globs and clumps and a huge fountain. It caused a dark, foreboding shadow as it rose. It reached apogee, tumbled and fell, right behind the berm.

Twelve tons of concrete "mortar" wasn't quite what he had in mind, but the wreckage against the berm made a convenient step, and there wasn't any enemy fire in that area. The steel flower of the blown drum tumbled and fluttered down to land atop the glop.

"Well done." Alex couldn't say anything else. "We'll need to detour north."

Bart took point and let the guns swivel. He chose targets near people but legitimately kept the casualty count low, though there were always collaterals.

Like that pair with what looked like a crude rocket launcher. It might be effective and it might hit, so he tagged them for a grenade and felt it kick the harness as it launched. It was an incendiary. He was out of the antipersonnel rounds.

It splashed in sparkly white, ripping one in pieces and sending the other shrieking in basso wails until he fell over and convulsed and stopped.

"Keep moving," Alex said. "We're following."

He did so, lumbering along, and something sailed past him. The visor flashed a warning, but it was outgoing, something on a string, so probably Elke's. That was confirmed when it hit the ground and cascaded in stages, from a first brilliant flare to gleaming fires, to flashing sparks and embers. Something overhead arced into the conflagration at high speed and exploded. She'd decoyed it.

Bart said, "I think they've escalated. Elke successfully shut off this section. The others are increasing fire."

Cady asked, "Do we have any idea which faction it is?"

Jason said, "I'd almost say army, except the fire is almost too good and all lethal. Aerospace Force doesn't have that kind of hardware. It's not Marines, in this sector, so it's a local faction. I'd guess that's the Sufi. They're about the best local."

"Well, if we can keep that up, we've got a semi-professional contact approaching from the north."

"Interesting," Aramis said. "That's Amala territory, and they're certainly not anything professional."

Helas asked, "Suborned? An elite group? Infiltrated?"

Elke had some kind of scanner, and said, "Munitions are Croatian. So they may be anyone's."

Jason looked frustrated as he said, "Who cares? We knew it wouldn't go as planned. Move!"

They clustered up around Highland and Jessie and ran east in a crouch. After the berm there was a ditch, then debris where annexed property had been demolished. He presumed that was their immediate destination. It was a solid kilometer, and he was already breathing hard, with the weight of the Medusa, and Highland's drag.

Jessie was keeping good pace, though. She certainly had been a runner.

The occasional fire increased. Then another drone rose behind them. He heard it, but it had to have already logged them. He turned, sighted, let the #2 gun slap a burst into it, and resumed.

Alex said, "Bart just killed a drone. Assume we're compromised."

"That wasn't a military drone," Elke said. "Do we have a photo?"

Bart said, "Yes, but I'm not sure how to get it from the system. Is it important?"

"It might be," she said.

"Then I will try." He was running, would soon have to actively dodge fire, half-carrying a weakened noncombatant and thirty kilos of Medusa. Now they wanted him to do technical work while avoiding debris and craters.

He thumbed a control, then another. There it was, and then gone. *Scheisse.* Hopefully not lost. There. He leapt like a 150 kilogram ballerina over a large chunk of concrete. He found the link for network, confirmed it was the one Jason projected from his pack, and sent it.

"Sent," he called to Elke.

A moment later she said, "That's a Ranco Industries model, last generation. They lost the trials on UN military, but were declined export license. They were a little too good for that."

Highland said, "But Blanding was CEO of Ranco before he . . ."

And she'd been talking to him, at length.

Alex said, "He was a suspect."

Cady added, "He may not be the only one. Alliance? Overlapping?"

"We can't know."

Highland's voice was ragged as she hurled, "I want that fucker dead."

"Not in our power to do, ma'am," Alex said as he dropped alongside. He needn't have. She found renewed energy somewhere and surged. Bart let her move ahead.

"If you get a chance . . ."

"We will follow contract, law and rules of engagement. Isn't that what you wanted?"

"Fuck you, too," she snarled.

"Cover in there," Aramis said and pointed. "There are supposed to be tunnels."

"Tunnels?" Jessie asked.

"Power conduit tunnels, more than big enough to crawl in."

"I'll try," she said. Claustrophobe?

"That's our best bet at the moment."

A serious, aimed burst of machine gun fire chewed chips from the debris around them. They shouted, shrieked or grunted as they felt minded to. Bart tracked back as best he could, fired a burst into the building from #1, and followed with a grenade from #4.

Then he almost smashed Highland into the wall as he turned to go sideways through the door. He paused to let her shift, banged his weapon and his knee, but got through, dragged her carefully past the frame, as Aramis brought up the rear.

"Must . . . rest," she rasped.

Aramis said, "One swallow of water, three deep breaths, and we have to find the tunnels."

"Should we split up?" Cady asked. "We can do more damage?"

Bart wasn't sure where her advantage came from, but Cady hardly seemed winded. She rolled on the balls of her feet, ready to spring.

"Down, or up?" he asked, because more than that would tire him. Also, he wasn't sure about dragging the bitch—either Highland or the Medusa—through the tunnels.

It was Lionel who said, "Above offers sniping position. Under will be harder to locate. We need to be rats."

Alex agreed. "Even though we're taking the fight to them, we're twelve, currently ten, versus thousands. We want to instigate, not wave our arms and offer it up."

"Through here," Aramis said. There was a collective groan, sigh, murmur and agreement that moving was better than standing, and they all followed at a jog, which would be easy except for the exhaustion of the previous sprints.

This had been an office building, perhaps twenty years ago. On Earth it would have been replaced by now. Here, it had apparently become apartments, then offices again, and the structure was weakened by a combination of substandard materials, age and conflict. Yes, if the tunnels were of good depth, they would be much safer than any elevation in this derelict.

Aramis seemed to know where they were going, and it was impressive how many maps, charts and building plans he could have. It was almost as if he had an inertial tracker in his brain.

They took a turn, then another. They went through what had been an office but had only broken remains of fixtures and furniture left. The walls had been pried to access the wires and fibers. That led to another door, to a service corridor.

"Elke, door," Aramis said.

She stepped up, slapped on a patch, took a large step sideways, and popped the lock. Or rather, banged it. His goggles stopped a few sharp tatters of plastic, and he caught one in his teeth, which he swept clear and spit.

Lionel looked at Aramis, who nodded. He kicked the door wide, waved his carbine down the empty stairs, then took point.

Not quite empty stairs. They'd been used for storage once the tunnels were no longer used.

"Ears," Lionel said. Bart checked Highland was wearing hers.

In enclosed quarters, even moderated guns were loud. His burst shredded several boxes, that seemed to be full of paper copies of documents.

"Ah, crap."

"Let me," Elke said. "Back in the hall."

Bart was in the doorway and stepped aside. The front two backed out, leaving Elke to fish out something, toss it, then step aside herself.

"Fire in the hole."

A roaring nimbus erupted from the doorway, blowing cindered paper and heavier chunks. He felt an overpressure slap. Highland whimpered, JessieM yelped. The rest flinched and waited. Five seconds later, Elke threw a thumb up and led the way.

He turned in and found she'd made worthy headway, but there was more crap down there, the lowest levels at the bottom of the landing were molded and slimy. Down the next flight, some stuff had tumbled and slipped in a small avalanche, but by careful foot place-ment they could step and ease their way through hot embers, acrid smoke, clutter and trash.

At the bottom, Aramis had opened the tunnel door himself, with a pry bar.

From the rear, Shaman said, "Hear that?"

They froze momentarily, and Alex heard small arms combat.

"They're mixing it up now. Hopefully that will slow them."

"What's the plan?" Lionel asked as they trooped into the tunnel. A crouch was possible, but Alex knew he'd be crippled after a hundred meters of that. He went to his knees, as Aramis and Bart had.

They stirred up dust that was a combination of spores, grit and drifting insulation. He grabbed for a paper mask and dragged it over his head. Some still got through, and his breathing was hindered by the filter matrix holding his hot exhalations. Still, it was a hindrance, not a stoppage.

Aramis's voice was muffled by a mask, and echoed oddly. He said, "We go across the street, well, under it. That puts us outside the epicenter. We then go up, and wait to see who comes looking for us. They have to fight through the confusion, and we'll have a good position."

Behind him, it was Highland who asked, "What if they wait us out?" She coughed from dust seeping around her mask.

"They'll want to be fast, and take the opportunity. The longer it goes on, the more likely we are to get backup. Their resources are finite. This assumes they're logical and reasonable."

She said, "Huble will be. I don't know about Lezt."

"We'll hope others are, too, or that they make mistakes."

Elke's voice said, "Ready to close this end."

He really wasn't sure about that. They needed cover and concealment, and to stop pursuit. It was also useful to create the impression that they might be dead. Against that, though, was that they'd be trapped underground, hoping the other end was no worse than this one had been, and that if Elke missed a calculation, it might cave in on top of them.

"As soon as everyone is in, do it," Aramis said.

"No time," she insisted. "They're entering the building now."

"Everyone move! Babs, do it!"

Behind him came shouts and scrabbles, then a breath-stealing *bang!* That blew debris past him. The ground shook and rumbled and continued to do so, as he scurried like a rat, except a rat had proper feet and wouldn't wear out its knees the way he was, even with kneepads.

"Elke, it's still rumbling!" he said.

"The building was unstable. A large part is coming down. Think of it as free bonus destruction."

"Can it hurt us?"

"I accounted for it."

If he ever got married again, he'd never be able to trust even a wife the way he trusted Elke.

Aramis said, "There's already a news churp that Ms. Highland may have died in fighting in the capital."

She snarled, "Those crab-picking snot ghouls."

Alex said, "After last time, you think they'd learn not to—"

Aramis cut in with, "BuState denies dead in fighting, insists kidnapped by factions. I'm getting a feed of 'her' calling for help and demanding peace from her supporters."

Highland said, "You were right." It was so soft it would have been inaudible, except he'd been hoping for it, and hoping not to be right.

"Yes, ma'am, they're going to build you up heroically, try to kill you, and load your presence into the party. If they can't do that, look for some embarrassing content to make its way out shortly."

Elke apparently had reception on her gear. "The Sunni are offering a reward for her capture as a war criminal. The Amala are offering to match it, dead or alive. Highland Campaign Concordance is demanding the government arrest the preceding groups."

"They're in quite a frenzy. Good."

"Access ahead," Aramis advised.

"Open?"

"Welded."

"Shit. Elke, forward."

"I am the creeping thing," she said.

They pulled up and stopped, face to heel, almost face to ass. A minute later, Elke crawled past, brushing the wall as she did so.

"This is going to be loud. Cover ears, open mouths, stand by. Any alibis? Fire in the hole."

The explosion sounded deep and low, but felt like a kick in the guts from an elephant. The overpressure absolutely crushed him in the enclosed space. The dust turned opaque, and over it all was a ringing noise where the metal had yielded to Elke's ministrations.

It still wasn't open, though he assumed her blast had done as intended. She was neither cursing in Czech nor preparing a second charge.

A tug at his ankles was Highland, who crawled closer and muttered, "Alex, are there clean clothes available?"

He wasn't going to ask which way she'd cut loose. These things happened in war, and her expression was completely forlorn.

"Not at present, ma'am. I'll see what we can find."

"Thank you."

Aramis pried at the metal, Bart shoved, and shortly it shrieked and relented.

Aramis said, "Yeah, a lot more trash here, and ripe. Wow."

The stench indicated the stairwell at this end had obviously been used as a latrine, trash dump and general pit. There were coffee scents, rot, piss, fermented vegetables and god only knew what else.

Behind, another round of rumbles started.

Elke said, "That was not me. Someone just struck the other building."

"So they know we're in this area. Move."

Aramis said, "Yeah, there's a plastic pallet here. We can walk over that for a few steps."

"Whatever helps. Move!"

Fortunately, it was mostly stink, though the floor was slimy and disgusting. "Watch your step!" he advised, as he crawled through the hatch onto the pallet, stood and turned.

Bad news, they had a ladder, not stairs, though there was a small landing at the top.

"Okay, this place already stinks, everybody drain. That corner, ladies first."

Aramis and Shaman stood there facing out, creating some illusion of privacy. Highland looked embarrassed and ashamed. Jessie half-moved and hesitated, stuck between needing to and unable to, until Elke grabbed her and went back herself. Cady said, "I'm fine."

Several of the men took turns to unzip and drain, and Alex went last as Aramis ascended the ladder behind him. There was a respectable puddle, several liters, but the detritus on the ground was so squishy it didn't seem it would matter.

That done, he turned to the stairs and climbed up, hands on the sides to avoid gripping the muck left from Aramis's boots. Then he knelt, turned and offered a hand to Highland. As she came up, he could see she had wet her pants. Well, explosions and collapses could do that to one. He wasn't going to mention it. If they could find clean clothes later they would. For now, he helped Jessie up, and Cady made the small landing completely full.

The door was partly off the hinges and askew. Beyond it was a cabinet of some kind.

There was movement to the sides, and he got the impression there were combatants.

Aramis had a pen-sized periscope, and Bart slid a small probe through another crack. Good. Elke's shotgun-fired recon rounds would not help here.

Aramis whispered, "There are four routes underground we could have taken. That disrupts the pursuit. This appears to be local militia. Red bandanas with Arabic as their uniform."

From the ladder, Jason asked, "Does it say 'Arm of God'?"

"How the fuck would I know? I don't speak Arabic. Hold on. Bart?"

Bart nodded, fingered controls, and pulled an image. It meant little to Alex, though it was familiar. Jason said, "Yes, that's them. Sunni. Adequately trained. Looks like they have current generation gear."

Alex asked, "Estimate on numbers?"

"Possibly thirty in this space. Beyond that, unknown."

He sighed. Frontal firefights were a bad thing, even with the element of surprise. These guys had rifles, light armor, and looked ready to rumble.

"Well, we do what we have to. We can take them. But some discretion would have been nice."

Jason said, "My Arabic is good enough I can sound like an Amala."

"Will they believe it, the way we're dressed?"

"Shouting will do it."

"Likely. Then I guess we do. Judgment calls. Balance ammo with damage. Aramis and Bart split the front. I'll take forward."

Cady said, "I'm on the right," and shifted her carbine to a left-handed stance. She and Jason were both largely ambidextrous.

Jason said, "I've got right. Marlin, Lionel, take left. Ms. Highland, Jessie, huddle down in the middle while we clear some space, then be ready to sprint for cover. Shaman, Elke, stay with them, bring them up the rear"

Jason slapped his ankle, he prodded Cady and goosed Aramis. Aramis nodded, said, "Go!" and kicked at the door.

It didn't break cleanly. It splintered. It was plastic, not wood, but old and crazed and some kind of extrusion. His boot went through and he wasn't going to be able to pull it back out. Bart slammed his forearm against the upper section, and it gave way, and the two tumbled through, shoving the cabinet until it caught on the floor and fell over. They tumbled, rolled and came up.

A bullet came between them, right over Alex's head, and he swarmed forward, high-stepping over the wreckage.

Then Bart opened up with the cannon.

Peripherally, he saw two men on the left explode into meaty goo. The cacophony echoed. Aramis fired three bursts right. Cady fired. There was a momentary pause for targets, and Jason started wailing something in Arabic, of which Alex only recognized, "*Allahu akbar!*" *God is great.* Well, that depended on whose god and the circumstances.

Ahead of him, someone kicked a door in, and started to spray the room. He pointed, filled them with a burst, and fired another, slightly sustained one down the corridor. That was about twenty rounds of his fifty-round mag gone.

Bart fired off some kind of grenade. Or maybe it was Elke. But the concussion was painful. Even moderate charges were brutal with reflective surfaces. Fire picked up all around as the eight mercenaries filled the space.

Alex realized there weren't any more targets for him. The room was a dusty, smoky, choking haze of debris with the acrid smell of propellant and the salty tang of blood. Computers were shattered, a respectable commo unit had been expertly hit. The mic and headset were shattered by pinpoint shooting—probably Jason's work.

Elke said, "Light military vehicle outside."

Aramis said, "My map says there's a perfect position for an OP at the top of this building."

"Then we're definitely not going there. Suggestions?"

"Yes, take the vehicle. I recommend frontal drive south."

"What's there?"

"More Sunni, then the army. There's a peace control point about three kilometers ahead."

"And Paramils overhead."

"Bart can handle them, or Jason."

"Yeah, and they won't want to be seen in that mix. Though same rule applies." He pointed in the direction of the door and started moving as he spoke. "They'll be unseen in the mayhem. Also, contact forward."

A squad of someone was arriving on the street front, taking up position across.

Alex ordered, "Block in principal, advance with cover fire, move."

Shaman and Lionel stood directly in front of Highland and Jessie. Bart and Aramis opened up until it sounded like the world exploded. Elke and Jason did something on the left, Cady went right, and Alex followed. There were tens of troops, at least, advancing leapfrog, though most of them did dive for cover when shot at. He picked one, and his first shot grazed and creased the man's back. Second shot was through the top of his helmet, and the man jerked like a frog. Two others shot back, and he flinched, but they weren't close. It was always good to be a moving target.

The vehicle was some equivalent to a Grumbly. Unarmored, unarmed at present, but decently mobile. The block of protective meat flowed and climbed the back, and Lionel dove from the open bed, through the back hatch, into the cab. Jason ran up the passenger side, waving a tool roll, fired a burst from some locally procured dump gun, dumped it, yanked the door and jumped in.

Alex waited for the rest of Cady's team, and she boarded second to last, then helped yank him up into the bed. They did not present a low profile, but they presented a heavily armed profile. Marlin had acquired some local machine gun, and Bart stood up against the cab as support and antiair.

"Roll!" he and Cady both said at the same time.

They were driving into an approaching mass of armed people, heading east again, and needed to turn south. Troops spilled into the street, mostly second-rate militia, though that was probably generous. Little of this planet deserved the sobriquet of second rate.

They'd planned for action, even if they didn't want it. They were about to get it.

✪ CHAPTER 26 ✪

HORACE MOVED FAST ENOUGH to keep Highland's grip under tension, so he knew she was following. Outside, bullets cracked, but none close enough to worry him terribly. At the curb, he swung, detached Highland's hand, and helped her into the bed with a shove. He frowned. She was soaked. Not critical in the field, but it had to be unpleasant and disturbing for a civilian.

He swung up after her, no longer being young enough to spring, and rolled ungracefully to a bench.

"You stay down, ma'am, miss," he insisted. Then, holding his carbine over the rail in case of targets, he dug into his kit. Right side, lower, angled pocket, and . . . there.

He handed her a flat packet.

"Super absorbent gel. Pour it in your hand, and it will soak up the spill."

She looked overwhelmed from the fire, but she recognized that, seemed to come back to ground, and said, "Thank you." She started dumping it and applying it.

Technically, it was a clotting agent, but principal's mental health mattered, too, and they'd already given this woman more adventure than her press releases had ever dreamed. The overload was apparent in her face.

Bullets cracked past, occasionally slapping into the sides. Marlin twitched and threw himself prone. Horace ducked, checked, saw a crater in his armor, and slapped him on the shoulder.

"You're fine, just a spall."

"Roger, thanks."

Bart fired forward, something from each tentacle. The man was really getting good at controlling that beast; if only they made them less monstrous, but of course, batteries and ammo took volume and mass. One gun pointed to each side, ready to hose buildings. One pointed straight up against drones, and at that moment it swung and stuttered. Light pistol rounds were all that was needed to take down most of those things. The grenade launcher he kept pointed forward. He also had a dump gun under his left arm, for close-in hosing.

Elke shouted, "Recon!" and slammed a shell overhead. "Heavy foot traffic ahead, and fighting between vehicles. We'll be dismounting in two hundred meters," she said.

Alex shouted, "Understood, stand by."

Cady said, "Edge and Helas are well-covered and safe. They'll keep activating repeaters. Five left."

Alex said, "Understood. Every ten minutes should do it."

Horace kept his eyes on his sector. Until there were casualties, he was a gun. It always amazed him how few casualties there were. He had first-hand experience on how effective training, movement, and avoidance could be. Right then, a man, head wrapped in a rag and pointing a rifle, rose above the sill of a broken window. Horace twisted his gun that way and fired a burst. Whether he hit or not he was unsure, but the man didn't shoot.

He heard sobbing. It was Jessie, not Highland. By touch, he located a mild tranquilizer and a mild stim. He reached back and said, "Slap these on your neck."

Fingers clutched at them. It took her three tries. That was about right for the level he'd prescribed. Then she grabbed that small wooden penguin again. Good.

Bart called, "Obstruction in a hundred meters, checkpoint two hundred past that."

Alex asked, "Hostiles?"

"I presume they all are."

"Then feel free to target any threats. With prejudice."

The battle was fairly intense by local standards, with several hostiles per block. Of course, they'd just hit someone's headquarters.

Alex said, "Jessie, churp our location."

"Oh," she said, and pulled at her phone. She seemed lucid, but slowed. That wasn't the trank, that was shock.

"Corcoran, cover me," he said and slid down next to her. He took the phone from her, unshielded it, slid in the battery.

She still had trouble focusing.

"Big battle. Current location. Ms. Highland fleeing antigovernment factions. Trying to reach friendly lines of the Sufi."

"We're trying to reach the Sufi?"

"That's what we're saying."

"Oh."

She got it done, and he wondered about disabling the phone again or letting her keep it live. Their location would be known in moments anyway.

Lionel shouted, "Traffic stop, prepare to unass!"

Amidst the rattle of weapon checks and reloading, Horace turned to Highland. "Ready, ma'am?" he asked, coaxing her from a sit to a squat.

"Yes, I am," she said. She brushed residual sorbent off her pants and strained into position.

A glance confirmed there were a lot more combatants around here.

"Listen to me," he said, and waited for them both to face him. "I will debark first, and help each of you down. Marlin will front for Jessie. Ms. Highland, you follow me. We will move quickly to improvised cover. Then we can expect to be moving under fire constantly for a while. If I go down, follow Marlin until someone else gives instructions. If he goes down, follow me. Understood?"

"Yes."

"Uh huh."

"Stand by."

He craned enough to get another glimpse. There weren't a lot of hostiles, though there seemed to be quite a few snipers. There was a crush of vehicles that would stop any progress.

"Here we go," he said.

The vehicle stopped fast but relatively smoothly, given the damaged road and trash. He leaned far back, and grabbed Highland's shoulder to stop her falling forward. Corcoran did the same with Jessie.

As the momemtum slackened, he slid out the back. Corcoran and

Marlin dropped off on either side and fired suppressive bursts. Then Highland slid off the deck, followed by Jessie.

Elke was ready to have fun. She had shotgun, carbine and toys, and no one to stop her until they reached cover. She sprung over the side of the truck, soaked up the impact sting in her feet, and tossed a smoke forward. She raised the shotgun, selected smoke-bangs and fired both, one each way down the street. The two teams swarmed past her into a building, and she brought up the rear seeking anything to shoot. She tugged the lanyard off the present on the truck.

A shot cracked the concrete next to her. She followed it generally back, looking for the source. Across the street and up three floors, a rifleman leaned out a window. Silly, silly. She thumbed for antiarmor and shot. Bart did, too, with a burst of mid caliber, and Jason swung for a shot. The man exploded into goo, but she was fairly sure her charge had blown his armor through his chest a moment before the others.

As she backed through the door, she heard, "Through that?" from an incredulous Cady.

Aramis and Alex stood together. Aramis had a route projected on a filthy gray wall.

"Yes," Alex said. "En masse, shooting anything in our way, straight along the alley. Then turn left and meet the checkpoint."

"How do we stop them shooting us?"

"Yeah, I'm working on that," Aramis said. "Hopefully they'll recognize some combination of us or Ms. Highland."

Lionel asked, "Did this seem like a good idea at the time?" while he and Jason loaded more ammo into Bart's rig.

Alex said, "Still does, barring any new ones."

"No, I have nothing. Except ammo."

"Let's move."

Elke checked locations of her accessories by touch and fell in behind Bart and Aramis. It was always best to lead with firepower.

As they left through the south, someone finally got courage to go for the vehicle. She heard the boobytrap hiss in that sibilant white noise, which presaged a shrieking scream of anguish. Flammable metals didn't stop for much, certainly not textiles, and moist flesh just made them react more.

They made it across the street as a mass before anyone caught them. However, as they entered the alley, fire behind them erupted.

"Man down! Man down! Corcoran is down!"

Cady shouted, "Marlin, stay with him, get to cover."

They might lose a lot over this. In the meantime, though, Elke turned and shot her last three obscurants to the alley mouth, and dumped a gun into the haze. It ran empty, she slid a prepared case into it, and pulled the trigger. She tossed it aside for some local to find. When he opened the breech he'd be without a face.

Peasants never learned not to mess with strangers. Perhaps, though, she could improve their manners a bit with gentle reminders.

Her load was significant and she panted. Thank god she didn't have the principal, the hanger on, or the Medusa.

At that moment Bart splashed something else overhead. Another drone.

Aramis said, "We have lots of recon. Active searches right now."

She pulled her monitor from her chest pouch and looked. There were lots of feeds, lots of scans.

"They're searching all frequencies and nets. They'll have us in a moment."

"A hundred and fifty meters," Bart said.

Alex said, "Good. Ms. Highland, please look up in the air for a few moments."

"Uh?"

"Look up. We want them to see you. We'll go between these buildings single file, and fast. That will put us one street from the CP. Okay, that's enough." Highland was still staring up. She seemed completely broken and pliable now. It was amusing how impending death changed people's self-assessment.

It was also interesting how far one hundred fifty meters could be in hostile territory.

"We should go active," Elke said.

"How?"

"Bart and I clear the route, loudly. After all, we want notice."

Alex said, "Do it. Formation, check loads, thumbs up, and go."

Elke led the way down the gap. It wasn't even an alley. If some-one collapsed the building, they were all fucked and forgotten. She went at a sprint. Behind her, Bart scraped and banged the walls. He had only two functional guns now, one carbine, one rifle. The long-range and grenade guns were dry.

"Dump that in the street," she called over her shoulder.

"I plan to," he huffed.

The view ahead wasn't encouraging. She turned over her shoulder and shouted, "I'll need to create a new door over there."

Alex was behind Highland this time, against his better judgment, but the firepower was up front, the principal in the middle, and he needed to ensure she made it. The rest were expendable. Meat shields were useful, but they'd get in the way of the firepower.

He heard Elke's statement and knew that meant explosives. Shit.

Elke reached the street. He knew because it got loud and smoky, then louder still. Bart fired a long burst, then unslung the Medusa.

That was a hint to hurry the fuck up.

He burst into light followed by Cady, and a scan showed the problem. They'd come out exactly between two factions, right in the middle. He'd thought Aramis meant that as a hypothetical, not to actually do it. Both sides tried to fire through the smoke.

Elke fired two rounds one way, turned and fired two the other, yanked something on her shotgun, and threw it. She slung two things on slings each way, and sprinted across the street.

Aramis and Shaman had Highland and rushed her behind. Lionel scooped a finally exhausted Jessie over his shoulder and followed.

Alex shouted, "Run you fuckers! Fire in the hole!" He made a quick head count by eye, and charged for cover.

Ahead, the world exploded. Again. This couldn't be healthy.

He groggily cleared the street just as the Medusa went into self-destruct mode. It locked onto anything moving and fired until it ran dry. Ten seconds later it exploded. So did Elke's shotgun. Enough explosive should dissuade anyone. It was certainly dissuading him.

The building he entered had been secured by barriers until Elke had cut her way in. The concrete still smoked from whatever she'd used to pierce it. He jumped over the rubble to find a door-shaped hole blown in the building's extrusion, if doors were round and cut by platter charges.

Inside was barren, stripped of all but structure. He strode fast to catch up with the others, halfway across.

"I'm surprised they didn't just demolish it," Cady said.

Indeed. It was a shell of metal and plastic struts, decaying concrete, with occasional weeds growing through the debris.

Jason said, "Rules. Cultural and environmental protections. Even a mundane dump like this can't be demolished, but it can be stripped."

"What do we do outside?"

Cady said, "There should be military barricades and interdiction weapons. We can call and negotiate, or disarm and not present a threat."

"Jason, Elke, can you jam them for a moment?"

Jason said, "Hah. No. Spoof, possibly. Throw up enough chaff, we can distract the automated systems. But someone has to go out unarmed."

"I will," Cady said. "I'll take Jessie."

Alex looked at Jessie. She nodded nervous agreement.

"I'll call first. Stand by."

He pulled out his other phone, punched in the number manually and connected. When the operator answered he cut the man off with, "This is Chief Marlow."

"Yes, sir, please stand by."

A moment later he heard, "This is Consul Beaumont. Your request is approved. Where would you like to meet the Special Service detachment?"

"We're still working on that. Who should I contact?"

"Senior Agent Machac." Alex memorized the number and recited it. Elke nodded acknowledgment that she had it, too.

He closed the connection, put out a hand for Elke's spare phone, then used that to call.

"Agent Machac."

"This is Marlow."

"Yes, sir."

"We need to meet with you to transfer Minister Highland to your protection. Is this agreeable?"

"Absolutely. We will accept responsibility on transfer."

"Yes, did they tell you we're under attack right now?"

"They did not, but I can follow the news. We can come to your location."

"Thank you. Sir, I trust you implicitly once we connect. I do not trust our communications or other agencies. We will meet you. Stand by, please. I will be in touch."

He closed again and looked around.

Elke said, "I have little left at this point. We'll have one shot and it better work."

Cady said, "Let us go first. Use it if we need to retreat."

Alex said, "Go ahead." To himself he said, *if we need to retreat we're pretty much dead. Highland's fanclub are squawking chickens, the army won't help or will be stuck in a bureaucratic loop, and the administration is trying to get her dead.* No joy. He'd have words about this with Meyer when they got back. If.

"Jason, keep us secure, I need to watch this."

"Roger."

Cady pulled releases and dropped her gear. Two of her team took it. She and Jessie raised hands and carefully stepped through rubble, into the street.

The peacekeeping position was a small-scale fort, with concrete and fill walls two meters high and broad, wire, sensors, observation platforms. One of the buzzing drones circling around dipped low to look at them. Cady kept leading Jessie forward, toward what was officially an "Interaction Point," where locals could meet for advice, to report incidents, or ask for help. They didn't often, and Alex had the impression this was actually a first for the unit on shift.

The drone extended a mic for her to talk. Then someone came to the gate, into an entry alcove.

"How are we doing back here?" he asked.

Jason said, "I have a perimeter of Lionel and Bart. Aramis and I have Highland. Elke and Shaman are roving."

"Threats?"

"I don't think anyone saw us, or if so, they're reluctant to enter the building. I've got that covered."

"Good," he acknowledged. Cady and Jessie had been waiting, and finally someone was coming out in person. Several someones. A squad.

"Troops inbound on foot. Squad strength. Current armor, camo and weapons. Officer accompanying."

Alex asked, "Are you going out to meet them?"

"If they ask, otherwise I'm right here."

The squad approached at a light trot. Cady and Jessie had hands on head. They were going to come in, he figured.

"Expect dynamic entry at this location, by friendly forces."

"Understood. Arms down on my order," Jason told the others.

He moved farther back, left his carbine slung low, and watched them approach.

They could probably see him by now, despite the brightness differential. The door was large and open for exactly that reason. The first two flanked the opening and poked carbines in. The next pair came in, weapons high, pointed at him, then the others.

Jason said, "Unit, arms down."

This was a very tense moment. Ripple Creek were all professional. Were all these troops experienced?

Cady led the rest in, arms still up, followed by a sergeant and a captain.

The captain said "You!" and grimaced in distaste.

It was Captain Roye.

"Us," Alex said.

The standoff between troops and mercenaries lasted fifteen seconds.

"Talk fast," the captain said.

Alex did so. "There are several threats to the Minister. At least one has hacked her feeds, and at least one is manipulating the opposition. Nothing reported is accurate. We have her here, of her own accord, and have been fighting through factions to keep her safe."

"Why did you feel the need to fight?"

"Some of them are trying to kill her."

Roye raised his eyebrows and said, "As I'm informed, most of them are trying to find her."

Was it possible the signals they'd received had been localized for them only? Possible. If it was narrowcast to a few blocks, there'd be few to receive, or notice, or care, except themselves.

"I can assure you that is not the case in actuality."

"Well, that's not my problem. What is now my problem is that you've started a massive fight, which is going to require me to fix."

"If it keeps the Minister safe, we're available to help."

Roye did not look happy. "Agent, with respect, every time you try to help, we have another disaster on our hands. I can furnish you a ride back to base, and in fact, I officially suggest so, or you can clear the hell out of my line of fire. Bureaucratic BS following that rescue of your man is why I'm in this tasking now."

That explained the hideous camo instead of the gray splinter he'd had previously.

He couldn't fault the man's position. Given conflicting information, the fact that the difference in their structures and goals had caused problems, and the government's habit of blaming the officer on scene for everything, it was quite understandable. Nor did he have any idea what he could offer.

Highland said, "Captain, I am here voluntarily now, and I do trust my guards. Any help you can give them is appreciated. I prefer not to return to base just yet."

Jason shouted, "Contact north!" as fire came through that entrance.

The sergeant repeated, "Contact north!" as a round came his way, and added, "And east! Multiple contacts!"

Aramis and Jason swarmed Highland and pulled her down. Everyone scrabbled for weapons. The troops dove into the building and took positions around the door.

Roye was angry.

"Have you really stirred the natives up to attack a UN position?"

"Sir, it wasn't us. Really. Someone is playing all of us for power. Highland has supporters, detractors, enemies, people willing to fake attacks for image, possible assassins, disputes with other agencies. She's somewhat contentious."

"And this sounds like a paranoid conspiracy theory."

"It's not paranoid if they're actually shooting at you," he said, just as a burst of something chewed the floor.

"Yeah, we'll sort it out afterward," Roye said. "Call for support."

The sergeant said, "Already did, sir. Advised delay. Other attacks all around."

"I'd blame you for this," Roye said. "Except it happens every couple of months." Then he spoke into his mic. "Understood, and thank you. Grid as shown. We're two five zero meters from the gate." He looked up and said, "A vehicle patrol is coming in. We can fall alongside them and through."

Two hundred and fifty meters. That was the distance to safety, and once there, someone still wanted Highland dead. What had they accomplished other than a runaround?

Well, they'd taken out two BuIntel paramils, and a bunch of her opposition were tied up killing each other. Maybe they'd drawn enough notice.

The two vehicles rolled in in a hurry. One Grumbly, one stretched light truck. The gunner on the Grumbly had a neural inducer and kept sweeping the area around them. Sure, induced pain would stop people, but only those not behind the lightest of cover, or in immediate visual range. The rear truck had a proper gun, but the odds of them being allowed to use it . . .

Not for the first time, Alex felt sorry for the military, hamstrung by all those feelygood regs and not equipped with enough lawyers to fight them.

In the meantime, though, they had another vehicle. They'd spent the better part of a day swapping from foot to vehicles and back.

The trucks slowed in the middle of the street, then guided slowly over to the right.

"Move," Alex said, and they formed a block around Highland, with Cady's team around Jessie. He wondered if Jessie knew she was a decoy.

The crossfire was a bit reduced by the neural projector. That reduced threat concerns, but not of random fire. There was enough going on all over . . . the locals seemed aware that the troops couldn't really do much to them, and flaunted it.

"Got air support, Captain?" he asked.

"We have recon drones to document incidents, so charges can be pressed," Roye said. "They've never caught anyone to press charges against, of course."

"No combat craft?"

"No. Some drones are armed, though not officially."

As much as he tried to be apolitical, that's what he should have expected from this administration. They were the most violent, militaristic pacifists possible.

He wondered if their aerial antagonists planned to avoid the drones, erase records afterward, or just plan on bullshit to evade the issue. Anything was possible.

"How far do we need to get for support?"

"The plan was for them to send a drone chopper. There are problems. So they're supposed to be sending a live pilot."

"To meet where?"

Roye said, "That's a great fucking question, since your trouble-making has made our base untenable. They can't land with the fire levels coming in, we don't have enough lethal weapons to secure the area, and now everyone knows where it's all going down. I've suggested a rooftop."

"Good, which one?"

"The one right above us, but now the UN Aviation Agency is insisting it's not an approved flight corridor."

That was ridiculous, petty, bureaucratic and no doubt true. "What, then?"

"We go back and buckle down until they get us."

Alex had to make a tactical decision fast. They'd be surrounded by troops, which would boost their defensive numbers, but, they'd also be a fixed target. There'd be more incoming fire, and it would be too cute and convenient for someone to lob in a charge, kill Highland and blame any number of local factions and Ripple Creek.

"Go ahead. We'll relocate and try again."

"Dammit, contractor, first you call me out, expose my position and divide my forces, now you think you're going to waltz away?"

Alex shook his head. "Our job is to protect the minister. That is all."

The captain shrugged. "Well, now we have to manage. How much ammo do you have?"

"We're pretty much full. We haven't actually engaged much."

"Good. I'll need to redistribute that among the rest of us who do have lethal weapons."

Alex's eyes widened. "I don't fucking think so."

"Excuse me? I believe I'm the ranking officer here."

"We're not military."

"I have the authority to commandeer what I need for the mission."

"So do I. I also have an unlimited license to kill people."

The captain furrowed his brow. "Is that a threat?"

"Yes."

Elke was moving around behind him. If this got ugly, it would be loud and violent.

Highland snapped, "Oh, don't be ridiculous. You're not taking my guards' ammo, like some Social Democratic activist."

Apparently it was true the different arms of the statists didn't get along. She was fine taking assets from others. If she needed those assets, though, or thought of a better place for them . . .

What an elitist bitch.

Luckily, she was their elitist bitch for now.

Rowe looked around, making his own summation.

"They told me to stick with Highland. They say they don't trust you."

"Hah. Don't trust us to let her conveniently die. I think they're actually willing to take us out to get to her."

Cady said, "They can still use her as a martyr. Massive uprising. If I can figure out how to exploit that, so can they."

Alex said, "Of course. That lets them play the rebellion against the UN card and move in in force."

Rowe asked, "But what's here?"

"Settling room, distraction, factions to play off against each other endlessly. When was the last time the government tried to solve a problem?"

"That's not true, you know," Highland said.

He looked at her. "Oh, really?"

"The problem is no one wants to pay the cost of solving the problems. I wanted to make a difference when I started. Then I realized that the only way to get elected was to lie my face off, then juggle things until the next election, betting on short memories to save me. Now that I'm appointed it's much more dangerous. I have to do what Chief Fuckup wants, regardless of what it might do to my career. In between, occasionally someone gets something done for one of their power blocs, and the whole mess restabilizes like collapsing rubble."

"You really think that's what people want?"

"They keep voting for it, so yes."

He would really have to consider that.

Jason said, "Why do you think anyone with the assets moves to the far colonies? Hell, that's the whole reason my adopted colony was created."

"That was one of the huge readjustments," she said. "Your founding corporations have a lot of assets. They're now increasingly off Earth and harder to manipulate."

Jason almost smiled. "Pardon me for liking that, ma'am."

"Eventually the General Assembly is going to make you share all that wealth."

He didn't want to argue politics, though she did need distracted.

"Yeah, well we need to move and fast. We have the military vehicles. I'm taking them." He looked at Rowe, who shrugged.

"They'll argue it out afterward. My safest response is to agree to an allied civilian force with the Minister here."

"And I'll need whatever ammo you have, and your troops' guns."

Rowe gaped.

"I don't fucking think so."

Alex snickered. "Interesting turnabout. So, are we going to work together here, or do we leave you sitting? I can move faster than you. Unless you plan to fight us—the locals will love that."

"We're going."

"Your troops must drop their lethal weapons. Now."

Rowe seethed openly, but he seemed to understand the rule. Frankly, Alex didn't need them except as bullet stoppers. He turned and pointed. His troops very clearly did not like it at all, but complied. They clutched their nonlethal weapons and looked ready to use them.

"Aramis, where do we go?"

"There's a substantial bazaar three kilometers west."

Rowe said, "Yes, we patrol there."

Alex looked around. "Good place for a handoff?"

Aramis said, "It's public. Start with that."

Cady said, "There'll be lots of witnesses, if we can avoid scaring them. Keep Ms. Highland masked until we're ready? Then we have instant video attention."

"I like it. Let's move. Captain, I would like troops in the rear." He started walking, and signed for the others to fall in to formation.

"In the rear?" Rowe seemed surprised but gratified.

"This is executive protection. We want not to get in a fight if we can avoid it, and to be discreet."

"I do not *believe* that *you* are lecturing me on discretion."

Alex didn't either.

"There are different levels of discretion. But we may need backup."

"With nonlethal weapons," Rowe clarified. Or was he complaining?

He shrugged. "Yeah, it's fucked up."

"I never thought I'd say this, but you guys don't get paid enough."

"Remember that in three thousand meters."

Ahead, Bart and Aramis broke trail, Lionel and Marlin flanked, Jason did overwatch, Alex and Cady brought up the rear. Alex could see all that, and Elke helping the two women scarve their faces as they moved. Shaman was nearby and ready. Behind, twenty angry young men were ready to shoot anything that annoyed them, including Alex.

The sporadic fire dropped behind, encouraged to do so by Jason and Cady. Cady was one hell of a marksman, possibly almost as good as Jason.

However, the horrifically bright uniforms marked the unit clearly, and even without that, a platoon-sized group of armed adults was clearly a platoon-sized group of armed adults. It dissuaded random potshots, but it meant they were certainly being tracked. That was fine for now.

It was hazy and hot. Slightly lower gravity didn't help much. There was an increasing amount of dust and other pollutants clogging the air, then the nostrils. Alex's straps cut into him, and his feet were sweating lumps. He pushed on.

The streets resumed habitation in this area. There were little shops and some larger businesses in random assortment, with two large apartment blocks ahead. Small dwellings were above the shops, some with laundry out to dry, dosses and cooking grills on small balconies. The vehicles varied from average to scrap, with some obviously mobile lodging.

Still, no one wanted a fight, or perhaps the following uniforms actually helped. They strode briskly along, crossing an intersection in bunches at a jog, then waiting, weapons low ready, for the rest.

That was when they were attacked. Bunching couldn't be helped, and in fact, offered offensive advantage. But they started taking fire from one of the blocks, and from across the street.

There was little cover, so four mercs clutched around Highland and ducked behind a car. The rest swarmed around and returned fire.

Jason said, "LMG in the building, fourth floor, second window west. Got him distracted."

"Pin them down, Elke, make them scared."

She already had a grenadelike thing in hand and arced it up and out. It flashed into howling, screaming, spinning pyrotechnics that tumbled down nice and pretty, then cracked out neural tingles and, apparently, light frag. The group of young males departed in several directions.

"Mudslimes are Satan's whores!" one of them shouted.

Alex muttered, "Well, good thing none of us are Muslim."

Another burst from the building made him duck and flinch. Whoever was up there was a respectable operator.

Next to him, one of the soldiers, looking inordinately mean for someone wearing neon colors, shouted, "If I had my grenade launcher, that asshole would not be a problem!"

"Noted," was all Alex could say. "Jason, paint it, all troops, fire on his mark."

Jason stood, snap shot and continued. Puffs indicated bullets cracking on the extruded concrete. Four others joined in, along with Highland, and two of the troops had apparently completely disregarded the order and brought carbines from their gear. Jason shrugged, capped off ten quick shots, raised a hand and shouted, "*Cease fire!*" He tapped Cady, then Shaman, and the code propagated out. In two seconds, the mercenaries moved with Highland secure in the middle, and the troops tapered off fire and fell in behind.

Rowe said, "I have two light casualties, detailing two to drop out with them and follow, or shelter in a building."

Alex said, "Noted. Aramis, tag it."

"Marked."

"We'll have someone sent, too."

He wasn't sure if anyone had hit the gunner, but the volume of fire seemed to have chilled his ardor. Nothing further came from there.

They crossed another street. The thoroughfare they followed tangled up after the gunfight. Cross traffic came in.

Bart swore in German.

"Talk to me."

"*Hurrensöhne* springbladers. Two. Forward left forward high."

He looked forward and slightly left, on roofs. Yes, there they were.

Highland said, "They're supposed to be called off! He lied again!"

"Keep going," Alex ordered at once. "Move now, talk later. Ma'am, I think it's a last gasp attempt. If they kill you, they deny it and blame anyone they wish. If they don't, they meet as planned. With churps reporting you're about to meet with rescue, they can't openly drop you."

A flash and a dot turned into a *woosh*, into an incoming mini missile.

"Scatter!" he shouted and dove to cover Highland, along with Lionel and Aramis.

He realized his ears were ringing and that blast had been all concussion, not far away. His vision was blurry, his ears numb and his body tingled.

"Track them," he mumbled. "What do we have?"

"Casualties," someone replied, sounding tinny.

"Elke, Jason, Bart, someone . . ."

"On your feet, Alex," Shaman said. He felt a sting that turned into coolness trickling through his neck. His brain thrummed, his skin burned, but he resumed functionality.

"Let's move fast," he said.

Rowe said, "Chief Marlow, we have several casualties."

He looked around and saw Rowe referred to the troops specifically. Several had taken frag or been slammed by percussion.

"Elke, cut them a door."

She snagged a charge, slapped it on a doorplate, rolled aside and thumbed her detonator.

It was a small charge, but after the previous one had shaken him up, it still hurt. However, they had an open building of some kind in which to shelter.

"Good luck," he said. "We're moving. Help Witch."

A moment later he said, "Oh, and Jessie."

Yeah, the young woman was holding up well. And at least the publicity paid off in the end. So far.

"Where'd the son of a bitch go?" he asked.

Aramis said, "Unknown. They headed south and kept going."

"They'll be back. What do we have for long range?"

Jason said, "I can possibly make three hundred meters."

"Do it if you can. Hostile to be shot on sight."

"Will do, and I'll call for volley fire."

"Right, can't hurt."

He thumbed his phone and said, "Last contact."

The connection beeped and at once he heard, "This is Machac." The man still sounded cultured and unhurried.

"We're going to meet at the Garden Bazaar, three klicks north of our recent location."

"I know where that is."

"Well, there are still two guys on the springblades. You don't know who's behind that yet, do you?"

"Not at all. Do you want us to meet you sooner?"

"The bazaar will be fine. We're five minutes out."

He disconnected without waiting for a response.

He wasn't the only one staggering, but Highland seemed reasonably stable, so they'd done their job properly. Could they finish up now?

"Elke, how are you set on smoke?"

She counted by touch. "A couple of minutes' worth."

"Can you hold one as we travel?"

"Make us an area target instead of points? Hold on."

She fumbled with something, pulled out a bandage and started wrapping it around a smoke grenade.

"It's going to catch on fire, but I can hold it for the duration."

"Pop it. Contact movement. Ms. Highland, grab onto Bart's harness. Let's move."

Elke pointed Aramis to the front, with Lionel, then took the number three position. Alex followed her, then Bart and Highland. The others gripped off the sides and back.

Following a concussion with lungfuls of ammoniac smoke was not the best thing for either health or concentration, but with the group clutching into a chain, they could move well enough. But were they concealed from outside, or just blocking their own vision?

"Time to waste the flashbangs!" he called. "As interruptions." He let his carbine hang while he reached into a pouch and pulled his free. He strained his thumb forcing the cap loose, then caught the lanyard in his teeth, yanked and tossed it to the right. "Every ten or fifteen seconds, and fire in the—" BANG!

His ear got punched again and the smoke eddied in ripples around him.

Off to the side, Jason said, "Contact airborne! Right forward forward high!"

Elke shouted, "Take this!" and shoved her shotgun over. Jason fired his, dropped his, took hers and raised it.

Alex had his own up, saw the figure, shouted, "All fire!" and started shooting. Maybe enough bullets in the air would get lucky.

The figure leapt across a building roof, about fifteen meters up. He did have to acknowledge that was one hell of a brave way to travel, and not something that would catch on generally.

Whoever the guy was, he seemed to be raising some other weapon, and relying on speed, angle and altitude for protection, along with distortion effects and armor. He was probably pretty safe, unless . . .

Whatever Elke had loaded, Jason fired. Shotgun. It must be one of her tungsten bore-riders, that would breach almost anything. The recoil staggered Jason back, but the shot hit. Their antagonist tumbled and twisted, the impact disturbing his trajectory enough, and tossing his leg off line. Instead of landing, he cartwheeled across the roof, over the edge and landed with a cracking thud a few meters ahead.

Cady and Lionel dropped out of formation, sprinted hard, caught up and stomped on him. They pinned and twisted his arms, Cady reached down with a pistol, and put a round in the crease between his body armor and helmet, right through the cervical spine. He convulsed twice and stopped.

From the front, Aramis said, "Through that alley will put us right in the bazaar."

"Keep moving. Lionel, Bart, I need you two to flank front. As we pass, take our weapons. We want to look nonthreatening to the public, blend in, then meet these people. Cady, Jason, you'll have overwatch, and be prepared to do something violent. Jessie, peel out and start recording as soon as you're through the alley. In the meantime, everyone watch top."

Elke's smoke was still pouring out.

"About thirty seconds left," she said. "Take it aside?"

Alex said, "Yes. Walk that way down the street. Everyone else into the alley. Move."

Elke moved the flare gingerly and winced. Yeah, the stink of scorching fabric indicated how hot it was. Alex went left at a walk with Aramis. The rest moved into the alley, shifting from tactical movement to a nonthreatening walk.

It was long and dark. There seemed to be a couple of small lanes crossing ahead, and it looked to be about two hundred meters to the bazaar itself. They kept weapons up, trained instincts leading them to create overlapping fields of fire.

Alex pulled his phone up. "Mr. Machac, are you there?"

"Here," the man replied. "Are you arriving?"

"It'll still be about five minutes. We've been delayed," he lied. "We'll be coming in north of you. Stand by."

He closed the connection and disconnected power again. The phone dropped back into its shield.

The group crossed one lane, which had everything from trucks to donkeys and a Mercedes, then back into the alley, narrower here and nasty. They were alone, though, and no one seemed to be aware of them.

Aramis said, "Shit, it's widening out. Conceal fast."

There was a clatter and shuffle as they all handed weapons off to Lionel and Bart. Rucks went too, into a pile. There was just enough room to squeeze by, and the two men stood over it all, shotguns ready. As he passed, Alex unslung his pack, passed over his carbine, drew his pistol and concealed it under his hands.

"Here we go," he said, taking a deep breath to steady himself.

The alley widened because whatever had once stood here had collapsed. The pieces were gone, probably for reuse, but the remains of a foundation were irregular underfoot. There were booths here, selling very questionable items for any culture on this planet—tattoos, porn, mild drugs. Ahead was the bustle of the bazaar proper, stalls, trailers and shops, noise and shouts and haggling customers.

"Find them," Alex ordered in a calm voice.

Aramis said, "Twelve people in suits, standing in a defensive circle around three limos, forty meters ahead, mostly facing north."

Reactively, everyone started to surge forward.

"Steady," he said. "Don't surprise anyone. Jessie, start sending. Elke, slave your photos to her feed. Walk slowly."

Elke said, "I've also got the photos of the bladers. That should prove interesting in a press release."

Highland said, "Oh, my, yes, thank you."

Yes, that would pretty well cinch the election for her. And how had they come around to actually caring and supporting that goal, at least on paper?

Because the administration was that corrupt and incompetent that even a bitch like Highland looked good in comparison.

He remembered the BuState security chief saying that Special Service were not that special. They got within ten meters before someone positively IDed them. Hands came up to indicate "halt," and people shuffled around.

From there they did okay and it was anticlimactic. One man stepped forward. "I'm Machac."

"Marlow. Glad to see you. Here's Ms. Highland."

"Ma'am."

"You are officially accepting responsibility for her safety?"

"I am."

"Then good luck to you. And to you, ma'am."

"Thank you, Chief," she said, looking wrung out and worn. "I do appreciate it. I . . ." she seemed about to make a speech, then just said, "Thank you."

"Glad we could be of service. We'll just see you into the limo," he said, with a glance at Machac.

The man didn't smile, but it seemed to be professional mask, not personal. He opened the door, Highland sat in heavily, and another agent took a seat next to her.

JessieM stepped up, held her phone in front of Alex. It showed a load of Highland being transferred into the limo.

"Check with an outside feed," he said.

She thumbed and gestured and said, "I have a feed from Georgie Ortiz. She's known and reliable. There are ten copies and forwards."

"Good. Then we'll call you officially transferred. Thank you very much for your help. Ms. Highland should be proud of you."

"Thank you," she said with a tired smile. "I need to sit down now." Then she sat heavily on the seat, and had to lift her legs in by hand, she was so wobbly.

Machac touched his earbud. "Yes? Stand by." He spoke to Alex.

"Relaying message that the lifter will not be able to meet you. BuState has a truck arriving in ten minutes. If Ms. Highland consents, we can remain to protect you until then."

That was both generous and a bit insulting, though probably not intentionally.

"We'll be fine. Thanks for the support."

"Understood." Machac nodded, climbed in, and three limos drove away slowly.

That left Ripple Creek on their own.

As usual.

As they preferred.

❁ EPILOGUE ❁

ALEX SAT IN HIS BOSS'S OFFICE and relaxed. They had a good relationship at this point. As long as the principal was safe, the lawyers informed and the checks cashed, everything else could be dealt with.

Don Meyer looked at him and said, "Rough one?"

"No worse than others, just tiring, grinding, wearing, and becoming more political. Okay, yes, it was disgusting."

"They paid well."

"I figured. What else was involved, though? You never said."

"What else would be involved?"

"Really? The third highest person in the UN, there's got to be something involved."

Meyer sprawled in his chair. "Yes, potential goodwill. And in the meantime, they couldn't touch us because we had her, or they thought we did. We've piled up some contracts for future benefit."

"How long do you think her goodwill will last?"

"If she wins? Quite a bit. We have some intel; she knows we can help her. If she loses, she won't have as high a risk factor, and we still have some intel."

"And the administration?"

"They haven't liked us since Salin. We needed some kind of pull with someone. We were never going to get any with Cruk or his pack of idiots. Highland's a brutal bitch, but at least competent."

"I don't know if I'd call her brutal, but vicious would apply."

Meyer said, "Able to face facts, though."

"Eventually, when they punch her in the face."

"That's more than Cruk."

"True." Yeah, there was that again. She wasn't good, but she was better than bad. "So we're okay with the fact that we've massively helped her campaign?"

"I'm glad of it," Meyer assured him. "We're higher up the chain now and need the support and credibility."

"I figured some of this was the case. I didn't plan to help her popularity."

"It was hard to avoid if she stayed alive. But keep in mind, this was a bad one. We've proven we can defeat anything the government has. Repercussions are not going to be good. Hide your money off planet in several accounts, Marlow. Well done, but we're going to have to have some major discussions. I'd stay armed, and together, and ready to bug out in a second."

He'd anticipated that. Jason had leads to several discreet banks. "Yeah, it doesn't look good. What about the company?"

"We'll be fine. I'll offer what I can in support, if it comes to it."

"Are we going to market ourselves as campaign promoters?"

Meyer said, "You joke, but I've had inquiries. Hunter, among them. He didn't like my quote."

"Hah. You're going to need the money for the lawyers when the administration figures out it paid half the money for a debacle that supported their leading opponent."

"That's the beauty of it. If she wins, we don't need to. If she loses, they don't care."

"In the meantime, I may drink the balance."

Meyer reached over and opened the cabinet next to him.

"First round's on me." He pulled out a bottle of Welsh whisky.

"A gift from a friend," he said.

Alex said, "I'll call Aramis to send more. He's on site now."

❈ ❈ END ❈ ❈